SECOND WORLD

Eddy Shah was born in Cambridge, and after a drifting education at various schools decided he wanted to write novels. He wrote his first novel at the age of sixteen (67,000 words, unpublished), then worked in the theatre, television and newspaper industries. In 1974, after being made redundant by the *Manchester Evening News*, he went home, told his wife Jennifer and one-year-old son Martyn that he would never work for anyone again, sold their house and started a newspaper. He then built a newspaper empire. On the way he fought the print and television trade unions, launched a national newspaper and introduced desk-top publishing to the print industry. He sold out in 1988 and started writing again. After having four books successfully published, he decided he wanted to write thrillers in a modern technological genre. His ideas for books were not trendy at the time so he quit writing and set about building a golf and hotel group with Jennifer. He also builds eco-friendly, affordable homes. 'All I ever wanted to do was write,' he says. 'And I'm now back doing what I always wanted to do.'

Second World was completed eleven years ago and Shah waited for the moment when he felt the time for publication was right. He approached Pan Macmillan in 2007 and they immediately decided to publish it. A second novel, continuing his 'Second World' theme, is near completion.

Visit Eddy Shah's book website at
www.eddyshah.com

PRAISE FOR EDDY SHAH

Ring of Red Roses

'As art as in life, Eddy Shah is a born story-teller'
Anthony Holden

'A well-above average book of its kind – he deserves being labelled a writer, not just a celebrity who has written a book'
Marcel Berlins, *Sunday Times*

The Lucy Ghosts

'A breathless, racy thriller' *Sunday Express*

'Eddy Shah has done it again' *Manchester Evening News*

Manchester Blue

'A tough riveting book. *Manchester Blue* is convincing and timely' Michael Hartland, *Daily Telegraph*

'Like Jeffrey Archer he keeps you turning all the pages'
Sunday Telegraph

'There is no denying his talent. The story-telling is on a par with almost any thriller writer, well-paced, with cliff hanging breaks that force one to read "just one more chapter" '
Oxford Times

Fallen Angels

'Shah has the skill and passion of a born storyteller. The scenes on the streets of Belfast click like the safety catch on an automatic weapon' *Sunday Telegraph*

'A classic of pace and excitement' *Daily Telegraph*

'An exciting, well-researched story' *Daily Mirror*

Also by Eddy Shah

Ring of Red Roses
The Lucy Ghosts
Manchester Blue
Fallen Angels

SECOND WORLD

EDDY SHAH

PAN BOOKS

First published 2008 by Pan Books
an imprint of Pan Macmillan Ltd
Pan Macmillan, 20 New Wharf Road, London N1 9RR
Basingstoke and Oxford
Associated companies throughout the world
www.panmacmillan.com

ISBN 978-0-330-46163-4

3 5 7 9 8 6 4 2

A CIP catalogue record for this book is available
from the British Library

Typeset by SetSystems Ltd, Saffron Walden, Essex
Printed and bound in the UK by
CPI Mackays, Chatham ME5 8TD

To Shep – who has fed both my inner and outer man

To Spurls – who showed me that Africa wasn't just a name on a map and that Charity begins with the young

And, as always – to Jennifer, Ardi, Tims and Alex, the true loves of my life

And to Mum – who has finally come home

BOOK ONE

AD 2044

'In freedom, I am lost in a myriad of choices.'
**Natan Sharansky. Russian émigré
and Gulag survivor
1980s**

'In freedom I am lost.'

**The GameMaster
2040s**

INTRODUCTION

THE WEEKEND STARTS HERE
OUTSIDE THE HOTEL GALLIPOLI
THE BRICK
SECOND WORLD
TIME: BEFORE COUNTDOWN

This was when he was most at peace.

On the Brick; it was still and quiet, clean, a perfect picture, just as he'd always imagined it in his mind. It would soon change. The clock was running down before the Weekenders hit, before they came tumbling onto the street, a trashcan of restless humanity dumped into the calm world he'd helped create. But for now it reminded him of childhood days on those Californian beaches, watching the water get sucked out in the undercurrent, seeing, for a brief moment, the clean sifted sand bare and pure – beautiful clear levelled sand – just before the next wave crashed in and brought the debris and turmoil and driftwood, as it always did.

He'd once calculated that the Brick was more than forty thousand earth miles long. And even now, after it had grown way beyond where people, including himself, had ever imagined it would, it had still used less than twenty per cent of its capacity. The Brick was the alternative world, an escape route out of the reality of life.

While RealWorld, where people really lived and worked and fucked and died, staggered along under the weight of nearly nine billion people, Second World had become the great escape, the place where dreams and reality merged. Alpha World, before the turn of the last century, then Second Life, were places where alternative cities and homes had been built on the Web by the internet pioneers. But, by 2008, it had all started to change. It became wildly popular and groups formed and brought about the nasty excesses of RealWorld. Groups formed to rape and plunder and hurt their neighbours. But they were harmless days, a time when the only person who got hurt was an unconnected avatar, a cyber image, on a computer screen. There was the odd divorce, the occasional group suicide, but these were in a minority. For most it was just a giggle on the net.

Virtual Reality had made it all possible. The ability for people to switch on their computers, connect up their SensoLinks, sit back in their chairs and just glide into a Virtual Reality parallel world in the Web. The SensoLinks caressed the sensory nerves that registered touch, feel, sight, sound, hunger, every sensation that ran through the human body. A Web meal was just as enjoyable as the real thing, often tasted better – except it left the consumers still hungry once they returned to RealWorld. Every sensation, from sex to sadism to sentiment, was now catered for in the Web.

At a price. Nothing was ever free. Apart from just walking on the Brick.

It was an easy system to navigate. One long wide yellow road, lined with boulevard pavements and buildings that ran on as far as the eye could see. Tall buildings, modern buildings, older single-storey buildings, churches, vast entrances to various theme parks, shops, beauty parlours, restaurants, all the paraphernalia of everyday urban life. Open to all, so long as they could afford the entrance price.

Then governments had moved in and taken over the Brick. It was that which disappointed him the most. He, and the others, had built it because it was their dream. They had built it so that the great melting pot of humanity, under the constraints and pressures of life in RealWorld, could have somewhere they could meet each other in friendship and fun and togetherness, well outside the ever-binding tethers of governments and bureaucrats and officialdom.

But nothing that promised freedom could ever be left alone. *That*, he shook his head, *was the most unnatural rule of nature*.

Following an intervention by the United Nations in 2011, each country was given access to their allotted areas of the cyber network, the old World Wide Web, the 'www' of the now defunct internet days. The fibre optic-based broadband networks had all too soon proved too slow for satisfactory information retrieval, and, after a series of missed turnings, the quantum network had eventually superseded the old atom-based optic network, and in turn had revolutionized the Web. For a fee it paid to the UN, to support their worldwide humanitarian policies, each country then leased out its section of the network to companies or individuals. The more economically advanced the country, the higher the price it paid. The more usage a country took, the greater its coverage on the network.

It was a never-ending world of computer software; a graphics protocol that might not exist in reality but was as real as RealWorld on which it was based. Its ultimate potential exploded as Virtual Reality and real-time avatars became the currency of the Brick.

The network providers started to build on the Brick in 2015, and it grew rapidly as more companies came on board. The French Zone redesigned its section of the superhighway as the Boulevard Champs-Élysées, the English Zone copied Oxford Street with the Globe Theatre at one end and Marble Arch at the other. The Europeans, with their traditional values, insisted that all new builds must seek governmental planning permission, copying a stricture that still dominated RealWorld. In contrast, America, with few zoning problems and a more robust approach to life, just let it all rip and allowed developers to build whatever they wanted. Some developers created small side streets and built their own community zones, others would simply slap something up on the Brick and offer whatever services they could to the public.

In the old days avatars could fly; it was a great way to move around. But that stopped. People could still fly, but only in the safety of a game park. On the Brick, people either walked or got a transporter, which was automatically charged to their credit account. Even cars using the Brick were eleven credits per six million cubits.

Still only twenty per cent of the network was developed, those areas still not utilized being known as the Dark Areas. They hadn't yet been mapped out, were just areas of empty digitless space, without light or energy or even the ability to carry sound.

Eventually, as the Brick grew, such areas too would have power and utility services laid to them, the network then expanding into them and creating fertile new areas where Web developers could move in. But, for now, the Dark Areas didn't exist, because they hadn't been 'invented'. Most of the megacorps, the larger network providers and developers, had already taken options on these sections, working on the premise that one day they would become valuable and would need to be developed. It was a simple system, but made possible only by massive investment and technological wizardry.

He now watched the CREEPs go about their business, cleaning and repairing the Brick, ready for the next public onslaught. He noticed a webcam, high up on the side of the building, swing round and focus on him. Immediately he turned and walked away, as if he were an ordinary Weekender who had arrived early and was just exploring the neighbourhood. He realized his step had automatically quickened so he slowed his step, calmed his anxiety. Now was not the right time to be noticed.

He looked at his watch, which was set to Brick Time: the same as Eastern Seaboard Time. It told him the moment was approaching, Convention Hall would be filling up, and billions tuning in at home to meet *The Man*. The elections were over, electronic votes counted, and it was 'Good Ol' Teddy Dixon' for another term – President of a United States which stretched from Canada to halfway down South America. The leader of a billion people.

He shook his head, and headed for a local cafe. He looked forward to a fresh, hot cappuccino. He'd watch it all on the cafe TV screen. He'd watch the action via the digital information that poured down the wire from RealWorld to Second World.

He'd watch it and know he was about to change the world.

BOOK TWO

LET THE GAME BEGIN

I already knew they were going to lose, that they would soon feel the pain. I smiled. That's me, Conor Smith. *Mister Cool and In-Control.*

I watched the Great Earth Dragon, or 'Draco Rex', snake across the stone kitchen floor towards Icarus, its flat-topped, slit-eyed, menacing head rearing back, ready to strike. They call it a game, but the trouble with Virtual Reality is that it's only a game until you step on the Brick and start to play. Then it becomes *real*. If you lose, it's *real* pain you take home with you, a sharp twisting pain that develops into a steady deep piercing ache that would last for days.

All of them knew that. The pain was part of the game . . . and it was being on the edge of danger that gave my players the buzz. I watched. They waited. Tajo, the samurai, crouched to Icarus' left, hidden from the dragon, and waiting in the dungeon alcove for the monster to get within range. The Viking girl, Nomuna, was out of sight on the opposite side of the kitchen; she knelt, her broadsword gripped tight, ready to strike, behind the huge cast-iron stove with the metal boiling pots hanging above it.

The three of them had tracked the dragon for nearly an hour through the old, medieval castle; had followed the telltale signs and marks that had given up the dragon's secret. They had seen the light green powder left on the walls as the dragon's scales scraped past them, the scorched

13

wooden beams where it had bellowed its defiance, the upturned furniture it had knocked over in its flight.

And it had finally waited for them here, in its chosen battleground, the large kitchen deep in the castle.

They had entered the room carefully. They moved warily, were ready for it this time. They had reached this point twice before. It was the first peak. And it was also where they had died. Icarus went first, his task to lure the dragon. He was the nominated sacrifice.

The other two slipped in and found their own hiding places. They had all seen this dragon before. It was smaller than they expected, no more than two metres high, some ten metres long. But it was the most ferocious one they had ever seen. Most Great Earth Dragons could measure over thirty metres in length, with an equal wingspan. But this Earth Dragon, Draco Rex, made up for its lack of size with a tremendous agility; it defended itself with surprising speed and ferocity. Unlike its larger cousins, it had a cunning and intelligent mind, was almost human in its preparation for the combat. The hunters knew it had deliberately left its trail for them to find. They knew this was where it would lead them, into a battleground of its choosing. This room was large enough for it to make good use of its natural ability as an expert flier, glider and fearless fighter.

Their real advantage was that it was alone. Draco Rex was an introverted and reserved beast, always shying away from the company of other dragons in order to lead a solitary existence other than during its mating season. Even then, the Great Earth Dragon was impelled by an instinct to avoid disputes over mating rights or territorial feeding grounds. Just as it mated only once every two years, so it ate sparsely. Two or three meals a year would suffice a fully grown Draco Rex.

It was that same time-to-feed instinct that had encouraged Icarus to lure the dragon into its favoured lair. Icarus now waited, seemingly unarmed, as the dragon suddenly rushed towards him. When it was still some thirty metres away, the dragon spat out its first fireball. Less than a metre across, the fireball tumbled through the air towards Icarus, who moved aside at the last instant to avoid it. It crashed into the table behind him, consuming it instantly in a bright orange flame. Two more fireballs followed, each missing Icarus as he swung away deftly to avoid them.

The dragon, now no more than ten metres off, haunched up ready, its talons ready to rake through Icarus's flesh, its teeth bared eagerly to feast on the young man. Icarus drew the crossbow that had been slung over his shoulder, ready cocked and loaded, and aimed it straight at the dragon's muzzle. He released the bolt, but the dragon had sensed the danger and was moving even before Icarus could pull the trigger. The bolt flew harmlessly past as the creature whirled up into the air and flew over and behind Icarus. It landed before he could fully turn, and was then on him, teeth ripping into his exposed back, tearing at the flesh.

Time to get him out before any serious injury, I thought. I punched the JetPax and instantly released Icarus. He screamed once before he evaporated from the dragon's grasp.

It was now up to the other two. Tajo and Nomuna were on the dragon immediately, hacking at it viciously with their swords. The beast had not expected them and reared up in pain. It gnashed its teeth at them but they easily moved out of harm's way, knowing the monster's strength was weakening. They moved forward, driving and slicing their swords into the great beast. In one of his attacks, Tajo severed two of the dragon's talons from its right claw, on another he drove the blade deep into its shoulder. The dragon was seriously wounded under the onslaught and now bled profusely, its green-blue blood spurting across the stone-slab floor. Sensing its weakness, Tajo and Nomuna grew braver and surer, attacking the beast from all sides, confusing it as to from which direction it should defend itself. As they hacked away, the two warriors slid on the floor, fighting to keep balance on the bloodied slabs.

Screeching wildly, the dragon turned to fly away, its great wings clawing at the air. It was difficult, though, for it lacked the distance to take off, to gain sufficient lift under its wings. It was too late, it seemed, and now Nomuna slashed at its right wing, severing the tip. The dragon managed to half lift itself off but now, with only one usable wing, crashed to the floor again. Pushing back against the grey stone wall, it readied itself for their final assault.

Tajo and Nomuna approached warily, their swords poised to attack. The dragon's bared teeth were still stained with Icarus's blood. It spat another fireball at them. Propelled with only a fraction of the power of the earlier ones, it floated across the room slowly, allowing the two humans to effortlessly avoid it.

'Careful,' warned Nomuna. 'We're not there yet.'

Tajo nodded. It was tempting to rush now, to get past this wounded dragon, to drink the cup of victory and join those few who had searched out the real prize, the Golden Dragon, and claimed it.

In their eagerness they made their fatal mistake. A second Earth Dragon, much larger than the first, moved in behind them. Twenty metres long, twice as fearsome as its companion, it bellowed out a great roar that shook the very foundations of the castle. Tajo and Nomuna whirled round, their raised swords suddenly no more than useless tinfoil in their hands. They instantly knew they were doomed. Behind them, the smaller, wounded dragon lifted itself up, regaining strength as it recognized their weakness.

The two warriors looked round for me, with panic in their eyes. They couldn't see me but knew I would be watching. I waited a few moments more before releasing them. I wanted them to feel real fear, to understand how truly dangerous it was in the Valley of the Dragons. The two fire-beasts now had them trapped, were starting to circle the game-warriors, were drawing back their heads, like pistols being cocked and preparing to rush forward. As the second dragon let out another blood-curdling roar, Tajo and Nomuna moved closer together.

I saw the panic, sensed their fear, waited a few more seconds as the mighty dragons circled them, bellowing as they closed in for the final kill. As the dragons both sprang forwards belching flames through shark-sharp teeth, I grinned and pressed the remote JetPax – and jettisoned the two cyber warriors to safety.

A moment later all I could see there was the male dragon licking the smaller one, nuzzling it, now eager to mate. In their closeness they had already forgotten the danger that they had just faced. The warriors had faded away; life had returned to normal.

I switched off the plasmatic wall image and flicked it back to the Conference Room where they had started the journey. They looked a sorry lot, heads drooping, despondent in their failure. Icarus shook his head in frustration; he had watched it all on the large wall screen that dominated the Conference Room. He rubbed his back; it still stung even though there were no apparent marks from where the dragon had gouged him.

'You OK?' I asked him.

'Just very sore.'

'You weren't at risk for too long, and it'll be fine in a couple of hours. The pain's in your mind, remember, and your back's responding to that.'

I turned to the others. 'So what went wrong?'

'We had him,' Nomuna blurted angrily. 'Where did that second one come from?'

'He wasn't a him,' I retorted. 'He was a her.'

'What's the difference? Where did the other one come from?'

'You didn't do your homework. You didn't research it properly.'

'We did,' Icarus snapped angrily. 'We *all* researched it.'

Tajo suddenly groaned, slumped in a chair, his head in his hands, as he rocked from side to side.

'Did you see something we missed?' Icarus demanded of the samurai. 'What the hell was it?'

'The obvious,' came Tajo's mumbled reply.

'Tell us,' implored Nomuna.

The samurai lifted his head. 'We accepted the fact that Earth Dragons always live and move about on their own. They do, of course. They don't even hunt together for food.' He looked at me and smiled weakly. 'So obvious really. So foolish of us.'

'*What* is?' demanded a frustrated Icarus again.

Nomuna joined in with a shrill self-mocking laugh. She, too, now knew why they had failed. 'It was the mating season, and that's when they come together. Every two years. Always the end of January and on into February.'

'The smaller dragon was a young female,' I volunteered. 'The second one was the male. He was protecting her.'

'Are we ever going to get out of this castle?'

I shrugged. 'Up to you. All I can tell you is that the higher you get, the harder it is to succeed. There's always a new danger, but also new clues to prepare you. Research is everything, remember. It's all in the detail. This is the third time you've reached this stage. Maybe, like most people, you'll never get beyond it. Because the higher you go, the deeper the pain, and the longer the recovery. What now takes just hours to recover from could take weeks, even months as you climb further up that ladder of success. This little dragon's beat you twice before, and now its companion finished the job. I'm disappointed in you because, with research and proper thought, you could've been up on the next level. I reckon you need a break – at least two weeks – to refresh the mind and reaffirm your commitment.'

I waited for their disappointment to die down, ignoring

their pleas to reinstate them. They understood why they had failed, but they *should* have read the signs.

Understand the enemy and victory is yours.

Icarus, though not the smartest of the three, was the bravest and most honourable. He'd been prepared to sacrifice himself, hadn't needed any prompting to do so. It was a good team and they could, if they trusted me, ultimately get to the higher levels. Their teamwork – and liking and trust for one another – was their strength. But I knew they still had a long way to go.

'Those are the rules. And it's all for your own health and safety. We'll fix another day, but you'll have to start right at the beginning again, working yourselves back to that kitchen on the fifth level.'

'How many levels are there, Conor?' asked Tajo.

'That's up to you to find out. And don't keep asking me, because I won't break the Code. But you've still a long way to go. Research everything properly and you'll get there quicker.'

'The Golden Dragon,' prompted Icarus. 'What's it like when you do get there?' He knew I liked talking about it, as the only GameMaster rumoured to have ever reached the Eventual Level, which only I knew wasn't just a rumour. 'I mean . . . to actually see the Golden Dragon.'

But I was tired, bored and a little disappointed in them. They were right to have sacrificed one of the team in order to slay the Earth Dragon, but to have not watched their flanks, to have let the second dragon take them by surprise, that was sloppy and also unnecessary.

'Just remember what the Code Book says: "His scales and wings are golden and he possesses great beauty, intelligence and bravery. He defends the Enchanted Castle, deep in the Hidden Wood, where a pure-hearted ancient knight stands watch over the Golden and Sacred Chalice. And they will both guard it until the world has become pure and worthy enough for the Chalice to be brought out of hiding and drunk from. Then the fear and the hatred will disappear from the world and we will live in the Golden Era that all good men wait for. And all other dragons – Earth, Water and Fire Dragons – shall fly to the Enchanted Castle and pay homage to the Golden Dragon." The legend is that no true warrior would ever want to kill the Golden Dragon – only those intent on evil. And therefore I will defend the Dragon from you, which is why, if you achieve the higher levels, I'll always be with you.'

'To protect us, or protect the Dragon?'

I laughed. 'To protect the Game. If you kill the Golden Dragon, there's no more Game. And if you die, there are no players.' I looked around at the three of them. 'Don't run before you can walk, therefore. It's a long way yet. And most people don't ever get to the end. They give up because it's either too scary, too painful, too expensive or just plain impossible. OK, I'll email you soon with the times for your next appointments.'

'How about tomorrow?' asked an ever-eager Icarus.

'No,' I said firmly. 'Anyway, the park's closed tomorrow. All day. For maintenance work. See you, then.' I hit the switch, faded, and was gone from them. But I could still see them. The trio, as disappointed as I was, huddled together to share their failure. They were all young, however, and their disappointment would soon dissipate. They believed they would see this through to the end.

I, of course, knew better; but they were among the best I'd ever taught. Who could know, they might just make it.

That was for the future, however. Right now I was also very hungry. I walked from my computer control room into the kitchen. I went first to the fridge for a snack before the next group arrived. It was a rum way to earn a living, being paid for doing what had been a hobby all my life. In my dad's day, billiards had been the token sign of a misspent youth. When I was young it had been video games and PlayStations. Yet it was exactly that which had made me a fortune. I reached for a slice of cheese and felt a sharp pain in the top of my right arm. I pulled back. This pain had been there, on and off, for two weeks now. If it continued longer I'd have to visit the doctor. Not something I relished, or believed in, but that was the price you paid these days; because it was what the insurance companies demanded. All that health cover had been free once, now you just paid for everything.

I lifted my arm tentatively and took out the Cheddar cheese, peeled off the wrapper and bit a chunk off – for energy. I went back to thinking about the three warriors I'd just left. I'd witnessed their type of deep disappointment so many times before. Disillusioned, defeated warriors they were. I smiled as I thought of the trio when they had first met me, three months earlier. Young and clearly eager at meeting me, old-fashioned Conor Smith. One blue eye and one green, two large, round, platinum earrings in my left ear and a face that looked a lot older and more battered than I really was; the only recon surgery had been done on my eyes, so I could see more clearly through my tired, sagging eyelids. My hair was thin and trimmed very short, but I'd never bothered to visit the Youthness Boutiques that proliferated in RealWorld. I had been wearing my usual garb of black T-shirt, black cord slacks and cowboy boots with worn, well-rounded heels. The boots, like me, were battered out of shape, re-heeled and re-soled long past any useful repair date, and always seemingly covered in a thin layer of dust which I habitually wiped off on the backs of my cords. The right sleeve of my T-shirt was rolled up round my biceps with a packet of cigarettes tucked into the fold, over a tattoo that said 'Baby' and another that just said 'Hey'. I never smoked, *never* had, but it was part of my statement from the early days when I raced cars on the newly built Brick.

I was all Jim Croce's 'Stock Car Boy', and maybe that's how I still see myself some times.

> Oh Rapid Roy that stock car boy
> He too much too believe
> You know he always got an extra pack of cigarettes
> Rolled up in his T-shirt sleeve
> He got a tattoo on his arm that say 'Baby'
> He got another one that just say 'Hey'
> But every Sunday afternoon he is a dirt track demon
> In a '57 Chevrolet

I guess I'd become a pastiche of myself. But who gave a damn? I certainly didn't.

In fact I was contemptuous of those obsessed with their appearance. The quick surgery techniques, especially the increased use of laser mixed with regenerating new drug and DNA technology, kept men and women in a continual state of freshness and youth. My dress was an expression of contemptuous disregard, based entirely on what had long stopped being fashionable. I felt it gave me my own identity, so different from the fops – as I saw them – around me. I was a techno-hippy in a world where I was considered one of the very best. That's what confused those who came to learn from me. No fashion studs in my tongue, no body jewellery, no tattoos to hide my real character, but by the time my students left there was never any doubt as to my true ability. I hope, by then, they saw the man and not the kind of façade that others used to hide behind.

They learnt to trust me. With Conor Smith you got what you saw. For I looked the world right in the eye and said what I believed. Then I grinned at the thought. Who was I trying to kid? I am what I am: a fuck-up trying to be different, just like the rest of the cretins out there.

I recalled the easy days, when Second Life was all the rage

on the internet. I used to go down to Abbotts Airfield and watch the planes land. Most of them crashed, piloted by keyboard pilots who couldn't hang two movements together. It was great spectator sport. I even remembered the SLURL. http://slurl.com/secondlife/Abbotts/160/160/70. That didn't happen now. Abbotts was an international airport with transporters that flew from one end of the Brick to another. Flying lessons, jets, space travel; it was all there at Abbotts.

All too sophisticated. No pioneering any more.

A sudden despondency settled over me, thudding right down into my stomach. Because I knew the warriors' failure had only exacerbated my own frustrations, highlighted my own disenchantment at my ultimate lack of achievement.

What do you do for a living?

I build games.

And what else?

I play games.

That's it, huh?

Not so bad for an ex-hacker, ex-criminal, ex-stoolie, ex-gaolbird and ex-software pirate.

So where did that get you?

A black platinum Amex card.

That's seriously rich. For playing games?

I get a cut from every one of my games that's sold. Last year ThemeCorp sold nearly half a billion games and tickets to the Brick from my designs.

That's a lot of games.

That's a lot of money.

How much?

No idea.

You don't know?

Who cares? I gave up counting a long time ago. Me, I'm just one of an elite handful, a regular 007 of the game world.

Conor Smith. Licensed to thrill.

God really does move in mysterious ways.

I felt the surge of uncontrollable anger build in me. From nowhere ... it always came from nowhere. 'Fuck everybody!' I said to the fridge and no one in particular.

Another day gone. Another day lost. I was the GameMaster, and the fact was the GameMaster had long since grown tired of the Game.

I flicked on the wall plasma to watch the news. The picture appeared instantly, and I watched the President of the United States walk into a packed Convention Hall.

As the President looked around, he could see only about a thousand people present, but he knew that millions more were watching, and were in there with him. He could feel them, pressing up against him, even though the nearest stood at least ten feet away, at the base of the large podium. He loved the new technology and how it helped him reach out to his supporters. Ever since Virtual Reality had run beyond games, it had been the politicians who were first to utilize its popular appeal. It was in their nature to use a medium they sincerely believed they controlled.

These were the moments he loved, when the American people, *his* people, came out to show him just how much they were on his side, and how much they loved him. But, then, he realized how much they owed him. He'd been the one who eventually picked up where George Bush and his liberal successors had left off, before the time of the Great Islamic Wall, as terrorists and suicide bombers grew in their numbers and killed innocent people in cities throughout the world, mostly in the USA, in Britain and some parts of Europe. It had now all become so commonplace that a new suicide bomb rarely even made the front page. But the fear was always there: the fear that it might be your neighbourhood, your best friend, your family that was on the next hit list.

Then, when the Islam for Islam jihad group had been

discovered with a small nuclear device, primed and ready to go, in Chicago, intending to detonate it in the Holy Name Cathedral at North State Street during the Sunday Mass, he had no hesitation in taking action. The biggest surprise was that all the bombers, fifteen of them each prepared to die as they triggered the bomb, were third-generation Americans, who had been through high school and college alongside many of those they were planning to murder.

Within days the USA had macro-nuked three Iranian nuclear plants, two major Iranian government buildings, and three small towns, two in Syria and one in Libya, which were considered the major training ground for Islamist terrorists. In all, six thousand people died, but America's military strength prevailed and the great powers that were Russia, China and India accepted the need for action. They could wait; aware that America's declining power as the senior economy would one day give them a better opportunity to flex their muscles.

But it also stopped the bombings overnight.

Then the West put up military fortified borders and encouraged many Muslims, some of them third and fourth generations, to go back to their indigenous homelands. There were no more dual nationalities, no more political immigrants. The rule strengthened the Great Islamic Wall that ran across Europe. The rule was simple. *You're either with us – or against us.*

But these things were far from the President's mind right now as he felt Annie's hand slip into his, give him a gentle squeeze. He turned and smiled at her. He was the man. He was back in the White House for a second term. She was part of his winning team. Part of everything he had become.

He squeezed it in return, then let go of her hand, looked round the massive Convention Hall ... and smiled his famous smile. Then he raised his hand slowly towards the chandeliers and gave the crowd that warm *we're-all-on-the-*

same-side-fighting-the-same-enemy gesture, showing he was putting his arm round them all, protecting them from the big world outside.

The cheers exploded and his smile got bigger, the wave of his arm more expansive, now reaching out to them. His victory, for a second term, only four weeks earlier, was theirs and he was sharing it with them. Good old Teddy Dixon; man of the people. They understood and accepted his strengths and his weaknesses. Good old Teddy. One of the boys. And they were all here now, come to celebrate his sixty-third birthday, all white-tied and tailed for this Gala Celebration.

Don Clancy stood behind the President, just to his left, his eyes scanning the crowds. Clancy knew there was little danger out there, not in this room. And, to make things safer, it had been an all-ticket event. But, as Senior Agent on duty, he couldn't ever allow his guard to drop. He looked round at the other agents spread through the room: Jackson, Smythe, Wallenski and Smerton. All in place, all alert. Clancy checked his watch. Three minutes to seven. 'Three minutes to go,' he spoke into his sleeve mike.

On the platform, President Dixon held up his arms for silence. He thought of this room he was in, as he waited for the sounds to subside. It had been built and decorated at his own request, an exact replica of Madison Square Garden where John F. Kennedy had been hosted with a gala birthday party in May 1961. A vast room, a brightly lit, welcoming room. Great for an evening of celebration.

The crowd's cheering died away into complete silence. Dixon lowered his arms, the smile now a big grin. 'Isn't this a great country, or what?'

The crowd erupted at the familiar phrase he had used throughout his election campaign.

'I mean, isn't this really a great country ... OR WHAT?' The same phrase, repeated, was louder this time, almost shouted at the crowd.

The response was overwhelming; Dixon stood un-ashamedly enjoying the adulation.

'Two minutes,' said Don Clancy. He didn't check with the others this time; his eyes instead were scanning the crowd in case of anything untoward. It looked OK: no threatening behaviour, nothing hostile.

'YEAH!! THIS IS A GRRREAT COUNTRY. And it's going to be even greater when we re-open the Summit with those Muslim countries. Now they know they need us. Now they know that what we have is worth having . . . for them, too. And we can learn something from them. *Absolutely*. We have to return to family values. We have to get back to our roots. That's the next stage. Right now, we've got to guar-antee, and I mean *guarantee*, no more terror. No more fear. That's how we're going to run these next four years. World peace, at last. AT LAST.'

The crowd went wild, arms reaching forward towards their President, the elected Protector and Father of the Nation.

'One minute!' yelled Clancy. He suddenly felt foolish, carried away with the emotion of it all. Smerton was grinning back at him. *No need to shout*. Not in this room. Every one of them could hear what he said, even if he'd whispered.

'One minute,' Clancy repeated unnecessarily, quieter this time but still firmly, as if to emphasize his seniority. 'Thirty seconds.'

Annie Dixon, the President's wife, turned and smiled at Clancy. He nodded back. The surprise had been her idea, planned meticulously and as secretly as possible. He had helped her, because the most difficult part had been keeping mention of the White House out of any negotiations with the suppliers. If they had found out who their customer was, it would have been blazoned on every front page in the nation, probably in the world. Tomorrow's papers and newscasts didn't matter. Because in a few seconds it wouldn't be a secret any longer. Annie Dixon turned her gaze back to where she knew the whole room's attention would soon be focused.

'Happy birthday to you.' The voice was thin, soulful, yet melodic. It was a voice everyone remembered.

The first strains of the familiar song burst over the room, the soft voice cutting through the applause for the President, overtaking the room's energy with its own nostalgia. The crowd, even before the first phrase was finished, were turning around, looking to the back of the room.

A single spotlight picked her out at the back, alone and vulnerable, in that same dress, standing in front of a single microphone.

'Happy birthday to you.'

She stood on a podium; the silver shiny dress closely moulded to her, inviting the belief that she wore nothing underneath, clinging to the body so many had craved and she had died for; the star she was: Marilyn Monroe.

'Happy birth-day, Mr Prezz-i-dent.'

The pout and the mischief in her eyes absorbed every man in the room. She leant forward, her hand caressing the solitary microphone on a stand in front of her. Even that small movement detonated a deeper avid excitement and hunger in the men watching her. The women sighed for what they could never have.

'Happy birthday to you.'

The little fluttering wave; then she turned, dreamlike, and was gone.

The crowd were ecstatic. Not just those in the room, but the millions who had joined in from outside. It was incredible. That was no actress or double. That really had been Marilyn Monroe.

President Dixon turned to Annie and hugged her. He knew it was her special present, only she would have thought

29

of that. She knew what he thought of Kennedy and that whole Sixties scene. And Marilyn, who had embodied the newness and energy of it all.

The crowd were pushing towards Dixon again, all wanting to shake his hand, to take something from the winner. The White House aides moved forward, clearing a path to the dance floor for the President and his First Lady. As they stepped off the podium Clancy followed, silently staying close but never intruding.

The first notes of the 'Tennessee Waltz' began as the Dixons reached the cleared dance floor, and the President put his arm around Annie's waist and led her into a sweeping waltz. They were both good dancers and the crowd watched and admired from the edge of the floor.

'That was some trick,' Teddy Dixon whispered to his wife.

'You approve?'

'Only you know what that means to me,' he replied. They both knew that what they said out here was instantly transmitted to millions. No secrets. That was the new style of modern democracy. Except for out there, once away from public scrutiny, everything was concealed. 'Only you come better than that lady. Only you . . . ever and always.'

She smiled, and the millions who overheard sighed along with her. They danced through the number, and others joined them on the floor. Soon the whole area was a swirl of dancing couples, all attired in dreamlike party gowns and dress suits, all enjoying the formality of an evening at the White House, or at least its Annex.

When the next dance started, the Dixons split up and went instantly about the business of politics. Annie worked the right side of the room, shaking hands, meeting people; the First Lady amongst the adoring citizens. The President mingled with those on the opposite side.

'Congratulations, Mr President . . .'

'I'm from Ohio. Senator George . . .'

'Say, are you only forty-nine? Sure look a lot . . .'

'I met you before in Los Angeles during the . . .'

'She sure is a great First Lady. I mean you are one . . .'

'Happy birthday, sir, to . . .'

'Did you know . . .'

'Congressman David Shaw-Murray. He's our . . .'

'They need you in the Oval Office, sir.'

Dixon looked up at Joe Meisner, his Chief of Staff. 'Can't you see I'm busy with these good people, Joe?'

'It's a matter of some urgency, Mr President,' insisted Meisner.

'We being invaded by aliens?'

'No, sir. More important than that.'

Dixon laughed. 'Nothing can be more important than me saying hello to a few more of these nice folk.'

'You can be back in just fifteen minutes, Mr President. Then you've got time for everyone.'

'You're a hard taskmaster, Joe.' Dixon turned back to the elderly couple from Nebraska he had been shaking hands with. 'Will you folks excuse me for a few minutes? If you stay right here, then when I get back, I'll carry on talking with you.' He turned to Clancy. 'You bring me right back here when we return, Don?'

'Yes, Mr President,' acknowledged Clancy, as Dixon's gaze turned to the other side of the room.

'Annie OK?' he inquired.

'Yes, sir. Got my secretary, Mary, helping her with the crowd.'

'OK, let's go.'

Meisner led the way with the President, both followed closely by Clancy. They pushed through the ebullient throng and entered the ante-room which housed the elevators.

'Which Oval Office?' asked Dixon coldly, all pretence stripped away now that the crowds weren't present.

'Twelfth floor, sir,' confirmed Meisner. The huge White House Annex had four exact Oval Office replicas spread over

31

its ninety-six administration floors. These offices enabled the President and his entourage to move around the large administrative block whilst still being able to find the privacy offered by his own office, for a variety of reasons. As most communications occurred by visual imagery contact, either on a video phone or through a video link on the internet, few of the President's callers ever knew that he wasn't sitting in the *real* Oval Office.

The small group stepped into the elevator, where Dixon put his thumb on the security recognition pad and punched the button. They stood quietly as the elevator dropped seventeen floors. It opened on a smaller vestibule than the one they had just left.

Smerton waited for them as they stepped out of the lift.

'OK?' asked Dixon.

'Yes, Mister President.'

There was a glass door, bullet-proof and shockproof, set in a similar glass wall, halfway across the area. To pass through it, each person needed to step up to the security faceplate and have their eyes scanned before the door would open, allowing access to the small glass cubicle on the other side of it to only one person at a time. The President went through alone. The others, with the exception of Clancy, entered a second, smaller waiting room.

Clancy now stayed in the vestibule to secure the area against anyone who tried to enter the Oval Office suite. He pulled up one of the velvet upholstered chairs and positioned himself facing the elevator doors. He switched off his multi-way communication system. This was not a time he needed to be available, to be in contact with the outside world. He relaxed. He knew the President's habits. They were all safe in this place.

I then made myself an organic-farmland cheese sandwich, then went back in time to watch the legendary movie star sing to the President.

The Great Crusader, that's what they called him. More Lucky Crusader. Real lucky that we didn't end up with the Third World War. It was only because the Chinese and the Russians were getting used to the soft life, now that their own economies were booming past those of the West, that they hadn't retaliated in traditional fashion. And the oil wasn't that important any more, now that the West had nearly ended its dependence on fossil fuels through all the new eco-energies. It's amazing what necessity and fear can produce: how quickly it galvanizes purpose.

No, I didn't like ol' Teddy Dixon, didn't trust him. He was a known womanizer, but the Yanks seemed to accept all that. Not the sort of chap I'd help out in a spot of trouble. More like, enjoy seeing him stew.

I watched Monroe sing. I'd seen clips of her singing to JFK and knew how accurately the image-makers had replicated that event. Her sexiness was obvious; they didn't move like that any more. I now realized why so many who visited the Brick were always wanting contact with the old movie stars. Even ThemeCorp, my employers, had hoarded some of the biggest copyrights on the great names of the past and their images.

I lost interest once she finished singing, took a bite from

my sandwich, switched off the screen and headed for the lounge. I looked forward to the quiet of the evening, though boredom was setting in again. Maybe it was time to close down the cottage and just walk around the countryside. After all, that's why I'd bought this place far away from the Sprawl where everyone else lived. To get away from the outside world. To get away from the Brick and everything it now represented.

Dixon closed the door to the Oval Office behind him as he entered. He loved this room. It represented so much of the contemporary history of the country he now led. Since 1800 the official residence of the President of the United States, the White House was the symbol, sometimes loved, and often hated, of the most powerful nation in the world. It was even more powerful than the United European Republic that had been spawned to counteract the USA's strength in the earlier twenty-first century. Europe had meanwhile withstood its own Great Ethnic Wars between its own citizens and the millions of illegal immigrants who had broken across its borders looking for a better life. Eventually, after years of Islamic terrorist activity from those who had come across as asylum seekers but had developed more sinister and revolutionary motives, the borders were closed and an armed, mined, thirty-foot-high concrete and steel wall was built from Albania right across to the Russian Republic. The old Berlin Wall was now well exceeded by the Great Islamic Wall, which had been the first step to securing Fortress West.

Meanwhile, Fortress USA secured itself, too, after continuous terrorist attacks. They had started with the destruction of New York's Twin Towers, which brought about the Middle Eastern and other Liberation wars. The deaths of their own soldiers, the lack of success against an unseen enemy, the burgeoning of a war with no frontiers to cross, had shocked America, so it had slammed up the barriers against all outsiders, even Europe. It wasn't until the Great Islamic Wall across Europe was completed that America reopened its doors to its allies.

The world had polarized. Each faction had become polluted by its own ideology, its pious belief that it served the one true God.

On one side of the fence was the modern consumer-driven culture of the USA, the United European Republic, the expanding South American continent, also Japan, the Russian Republic and Australia. Ranged against them were the Muslim-dominated Arab, African and Near East countries who had abandoned the West's dream of democracy and returned to a culture motivated by religious zealotry. Israel had survived as a small oasis of democracy because of the armed support and destructive rocket weaponry placed on its borders by the USA. China and India supported the West because they needed its trade to feed their millions. But they otherwise remained neutral and waited to see how the world would resolve itself.

Teddy Dixon was the keyholder of that great power. He hugely enjoyed being the most powerful man in the world. But at this moment his mind was on other matters.

She was already there, waiting for him. Sitting in his chair, with her back to him, she stared out over the lawns that led to the Ellipse. Her blonde hair rested on the top of the high-backed chair. Marilyn. As real as ever she was. She swivelled round and faced him. 'Good evening, Mr President.'

'Marilyn, my dear,' he acknowledged as he crossed the room to stand in front of the desk. She was still wearing that famous dress, the one that seemingly had no room for anything underneath it. 'May I call you Marilyn?'

'You're the Prezzident. You can call me anything you want . . . honey.' She purred the last word as if it melted on her lips.

'What did *he* call you?'

She smiled, coy and mischievous. That was what they all wanted to know. 'You mean Johnny?'

'You know damn well who I mean.' Over three-quarters of a century since his assassination and JFK was still the President they all remembered, all revered.

'Naughty ... using those bad words ... and with me here to please you,' she admonished playfully. 'But then you can,' she squealed. 'You're just *sooo* big. You can do anything you want with little me.' She uncurled and stood up from the chair. 'Why don't you come and sit down, Mr President.'

'What did he call you?'

'Just his baby. And his honey. I was always Johnny's honey.'

Dixon moved round the desk. 'You can call me Teddy ... honey.'

'OK, Teddy baby. My little honey. Just sit down, just relax.'

He eased past her, felt her firm, sensual shape under the dress. He couldn't restrain himself from letting his hands slide over her body before he settled into the chair. She smiled at him, as if secretly mocking his weakness. But, then, they both knew she was a goddess.

The goddess sat on his lap, put her arms round his shoulders and pressed her lips against his. His head went wild as her tongue probed his mouth, licking it from side to side, entwining his tongue with hers; soft lips, moist lips, drowning him in her passion. His erection was instant. She squiggled and wriggled on his lap as she felt his manifest interest. The goddess intensified her attentions on his mouth, then slipped her tongue into his ear. She knew, from his immediate reaction, that she'd done the right thing.

Dixon started to stroke her body fiercely, explored her breasts, soft with a young woman's firmness under the silver dress. Then his hands moved lower, covered her mound, stroked it frantically through the thin material. He knew now for certain she was wearing nothing underneath. Just as he had always imagined. She moved her lips back to his and started kissing him deeply once again. This time she was so fierce in her probing that he had trouble breathing. He pushed her away to catch his breath.

The phone rang. They both froze, startled by the suddenness of the ringing.

'Leave it,' he said, as he returned to her kissing, but the phone kept ringing insistently. He pulled away again and tried to regulate his breathing. Once he had brought it under some degree of control, he picked up the handset. 'Yes,' he said sharply.

'The First Lady's asking where you are.' It was Meisner from next door. 'She's got the Secret Service looking for you.'

'Just say I've had to take a call. International. Say I'll be back soon.'

'OK. But, please, don't be too long.'

'Anybody know I'm here?'

'Only those of us out here.'

'Keep me covered. And don't disturb me again. *Unless . . .*' Dixon put down the phone, his last words unsaid but understood by Meisner.

'Just like Johnny. Always on the run, from Jackie.' Marilyn smiled conspiratorially. 'Bobby always protected Johnny. Bobby always knew where he was. But then, Bobby always knew where I was, too.' She giggled and tongued his ear again.

Dixon gripped her shoulders and pushed her away from him. Then he forced her down onto her knees in front of him. The force and sharpness of his grip made her wince; her eyes softened with the tears of pain which she struggled to hold back. Holding her with one hand, he unzipped his trousers with the other. 'Come on,' he ordered. 'You know what to do.'

'I'm not just any cheap hooker,' she protested.

'Do what you're here for,' he shouted, then slapped her sharply across the cheek with his free hand. She reeled back but didn't fall as his hand still gripped her shoulder. 'Do it,' he commanded again.

'Johnny never hurt me like that.'

'I'm not Johnny.'

'And I'm not Monica-sucking-Lewinsky,' she purred back. 'If you want me, then do it properly. Let's go where I went with Johnny.'

'Here? In the Oval Room.'

'No, never in here. We had our special place.'

'I haven't got time.'

'You're King of the Hill, so make the time.' Through the open zip, she stroked the hardness under his pants. 'Come on, baby. Who's going to call time on the Prezzident? Just ten minutes, baby. And you'll get everything you want in that time. I'm the best. I always was. That's why the world loved me . . . that's why they all wanted me. The best, baby. Just for you.'

Dixon reached over, picked up the receiver and connected to the waiting room. 'Fifteen minutes. Buy me fifteen minutes.'

'Yes, Mr President,' replied Meisner, but the phone had already disconnected. He pressed the switch on one side of the phone that stopped any recording of the conversation. Meisner was a man who liked to cover his own back. As far as he was concerned it would only be a matter of time before Dixon walked into trouble; that was the problem with having an unguided missile for your boss.

'So tell me more about you and Johnny,' Dixon said.

'Not here,' she gasped, her breath heavy with anticipation.

'I can't leave.'

'We'll be there in seconds. Just out of here and down West Executive Avenue.'

'Where to?'

'You'll find out.'

'Not the Old Executive Building?' He vaguely remembered it was on the other side of West Executive.

She giggled, her voice husky and inviting. 'I'll surprise you.'

'I can't leave here. Security.'

'That's why Johnny used the secret door. So we wouldn't get caught.'

'You know that?' Dixon was surprised.

'I know everything, Mr Prezzident.' She knelt forward and nuzzled the pronounced bulge under his pants. Then she zipped him up and stood, holding out her hand, inviting him to go with her.

'I can't . . .'

'You can. Anything you want. Just ten minutes. Then you'll know everything that Johnny liked.'

'OK. You really knew there was another back way out of here?' he repeated incredulously. 'I'd like to see the Secret Service faces when they find out about that.' He chuckled.

'He told me everything.'

'OK. But let's make it real short.'

'As short . . . or as long as you want.'

He held back momentarily. 'But you're not . . . I mean, not Marilyn . . . How do you know what really happened?'

She laughed. 'Cos I just know, silly. That's why you got the best. I know everything.'

There was a message light flashing on the old phone I kept for nostalgia's sake. I knew it was one of my country neighbours. They still liked using the landline, even if there was no landline; they'd been phased out decades ago. Everything passed through the air, all data, all conversations. The phones they used were just handsets with old-fashioned dials that looked like they were linked to something solid beyond that plug in the wall. *Looking at them, you wouldn't think mobiles had been around for over seventy years.* Norfolk folk liked something dependable in their hands, something grounded. That's how the farmers preferred it. Old fashioned with old-style attitudes.

'Conor,' started John Mathews on VoiceMail, 'if you're ordering anything from Sainsbury's could you please add the following?' Mathews then listed several items he needed at home. As he finished his list he added, 'There'll be someone in all day to take delivery. And, if you do come over, your bacon's ready.'

I replayed the message, recording it on to my Compu-Phone. Mathews was a pig farmer two miles down the road and, when I'd first moved here, he'd been the slowest to accept the new incomer. But, once he realized the Londoner in me had transplanted to their midst because I simply wanted to live as plainly as they did, we became firm friends. That relationship had taken more than ten years to forge, by which time the local community didn't regard me as a 'furriner' any longer. In his late seventies, Mathews was one of many in the rural areas who didn't even own a simple computer, save the MediJacket that linked him to his doctor. He regarded most modern technology as the scourge of civilization.

He'd occasionally drive over to Rose Cottage for a game of cards and a few glasses of mulled wine to help while away late evenings. He was one of my rare visitors and we always played in the kitchen, the one room where there was very little technology on show. Our games were interspaced with long, comfortable silences, interrupted by trivial comments that happened to cross our minds. I enjoyed the trivia. No competition, no envy, no attempt at outdoing each other.

Mathews took solace in our sessions for another reason. His wife had died twenty years earlier of a cancer growth, just before DNA clone-surgery was introduced, and he had subsequently locked himself within his own sorrow.

'What I miss most', he told me once, 'are the little things. Not the big events but small . . . incidents. Things like seeing a woodpecker climb up the balcony railings to steal a peanut from a bluetit, or tiny ducklings following their mother across the lawn towards the river. There's no one for me to share these moments with, no one to whisper to so the birds won't hear me, *Hey come look at this; hurry up before they go*. That's what makes you lonely. Little, personal things, things that nobody else would give a damn about.'

Thus we shared the inconsequential and made it personal, and it became the strength of our friendship.

He rarely asked about my past. But he sensed my loneliness.

'You've never loved, have you?' he'd once asked, surprising me with such a personal question.

'My parents. My job. Things I've done.'

'No, I mean another person. A woman?'

'Messed around with a few.'

42

'I don't mean that,' was his dismissive reply. 'I'm talking about love . . . you know, jealousy and pain when you think they're with someone else, and sheer joy whenever you're with them.'

'Not yet.'

'Loneliness isn't good, you know.'

'*You* should know,' I'd snapped. I'd hit back, felt a rush of anger, then instantly regretted it.

'Don't matter,' came the unconcerned reply. 'At least I had it – love – most of my life. You're never really lonely after you've had all that. Bit sorry for yourself, sometimes, maybe, but nothing you can't cope with. *You* take life too seriously, let the wrongs of the world get on top of you.'

'It's a messed-up place, so who cares?'

'You snap too easily. You're not like that at work, are you?'

'Of course not. I'm the one in control there.'

'Don't think I'm getting at you, but you've got to bring your anger – or maybe it's frustration – under control.' His next question was even more surprising, from one usually so reserved. 'Who hurt you, Conor?'

'Nobody.'

'Then why?'

'I wish I knew,' I interrupted him. Yet he was prising me open, and I suddenly felt a need to share myself with someone else. 'I sometimes think it's because I've never had a real purpose, never done anything that mattered. I had a great family, was successful at everything I did, and none of it took much effort. Success just happened. I've got everything most people want. Apart from my parents dying, nothing's ever really affected me. It's all too easy, too boring. That's how the world is now. Everybody lives in Fantasy Land. Nothing's real any more. All this Web stuff, it's the great escape from life, isn't it? And yet I'm one of its architects. One of its Gatekeepers.' I sighed with frustration.

43

'I know it's all wrong, yet I can't walk away. I need something real, John. I need to do something that makes a real difference.'

I sensed him looking at me searchingly. I had kept my gaze averted while I'd been speaking, but I now looked him directly in the eye. 'I think that's why I escaped out here,' I added eventually. 'Rose Cottage, here, it's my stab at reality, of staying in touch with what life's really about.'

'This place needs a woman's touch. It's all too spartan and clinical inside, too simple, too uncluttered.'

Mathews's grin annoyed me. It was patronizing: an older man's certainty that he knew all the answers because of the few years longer that he'd lived. More than that, we both knew I'd revealed more than I ever had with anyone else. Then I grinned, realizing he'd beaten me because he was right. I leant back in the chair and shook my head. It was not often someone got under my defences.

'You need debris in your life, Conor,' he had then continued. 'Things to remind you that you've been hurt . . . that you've got some things wrong.' Mathews had waved his hand round to encompass the room. 'It's a beautiful cottage . . . but it needs to acquire a soul.'

Rose Cottage itself had been a small farm-worker's two-storey house, high on a whale-shaped hill overlooking the undulating farmland that makes up the countryside of Norfolk. I'd bought the dilapidated place in 2019, just after the United Kingdom had finally become a full member of the United European Federation. It was to be another ten years before the Kingdom finally disowned its monarchy and each of the countries that had once made up the Union became separate regions within the new United European Republic.

I'd lived at the London end of the Inner Sprawl, that mass of urban concrete metropolis that stretched from Southampton through Birmingham to Manchester and Leeds along the old motorway system, on a comfortable salary that provided an equally comfortable lifestyle. But once the politicians had stripped away England's heritage and identity in the cause of political modernity, I decided to move out of the Sprawl, away from the increasing European influences that I knew would follow. Government by bureaucracy was not something I felt comfortable with. I was tired of 'political correctness', of the constant withdrawal of personal freedoms, of the power of a few to control the lives of the many. Government did now, especially in the big cities, watch and control every aspect of everyday life. Technology and bureaucracy had merged into one. It had devolved large groups of people into small ones. It forced most people onto public transport, so it became difficult for individuals to travel at their own convenience to wherever they wanted. A static population, after all, was a controllable population. This created an environment where people spoke to each other via emails and text messages instead of face-to-face. It had most of them working from home where they rarely had the opportunity to meet, and could only communicate through electronic routes set up – and monitored – by the government itself.

It was a regime I found increasingly unacceptable. Yet I'd been one of those who had brought about those new technologies. But, despite the rewards, I refused to be a contented slave.

I sold my house in super-fashionable Richmond and moved to the country. I hired one of the city-rent cars which were available at all main train and bus stations. These had become necessary once residential parking and congestion charges had priced the majority of Inner Sprawl dwellers out of the car market. Only the very rich and the megacorporations could afford to use their cars inside the capital. And that included all the politicians and civil servants who had overcharged the residents in the first place. I hated the Sprawl anyway, both Inner and Outer. Grimy, dirty, a shabby place, always wet underfoot in the perma-rain that had become the norm in the northern hemisphere during global warming.

The car I chose, a BMWRover Upright Classic – a simple two-seater powered by a 1.1 litre engine – was the standard vehicle that EuroHertz hired out. With a full tank of hydrogen fuel it could run for over eight hundred miles.

I headed for East Anglia, a part of England that had suffered least change since the millennium. It lay on the eastern edge of the Outer Sprawl, that suburban belt that had stretched its tentacles over most rural areas. Over the years, to escape the city, the Townies had moved out of the Inner Sprawl, into second homes, leaving decaying and disintegrating communities behind. All they achieved was to take with them the very hopelessness they had left behind, the chief difference being they now lived in houses with gardens instead of window boxes. These hapless communities moved further out in suburban convoys, and it wasn't long before crime and government restrictions had overtaken their desperate dreams of freedom.

It was no Golden Age, in spite of the government messages that filled the media. Yes, people lived longer, were fitter, had nice warm identical homes, were perpetually young and never did without. They saw real life on television, watched wars and disasters and tragedies unfold from the comfort of their armchairs and their secure warm sheltered lives. It was real Reality TV at its best: watched by the masses, all huddled in front of their latest plasma widescreen Reality Screens.

It was how the world had become. Evolution. Nobody knew how to change it. Nobody could be bothered to change it.

Trouble is, as John Mathews always said, *people just don't know any better any more. It's a soap generation acting out their favourite soap TV shows. I reckon the actors should stop acting and watch the damned audience. I don't think they'd see any bloody difference.*

I had driven through the Outer Sprawl, past the myriad of ever-changing billboards that littered the motorways, past the girls in their Tesco dresses under their Tesco macs, past the dull streets watched by the ever present street cams, and towards somewhere different.

East Anglia, one of the few remaining protected rural belts in England, became a pleasure for me with the sights and reminders of its medieval history, and I had later spent many happy days learning all about the region. I was lucky to have the eurodollarcredits to afford such an individual lifestyle.

Even the weather was easier, as the perma-rain seemed not to affect East Anglia like the rest of the British Isles and Central Europe. Most people didn't really mind the permanent damp – after all, it kept the country warm and lush and everything grew well in that climate. Not like in southern Europe, in Greece and Spain and Italy, even southern Germany, where the deserts had begun to spread in the infra-heat of the endless dry sunshine.

The small house I bought was basically a ruin, the shell still intact but the interior floors long since collapsed. A two-bedroom cottage with a large family room on the ground floor, it stood up on a hill from where the views were exhilarating. The moment I decided to buy it was when I witnessed my first East Anglian sunset, a brilliant gouache of pastels spread across a vast Norfolk sky.

I had the place converted and moved into it five months later. There I soon grew accustomed to the silence of dark nights, to the fluttering and rustling of nature, to the storms that shook the ground then burnt themselves out, and used to being alone in a lonely place.

My first purchase was a new mid-range PeugeotFiat four-wheel drive EconoCruiser. I'd always loved driving but never had the opportunity to own a car before, that being how it was in the Inner Sprawl. Pro-car there meant anti-social. Within the Sprawls, everyone travelled by MetroTube for long distances, in trams and mini-buses for local journeys, or in Hi-Speed People Movers which covered the medium distances within the Inner Sprawl at over two hundred miles per hour. Those in the Outer Sprawl used low-end electric cars with a maximum speed of 25 miles per hour and a range of ninety miles – enough to get them to work and back and maybe occasionally the shops. That's how the government controlled people. Limit movement and you limit the spirit. And blame it all on protecting the planet.

That new car was my expression of freedom.

I took my work to Norfolk with me. I also took time to determine a new career. Business and all the other opportunities open to me, including being a super snoop for Britain's spy centre at GCHQ, were not for me. I liked being on the outside, doing my own thing, so I decided to become a GameMaster.

Never married, or even interested, my one love had been computers. An only child of working parents, my best friend and teacher had been the Apple Macintosh my parents kept in their study. At five I was playing games on it, by eight writing programs to design my own games. No one taught me, I just had a knack of picking things up. By eleven, when I left primary school, I was hacking into my school reports, company finances, and anything else that happened to interest me.

I was first arrested when I was fifteen. The Ministry of Education objected to my infiltrating their main system and thus trying to change my grades. Whilst doing that I'd also pulled up all the personal files on those teachers I disliked, including their salaries, and emailed them to all the pupils, the parents, other schools and to the teachers themselves.

'It took us eleven weeks to trace you,' admitted the police sergeant from the Technological Crime Prevention Unit, as he confronted me in the Headmaster's study. 'It usually takes three, at the most, so you've clearly got a talent, but you can't just break the law when you feel like it. I want your word that you won't do this again.'

I nodded; with the long arm of the law pointed directly at me, I would've agreed to almost anything.

The sergeant pushed a form across the table and held out a pen. 'Sign that. It's an admission of guilt, but it also confirms we're not prosecuting you *this* time.' I quickly did as I was told. 'Next time you'll be put in His Majesty's custody. To you, that's jail, and being fourteen won't help you. Straight in, as a young offender you'd go. We need to do that, son, otherwise you'll end up robbing people and generally messing up society. And we can't allow that, can we?'

'No, sir.'

'You do understand you've done wrong, don't you?'

'Yes, sir.'

'Good. Now . . . how would you like to work for us?'

And that is how I started working, part-time, for the TCPU. At a very young age, the poacher had turned gamekeeper. Hacker was now cracker.

My inquisitive mind was suited to this new work perfectly. I found ways into hackers' computers in a manner that surprised even the most experienced police experts. By day, until I was seventeen, I attended school and walked away with a high-grade baccalaureate. My maths and IT results were almost perfect passes. The rest of my results were failures, until I hacked them and changed them. The education authorities reported me but my Team Sergeant at TCPU, the division investigating the misdemeanour, simply stated they had found no evidence to convict me. They tut-tutted me, then said I anyway had the minimum qualifications required to be fully employed by them.

I declined the opportunity to go on to university and by the age of twenty was the TCPU's senior programer at Scotland Yard. I devised a version of specific computer languages, a stack-based threaded interpretive language which meshed together the protocols on various systems and gave me the opportunity to command prompts while the graphics and other information were still running. It meant, as I explained to my uninformed supervisors, the fishhook was in the fish even before it had taken the bait.

But, the gamekeeper missed poaching, as few of the hackers ever got past me. I had no desire to make millions; money was an irrelevance, only a necessity in a confused world. I turned down offers to go to Silicon Valley and Cambridge. My spare moments were spent in internet cafes, mixing with those who had the same interests. My relationships with women were rare; I only found really interesting those who challenged me intellectually. Sex was a way of connecting, a final coming together of two like-minded people. Once that was achieved, the friendship remained, but the sex itself just faded away.

I never wanted to stay with them more than one night. And they were much the same. In the modern world, real relationships didn't start until most were well into their thirties, or very often their forties. When they said *make love to me* I translated it into *fuck me*. I always left the bed angry; slightly ashamed but not knowing why. There had to be something more than one-nighters. It all seemed so pointless somehow.

I roved the world on the internet and the newly expanding Web. No place was spared from me, no file or organization safe. I wasn't vindictive with the information I unearthed, never misused it for personal gain. The joy was in the success of exploration rather than in the result.

On my twentieth birthday, after a morning of headaches and inner anger, I decided it was time to move on. I went to work in the morning and hacked into the TCPU's most confidential files, the very ones I already had access to. The trail I left led via various countries, internet service providers, websites and the computers of some of the largest corporations in the world. My aim was to let the TCPU know that they had been accessed, but leave them unable to trace the perpetrator. The information I downloaded was sent to every newspaper in England. By lunchtime, with my colleagues going frantic as they tried to trace the hacker, I switched off my machine, after wiping out all evidence that could be traced back to me, spiked the source to 10 Downing Street as being the zone where the hack had been created, handed in my resignation and left Scotland Yard.

They always suspected it was me who had unloaded their files into the public arena.

'People get killed for less,' my superior had warned me over the phone a week later.

'Or get left alone simply for what they know.'

But they knew they'd never pin it on me; they'd trained me too well.

The headaches and rages then disappeared until the next time.

Don Clancy sensed something was wrong even before the First Lady herself came down to the 12th floor.

Meisner's instructions had been clear. 'Don't go into the Oval Office. Those are the President's specific commands.' Then Meisner had played the recording of Dixon's last orders on the phone to confirm this instruction.

The Secret Service had changed little over the years. Since the unsuccessful attempt on Ronald Reagan's life, it had become the ultimate protection squad. Trained to 'cover and evacuate', to instinctively hurl himself in front of bullets, each agent was highly skilled in many disciplines and possessed exceptional physical fitness. However, the truth was that, because of a lack of real contemporaneous experience, the Secret Service still lived in its past. Since the raising of the Great Islamic Wall there had been no real threats against any President, and they were now as much merely an emblem of his power as was AirForce One or the Great Seal behind his desk in the Oval Office.

The agents had developed their own style in work-wear, most of it deriving from the image of them that was portrayed in the movies. They invariably wore reflective shades, dark suits and black shiny shoes. Their jackets were long, as fashion now dictated, and went down to the knee, shades of an old cult film called *The Matrix*. They were all wired to the same communications system and could speak normally, not whispering into their sleeves as they had done at the start of the millennium. New technology meant that a mini microphone on their lapel was programmed to pick up its wearer's voice alone and delete all background sounds.

They were serious and smiled rarely; purposefully trained to be paranoid. It was that instinct above all that was supposed to keep them constantly alert. And it was this culture of paranoia that made Clancy nervous of his own men.

Twenty minutes had elapsed since he'd been left waiting in the ante-room. He was used to clandestine trips to various parts of the White House, both in the Annex and the Real White House. The President was addicted to the buzz of danger and, even though he had complete anonymity in Second World, he still enjoyed the odd sexual exchange in the confines of the real Oval Office with his lady visitors. All the Secret Service agents who bodyguarded the President also protected his amorous eccentricities. It had been that way with all Presidents since the Secret Service was founded.

In RealWorld, Clancy knew, these assignments rarely took more than ten minutes, passing opportunities grabbed in strange dark corners. Out here, in Second World, they could last for anything up to half an hour; it was a place where the President had little chance of being discovered. Unless the First Lady was nearby. And twenty minutes was beyond the safety margin. She could walk in the door at any moment. Clancy rang Meisner.

'He said he didn't want to be disturbed.' Meisner was adamant. 'If you think it's a security problem then you act accordingly.'

Clancy hung up. He was annoyed with himself for ringing the Chief of Staff. He'd already known the man wouldn't make a decision, just pass the buck back to him. He decided therefore to give it another five minutes. As he sat down again the phone rang. 'Yes.'

'I've been trying to get through.' Clancy recognized Wallenski, one of the agents accompanying the First Lady. 'I was onto Meisner.'

The door opened and the First Lady herself walked in, even as Wallenski continued. 'She's on her way down now. Said she was going to—'

Clancy put the phone down without answering. 'Mrs Dixon.'

'Where the hell is he, Don?' she demanded.

My VISI-Message screen flicked itself on. It was Theme-Corp's London office listing my appointments for next week. I glanced through them; things were quiet as expected with the maintenance schedule closing the park down.

ThemeCorp – I'd joined them just three weeks after leaving Scotland Yard.

The largest Virtual Reality company in the world, it had been launched only nine years previously at Cambridge University's Bill Gates Uni, the dominant information technology campus in Europe. ThemeCorp was funded and run by a group of scientists who had worked for the US government, got tired of the snail-like progress of official bureaucracy and decided to branch out on their own. With an R & D budget of four billion dollars, raised by willing Wall Street and City of London stock markets, both eager to cash in on the new brainpower that had been released into the commercial world, it leapfrogged all its competitors in linking the World Wide Web with Virtual Reality. It was the first major theme park on the Brick, growing faster than the more established companies like UniversalDisney and ActionCorp.

Two years later, at the age of twenty-two, I myself joined them. I was once again the bright kid on the block, one of their top designers. My WebName, Condor, which I'd adopted when I first went on the Web, was forgotten in favour of my own real name. It was how things were now:

people didn't need WebNames any longer. Not when they had avatars they could live in. The avatar had been the real breakthrough. And the avatars were Real Time images in the VR, puppets in the likeness of their controlling masters who could jump through the Web, from situation to situation, from VR activity to VR activity within milliseconds. It was the start of Second World, the jumping-off point where ordinary people could become supermen without leaving the comfort of their homes.

I'd tested the first practical biosensor, one that tracked my eye movements by measuring my muscle commands. In time, as more biosensors were added, body movements worked in conjunction with eye directions to create complete coordination in the VR. Further biosensors, in touch with separate parts of the body, sensed movement and translated them into action. So it was that a person could sit or lie down and watch their avatar, or puppet, moving in Second World, reacting as they imagined, moving in all directions with full coordination, yet themselves never moving physically from where they lay.

When this was combined with the vast video game technology that produced graphics engines capable of generating a minimum of seventy-five million polygons per second, the basic requirement of 3D modelling, VR characters lost the angular geometric toy-like appearance they had been known for, and became thoroughly lifelike. It became impossible to tell the difference between Buzz Lightyear and your mother as graphics engines increased their capacity at phenomenal rates.

There was also Alpha World, created back in 1995, which had become the largest and most populated township in the new Active World's universe. As the first step to where people could meet via their avatars, outside of the normal chatrooms that had proliferated, it started slowly and was initially used only by WebFreaks and techies. Alpha World was a flat featureless plain, with no natural landmarks, which spread in all directions for hundreds of cyberspace miles, approximating to the size of California. Before long it attracted settlers from RealWorld, mostly individuals who ran the Web and there built homes for themselves, to escape into. Their avatars looked lumpy and their blobby movements eventually improved as technology marched on. Some built forests and gardens around their residences, but the technology of the time made them look like kids' drawings – in out-of-focus 3D. Soon, hundreds of thousands had homes in Alpha World and there communicated with each other with their ideas and their dreams. It was the days before avatars could speak as they now did, fluently and effortlessly.

Second Life had also grown during this period and these two visual landscapes were pioneered and developed by millions of people across the world, all intermingling through their computers, through the biosensors. The newlands became even more important when the Great Islamic Wall went up; people could meet and talk without leaving their own countries. Many saw it as a way towards a peaceful future, where ideas could cross borders and ferment in order to bring about understanding and tolerance in the future. Churches and mosques were built in all these newlands and the violence of RealWorld stayed out of Alpha World and Second Life.

But commerce, which was suffering in RealWorld, recognized the growth of the Web. Big corporations invested heavily, and rushed to invest in this new Second World. They realized how they could carve it up and rent it out. To them, it was just another profitable piece of real estate.

Their key to success was the technology in which they now invested to speed up growth. The first breakthrough was the ability of cable-free computers to pass information between themselves at speeds in excess of sixty gigabytes per second, which meant that life in Second World was catching up with that in RealWorld.

I'd tested the third full bodysuit on the newly expanded Web. Both UniversalDisney and ActionCorp beat Theme-Corp and NintendoSony to the punch. The bodysuit was a complete human covering which supported VR sensors and effectors. The human body contains ten trillion cells and one trillion of those are in the brain alone. The new bodysuits only managed to have a billion sensors, so movement in VR remained jerky to say the least. Originally known as DataSuits, a name too formal for the evolving market, they soon became known as WebSkins. Within three years, the WebSkins had gone from clumsy, tight-fitting rubber bodysuits with sensors attached to the wearer's skin to simple, loose-fitting cloaks that were as thin and light as cotton. These cloaks also had over five trillion sensors attached to them and VR movement became less jerky and more comfortable. The market grew dramatically with these new garments. The same technology that had freed the common computer from the limitations of its cables now had sensors that could translate every small electrical movement in a person's muscles.

The unique strength of the brain is that it is the only part of the body that is totally contained within its own protective shell. The only outlet for its information sensors is down the back of the neck and through the vertebrae. It was this area the designers concentrated on next. They developed an electronic shank that, when placed on the back of the neck, just under the cranium exit, picked up the brain's pulses that were being pumped around the body. This shank was then connected wirelessly to any computer within fifty feet, and this gave its user the opportunity to link his brain patterns directly to the Web.

Having freed the user from the cumbersome and clumsy helmets of early VR, Second World became open to anyone and to everyone.

Movement in the Web was, at its very slowest, in Real Time. As people thought, so they moved. The loss in time was counted in nanoseconds. Think Time was the next breakthrough. Users only had to think of movement and, as long as they satisfied the entrance criteria, could immediately catapult themselves from one location to another. Commercially that suited the megacorporations. They charged membership fees for their various locales, whether it was a theme park, a hotel, a meeting room or any of the thousands of other venues on offer.

The problem for many became differentiating between RealWorld and Second World.

The megacorporations set out to recoup their investments and rushed to build sites on the Web.

Alpha World and Second Life developed into communes, their amoeba-like spread by now too large and too far-reaching to become a controlled zone.

So, determined to control the Web, Western governments bypassed the two earlier communes, banded together and created the Yellow Brick Road. Known as the Brick, the road, a yellow-tiled highway, stretched on into infinity, a never-ending boulevard in cyberspace. The Chinese and Indians, and through them the Muslim world, now flocked to join the Web. Governments had taken over sections of the Brick and leased them out to the corporations, some immense, some small. Space on the Brick was bought up by all manner of businesses who found that the VR created vast new markets. If people could visit the Brick, then there had to be something for them to visit. Soon there were restaurants, hotels, theme parks, sports centres, offices, meeting rooms; you name it. If it existed in RealWorld then it was duplicated in Second World.

The world there felt safe from the terrorists. Everyone met on the Web and nobody crossed the RealWorld borders they weren't entitled to. The West knew that the Islamic fundamentalists, who kept a hold on their power by subjugating their peoples in harsh conditions, were blocked out in RealWorld from the areas they might attack, yet they could trade ideas and goods though Second World, whilst still giving vent to their ideologies. There were mosques and synagogues and churches along the Brick, built right alongside the theme parks and hotels. It was a system that suited all and made money for everyone.

Millionaire entrepreneurs came and went; the upsurge in billionaires in the late 1990s, when the Web first started, was a gentle ripple compared to this explosion. Stock markets crashed and rose again. Whole economies were thrown around like ships in a force ten gale by new waves of technological change.

By now I was a freelance Accelerator, specializing in hardware and software that increased the speed of graphics manipulation. It changed my thinking of a slower Real-World. I became a test pilot for the Web, hiring myself out to the companies who raced each other to invent and sell the latest VR kit. My personal fortune rose, built not on the whim of investors but on the banking of hard cash paid for my old hacker talents. But money still didn't interest me. I just wanted to be the best on the Web, to understand its future, to go, like starship *Enterprise*, where no man had gone before.

By the age of twenty-four I was one of the few Accelerators who got a licence to wire a SmartChip under my skin at the base of my neck instead of clipping on a shank. Unlawful for everyday Web users, the SmartChip meant that I could enter the Web at any time and at any speed, as long as I was within one hundred and fifty feet of a cable-free wireless computer. All I needed was a pair of sunglasses that carried the batteries and switching units that triggered the chip into operation. The shades helped because it was easier not to be distracted by RealWorld once I entered Second World. The chip itself was a licensed item, designed to prevent hackers and other unauthorized users from entering private and work computers. Anyone found with an unauthorized SmartChip could expect a prison term of at least five years.

The final frontier had been breached in 2012, when quantum computers and nanochips came of age. Quantum computers worked differently. Based on the theoretical constructions of Paul Benioff, David Deutsch and Richard Feynman during the last few years of the twentieth century, these computers didn't queue each request, but instead performed mammoth parallel computations. This, in conjunction with the latest nanotechnology, where conventional silicone-based microcomputers could still be used, entirely changed the technological world. Speed was instantaneous. Contact happened with the blink of an eye. Within ten years, every personal computer was a quantum machine.

The security services were the biggest winners. They could now break through personal security codes. Prior to quantums, security, for decades, had been based on a variable password system called PGP, Pretty Good Privacy. That now changed and the security services could identify and track all personal computers unhindered. It was, of course, unlawful for them to do that without an InvasionWarrant granted by a high court judge, but the reality was that their access to the Web was total. Security wasn't the motive for the technodreamers like me, however.

Multi-programmed silicon chips, as fast as they were, had hit a brick wall with their limitations on speed and miniaturization. Copying human DNA and cells, the natural organic supercomputers that exist within all of us naturally, the technodreamers moved on to single-cell computers that rivalled atoms in size and could format to any planned molecular structure. Each nanocell had a simple unitary function that, when linked in any specific DNA mode with other nanocells, became sophisticated programs that were fast enough and small enough to make quantum computers utilize their full powers.

This nanotechnology was first developed and used in medicine, where nanomachines (as the DNA strands were called) could be injected into the body, carried along the bloodstream to a target such as a blocked artery or some diseased tissue, and then repair the damage with non-invasive surgery. These methods changed everything from the treatment of diabetes to the cure of mental illness, and even the daily use of medication.

The final frontier was in information technology. Its new microscopic molecular computers were designed not only to calculate and compute, but also to replicate themselves under certain circumstances when so programmed. They could also replicate the computer user in areas like Alpha World; except these were no blobby soft-movement avatars, but real, talking three-dimensional images that were no different from the host who controlled them in RealWorld.

The Web, with these technological breakthroughs, had finally become a mirror-image of RealWorld. And the problems were immense. Most Web users didn't have the physical and mental capacity to cope with the sudden speeds and changes of pace that took place in VR, even with support from the nanotechnology they had invented. WebFever, mind destroying, sometimes permanent, was in danger of becoming the new AIDS, as an incurable epidemic.

The United Nations stepped in and, with agreement from all the nations involved, created a set of laws that all countries must adhere to. Natural barriers were introduced so that avatars couldn't cross through walls and had to enter sites through approved entrances. Travel speed was limited so there was a semblance of reality, the senses of touch and feel and sight and sound imitated exactly those of the host user.

To safeguard the health of Web users, by law and because of medical opinion, most users could only enter the Web as avatars for no longer than six continual hours in twenty-four, or twelve continual in seventy-two. Any more than that legally required a rest period away from the Web of at least a week. Users could rest in the Web, however, and thus extend their usage hours considerably. Hotels sprang up to accommodate this necessity and the growth of private homes along the Brick flourished. The new houses, with cyber trees and gardens that grew and died with the seasons, were often more expensive than those in RealWorld, but the ability to have sustained rest periods in controlled Web-Environments ensured that users could stay away with their friends in secure surroundings for days.

It was proved that any normal Web user could last no more than thirteen continual hours of activity before the mind gave up and the user descended into WebFever and often madness.

One of my experiments, which lasted over twenty-one hours of active movement in Second World. took me three weeks to recover from. WebFever played havoc with my mind and body and without the help of the MindDoctors and their nanomedical support, I would almost certainly have stayed comatose. I knew it was time to leave the Sprawl. I was tired and jaded – in a loop – and what had once been challenges weren't challenges any longer.

ThemeCorp, always on the lookout for experienced Accelerators, suggested I rejoin them as a GameAssistant. It was a backward move, but I relished the opportunity of rising to GameMaster, since there were no more than forty of them throughout the world. They commanded enormous salaries, were on the front pages of celebrity magazines and were regularly being interviewed in the media as showhosts probed to find what future project would next revolutionize the Brick. But some were like me; the game was the thing, the attendant celebrity a nuisance. The GameMasters were the real pioneers of Second World, the ones who went out and pushed the frontiers. ThemeCorp, one of the giants of theme parks both in Second World and RealWorld, needed new ideas for their customers on a continuing basis.

The sense of urgency as I learnt new crafts and discovered different routes through the computerized maze, spurred me on. Within two years I was elevated to GameMaster, and, just before my thirtieth birthday, I realized I'd reached the top.

From then on, in the comparative peace of Norfolk, I concentrated on staying ahead of the field, developed training programs and worked with those who wanted to achieve GameNirvana. It rarely happened. Once or twice a year I'd test the latest games and theme events for ThemeCorp, but it didn't take long to unscramble their secrets. Other than that, I trained those who came to ThemeCorp and paid fortunes to play the various games. The Valley of the Dragons was only one of a hundred and twenty games. And I myself had mastered them all.

There was the one trip to Portofino. That was my real final adventure. I only needed to go once and, with the satisfaction of having there achieved what was termed the impossible, settled down to live life simply and on my own terms.

I occasionally helped the Security Services in Europe and the Americas, too. It was a carry-over from my police days, and one that helped me stay in contact with the hackers' world. Those guys were still pushing the boundaries and helped me keep ahead of the technology. More than once I let one escape with a warning before I shut him down. There but for the Grace of God and all that stuff.

In truth, I was soon bored once again. The headaches and rages returned. Life became inconsequential; I lived in a dream from which I would never wake, a dream I was somehow in control of. Thirty-nine years old and still playing video games.

I mixed with people I never met, just their avatars in cyberspace, in some digital scene of life and death that they could all escape from when the danger became too great.

Just bang the Jettison Passenger button they all carried on their wrists like a wristwatch and you were out of danger, back in your everyday suit in the comfort of home. *JetPax out of danger*: if only life were that easy.

Life in RealWorld was orderly, efficient, and sanitized, in spite of the Inner Sprawl. The excitement now lay in the disordered and distracted efficiency of the occupants and buildings on the Brick. The fun was in that which wasn't real; I lived and yearned for a world that I already inhabited, had helped create, but which didn't really exist.

I was ready for another challenge. Or, as Mathews pointed out, a real relationship. I'd stumbled into one, though, but not one Mathews would appreciate, or approve of.

I'd found an old pistol, a black 1914 Russian Nagan revolver, in one of the many antique shops that littered East Anglia. It was rusty and pitted with age and being sold only because it was non-serviceable. I found a gunsmith through the Web and had the Nagan restored; even managed to get the gunsmith to supply me with six bullets. It was an illegal transaction but cash was still king of the universe. I don't know why I bought the gun, but I was attracted to its deadly sexuality, its sole purpose to destroy, its lethal stillness that could only be woken by its owner, its sense of a foreboding and violent history. *What had it been used for? What evil deeds had it been party to?*

I loved it, for it was one of the few things that was more powerful than I was, one of the few things that could hurt me. I used to carry it loaded around Rose Cottage. I'd put it on the dining room table and watch it as I ate, brooding over its past, at times jealous that it had shared its malevolence with others. Later, I'd put it on the coffee table next to my armchair, lay the bullets in a fan shape around it, and then watch TV. My eyes would wander over to the black revolver and I trembled at its deadly calm, its power to meaninglessly destroy, its total lack of concern with those it obliterated. Yeah, then I'd take it to bed, slipping it into the bedside cabinet just before going to sleep.

On the morning of my fortieth birthday, I opened the drawer and looked at this gun.

With no forethought, as if it were a normal occurrence, I suddenly picked up the Nagan, emptied all the shells from its chamber, put one bullet back in, spun the chamber, snapped it shut, cocked it, put it in my mouth and pulled the trigger. It merely clicked. Then I put the gun down, filled the chamber with the remainder of the shells, and put it back in the drawer. I showered, shaved and went downstairs for breakfast.

I didn't get the shakes until I was eating my second slice of heavily buttered toast. Suddenly I broke into a sweat and felt a massive surge of excitement wash through me, in a real rush. Then I burst out laughing. Wow. I'd finally achieved something. Double Wow!! Something real, something that mattered, something I could feel and touch. I never carried the gun around with me after that. It stayed, fully loaded, in my bedside cabinet.

On every birthday, when I wake, I now take out the old Nagan, load it with one bullet, spin the chamber and pull the trigger with the barrel in my mouth. I've cheated death nine times. It is my greatest achievement. And three months to go to my next birthday. I can't wait.

'Tell me, Don,' she repeated, 'where is the President?'

Jackson, the other agent on the First Lady team, stood behind her. He shrugged at Clancy to indicate he'd done his best to keep her in the Convention Room.

'In the Oval, ma'am,' answered Clancy. 'He's taking an important call.'

'Is Joe with him?'

'No, the Chief of Staff's next door.'

'Why?'

'I don't know. That's how the President wanted it to be.'

'Are you going to let me go through?'

'I'll just check with . . .'

'You don't check with anybody.' Her voice tightened in anger.

'No, ma'am.' Clancy backed off. He turned to the glass protection door and put his eye close to the scanner. When it cleared him he opened the door. 'If you'd like to follow me, Mrs Dixon. I'll just go ahead and tell the President you're here.'

Her voice stopped him. 'There's no need for that. Just tell him I'm out here.' Annie Dixon was no fool; she knew her husband better than anyone else. 'I'll wait right here.'

'Yes, ma'am.'

Clancy crossed the vestibule and knocked on the Oval Office door. There was no response. He knocked again, louder. Still no response. He turned towards the First Lady, just as Meisner came into the room behind her. He saw the shock register on the Chief of Staff's face when he saw Annie Dixon standing there.

Clancy knocked again, his worst nightmare unfolding. 'Mr President,' he shouted through the door. 'This is Agent Clancy. Do you hear me?' Still nothing. 'I'm coming in, sir.' He turned the handle and slowly opened the door.

There was no one in the Oval Office.

I switched on the TV, a plasma screen that filled the wall. Where there had been a large print of a Farquharson Scottish snow scene, complete with sheep, there now appeared a selection menu.

'Sainsbury's, Food Department,' I said loudly. When the supermarket menu appeared, I continued. 'Conor Smith. Account and PIN number XK222KX, Rose Cottage, East Harling, near Norwich. Delivery within four hours. If not, possible contact on mobile CS 412412.'

Thirty seconds later the screen changed to the interior of a supermarket, as Sainsbury's accepted me as one of their registered customers. 'Delivery will be within one hour,' said a friendly electronic female voice. 'We have three other destinations in your area and will depart as soon as you have placed your order. Thank you for using Sainsbury's and have a good day, Mr Smith.'

'Meat,' I began.

The screen jumped to the meat counter. The produce was laid out exactly as if I'd been making one of my rare visits to the shop itself. I walked over to the screen and pressed a fillet steak. 'Sixteen-ounce, please, I'd like that one – it's got good marbling.'

'Four dollars and sixteen cents, Mr Smith.'

'To shopping basket.' He touched the Suffolk pork sausages next. 'Two packs, please.'

'Two dollars and twelve cents, Mr Smith.'

'To shopping basket.'

Five minutes later, I had completed my week's shopping. In the early days, like so many others, I'd used Virtual Reality to shop in the cyberspace superstores and supermarkets. But, once the novelty had worn off, most shoppers began using their TVs and touch screens. The system had grown so sophisticated since its inception in 2015 that the items on display were the actual ones delivered. This worked because all supermarkets and large stores had local branches which ensured delivery schedules were met. The latest fad was for shoppers to actually go shopping in real stores. TV selection was too easy, and now people wanted more, though the supermarkets charged higher prices for those who walked through their doors. I went to Sainsbury's at least once a month, as I enjoyed the interplay with real people, which brought back a sense of community. In a world where most people worked from home, more and more people were missing the ability to go out and mingle with their neighbours. A short trip down the road had thus become a big adventure.

I switched the screen to the TV listings; in spite of the hundreds of channels there was little of real interest. The wall, filled as it was by the large hanging screen, became a myriad of contrasting images as I scrolled through the programmes. After five minutes of searching I was bored, no Dial-Up Movies or hits from the West End or Broadway that I liked the look of. Even the Reality TV soaps, where you took part in the action from the comfort of your sofa, had become mundane.

The gaggle of religious programmes, between channels 340 and 371, finally focused my attention. These ranged from the wild and wacky to orthodox Muslim, Christian and Buddhist.

I logged on to the third religious channel listed: the 17th Baptist Emmanuel Church of Piety and Prosperity. A caption blared across the base of the screen: 'CALL NOW ON

THIS FREEPHONE NUMBER AND HELP THE REVEREND
JEREMIAH POST MAKE YOUR OWN PERSONAL MIRACLE
HAPPEN WHEN YOU PLEDGE YOUR MIRACLE-AND-WOR-
SHIP DONATION TO US.'

'Don't worry about the amount,' the Reverend Post
himself purred from the screen. 'Small miracles still happen
for however small an amount you donate. But if you want
the Good Lord to try harder and make a big miracle happen,
then that little bit more money – that more meaningful
donation – is going to give you a bigger chance of receiving
that miracle that you truly deserve.'

I picked up my keyboard and tapped my first link. 'Fuck
you and amen,' I swore at the Reverend Post. Robin Hood
was back. Robbing the rich to help the poor. I detoured
money currently being cyberwired to the Church of Piety
and Prosperity to the bank accounts of Oxfam instead.

The phone vibrated in my pocket. It was a new system,
one that could work in both RealWorld and Second World
as well as communicate between the two. Sales of the
multiband unit had rocketed. It meant that users could keep
in constant touch with RealWorld business whilst exploring the Web as avatars. It stopped as soon as I took it out
and flipped it open. The message said *Unanswered Call.* I
punched in a code, knowing how to decipher anonymous
callers. *This call is non-traceable. Any attempt to trace this
call could lead to criminal action.*

So, it was a government office that had just rung me,
possibly even one of the Security Services like the FBI. I
knew Security Officers from all over the world, even from
behind the Great Islamic Wall, but those chaps always left
their numbers. This caller wasn't allowing his trace code to
operate. I put away the phone. Whoever had called me
would call back, if it was that important. Or maybe someone
was running a trace on me. I felt uneasy as I returned to the
Reverend Post and his pocketful of miracles.

Clancy didn't bother looking through any of the other connecting doors. He knew they were fakes, didn't open anywhere. Except for that cupboard on the far right. He turned and shouted to the others. 'Alert the White House security teams. Is the President known to be anywhere else in the building? Check his suite, too. Is he back in the White House? Jackson, check the Annex now.' He saw the First Lady, her hand up to her mouth in shock as she realized her husband was not where everyone expected him to be.

Clancy entered the Oval Office just as Meisner came through the security door behind him. Smerton was already on the phone.

'He must be in his suite,' said Meisner nervously, as Clancy crossed the room and opened the cupboard door. It was empty, as he expected.

'Check his suite,' repeated Meisner behind him.

'Being done,' answered Clancy. He stepped into the cupboard, his hands pushing against a wall at the back.

'What're you doing?'

'He's still in his suite,' yelled Smerton from next door.

'Get in here,' commanded Clancy. He continued pushing against the wall with the palm of his right hand, feeling for something. He ignored the protests of Meisner, as Smerton came through into the Oval Office. 'They might've modelled all the safety systems out of the White House in here, too.

Look for the escape mechanism.' The second agent joined Clancy and they both pushed against the wall.

'I've got it.' Clancy stepped back as a section of wall, no more than six inches square, slid back, activated as the agent had pressed against a small pressure pad. A numeric keypad folded out. 'I don't know the code. Dammit! Ring up and get it.'

'What the hell *is* that?' asked Meisner, as Smerton left the room.

'Escape route. Just like in the real White House. It's a bombproof tunnel that leads out of the building, under the West Wing and through to West Executive Avenue.'

'How come I didn't know about it?'

'I have no idea.' Clancy tried not to let his irritation show. This was no time to discuss White House security policy. 'It was an emergency escape route put in during the late 'fifties when McCarthy was running everyone scared of the Commies. It's been there ever since.'

'The President knew about it?'

'Of course.'

'He never told me.'

'Nobody knew, apart from the President himself and the Secret Service. That's how it was.'

'Why would he go out through there?'

'No idea. I just know he didn't came past me.' Clancy shook his head in disbelief. 'This Annex is totally secure. It's ringed with more electronic protection than anywhere on the planet.'

'We don't have a West Executive Avenue on the Web,' said Meisner chillingly. 'So where the hell does this lead to?'

Clancy shrugged. 'Let's see if it's operational first.' Clancy saw Smerton re-entering the room. 'Got it?'

'Today's White House code is 68735. So I guess it'll be the same over here.'

'If it works,' grumbled Meisner.

Clancy punched those numbers into the keypad. As soon

as he hit ENTER, a larger part of the wall slid back, big enough for a man to pass through. 'So far so good.' Clancy unclipped his webColt laser-gun from his shoulder holster. 'You stay with the First Lady,' he instructed Meisner. Clancy then stepped warily through the opening, Smerton following, his weapon also at the ready.

'What's going on, Joe?' Annie Dixon asked, as Meisner rejoined her.

'Teddy's not here. We thought he was – '

'Taking a phone call?'

Meisner ignored her question. 'He'll be somewhere safe. He's going to be OK. You know Teddy.'

'I know Teddy,' came the knowing response. 'Who was in there with him?'

'No one, that I know of.'

'Why did he come down here?

'To take a call.'

'From whom?'

'I'm not sure.'

'Don't lie, Joe. You're his Chief of Staff, so you know who he took a call from . . . or who he was with.'

Meisner shook his head. 'Let's find him first, huh? I'm sure he'll explain everything once we do. No point getting all wound up until then. Priorities . . . like Teddy always says, priorities.'

The secret corridor that Clancy and Smerton followed was nothing like its counterpart in the Real White House. While that was concrete-walled, painted white, clearly lit with clear red directional arrows painted on the walls and emergency foot-lighting guiding its escapees down the long winding stairs, this one was dark with no feeling of walls, as if leading into a nothingness which was only highlighted by a small bright light in the distance.

'Shoulder to shoulder,' commanded Clancy once their eyes had adjusted to the darkness. He waited until Smerton's shoulder was pressed against his. 'Head for the light. Let's not rush it.' As he moved forward he felt the other agent keep pace with him. Both men held their webColt lasers at the ready. The darkness turned into a soft greyness, the whole area partially illuminated by light from the open cupboard door behind them and the small distant beam ahead. As they moved forward they realized they were not in a corridor, but in a vast area with no walls, no ceiling, nothing solid apart from the floor.

'Think Web here,' said Clancy. 'If anything rushes you, JetPax yourself out immediately.'

The two men moved together, each searching his side of the cavernous area for any signs of life, each ready to protect the other if danger threatened. They both knew they were now deep in cyberspace; but they also knew the danger was real. Lose out here and you could never return.

As they reached the end, the small light had expanded into an opening the size of a single door. Clancy went through it first. There was nothing. Just an empty space of white that had no ceiling, no walls and not even a floor. Clancy discovered that out as he went into free fall, tumbling down, twisting and turning like Jimmy Stewart in Hitchcock's *Vertigo*. His last thoughts before he hit his JetPax was a terrible sense of failure. He'd lost his President. He'd failed the one man he lived to protect.

Smerton watched his partner fall, then, after one more look into the empty whiteness, turned to work his way back to the Oval Room, now just a simple light in the distance. As he began his journey, the light went out and the floor disappeared beneath him. He fell immediately in the blackness, could see nothing as he hurtled downwards. He swore as he scrambled to find the JetPax button that finally released him from Second World. He hit it hard before he crashed to the bottom of whatever place this was, where he could die and no one would ever find him.

The clues they may have found were obliterated in the collapsing zone that should have led them to their President.

Clancy snapped the electronic shank off the back of his neck just as Smerton returned. Once the shank was off, he removed his shades, unplugged the brain biosensor earpiece and crossed to the bank of television monitors at the far end of the control room. There were fifteen in all, linked up to view every area in the Annex, and each monitor could simultaneously record over one hundred separate viewpoints whilst the security team studied individual areas.

A similar number of screens flickered in the neighbouring room, partitioned off by glass from the one Clancy was in. Those other cameras watched every section of the Real White House and its surrounds.

'Is he still missing?' Clancy asked.

'No sign,' replied Paul Gallagher, who was Chief Operational Supervisor of the Monitor Room and had previously been a field operative to the White House Corps, some fourteen years earlier. Being on presidential protection had never appealed to him, since his real love was computers and the systems they employed. They were like an extension of his mind and he spent most of his time seated in front of them, or in a WebSuit. That he preferred to the more streamlined shank. His natural abilities soon got him promoted to his present role as Chief Supervisor, equivalent in rank to Secret Service Senior Agent on the Presidential Protection Squad. Pale-skinned with almost ash-blond wavy hair, Gallagher was *the* expert in White House surveillance.

'You run the tapes yet?' Clancy asked him.

'Yea, starting with the Convention Hall.'

'Pick up anything?'

"Hey, we've only just started downloading. I didn't touch the Oval Office tapes, as I thought I'd better wait for you.'

'Run them now. Dammit, this whole area's meant to be totally secure. And anyway he's got a JetPax strapped to him. Nobody's ever broken a JetPax code – nowhere in the entire Web.'

'What do you want me to do?' asked Smerton, now divested of his Web equipment.

'Get as many agents as possible into the Annex, and search every room.' He turned to Gallagher. 'How many can we actually transport into the Annex?'

'We've got twenty suits left. That's it.'

'OK, get twenty agents. You stay and monitor it all from here.' Clancy turned his attention back to Gallagher. 'I need to run the tapes from the point when we went down to the Oval Office. While I'm doing that, I need some of your people to scan the crowds, looking out for anything else in the Convention Hall that could be suspicious.' He waited while Gallagher passed these orders on to his team. 'From now on we work on a need-to-know basis,' he instructed Gallagher.

'Apart from your group and those present in this room, nobody else knows the President is missing.'

'*May* be missing – and let's keep it like that. Run checks on all staff who're involved with White House security. Go back through everybody's files, including my own. See if there's anything that stands out. Check if there's been a power or technical crash, deliberate or otherwise, that dropped all the protection shields. Could someone have switched off the security for enough time to get the President out from wherever he was?'

'No, not without us picking it up.'

'*Nothing's* secure any more, as far as I'm concerned.'

'We're not allowing anyone out of the Annex or the Convention Hall. I can tell you, we're taking a lot of heat on that.'

'Tough, but hold them there. Just say we've got a technical problem.'

'Not possible. The press'll pick that up straight away.'

'Shit, we can't just let them go. Are we downloading all the WebNames of everyone who came to the party there in the Convention Hall?'

'Being done. There were more than a million guests. It's easy enough to verify because it was a ticket-only deal.'

'In Second World, you mean?'

'Yeah, in avatar form. Another thirty million were watching on TV.'

'I'm only interested in those actually present. How long to download?'

'Maybe eight, ten more minutes. Then we'll run the sort codes. We're splitting by names, religions, states, cities, age, political affiliations, criminal records, foreign nationals, diplomatic guests, immigrants who are now US citizens, socio-economic groups, government workers, opposition party members, those who've contacted the President's office by email, telephone or mail, had a record of any college demonstrations in their past, and about forty more categories that we reckon might throw up an answer as to who out there would want to hurt the President. And when we've checked, we'll restart those search engines and run them again. Cover everything. We've got the techno. We'll use it.'

'But whoever started this has got to be a fucking technical genius?'

'We'll get there.' Gallagher didn't sound too sure. 'We'll have our first list of possible suspects in a few minutes.'

'That could be a couple of thousand people. Maybe more.'

'It's a start.'

'OK, if anyone asks, say the President's not feeling too good – that he's resting for a while.'

Where the hell was he?

He wasn't the most popular President amongst his security staff. Always slipping out on them, always chasing the high-heels.

But that wasn't important to Clancy. It wasn't the man himself that mattered – the holder of the Office. Clancy had just lost the President of the United States. He broke into a sweat as he waited for Gallagher and his men to start producing results.

He had no idea where he was. When she'd taken him through the escape route, he'd expected to find stairs, some simple form of passageway. But there was nothing, just a grey darkness with one small light at the end. He'd hesitated, but she turned and smiled, inviting him on.

'It's only through the other door, Teddy honey. Right there, where that light is.'

He followed her, his arm ready to punch the JetPax.

'Nearly there, honey.'

God, she was like *real*. He looked forward to screwing her, wanted to know what her special tricks were, find out was she as good as a goddess should be. He felt a rush of pleasure through his body. He'd spent enough time in the special boudoir rooms you could rent anonymously on the Brick. It was as good as anything in RealWorld, sometimes even better after taking the SurgeSurge pills. He smiled; no wonder populations in the Western civilized nations were dropping. Who needed real sex?

They reached the light. It was a half-open door leading to a brighter, whiter area beyond it. She turned and sunk into him, wrapping her arms round him, kissing him deeply, exploding his mind into a kaleidoscope of lust and emotion, just as she had done back in the Oval Office. He responded immediately, his arms round her, gripping her firm voluptuous bottom through that skimpy, feel-through dress.

She suddenly seemed physically stronger; she wheeled

him round even as she kissed him. He lost his balance and fell backwards, the two of them still entwined, still kissing. They fell into the bright whiteness and tumbled down, falling, clinging to each other, still kissing. He knew he was in trouble.

With his arms still round her, he tried to punch the JetPax with his right hand. He couldn't reach it. She was wrapped tightly around him, so his hands were trapped and useless. All the time, she kept kissing him. He struggled to break free, still trying to release himself so that he could hit the JetPax.

Then she was gone ... the whiteness evaporated, too, and he was suddenly alone in a black void. So black, he couldn't see his hand, only knew it was there when he touched his face. He realized his watch was useless; time lost meaning when he couldn't see the hands, even with their luminous paint. He felt for the JetPax again but it was no longer attached to his arm. He took his lighter from his pocket and ignited it. Nothing. No light came from its sharp gas flame. He held his other hand out where he imagined the flame should be; it burnt him momentarily and he snatched his hand away. In his surprise he dropped the lighter. He cursed but he couldn't hear his own words in the emptiness. He was in a vacuum of silent blackness.

He started to walk and nothing obstructed him. He moved carefully, deliberately, feeling his way as he moved. He walked a long way before he stopped. He'd counted over eight hundred paces. Eight hundred yards. Half a mile. And still nothing. He sat down.

The President of the United States realized he was now beyond outside help. He was in the Dark Areas. Somewhere that didn't even exist.

'First Lady's coming back,' Smerton called out across the room.

Clancy crossed the room, past the rows of monitors with their eager-eyed operatives, past the rows of SensoBeds ready for those who needed to enter Second World, and into the small private, sealed-off section at the rear of the large Control Room.

There were six SensoChairs in the Presidential Transfer Suite, and three of them were occupied. Each person wore WebShades and was garbed in a simple WebSuit, a light-weight kimono-style wraparound made of microweave cotton with biosensors built into the weave. They were more comfortable than the neck shanks worn by the agents and by more experienced users of the Web.

The First Lady sat up, wearing one, now taking in her surroundings, as though waking from a dream. She, like many others, found WebTravel a slow and difficult process to master. It was all to do with the bio-rhythmic process. Being in Second World was no problem; it was the transporting to and from that was the most difficult for users to adapt to.

Clancy waited as a White House technician helped Annie Dixon out of her suit. On her right, Joe Meisner came back, too. He was an experienced traveller and got on his feet immediately. Clancy knew all about the Chief of Staff's Saturday Night Specials; his reputation as a serious party animal was notorious.

'Any news?' the First Lady appealed to Clancy.

'Not yet, ma'am.'

'Where are you up to?' Meisner asked.

'It only happened' – Clancy glanced at his watch – 'within the last ten minutes. We're moving as fast as we can.'

He waited while Annie Dixon crossed over to the third SensoChair where her husband now sat, still, and almost lifeless apart from a few muscular twitches and his regular breathing. She knew not to touch him because that could have terrifying effects on him wherever he was in the Web. She passed her hand gently around his cheek.

'I think we should leave this room to the technicians,' Clancy continued. 'Ma'am, I need to get back to the Control Center. Would you like someone to escort you to your private rooms while we work out what's going on?'

'If you don't mind, I'll stay down here for now.' She took one last look at her husband, composed herself and followed Clancy into the Control Room.

'Anyone call the Vice President?' Meisner asked Clancy.

'No. Not till we have some idea of what's going on.' The last thing Clancy wanted was news of this business to circulate.

'We're ready to run the tapes,' Gallagher shouted over from the Control Center.

Clancy knew the tapes might embarrass the First Lady. He turned and faced her, registered Meisner's concern over her shoulder. *Fuck Meisner.* He was the one who set these things up, so was just as bad as Teddy Dixon. It was Annie Dixon he wanted to protect. But they had to run the tapes, because the answer could be there. 'These tapes ... they record all the President's movements after he left the Convention Hall.' He paused. 'We need to run them.'

'Well ... ?' she queried.

'They might cause you some distress, ma'am.'

'Why?' Annie Dixon looked round at the others.

There was an embarrassed silence all about her. For a

moment she felt foolish, very naked and very frail standing in front of them all. But she stood her ground; these people knew what Teddy Dixon was really like, and were probably part of the conspiracy that protected him.

'If there's been some major accident, I don't know whether you'd want to see it.' Clancy gave her one last opportunity.

"I'm a big girl, Don. Why don't we just run the tapes?'

'Yes, ma'am.' Clancy signalled Gallagher to start the tapes.

Throughout the room, everyone's attention immediately focused on the left-hand one of the three central monitors.

'Concentrate on what you're all doing. Don't bother with what doesn't concern you,' Gallagher warned the other operatives and waited for them to return their attention to the other recordings of the events in the Convention Hall, looking out for any small clue that might help them in their search. The last thing he wanted was for the gossip to start spreading once everyone there had seen what really happened in the Oval Room.

The screen activated with an empty shot of the Oval Office ante-room. The elevator opened and Marilyn Monroe entered. She passed through the glass security door, using the eye scanner, and entered the Oval Office. The Oval Office camera then came to life on the second of the three screens. Marilyn wiggled her famous wiggle over to the desk, looked round the room, then sat down in the President's chair, swinging away from the desk and looking out over the White House lawns. She suddenly laughed, obviously enjoying the moment, the anticipation.

'She knows she's on camera,' commented Gallagher.

'Who arranged for her to go down there?' asked Clancy. He already knew it was Meisner, but the Chief of Staff said nothing. 'And who programed her into the eye scanner.' He looked across at Gallagher. 'Who OKed that?'

Gallagher answered softly. 'We were ordered to let her through.'

'You watched from here?'

'Only up to this point. I wouldn't allow anybody to watch after that. We're here to secure, not to spy.'

'So who gave clearance?'

'My office,' said Meisner.

'Why?'

'It was . . .' Meisner looked away from Annie Dixon. '. . . an authorized request.'

On the first monitor they all saw the elevator open and the President's party emerge from the Conference Room. The group, after some discussion, broke up and the President alone entered the Oval Office.

Clancy saw himself settling down to wait outside.

The second screen now went blank. 'The monitor cuts out automatically whenever the President's in any private room,' explained Gallagher. 'That's standard procedure.'

'But we're still taping?' stated Clancy.

'The tape keeps running. Then, once it's digitally transmitted to a secure recording room, it wipes itself clean.'

'We need to see that tape.'

'Only the President, or an Order from the Supreme Court, can authorize access to those tapes. It goes back to the Nixon days, I guess.'

'Do you know where those tapes are?' asked Meisner.

'Yes, sir.'

'I agree with Don. We have to see those tapes.'

'I can't release them.'

'For Christ's sake, Paul,' shouted a frustrated Clancy. 'This is no ordinary situation. While we're arguing here, or hanging about waiting for the Supreme Court to meet, which could take hours if not days, the President is obviously in immediate danger. Do you *know* what's on those tapes?'

'Of course not. But I still can't release them.'

'We have less than twelve hours to find him, Paul. To

find him and get him out. More than that and his brain's fried.' Clancy turned to the First Lady. 'Sorry, Mrs Dixon.'

'No, you're right, Don.' she agreed. 'We need to see those tapes.'

'It's your call, Paul. So what do you want to be remembered as? The guy who went by the book or the guy who saved the President?'

'OK.' Gallagher finally agreed. 'But I need authorization – from him.' He indicated Meisner.

'You've got it,' ratified Meisner.

'Let's see those tapes now,' urged Clancy.

'I can download from here,' said Gallagher. He called one of the other operators over and both men punched their personal security codes into the computer. Gallagher, under the eye of the other control operative, downloaded the sequence that all were urgently interested in. Once the specific Oval Office file was open, the two men locked out the mainframe to access by anyone else.

The screen snapped on again. President Dixon entered the office. They saw him catch his breath as he realized she was over in the chair, saw his excitement as he swung round. '*Marilyn.*' They heard his words as he crossed to the chair. '*May I call you Marilyn?*' He was at his charming best.

Annie Dixon looked away as his familiar voice, now intermingling with the blonde siren's, was heard across the Control Center. It didn't matter that it was in his imagination, that she wasn't the real Marilyn Monroe. It didn't matter that he was the President of the most powerful nation on earth and he was making a fool of himself. All that mattered was his desire for someone else, a desire he had never really felt for his own wife. She now wished she had followed Clancy's advice and gone to her rooms. To hear his lust for someone else, here in such a public place.

'Who hired Monroe?' Clancy asked.

'I did,' Annie Dixon replied, keeping her back to him.

'*I was always Johnny's honey,*' said the seductive voice on the screen.

'He liked Jack Kennedy, thought he was the greatest of them all. So I arranged for . . . *her,*' Annie Dixon barely got the word out, 'to sing to him for his birthday.'

'Where did you hire her?' Clancy moved up next to her, keeping his voice low. There was no need to share her embarrassment with the rest of them.

'Abbi helped me.' She was referring to Abbi Patrick, the First Lady's oldest friend and equivalent to her Chief of Staff. 'She got hold of a company that specialized in celebrity avatars, but she checked that the White House had used them before. And also she got the uniformed division to verify they were OK.' As all knew, the uniformed division of the Secret Service looked after all internal White House security as well as the entrances and grounds.

'Ring through to Mrs Dixon's rooms,' Clancy instructed one of the operators. 'See if they can find Mrs Patrick and get that information off her.' Then he added, 'Don't tell her what's happened. Just make sure she digs up that information immediately.'

'*The First Lady's asking where you are.*' Meisner's voice blasted out from the screen. Annie Dixon looked up again and saw her husband on the phone, Marilyn sitting on his lap in a state of undress. '*She's got the Secret Service looking for you.*'

She turned her attention to Meisner, but fortunately for him his face was turned away from her. She looked round the room but it seemed nobody was aware of her any longer. They were all gripped by images of their President and one of the greatest screen sex goddesses of all time. She turned back to the screen just in time to see Dixon push Monroe's head down between his thighs.

'I need a list of every company that uses a Monroe avatar,' Clancy informed Gallagher.

'OK,' came the answer as Gallagher forced his attention

away from the screen. He passed this request on to one of his staff.

Clancy himself was glued to the screen, in a mixture of fascination with what he saw and embarrassment for what the First Lady felt. He was determined not to catch her eye.

'*And you'll know everything that Johnny liked,*' purred Monroe.

'*OK. You really knew there was another back way out of here. I'd like to see the Secret Service when they find out about that.*'

'*He told me everything.*'

'*OK. But no more than fifteen minutes.*'

They went over to open the cupboard and Teddy Dixon, after searching for the keyboard, released it.

'*I don't know the number,*' they heard him say.

They watched as Marilyn leant forward and tapped the tiny keyboard, the door swinging open beyond them.

'*How did you . . . ?*' asked the surprised President.

She smiled and silenced him by putting her finger on his lip, then she kissed him. '*Johnny's waiting,*' she added after her lips released him.

Dixon turned and walked on through the opening. Monroe took one look back at the room, blew a kiss at the camera, and followed him. She closed the door behind her.

There was no further sign of life in the room until Clancy entered a few minutes later.

'Run it over and over again and enhance everything digitally. See if there's anything there, anything that doesn't fit in.' Clancy was speaking to no one in particular, his mind trying to come to terms with what he had just seen.

'He'll be back soon. Maybe he's just enjoying himself,' Meisner whispered in his ear, out of earshot of the First Lady.

Clancy gave him a withering look. 'I don't think so.'

'Why not?'

'Did you give her the code to the escape route?'

'How could I? I didn't even know it was there.'

'Did you know the code in the Real Oval Office?'

'No. Only the President and you boys do.'

'So how did she get the code?'

'Maybe he . . . I don't know. That's a pretty flimsy reason for you to be convinced he's in trouble.'

'Don's telling you we've been hacked,' Gallagher interjected. 'Someone's got all our codes. And if the President doesn't come back soon, it means that hacker's also found a way of negating our JetPaxs. That also means neither we, nor anybody else, can ever go into Second World and be sure of getting out again. That's blown the whole Second World security system.'

'Forget all that for now. You sure there's no trapdoor?' Clancy was referring to the hole that was very often left in place by designers or maintainers should they need to get back into a closed system for maintenance.

'None we know about.'

The doctor was his usual patronizing self. He sat on the other side of his desk from me, the computer monitor like a barrier between us. The doctor's office was sparsely furnished: just the desk and a blue filing cabinet behind him. The latter was only there for show, to give the office a traditional, old-fashioned look. Someone's idea of making the patient feel at home.

'You're spending too much time in the Web,' he said gruffly.

'But I'm active in there regularly. It's my job,' I protested. I hated defending myself like some addict promising to abandon a habit he couldn't give up.

'You need real exercise. You need to walk and work your muscles. I mean plenty of fresh air, that sort of old-fashioned exercise. You need to get fit.'

'I will. But what's wrong with me now?'

'Nothing much. Your muscles are becoming flabby. That's why you're straining them.' The doctor referred to his screen. 'Your DNA shows a potential for heart problems.'

'I know.'

'Rest of you is fine. At this rate, and with your DNA reading, I don't think you'll make eighty, and that's not old these days. Your blood pressure's way too high. You still taking those pills?'

'Yes,' I said truthfully.

The doctor tapped his keyboard. 'I see you get them delivered from the supermarket. You should go there yourself instead of waiting for everything to be delivered.'

'I do . . . sometimes.'

'How's your anger management?'

'OK.'

'What's that mean?'

'I've been OK.' I hated the MediJacket. It diagnosed all your faults, past and present.

'I can give you medication for that.'

'I don't need any.'

'That's why you've got such high blood pressure.'

'I'll join a fitness gym.'

'Sure, in Second World. They plug you in and pass electric currents through you, so your body jerks in Real-World. Some exercise!' the doctor snorted. 'Waste of time, waste of credits. You all think you can buy into your dreams through the Web. The truth is, the technology it creates does *not* guarantee satisfaction.' He looked at his Screen-Records again. 'You live in Norfolk. Now that's a good place. For walking, I mean. For getting fit.'

'I get the point, Doctor.'

'Then do it. Live longer, Mr Smith. We're in a world where medical techniques allow people to live till they're a hundred and thirty. You're not even fifty and you look twice your age. Get some recon surgery. Get rid of those lines on your face, more hair on your head. Dammit, you can afford it.'

'I like the way I am.'

'Nobody else does. That's probably why you never got married.'

'Hey, is all this necessary?'

'If insults get you fit, then yes. You need to get that DNA problem resolved. Nobody'll marry you anyway, once they've checked your charts. And you definitely won't get insurance for kids. Not kids with flawed hearts.'

'I don't want to be a perfect specimen.'

The doctor laughed. 'That you're not for sure. But you're always reporting aches and pains when there's nothing wrong with you. Just get out and take exercise. Don't waste my time, or yours, anymore. GET FIT, MR SMITH. Come back only when you've something seriously wrong with you.'

'That it?'

'That's plenty. A final word of advice, Mr Smith?'

I couldn't wait.

'Get a dog. One that walks you to death. It'll be a lot cheaper than coming to me. And it won't shout at you.' The doctor sighed and faded away

I velcroed the MediJacket off me. I hated wearing the damn thing, giving all my bodily data to an unknown doctor sitting in some office in the Sprawl, a hundred miles away.

I switched the screen off, swore loudly and went back to RealWorld.

'I've got that Monroe copyright info,' announced one of Gallagher's operatives.

'Go on.'

'There are twenty-six thousand outlets worldwide that can sell or lease out Monroe avatars. Fourteen thousand are in the US, while Europe and Japan eat up another eight. The rest extend into the developing regions. We're currently running checks to see who's actually got Monroes out on lease right now.'

'Who owns the mother rights?'

'ThemeCorp. There was a big auction about eight years ago, when all the major celebrity rights were sold. Theme-Corp took the lion's share.'

Clancy nodded. Some bright auction house in London had pulled all the copyright individuals together and auctioned the most famous names in entertainment history. Monroe, James Dean, Marlon Brando, Mohammed Ali, Sinatra, The Beatles, Streisand, Connery, Bogart and anyone who had been anybody in the world of sport and showbiz. Even Lassie and Francis the Talking Mule got cloned. It was a great coup for ThemeCorp. They then produced clones of the glamorous and famous, whom they leased out for whatever reason people wanted. So it was that you could go to eat at a famous restaurant in Second World and take Frank Sinatra as your guest. You could impress your friends by getting The Beatles to sing for your birthday. It was big

94

business, being seen out with someone who still rattled the world's emotional cage. And the greater the star, the greater the rental price. It was as socially defining as owning a Ferrari in RealWorld had been in the early years of the millennium.

The lure of vast profits had pushed ThemeCorp to spend immense amounts on research, whereby they could ensure the StarGuests – as they were dubbed – would react in every known situation in an identical manner as they would had they been real. The RealWorld actors who sat in their WebSuits and acted out these fantasies were highly trained and highly paid. They worked from home and most were trained to carry out at least ten different star roles, as requested.

The celebrity culture of the early part of the century had eventually bored the public. Anybody with plastic tits, no creative talent and an eye for the camera could become a star. The Web changed that; now everybody could be a celebrity. And it was the old stars, the big names from the past with a solid place in entertainment history, who were the biggest draws.

The software that ran these avatars was also leased out. Anybody could download it from the Web, at a price, and use the avatar themselves, becoming the star of their choice. It was in this way that the StarGuests became known as StarFuckers. They were used as sex objects, even found themselves in brothels and sex shops on the Brick. They were a big pull for the Weekenders, for the one-night-stand brigade. ThemeCorp, and the other companies who owned the rights for the stars, vigorously denied that their clones were abused in this manner. But it happened and probably accounted for seventy per cent of the avatars' usage, so the companies never took the problem seriously though avowing that they would do their best to stamp it out.

But big business was big bucks business. They knew the avatars were safe, were virus protected because each avatar, once its rental period was completed, simply evaporated into cyberspace.

Clancy presumed Monroe's avatar had been a single rental. No megacorp would ever consider running a stunt like this.

'We can't sit on this thing any longer,' said Meisner. 'Time we reported to the Vice President and the National Security Adviser.' He thought for a moment. 'And bring in the FBI.'

'I wouldn't do that yet. Not the FBI.'

'It's their jurisdiction.'

'Not if he's still somewhere in the Annex. That's Secret Service jurisdiction.'

'We just watched him leave ... your jurisdiction. On tape.'

'Doesn't mean he's out of here. We have to call in the VP and NSA. But not the FBI – not if you want to keep a lid on this. If that doesn't work, then what? The Chiefs of Staff? Send the Marines in? A million of them, all in WebSuits, fully armed? How far do you think they'd get? We'll never find him.'

'Prove to me he's still in *your* zone.'

Clancy pointed towards the small room where the President lay motionless. 'He's still here. Next door. In his WebSuit. That puts him firmly in my zone.'

'The FBI have more resources.'

'No more than us,' cut in Gallagher. 'They may have more manpower, but we have the same access to information and Second World that they do.'

'I'm going to contact the Director,' said Clancy. 'He'll want this kept local. Legally the President is still on White House property and under our jurisdiction.'

They both knew that Secret Service Director Bill Walls and his AD were abroad in Berlin, setting up a RealWorld visit for the spring. There was no way of his returning in time to lead the investigation, which left Clancy, as Senior

Agent, in charge of the President's security. And Walls, a young ambitious Director, always protected his own department.

Meisner clearly accepted he'd get no change out of Walls. 'What about WebCops? And SnoopCams?' he queried.

Meisner knew he was isolated, but at least he was in the clear. Nobody could now accuse him of not trying to involve the FBI. And Gallagher was right. Congress had passed a bill in 2020 that gave all security forces access to the army of cyber police, those digital-enhanced information gatherers who manifested themselves in many forms to gather information on the Web. The WebCops were hated. They simply snooped on everybody and everything. They were an army of electronic robotic puppets who walked the street spying on all the others, sending their visual images back to be recorded or to a RealWorld operator who worked a group of avatars. It was impossible to move in Second World without being noticed by a WebCop – a snooper in many disguises and forms. Those who lived in the richer societies were used to the cameras, since StreetCams inhabited the RealWorld much as did the SnoopCams in Second World.

On the Brick the WebCops were supported by SnoopCams, cameras hidden on walls and pavements and trees. These invisible data gatherers had become the most sophisticated surveillance system ever known. And all that information, when requested, was on tap for the government and its security forces.

'I want it kept off the SnoopCams,' explained Gallagher. 'If we put his photograph out, everyone including the media would be immediately alerted. Now is not the time to run that program.'

'Except the SnoopCams could pick up all the Monroe avatars out on the Brick,' suggested Clancy.

'OK, as can the WebCops. But absolutely no pictures of the President.'

'Meisner shrugged. 'I need to contact the VP and Marlin.'

Deke Marlin was the National Security Adviser to the President.

'I've located them already,' said Gallagher. 'The Vice President's already in the White House – and Marlin is on his way over. I'll ask the VP to join us.'

'I'm going to take the First Lady to her suite.'

Annie Dixon started to object but Meisner firmly stopped her.

'Annie, let me get all this under way. Please do as I say. We'll run regular updates to you.'

'Couldn't I stay in there' – she indicated the ante-room – 'with Teddy?'

'I don't think that would be wise. I don't want these guys being sidetracked.'

She reluctantly agreed. She desperately wanted to stay but knew her presence would indeed be a distraction.

'I'll be back in ten minutes.' Meisner took her arm. 'Brief the VP and NSA if they're here before I get back.'

Clancy and Gallagher waited while Meisner led Annie Dixon from the room.

'Prick,' cursed Gallagher to Meisner's departing back.

'Any ideas?' Clancy asked.

Gallagher shook his head in exasperation. 'We don't have a manual for this one.'

'Let's find out how they got in – and out – of the White House. And how the hell they overrode the JetPax.'

'Christ, that would be some virus to knock out everyone's failsafe.'

'You're the techie hotshot, so tell me what to do.'

'I have no idea. We just sit up here getting information. That's our role. Maybe we should consider the FBI – they wrote the book on kidnap crimes.'

'No,' answered Clancy vehemently.

'If the President's somewhere in the Web, then we need someone who knows every part of it. Someone who grew up in it. The best hacker there is.'

'Most of them're in jail.' Clancy puzzled for a moment, rubbing his cheek. 'And I can't see Meisner or the others playing ball and releasing them, not for a few hours in the Web. They know they'd never come back. Boy, would that create havoc.'

'They're not all banged up inside. Some of them have crossed the wire. Probably half the guys working in here came down that road.'

'You one of those, Paul?' It was a light-hearted question. They both knew Gallagher's early days had been spent running with the hackers, when as a young agent he'd infiltrated them. And then became fond of them and got to share their basic distrust of the establishment. He'd become one of the best, originated the term 'tracker', which was given to government agents who chased corporate computer fraudsters. When the authorities had found out, they blocked Gallagher's promotion route and he settled down to Government Officer Grade 4. That meant he had a good enough salary to prevent him from being poached by one of the megacorps, and a job title that gave him a respectable position in society. Paul Gallagher had reached the top of his corporate tree.

One of the Control Room operatives joined them. 'We've got a list of everyone who was at the Convention. We've got about three thousand guests who could be suspects.'

'Find out if any have recently hired, or purchased, or been in touch with a CelebHire Company, especially those interested in Marilyn Monroe. Use the SnoopCam Central Agency Archives for that. Feed the pictures through and see if the SnoopCam identifier can match anything. Then see if those suspects have further links with any other Kennedy-type avatars. Like that mobster Sam Giancana or the Judy babe they were both screwing.'

'Judy Campbell,' volunteered Clancy. 'She was also horsing around with Frank Sinatra.'

'You got it. Use Google to get any other links. Has

anyone already left the Annex? And if they have, where did they go? Are they back on the Brick and are they alone? Are they anywhere in the Web where a camera can pick them up? Maybe some have met up again after they left. And, if they have, where are they heading for? While you're chasing them, get any SnoopCam or WebCop that's picked up any Monroe avatars in the last hour. Hotel lobbies, bars, anywhere else on the Web.'

'OK, a lot of the Annex guests are leaving. The rest are impatient, but still waiting for the President.' The operative turned to go, then, 'There's an old couple from Nebraska said they were waiting for him to return, said he told them to wait for him.'

'I remember them,' said Clancy. 'Well, just get someone to say . . . explain he's not feeling too good.'

'We really do need outside support,' urged Gallagher.

'Any ideas?'

'I need a privateer. Maybe a team of them.'

'And?'

'The best man is . . . He's not American and he hates politicians and the establishment. Put him near Meisner and those guys and he'll just walk away. As a security risk, he's the worst you could expect, but he's the best in the Web.'

'What's he do?'

'He's a GameMaster.'

'This isn't a game.'

'No, this *is* a game. That's the only way we can play it.'

'Can we find him?'

'I already did.'

'You know him?'

'Yeah. He used to teach me, at ThemeWorld, when I used to chase dragons.' Gallagher paused. 'He's also a cracker.'

'No way.'

'The best there is. Worked for the Brits. Police and security services.'

'That's like giving the vault keys to a safecracker.'

'All GameMasters have the highest security clearances.'

'This is crazy.'

'We've only got between ten and fifteen hours. Any more than that and we've got a brain-dead President.'

'If he's really missing.'

'It's your call.' Gallagher's words were brutal and final. Clancy sat down. 'We need clearance.'

'We need to act. Hell, Don, we've nothing to lose.'

'No. Just our careers.'

'Shit, you've done that already. If you don't get Dixon back, you can kiss your pension goodbye.'

The doctor was right, and I was paying good credits for his advice. Sixty euro-dollars a visit. *So get out and walk. Just half an hour a day.* Hell, that's why I'd come out here in the first place. Maybe get a dog. Hey, that's good. A companion who can't answer back. I never had a dog. Maybe I could . . .

The mobile phone vibrated. Someone was scrutinizing me again, checking up on my location. When I tried to trace the call, it gave the same message: *This call is non-traceable. Any attempt to trace this call could lead to criminal action.* Then a second message appeared. *Logging on to Rose Cottage. Please see me. Galverston.*

I recognized the WebName. I reached over for my shades and slipped them on. I'd go for a walk later. Apart from the doctor I'd had a good day. I'd even siphoned nearly forty thousand US dollars from the Reverend Post. A good hour's work. I slid back into the Web.

Gallagher and what I presumed to be a colleague were waiting for me. The colleague looked at me as if I were rotten meat.

'Hello, Paul. Long time no see. If you'd stuck at it a bit longer you would've got closer to the Golden Dragon.'

'Good of you to remember me. After all this time. I always felt I'd let you down,' Gallagher said.

'No, you let yourself down. You could've gone a lot further, but you just couldn't be bothered.' I sat down on the sofa. 'Your friend looks very smart and very official.'

'Don Clancy,' replied Gallagher. 'Secret Service.'

'What've I done now?'

'We have a problem.'

'No, *you* have a problem. And you want to see if I can get you out of it.'

'Are you always this cynical, Mr Smith?' asked Clancy.

'I'm usually a lot worse.'

'Conor, is it possible to disengage someone's JetPax while they're in the Web?' cut in Gallagher.

'Yes.'

'How?'

'I don't know.'

'But you said . . .'

'That it's possible. I don't know if it's ever been done. But, whatever safeguards you put in, whatever systems, there's always someone out there who'll eventually break the code. The trouble with the JetPax is that everyone thinks it's perfect. So nobody's looked at improving the safeguards. Big mistake. It was bound to happen.'

'We didn't say it had,' said Clancy.

'Then why're you asking?'

'Like Paul said, we just want to know if it's possible.'

'Yeah, yeah. Look, do me a favour, if you want my help, don't treat me like a child.'

'Coming here was Paul's idea, not mine.'

'Then fuck off and leave us to it.' I stood up. The chap was a pain.

'We're wasting time,' Clancy said to Gallagher. 'Let's get back.'

'Just give me a minute,' pleaded Gallagher. 'Conor, have there been any stories about someone hacking the JetPax code? I mean, you know most of the big computer boys – the good ones . . .'

'He means hackers,' interrupted Clancy.

'I know what he means,' I growled. 'There's always rumours. Always someone trying to get past the rest. No, I've heard nothing.'

'I'm going back. This is a waste of time.'

'We need your help, Conor,' said Gallagher. 'We've lost one of our key people.'

'You don't have clearance to give that information,' warned Clancy.

'What do you mean . . . lost?' I was suddenly very interested. This was a real game.

Gallagher ignored Clancy. 'He was in the Web, in a secure area, and someone trashed his JetPax and got him out,' he continued.

'Against his will?'

'We think so.'

'You got anything on tape?'

'Right up to where he walks through a door in a secure area. A door we didn't know was there.'

'Trapdoor?'

'Not sure. Don't think so. There's no record of it anywhere.'

'Did anyone follow him?'

'Don?' Gallagher turned to Clancy.

'I did,' said Clancy cautiously. He then explained what had occurred to him and Smerton when they walked through the cupboard door.

'You were avalanched,' explained Conor. 'Big WhiteOuts. They lead out of the Web and if you follow you get trapped in a loop that goes nowhere. Then it collapses all around you. Just floods you in a brilliant white. Like an avalanche, leaving no trace of anything. It's a pretty common structure if you don't want to be followed.'

'Difficult to set up?'

'No, basic game programing. Actually illegal, under the UN code. You're still stuck in the Web. But your JetPax should get you out. How effective was the secure area?'

When Clancy didn't answer, Gallagher spoke. 'The White House.' He ignored Clancy's glance of warning.

'Now that's new. I thought the White House was totally firewalled.'

'It is, was. With all the latest protection protocols.'

'Then your man's a real expert. Unless it was an insider, someone who dropped the security fences for a few seconds.'

'We found nothing to substantiate that. All the system checks were clean: no power outages, no spike through the systems. We're running files on White House staff, especially new employees. But nothing's yet obvious.'

Clancy's bleeper bleeped. 'We're wanted back. Let's go.' He faced Conor. 'I'm warning you, don't spread this information on the Web. It was Paul's idea to come here, and I think he was wrong. So don't fuck us up. If you do, I'll come back and you'll never see the outside of a jail for the rest of your natural.'

Conor smiled. 'And I thought I lived in a free country. Outside the USA.'

'On this one your government will give us all the author-ity we need. Let's go,' he said to Gallagher.

'I'll follow you.'

Clancy hit his JetPax and vaporized.

'Sorry about that.' Gallagher apologized.

'Why? He's *your* arsehole. I don't have to work with him.'

'He feels responsible.'

'Who's missing?'

'Don't ask me.'

'Somebody the Secret Service is supposed to watch?'

'Listen, we need your help. *I* need your help. It looks like a Marilyn Monroe avatar was used to infiltrate the White House and break our security barriers. We have no idea what they want. Can you get out in the Web, Conor? You know everyone in the cyber cafes, on the Brick. Somebody's got to know something.'

'Is that the only clue? Marilyn Monroe. Christ, she's been dead for more than sixty, maybe seventy years.'

'See if anyone's broken the JetPax code. That'll take us straight there.'

'How long've I got?'

'Under twelve hours.'

'It's someone big, for you guys to be that worried.'

'That's a no-brainer.'

'I'll need the White House Web communication codes.'

'Why?'

'So that I can hear what you guys are coming up with. I don't want to be going down one road and find you've turned off behind me, chasing new leads.'

'No can do. I'll contact you through your mobile, as soon as we get anything.'

'OK, but remember one thing. It's Friday, so the place is going to be heaving with Weekenders in a couple of hours. That's going to make things very difficult. Most of my sources make their money in Second World. And it's the

Weekenders they make their money out of. I may need some credits to call in favours, but they're going to be expensive on a Friday.'

'I'll get that arranged,' said Gallagher. 'But my budget's only so big.'

'Do you want your VIP back, or not?'

'I'm counting on you.'

'It's the President?' I fired a shot in the dark.

'No comment.'

'One of his family?'

'Conor!' warned Gallagher.

'I saw it on the news: Monroe singing "Happy Birthday" to your President.' Conor grinned. 'I'm not that daft.'

Gallagher shrugged it off, but didn't deny the suggestion. 'I'm going. Thanks.'

I was intrigued and fired up. As soon as he'd gone, I went to work. It was a popular misconception that hackers, crackers and phreakers could cut into computers and hack their systems within minutes. To crack even one code could take weeks of diligent and painstaking effort, often leading up blind alleys that meant the hacker had to go back to the starting point. Even now, with the most powerful of intelligent, self-initiating search engines, it was a slow and ponderous task.

My strength was that I had been at it a long time. My favourite hobby had been hacking into as many world government and megacorp central storage bins as possible. Day after day, year after year, I'd meticulously leeched on their systems, never allowing myself to be discovered. By designing my own search engines, these were automatically updated as my targets changed their systems, just to avoid being hacked. Someone once called me a magpie, a hoarder who had never trashed anything in my computer. Right back to the day I'd first hacked into my school reports. I even kept the old games I'd played when I was five years old. One of my proudest possessions was a first copy of

Tomb Raider, one of the greatest computer games of the 1990s.

I pulled up my private files onto the plasma wall screen and began running through all the years of data I'd saved, probably the most comprehensive information on institutional and corporate bodies held by any private individual. Banking codes, police records, MI5, MI6, FBI, CIA and most international security files, NASA data, military top secrets and wage controls, anything and everything I'd hacked over the years.

Five minutes later, a file appeared on the wall screen: WHITE HOUSE ACCESS CODES. I hoped they were still current. They were. I accessed them. I found what I was after. I looked up Don Clancy's staff records, surprised to see the Secret Service agent was five years older than me, so the man was obviously a high spender at the Youthness Boutiques. Clancy looked about thirty and there were no signs that gave away the demeanour of an older person. *Apart from his attitude.* I recalled the diamond nose-piercing as well as the gold and emerald earring. Clancy liked to parade his wealth, probably had expensive body piercings under his go-to-work suit. *I live in an age where the character of a man is reflected by what he wears on his back.* The fashion amongst the young these days was for simpler tastes. More elegance, less ostentation. It was the older ones who flashed their wealth. I should've picked that up.

After that I trawled the confidential data to find out what was going on. It was another ten minutes before I confirmed that the ghost of Marilyn Monroe still haunted the White House. I dialled in to the Datakeeper, my oldest ally, and brought him up to speed, passing on all the information I'd got.

'You will keep me informed,' said the Datakeeper.

'Automatically. Everything I get will come straight through to you.'

'Do we need to inform anyone that we're working together?'

'Why? There's no conflict of interest. And something this big is better kept between ourselves.'

There hadn't been such a sense of united urgency in the Puzzle Palace since Dixon had ordered the bombings in the Middle East.

The National Security Agency's Puzzle Palace covered over 2,500 acres and was the nerve centre of the USA's largest intelligence-gathering organization, employing over 120,000 people with an annual budget that was larger than the CIA and FBI's expenditure combined. The NSA, started in the 1940s in a single office in Washington's Old Munitions Building, was now an antennae-bristling complex of forty vast buildings with links into satellites, the internet, and any other paraphernalia of modern-day snooping that included reading a car number plate parked next to Mc-Donald's in Moscow's Red Square. Signals Intelligence, or SIGINT, rapidly became the first recourse of the USA's intelligence, much to the chagrin of the CIA and FBI. The NSA, linked to receivers all over the world, from Turkey to Australia, from Puerto Rico to Antarctica, in addition to numerous satellites circling the earth, was solely designed to intercept radio signals and other telemetry. It had for more than seventy years regularly intercepted and read the secret communications of over forty countries, including all its allies.

The Interception of Ultra-Covert World-Wide Telecommunications section of the NSA was known as the Telephone Exchange. Its remit was beyond that of just telephone bugging. It had its own agenda and budget, and was responsible for the highest level of surveillance and interception on a global scale. The department had reached some notoriety in the 1980s when a report on the agency pointed to its 'extraordinary capability to intercept', and concluded that 'no other agency of the federal government undertakes such activity on such an immense scale'. But that was about intercepting phone calls and other forms of international communications, including faxes and satellite links.

The department was thus ideally placed to monitor the new internet technology that arrived at the turn of the century. The NSA, because of its previous long record of privacy violations, and now without the Cold War or the Middle East to hide behind, made a conscious decision to play down its role in net-tapping. But, while in public it presented itself as a modern government-monitored security service, it secretly enlarged the responsibilities of the Telephone Exchange to cover the new expanding internet.

The Foreign Intelligence Surveillance Act was then introduced to prevent the NSA and other services from extending their wide influences. It ensured that the NSA was no longer allowed to target or watch Americans without a FISA warrant, even from international areas, as long as that person was located on US soil. But that same person, once they had left US territories, was stripped of any protection from the NSA. After the 9/11 attacks in 2001, when Islamic terrorists flew into the Twin Towers of New York and killed over 3000 innocent people, the NSA decided to treat everyone as possible suspects.

The growth of VR brought new opportunities for the ever-hungry NSA. Once US citizens were on the Brick, the NSA considered them to be on foreign soil and subsequently open to being spied upon. With over fifty years of cooperation with GCHQ, Britain's equally impressive electronic surveillance service based in Cheltenham, the two snoopers declared open season on Second World. During all this, middle-class society moved out of the cities and back to the plains, back to the dream that was small-town America. Many big industrial cities degenerated and these areas became known as the JunkBelt, very similar to the Sprawls across Europe. But behind it all there was always the spectre of a major terrorist attack from the Islamic world.

The NSA was the front line against terrorists, but their control of information within America was a gigantic platform in bringing insecurity to the paranoia of a creaky Fortress USA. Eventually, as part of the Settlement Treaty, the government agreed to curtail the NSA's influence and promised that its vast information banks on private citizens would be destroyed. That ruling tied in with the international FISA laws being passed through the UN simultaneously.

By the time international laws were passed in 2027, the NSA and GCHQ had files on every citizen in their own countries as well as those in others nations, both friend and foe. With intelligent computers, scan guides, voice matchers, phone scanners, word identifiers and 54,000 words-per-minute printers, they could access any source they wanted and file information immediately. Voice analysts, data technicians, camera controllers and a collection of crackers, trackers, phreakers, cryptologists and cyberpunks watched the world, in the privacy of the Telephone Exchange, which had a direct link to GCHQ.

According to the authorities, the information collected before 2027, that on private citizens with no records and taken without FISA warrants, was destroyed. But the NSA and GCHQ still maintained the same staff and the same facilities. They appeared nevertheless to follow the guidelines required, and, as time rolled on, the past didn't seem to come back and haunt the citizens who walked the Web.

So, when Deke Marlin, the National Security Adviser, was informed of the President's disappearance, his first contact was Dwight Swilkin, the Telephone Exchange's Director.

They spoke on a secure Vuephone link.

'That's for your ears only,' Marlin said as he related what had taken place. 'Get a team together, best people. Pull in everyone you need, wherever they are. War rules apply. This is to remain a totally secure operation. No one goes home; they live on site. No contact with any other department.'

'Who else is in on it?'

'Secret Service – up to now. I'm going to try and get this contained between us.'

'And if we tread on their toes?'

'Usual disciplines. Protect us. Make sure we get the news first.'

Swilkin nodded. 'I need a warrant. Especially for the SnoopCams.'

'I'll chase FISA when I need to. In the case of a national emergency, like I believe this could be taken as, we do have the right to tap directly into the network.' He noted Swilkin's wry smile. 'Chase *everything*, Dwight.'

'It could open us up to more charges on privacy invasion. And the usual human rights outcry. We will have to go into past files.'

'Do what's necessary. We protect our President.'

'Even at the risk of damaging the Puzzle Palace?'

Marlin gave Swilkin a warning look. 'I would not expect our position to be compromised. We protect ourselves at all costs.'

The Voice jolted him, came out of nowhere, filling the empty blackness.

'Once upon a time, in the early days, all you got on the Web was porn and sex and all that stuff.'

Dixon jumped to his feet, startled. He had got used to the lifeless silence. It wasn't a voice he recognized. It came from no specific direction, but encircled him, trapped him.

'Now we're advanced and more civilized, and we've got avatars and VR and medicine for everybody, and Second World to take away all that misery and pain ... and the only thing we still get is porn and sex and all that stuff ... Not good, Mr President.'

Silence. No apparent movement from anywhere. Dixon waited with the miserable desperation of knowing he was helpless.

'She was a beautiful creature,' the Voice said eventually. 'Yet, even now, after all these years, she still can't get to sleep. No peace for that sweet little girl, sweet little Marilyn. Why? Because of people like you, Teddy Dixon. Poor Marilyn, do you think her being dead stopped the pain? Stopped any feeling? Is that what you think, Mr Prezzident? Are you really that stupid? No wonder our country's falling apart – because you don't care. Poor Marilyn. Poor baby Marilyn. She was just like the rest of us poor folk. Just shagged by you rich powerful dicks. Poor, poor Norma Jean.'

Dixon stayed quiet. Maybe the guy was a psychopath, some nut in love with Monroe. Maybe he could talk the guy round.

'Then again . . .' The Voice belched out laughter. 'I'd like to have banged her, too. Hey, she really was a sorry bitch, wasn't she? All those looks and nothing more than a trophy hole to fuck. Pitiful. Just fuck-me pitiful. No wonder she couldn't stand it any more.'

Silence.

'At least she had the guts to take her own life.'

Silence.

'Have you the same guts, Teddy Boy? Are you prepared to pay for what you and the rest all did to her?'

More silence.

'Four more years. Four more years. Tell me, Teddy Boy, why do you want four more years? You don't deserve four more fucking years.' Still the silence. 'Talk to me, Teddy Boy. Truth or consequence? You tell me the truth or face the consequence. You ever played that game, Teddy? Maybe when you were a kid?' The Voice let out a deep sigh, the sound cloaking Dixon like fog. 'I bet you never had to play with your life as a consequence? I mean, nothing like this.'

Teddy Dixon suddenly felt the blackness harden. Where he had felt space outside his body, he now felt pressure, pushing against him, like a vice forcing the air out of his lungs. He grabbed his own throat in despair, tried to breathe deeply and suck in the air. But there was nothing, just the darkness and the pressure crushing his chest. The dizziness rushed in.

'Time to say something, Teddy. You can't hide from me even in the dark,' shrieked the Voice. 'Just say . . . hello. Do that and I turn the air back on.'

'I hear you,' gasped Dixon.

'Can't hear you.'

'I hear you, I hear you.'

'Then say hello'

'Hello. Hello.'

'Now, isn't that easy, Mr President?'

The air exploded back into his lungs, he collapsed to the floor, sucking it in short, hurried breaths. The pressure subsided and his dizziness eased.

'Truth and consequence, that's the game. Teddy, did you ever consider what a shithole you're turning this country into? This was a proud nation once. We were going to show the world how to live in peace. We fucked up, didn't we? All that shit in Iraq and what it spawned. And you with your little macro-nukes, taking out all those people. Did you like the game, Teddy? Did you enjoy pressing the button? Fuck everyone up, bomb them to hell, blow their little mud houses to smithereens, then just walk away. Game's over, did you enjoy the hotdog? Or did little Teddy burn his tongue with all that mustard? We left them and we went back to what we were good at: feeding our bellies and fuck everyone else. That's the West for you. Shut every bastard out if he don't agree with you and leave him in his own excrement. Some civilization, eh? Half the world can't get enough food, and the other half's stuffing its face while it's blowing its mind on the Web.

Silence for a moment, till the Voice continued. 'I've heard of freedom of choice, but this is ridiculous. What happened to the law? What happened to the order? Christ, Teddy, you're letting it all go wrong and you're doing nothing about it – except chase nice girls like Miss Monroe. And now, having taken away most of our freedoms, having invaded all our privacy with your SnoopCams and Street-Cams, now you want to replace our identity cards with barcodes. Lasered onto the back of our hands from the day we're born.'

'That's for your own security,' Dixon shouted, instinctively always the politician, instinctively protecting their point of view. He paused, because the power of his own voice in the darkness startled him. He went on to justify himself, speaking softer this time. 'So our police and the cameras can scan you and make sure you're not hostile, that you're a clean citizen –'

The Voice cut across him, screamed at him again. *'YOU'RE DESTROYING OUR FREEDOM, MISTER PRESIDENT.'*

'What would you like me to do?' yelled back Dixon, desperately trying to work an understanding with his tormentor.

'How do I fucking know? You're the President. You tell me. You get paid for that shit.'

The air stopped again, the hardness pushed against his chest. He was ready this time and he held his breath. Forty seconds later he passed out.

'You get some sleep now, Mr President,' comforted the Voice softly. 'You just sleep and save your energy. Otherwise you won't last more than a few hours down here. Just relax and you might just live a little bit longer.'

The meeting between the Vice President, Meisner and Marlin was over. Clancy and Gallagher also both attended. Most of the discussion was on how to get information on all those who attended the Convention, and on White House staff, and on anyone who might have recently become an enemy of the President.

Marlin had insisted the perpetrators had to be an organization from behind the Great Islamic Wall. 'We've got to go on national alert straight away in case there's some dirty devices about to be used against us. Protect our cities. Close up all entry points into the country.'

'No. Not yet,' answered the Vice President, Nancy Sumner. 'I will not agree to the release of information that suggested the President was missing. That would create panic. We know he's in Second World. We know he's alive, physically anyway. We control this thing from the White House until we find him.'

'And if he's . . . *not* alive?'

'He *is* alive. He's next door . . . and breathing. That's a fact. Just give me a plan of action.'

They quickly reached agreement that the National Security Agency, and not the CIA, under the immediate control of its Director, would monitor all known foreign governments and organizations hostile to the United States or its President. All satellites would be reprogramed, where necessary, for surveillance of terrorist groups and their camps.

Information would be released only on a 'need to know' basis and that permission would come solely from the Vice President. Her office, in addition to the White House Security Control Complex, would be the analysis centre point for all information.

Once Gallagher realized that, because of a lack of information, the meeting was running out of steam, he again brought up the idea of using a team of crackers. Marlin, the NSA chief, supported by Clancy, was against it.

But Nancy Sumner, a hardened politician who had often stood up to Teddy Dixon and kept him committed to his election pledges, warmed to Gallagher's idea. 'According to everyone, we have less than twelve hours to find him,' she said commandingly. 'We have two major reasons for finding him. First, he is our President, and every possible effort should be made to ensure his safe return. That is, we've all agreed, the responsibility of the Secret Service, so we have to go along with their advice. Secondly, if the public, in the US and the rest of the world, get any idea that there's a virus that can knock out their JetPax systems, we will have major panic. Nobody would want to visit Second World, so Wall Street would crash. E-commerce, megacorps, small business, communications, would all suffer if their services were no longer being used. We'd then have a global economic disaster, and the cost of recovering that situation is unimaginable. We've little choice but to give Mr Gallagher's idea a chance.'

'I'll agree, but only if we can vet those names ourselves,' said Meisner.

'OK, Joe, I'll buy that.' She turned to Gallagher. 'Do you know how to contact these people?'

'Yes, ma'am,' replied Gallagher. 'I was on a task force that investigated hackers some years back. I can trace them pretty quickly.'

'Good. Get us some names as soon as you can.'

'Yes, ma'am.' He paused, then, 'I need a FISA warrant. I

have got to use the SnoopCams – and all the information they may already have recorded.' They all knew the rules. You could monitor electronic means of communication – with the exception of personal email – but not excessively.

'Joe?' Sumner turned to Meisner.

'I think we've got to take that risk and not chase warrants,' Meisner said after a moment's thought. 'Let's not forget that FISA doesn't apply until we actually process the communication into, quote, *an intelligible form intended for human inspection*, unquote. In other words, until we print or store the information, or use it. I would also add that we're acting in the public interest and not against it. We're protecting our right to defend our national security. FISA would have a problem calling that play against us.'

'OK. If the UN or any external monitoring systems pick up an excess of surveillances, make sure I know immediately,' agreed the Vice President.

Clancy helped Gallagher prepare the list. While they were going through the data files an operative reported through to Gallagher it was the 'As Good As it Gets' Copyrighted Puppets, Inc. company that had supplied the Monroe avatar. The company, owned by ThemeCorp, had so far received no notification of any problem with the avatar in question.

While Gallagher took the call, Clancy studied a sheet of paper lying on the table. He wasn't surprised to see Conor Smith's name at the top of the list.

The two buildings, side by side on the Brick, were totally incongruous, and at odds with each other. But that's what it was like on the Brick. No plan, no thought to overall form, just lease the next space and fill in the Dark Areas. It was a greedy world's final tribute to Mammon and the art of fast food, PunkArt, ExploMusik and turning a quick buck.

Number 6M278K3301 was a Lutheran Church, simple in form, its modern spire rising as a warning to those who would deny God and his teachings. A small church, as those on the Brick went, being no more than one high storey tall with its spire on top, it was a well-known landmark, because of its smallness, and therefore, one presumed, its integrity with its own past. Good people came and worshipped there; believers in their faith and in their pastor. They were of the old order, coming from all over the globe, seeking comfort and solace in a world where excess and selfishness were the new mantras of the day.

Next door, number 6M278K3303, was a modern building, shooting straight up to its eighty-fifth floor. It was a rectangular shape, tall and thin and coloured in black and white squares like a giant chessboard. Built three years earlier, 6M278K3303 was a hotel block and, as with all such blocks, the more expensive and luxurious accommodation occupied the lower floors. They had grand entrances and marble floors and five-star room service with food prepared by master chefs in wonderfully creative kitchens. The higher one rose, the cheaper and shabbier were the environs, and quality service became nonexistent. The reason was simple, because there were no views from the top. Only those specially built into the window frames by the occupiers. The lowest floors looked out onto the Brick itself and there was a constant visual intermingling with the life that coursed along it. On top of the building you just looked out on the Dark Areas.

The Hotel Gallipoli occupied just the top five floors of 6M278K3303. Its windows were small and curtained over. The reception area reminded one of those late last-century films; a single staircase, rickety elevator and a tired, couldn't-give-a-damn-so-help-yourself she-male receptionist who was more interested in the sports and betting pages than the customers who approached the desk. He was an avatar, looked like a faded Roger Moore with balloon breasts, and was controlled by a tired actor who was currently at home watching TV while occasionally glancing at the small monitor that covered the Gallipoli's foyer.

He saw her enter and, as she made her way to the stairs, went back to his TV. Marilyn Monroe didn't surprise him. He'd seen them all: Ava Gardner, Betty Grable, Jayne Mansfield, even Rock Hudson and Boris Karlof. As long as they were dead, they were fair game. He knew the ghouls were out there waiting for the Kylie Minogues and Julia Roberts to finally die off. *Christ, they make more money now they're dead than when they were alive.* He was beyond surprise when it came to people's private obsessions. The Gallipoli was a FuckHotel pure and simple. Even the WebCops rarely bothered him. It was the cheap end of the market. Dirty squalid rendezvous and MIWs. The cops gave up trying to trap the MIWs; they escaped into the Web before they could be apprehended. Rumour was they even knew how to move around the Dark Areas. The receptionist relaxed. It would be another three hours before the early Weekenders started to move in.

Marilyn Monroe, as arranged, headed to the 84th floor, room 58. She'd enjoyed the caper; it wasn't every day you got to be the heroine in a WebGame with the President of the United States, even if he was only an avatar. She'd researched the Kennedy affair thoroughly, studied the script and rehearsed it over and over again. The client had asked for that. That's why he was paying so much. Her bank balance would soon be doubled, and she wouldn't have to work for another year. Time to enjoy life and get off the Web for a while.

And she'd been good as Marilyn; she knew that by the President's response. He'd been part of the game. But his sudden reaction when they fell into the whiteness, as he fumbled with his JetPax and seemed genuinely surprised by her actions, this had worried her. She'd suddenly felt as if someone else was there, holding her against the President, not allowing either of them to escape each other's embrace. Scary. But she knew it was all in her imagination. Everyone knew you couldn't go invisible in the Web; that was one of the first laws the UN had imposed.

But it had perplexed her at the time. It was as if Dixon hadn't known where the game was going. It had shaken her, the whole experience. She'd been told Dixon was in on the charade. Then he was gone, not even a chance for goodbye.

She took out the SmartKey the client had sent her and opened the door. It was a simple room; one unmade single bed, no other furniture apart from a bedside table which had a lamp, a phone and a glass of red wine on it, a worn carpet, no pictures on the wall and a curtained window. There was something familiar about the bed, the way it sat in the room, the way the bedclothes were thrown back. She closed the door behind her and, because there were no chairs, perched on the end of the bed. Her client was late. The phone rang, shrilled across the bareness of the room.

'Hello,' she breathed as she answered it.

'Marilyn?'

She recognized the client's voice. 'Hi, Mister Onassis.' It was the name he'd asked her to use.

'You did well.'

'Thank you. Singing to that audience, that was fun ... mindblowing.'

'You were great. As good as the real thing.'

'Must've been fantastic, for Marilyn. She was a real star.'

'So were you. In fact, I'm going to give you a bonus.'

'That's great. Say, that puppet was just like the President.'

'It was a very successful game.'

'How come you got a puppet of the President? I thought that was against the law.' She regretted it as she said it. It wasn't her business. She hadn't been paid yet and she didn't want to upset the client.

'He gave permission. It was part of a White House security game.'

'Wow, isn't that something? The agency said the order came from the White House.'

'You keep that just between us.'

'Sure.'

'I'm sorry I can't meet with you, only ... you know, security and all that. But I thought we'd drink a toast together. To a job well done. And, you never know, there could be more. You just make sure you keep a lid on this.'

'It'll go no further.'

'Good. I'll pay the credits, and the bonus, to your copyright agent. Anyway, just lift up your glass – I've got mine here – and let's toast a successful and winning game.'

Marilyn picked up the wine glass with her other hand. She didn't normally drink alcohol or take any substance if she didn't know the source. But her agent had booked her for Mister Onassis and that meant he was OK. She was safe with him.

'Cheers,' she heard him say.

She sipped the wine. It was good, a deep cyberwine with body and real taste. 'This is expensive stuff,' she said as she felt it thrill the back of her throat.

'Only the best, Marilyn. For a great star and a great actress.'

The worm came at her during the third sip. She'd taken enough substances in her time to recognize the rush of AcidIce. In RealWorld it was a potent psychostimulant, based on methamphetamine and phencyclidine, or PCP. It was a staggering cocktail, both hallucinogenic and stimulatory. AcidIce was a favourite amongst the Weekenders. But, as most dealers knew, it was a controlled substance; after all they needed their customers back each week, and too much of this could kill.

She'd never known a rush as powerful as this. She watched the worm as it metamorphosed in her glass, draining the rest of what she had believed was red wine. Then it crawled onto her hand, and burrowed its way into her skin, just below the knuckle on the index finger of her left hand. She threw the glass away but it was too late. The worm grew longer, filling up with her blood, darkening into a rich lush deep brown colour. She dropped the phone and tried to squash the worm as it wriggled into her.

DV! Dammit he'd given her DV. A fucking sex disease. Anything but DV.

Then she remembered the JetPax she always wore, reached for it, hit the escape button.

'Too late,' said her customer. 'Too late, baby, but don't worry.'

'You promised me. I trusted you. My money.' The words came out in staccato bursts. She wrenched at the JetPax.

'Not you, Marilyn. You remember what you always said in real life. *I'm not interested in money. I just wanna be wonderful.*'

The worm entered and the rush exploded, unbelievably intensifying past where she had ever been before, seeming to have no natural end. The worm slithered into her bloodstream and she felt it growing through her, filling her arteries. She saw her father. He floated past, smiling. *Where've you been, baby? Come and play.* She turned away from him. She remembered the awful things he'd done, first to her mother, then to her. Things he'd forced her to do. She sobbed. The anxiety and deep uncontrollable emotion was building inside her, frenziedly as the worm filled her.

'That *was* the real President, Marilyn, so you nearly fucked more than one President.'

She didn't know what he was talking about. She didn't care what he was talking about. Then she remembered why the room she was in was so familiar, with the bed unmade. She recalled the photographs of the dead Marilyn, the ones she'd used to help her research. It was the same bed Marilyn had died on.

Her sobbing had now turned to screams, not of pain but of lost innocence, lost hope, the fearful and final realization that there was nowhere else to go. The worm filled her now; she was helpless now, her being taken over by the AcidIce. She felt it manoeuvring inside her, filling every crevice. Hardening as it did so. Surge of anxiety, surge of heartbeat, mind full of Father and the wasted mistakes of a life, while floating in and out of cyberspace and RealWorld and seeing the strands of telephone lines that weren't there any more – faster, faster, out of touch, out of touch, wandering into nowhere. Nothing real. No more dreams. The wire was taut, stretched, ready to snap apart and disconnect her for ever. She felt the worm squeeze into her brain, wipe out all the good and the bad stuff she had ever remembered. It sucked her into oblivion. The worm was alone at last. It died as quickly as it came.

'Goodbye, Norma Jean,' said Mister Onassis.

They were the last sad words she ever heard.

'He's gone. Smith's gone.'

Clancy rushed through, to find Gallagher alone on a monitor.

'He's probably started already,' replied Gallagher.

'We only just got permission.'

'He probably took off, on his own initiative.'

'What if we'd decided not to use him?'

'He would've done the same.'

'You're playing with fire.'

'Lay off, Don. We're never going to solve this with traditional techniques. Conor's probably out early because he wants to beat the Weekenders. Like he said, he doesn't want to be slowed down by the crowds, maybe even get any clues disturbed when millions hit the Brick.'

Clancy leant across the table. 'How many GameMasters are you pulling in?'

'For now, I'm just going with Smith.'

'Who the fuck agreed to that?'

'The VP did.'

'You went and saw her?'

'Sure. She asked me for a list. I went down, with a few names, and told her the best guy was Conor Smith.'

'Why him?'

'It's the contacts out there, in the Web, that count. He's got his and I can back him up with all the intelligence info he needs. We don't have time to go through all the megacorps finding out where their GameMasters are.'

'So she simply agreed, just like that?'

'Sorry, Don, but we really don't have time to chase the usual channels. Smith's good, and I trust him.'

'Big risk.' Clancy rubbed his forehead; things were rapidly slipping out of his control. But he kept quiet; it would be churlish to remind Gallagher who was the Senior Agent.

'Like I said to the VP, no risk can be big enough if we're to find the President. We don't have the luxury of trawling through a selection list and interviewing lots of people. No time-outs on this one, Don.' Gallagher leant back in his chair. 'I've asked Joe Meisner if we can go up with him and see the First Lady. In about fifteen minutes.'

'Why?'

'Maybe she could help us . . . give us a clue. We need to open every door.'

'I should've stayed closer to him.'

'Too late now.'

'I was responsible. And now, according to you, I'm just using old-fashioned procedures to chase the wind.'

Gallagher ignored the accusation. 'What about the guest lists?'

'I've got a team on that. But I need to interview them. Christ, Paul, it's impossible to interview nearly three thousand people in less than eleven hours, especially if you can't alert them as to why. We're running search machine after search machine. Anything that could link someone in a positive way. I've found nearly three hundred guests who've fucked Marilyn Monroe, but not one of them from the same supplier we used. Even Joe Meisner's taken a few celebrity puppets out for the night.'

'Any news on *our* Marilyn?'

'Still missing. And that goes for the actor driving her.'

'He must be some good programer, to override all those secure systems. He's got to be working from the inside.'

'Inside where? He's cracked the megacorp codes, the

White House codes, even the copyright codes. He can't be inside *everything*.'

'Then he's a tracker.' Gallagher swung away from the monitor and beckoned Clancy to follow him. When they were out of earshot of the rest of the room, Gallagher continued. 'We've got the best trackers in the world working for us. The National Security Agency, CIA, FBI, you name it. These guys do nothing but chase information going round on the Net. They're linked into SnoopCams and StreetCams, they've got bugs in places no one's ever heard of. They track emails and ecomms twenty-four hours a day, three hundred and sixty-five days a year. And all this information has to be stored somewhere. Don't ask where, I really don't know. But it's there. We need access to that information. Could Marlin get it for us?' Gallagher leant forward to drive home his point. 'We need that access. It could speed up this whole operation, Don.'

Clancy was silent as he contemplated Gallagher's views. An Act of Congress had fallen in line with the UN directive back in 2027. It was passed to protect US citizens from having their email and other Web information intercepted by the NSA or any other security or government service *unless judged to have a hostile intention towards a sovereign state.* To this day, no proof had ever been found that established otherwise.

Clancy decided to voice the same view. 'I don't think I can help, Paul. That's way out of my jurisdiction.'

'Which is why Conor Smith needs all the slack I can give him.'

'Too long a shot.'

'Give me an alternative. Anything that stops me working outside the system.'

Clancy shrugged. 'Don't drag me down with you if you fuck up.' Then he let out a shrill laugh. 'Shit . . . as if I could dig a deeper hole than the one I've already buried myself in.'

Unlike most previous First Ladies, Annie Dixon didn't set about rearranging and redecorating the White House as soon as she had moved in. She enjoyed it as it was, steeped in history and drama. Why change it, she thought, when she herself would only be another passing footnote in the book of American history.

A financially independent woman with her own successful media technology company, she took the trappings of being First Lady in her stride. She'd left her husband alone to chase his political career, supporting him where necessary, both emotionally and financially. She was surprised when he made it to the Presidency; his past was littered with indiscretions that had somehow never affected his career. It never much mattered to her. She was busy, neither wanted children, and this left him free to follow his political ambitions. Their marriage was sound mostly because they shared a tremendous sense of humour and of joint achievement. He revelled in her business success and was the first to praise her publicly, while she admired his political and people skills, and the fact that he really cared about the constituents he represented. In her eyes, that was what ultimately made Teddy Dixon the success he was.

She genuinely believed he was the one who deserved to fill the history pages, not herself, the partner who might have painted the White House walls a different colour. And now that would be shattered if what she had seen on those tapes were ever published.

She sat quietly in her living room, listening while Meisner reported the progress so far. Nancy Sumner, the Vice President, sat next to him. The more Meisner spoke, the more Annie realized how little they knew.

When he finished she said, 'When I asked for the Marilyn Monroe puppet, I told Abbi to make sure we dealt with a respectable company. Have you checked up on them?'

'Yes,' replied Meisner. 'Blue chip company. They're a subsidiary of ThemeCorp.'

'I know we don't have much,' added Sumner. 'But we're throwing every resource at it, Annie. Everything.'

Annie Dixon had little time for the Vice President, but she'd never let that show. Her intuition was that Sumner, a tough ex-lawyer who had championed employment causes, had never liked Teddy Dixon, that she linked with him only because she had an eye to the main chance. And, if they didn't find Dixon, then the main chance would now be within Sumner's grasp. 'I'm sure you are,' she replied, smiling then. She turned her attention to Meisner. He wasn't the best Chief of Staff a President could have, but he was Dixon's man and loyal to the end. With predators like Sumner circling, at this moment that counted for everything. 'Those tapes,' she said. 'What's happened to them?'

'Nobody's seen them since we did,' Meisner answered. That was the truth as far as he knew, but guessed that some of the outside help being brought in would need access to them. 'Except for Nancy, the National Security Adviser and the Attorney General.' He must have seen something in her expression because he immediately tried to calm her fears. 'The tapes are in a safe place and cannot be accessed by anybody. Unless authorized by the President or the Supreme Court.'

And you all have proof of my husband trying to fuck a celebrity puppet. 'Thank you,' acknowledged Annie with a warm smile.

The Vice President rose. 'If there's anything you need, I'll be in my office. Just feel free to wander over.'

'I will. Remember, I still live here.' Annie regretted it as soon as she said it.

'I meant into the security control areas. If you need to find out how they're doing.'

'Of course. Thank you.'

Sumner left the room.

'Did *you* arrange for Marilyn to visit Teddy?' The First Lady asked Meisner.

'It was harmless. Just . . . harmless fun,' came the embarrassed reply.

'We both know what he's like.'

'That's Teddy.'

There was a knock on the door.

'That's Clancy. I said he could speak to you. You might come up with something. They don't have a lot to go on.' When she nodded agreement, he called loudly. 'Come in.'

'Please sit down.' Annie acknowledged Clancy and Gallagher.

'We just wondered if there was anything recently that may have worried the President,' began Gallagher, remaining standing.

Annie shrugged. 'Like what, Paul?'

'I don't know. Did he seem restless in his sleep?'

'We sleep in separate rooms,' she reminded them. It wasn't a secret in the White House, only to the outside world.

'Did he mention anything out of the ordinary? About being fearful of something, or somebody? Did he get any calls that made him edgy? Was there any group of people, or any individual, who rang him more often than anyone else? Anyone who called up and he made an excuse to leave the room . . . any private conversations?'

'No to all of those.'

'Do you, yourself, have any business enemies who might turn on him?'

'I don't think so. Isn't that pretty dramatic?'

'The whole thing's pretty dramatic.'

'I'm sorry, you're right. We must examine every avenue. No, I don't think I have business enemies who would kidnap the President just to get at me.'

'Or embarrass him, and, through him, you and your company?'

'I think that's rather far-fetched but, no, I don't think so. From what I saw on the tape, he didn't need any help on that score.'

Gallagher remained unfazed. 'Can I have a list of the companies you do business with?'

'I'll arrange that.'

'Why did you choose to hire Marilyn Monroe?'

'Because Teddy has a thing about the Kennedys, so I thought it would be fun to duplicate the famous birthday song. You saw the response amongst the guests. It was a great success.' She paused and looked at Meisner accusingly before continuing. 'I certainly didn't arrange the little reunion afterwards. Did you think I had?'

'No, ma'am.' Gallagher wisely moved on. 'Your company is a media technology group with large advertising concessions on the Web?'

'Am I now a suspect?'

'No, ma'am, but you have pretty extensive links into Second World. Someone you know, someone you do business with, could have had access to the Monroe avatars and to the company who hired them out. That's why I need your records, and the access codes. To check any possible links. Right now, we're grabbing at anything we can get.'

'I'll have my office give you all our access codes immediately, and make sure my staff are at your disposal, if you need them.'

'Thank you, ma'am.'

'You two really do have a tough task ahead of you,' she said understandingly. 'Pray God you succeed.'

METROPORT 1703
BUDAPEST DISTRICT
HUNGARY INTERNATIONAL ZONE
DIAMOND PARK
9M436K2201, THE BRICK
REAL TIME: ZERO MINUS 10 HRS AND 25 MINS

I knew no one was better at understanding Second World and its darker side than the MIWs, those lost souls who were officially listed as Missing in the Web. There was little point in going to the popular or usual places where hackers hung out. If Gallagher was going to send out more people, which he probably would, I didn't want to be around while they were all falling over each other.

My first choice was the girl; I hadn't spoken to her for nearly three weeks. I'd first met her, and the boy who followed and relied on her, when I was tracking a Cyber-Drug dealer for Scotland Yard. We'd hit it off instantly and I often shared a coffee in some Starbucks or took her to Dragon Park or one of the other centres owned by ThemeCorp that I had instant access to. FerrariMania had become one of her favourites. The boy occasionally accompanied the pair of us, but always kept his distance, like a stray puppy, unsure and untrusting, occasionally putting his paw tentatively through the fence.

Andi Whitehorn. American. Attractive. The way I liked them. I'd developed a soft spot for her, enjoyed her company. She was a serious type, and that sort of suited me. Mum said I'd always be alone because that was my nature. She said I had OCS, Only Child Syndrome, said it made me obsessive about either being looked after or wanting to look after someone else. Andi fell into the second category. And maybe, during my darker moments, I realized I felt this way about her because I could always escape back to RealWorld and be on my own at Rose Cottage. But I definitely felt something for her; enjoyed having someone to worry about, someone to feel responsible for. She'd been twenty-six when she went MIW. That was nine years earlier. A slim, auburn-haired girl with a round face and short-cropped hair. Delicately featured and delicately built. She was now wearing a Mary Quant white outfit from the 1960s; expensive in the copyright world of the Web. She was always up to date with the latest fashions and changed her outfits constantly. I never asked where she got the credits for them.

Andi had been on CyberDrugs ever since she'd gone MIW. After helping me the first time, I got extra 'stoolie' credits out of Scotland yard for her. It suited them because the MIWs made the best stool-pigeons. It was a lot more than the measly welfare credits she lived on, and she promised me she'd get help coming off the stuff.

Confirmed druggies stood a good chance in Second World, since there were enough carers and counsellors located in small offices all along the Brick. Counselling was an industry that had taken off in RealWorld during the 1990s and grown through the first quarter of the next century. Now it was passé there; you were meant to look after yourself with the help of the latest computer-generated programs. Drink, drugs, sex, gambling; all excesses in RealWorld had self-help programs you could buy off a shelf. CLEAN – THE GOLD EDITION was the latest bestseller; a program designed to increase self-esteem and help its user beat those habit-forming destructive lifestyles. Others included LOST WEEK-END AND HOW TO REGAIN IT, SHOOT – THE CURE, and DROOP – FOR HAVING LESS SEX BUT MORE PLEASURE.

The result was that although more RealWorld counsellors were out of work there, they actually got busier as their former customers entered the Web looking for help that was denied them in RealWorld. Counselling had thus been driven underground. The authorities let them get on with it; it suited them because it allowed them to allocate public money to other services. The counsellors didn't ask whether their clients were from RealWorld or MIWs. They cashed their credits all the same.

One day Andi admitted to me that she'd escaped into the Web because she was a fugitive from the Long Beach Police Department.

'What did you do?'

'Killed my sister's husband.' She'd said that with no emotion, a declaration chilling in its innocence.

'Why?'

'He was no good. One night, when my sister was away with my dad, visiting relatives, he made a pass at my mother. She was very beautiful. When she turned him down, he beat her, then raped her. I was sleeping in my room, had no idea what was going on. She was unconscious when he finished with her, so he came after me. Did the same.' She'd given a tiny shrug. To me that dismissive action displayed her vulnerability despite her apparent coolness.

'You killed him that night?'

'No. He ran away. When my sister got home next morning she found my mother and me both in a pretty bad state. We were taken to hospital and they never found him.'

'Then how . . . ?'

'I was only fourteen at the time. Nine years later I ran into him in a bar in Long Beach. He didn't recognize me, and I let him take me home. He kept saying I looked familiar, but I never told him who I was. He'd grown fat, didn't shave, was a real dirtbag. Couldn't believe his luck that I'd gone home with him. I got a big knife from the kitchen; it was unwashed, sitting in his piled-up filthy sink. Had pizza crusts and bits of cheese and salami stuck to it. While he was taking his T-shirt off, was pulling it over his head, I just rammed it into his face as hard as I could. He couldn't see anything as he was trying to rip off the shirt but couldn't stop me jabbing it into him. When he finally got it off, it was too late. He was blind and pretty near dead. He lay there, on the linoleum floor, all the blood everywhere, trying to look up at me. He couldn't speak, was breathing real heavy. I saw him say *Why*? With his mouth, no words. He said it again and again. *Why? Why? Why?* I just stood and watched him die. I didn't want to give him the satisfaction of knowing why I'd knifed him.'

After some time, and my silence, she'd continued. 'I left my prints on the knife. I didn't know better . . . I should've wiped it. I went back to San Diego but the police came looking for me. So I went into the Web. I stayed MIW. I'm not going back to face Death Row for such a scumbag.'

Andi's friend, Tebor, was fourteen when he went MIW. A Hungarian youth, the boy had played in the Web ever since he could walk. His father, a programer in Budapest, had left his mother for a younger woman. He showed no interest in Tebor, and the boy made friends with other youngsters at the local internet cafe. One drizzly dank afternoon in RealWorld, while the sun beat down in a glorious seventy-five degrees in Second World, he simply decided not to go home again. His father, now living in Italy with a new family, still had no interest that his son was Missing in the Web, and Tebor joined the ranks of those whom no one wanted back. They were like Peter Pan's Lost Boys, except their escape world was bigger than the world itself. So their minds simply closed themselves down from RealWorld and only functioned in cyberspace, which had become for them the only reality.

Andi and Tebor teamed up and worked together. They had no idea where their Cadavers were; it didn't matter to them because they could never go back. Maybe one day somebody would develop the technology to haul them back to RealWorld.

The real problem was that a person's brain couldn't cope

with the continuous, ever-changing world of cyberspace for long periods. The result was that many early users, staying in Second World for days on end, would return to their host bodies in RealWorld in a state of WebFever; a condition brought about by the unrelenting confusion between reality and fantasy and so short-circuited itself into a catatonic state from which there was no recognized escape.

After a series of clinical trials, the World Health Organization realized that the host body was locked in this state of inertia and muscular rigidity because of Extreme-Schizophrenia. They also realized very quickly that, although the host was trapped in catatonia, the imagination was running amok in Second World, still very much in control of its actions and thoughts. It found that some MIWs, desperate to get back, had attempted a variety of wild exercises to break through the matrix and ended up being wiped out by it as they broke their tenuous link with their host. This condition, one of acute paralysis and high-fevered runaway brain activity, became known as WebMadness.

In conjunction with the UN and its Security Council, the WHO instantly produced new WebLaws set out to protect all future users of the Web, as well as those already trapped in it. The first step was to protect the bodies they had left behind. The official term for them was cadavers, and the resting place became known as a Catacomb. The cadavers of the MIWs were stored in these special Catacombs. Rows upon rows of temperature-controlled coffin-like storage units, each plugged into a central life-support system, each linked directly via a mini computer to the matrix of the Web. Though the bodies lay still, they were exercised daily by electric current systems, and were monitored by sensors inside each coffin. Nobody had ever returned in a sane manner. They were left plugged into the Web but they were kept alive until they died naturally.

The UN, in its role as the Grand Provider for the underprivileged, funded a social benefit for each MIW. This was paid as dollar credits, but because of Amnesty International's human rights dictum that the UN could not challenge the freedom of the MIWs, there were no checks on who was collecting benefit and who wasn't. As some of these MIWs had gone underground because of terrible crimes in RealWorld, the system was open to abuse. But, in 'politically correct' RealWorld, no one dared criticize the system. The MIWs, both dead and alive, were left alone to surf the Web for ever, paid for by the state.

After my visit from the Secret Service, I'd tried to contact Andi before I left Rose Cottage.

Eventually she acknowledged my call.

Yes she wasn't doing much right now.

Yes she was well.

Yes she was still with Tebor.

Yes she was still open to business and could help me.

Yes she'd meet me but could I remember where Tebor was born, and it would be the closest cup of coffee. And not to forget the diamond.

Finally, *why hadn't I rung her for three weeks?*

I felt safe in knowing I hadn't been monitored as I slid the mini-keyboard back into my watch. The message wasn't as complicated as most people sent. Even though breaking into email had been outlawed by international law, everyone believed that it still went on. They just didn't know how. Even I'd never come close to solving that one. The message she'd sent seemed meaningless; just one more sliver in the endless chatter over the optic tidal wave that covered the continents. The trackers, whoever they were, would have more interesting titbits to digest before they got to Andi's small message.

Tebor was Hungarian, so that meant they would meet in the Hungarian Zone. He'd been born in Budapest. The closest cup of coffee was the nearest TeknoKlub. The lives of MIWs revolved round the cyber cafes and punk coffee shops. That was on Margitsziget or Margaret Island, right in the heart of the city. The 'diamond' perplexed me until I looked up Wikipedia on Budapest. There was a Diamond Park on the island, named after one of the original VR villages in 1996. Built for the Mitsubishi Electric Sunnyvale Labs in Silicon Valley, the Park had brought together the first interactions, in Real Time, of speech sound and 3D animated graphics. As a result, when the Web became a reality, Diamond Parks were, with Alpha World and Second Life, amongst the first cyber villages.

There was a second coffee house, the Huszar, not as well frequented as the TeknoKlub. That was on the edge of Diamond Park, next to the Margaret Bridge.

I entered the Web and was transported to MetroPort 1703. The trip took twelve nanoseconds.

Visitors to Budapest in RealWorld and Second World commented there was little difference between the two. A tired city, but built on pride and hard work. So different to the shabbiness of the rest of eastern Europe, even after those countries had joined the United European Republic. In an attempt to build up tourism on the Web, the government had slavishly copied all the main streets that followed the River Danube and built there the same buildings as were in RealWorld.

There were fewer SnoopCams. That's how it was in the poorer countries. Their economies couldn't afford the sophisticated surveillance systems, or the staff that operated them. They were therefore a haven for cyberpunks, MIWs and anyone else not wanting to be noticed.

I came out of MetroPort 1703, walked the short distance along the Ujpesti River Walk and entered Diamond Park by the Margaret Bridge. The Huszar was no more than a grey-walled, small-windowed, summer cafe looking out on the Park. Not a place for tourists, its appearance was particularly unfriendly, as was the slouched man reading a paper behind the bar. I ordered a beer. The surly response and the slopped glass banged on the counter told me I wasn't welcome.

I paid with my euro credit SmartCard, then went to a table by the window. Each table had a simple monitor and keyboard sitting on it. The monitors were the latest IntelliVisuals; the hottest and most instantly reactive screens on the markets. The keys on the keyboards were well used and smeared with finger grease. This was definitely a hackers' bar.

'Hello, Conor,' she said from behind me. 'I was in the little girls' room.'

'Even in Second World?' I smiled welcomingly as she slid into the next chair. I liked the old-fashioned terms she used. 'You know why we all feel we've got to go to the john on the Brick. Not because we need to, but because you're automatically programed to feel you need to. Still carries on with MIWs.'

'I know, because everything down here has to pay for itself, and it's another way of getting the credits out of your wallet.' She considered for a moment. 'Just a thought. What happens up there to my Cadaver? I mean, all my bodily functions.'

'All taken care of, automatically. You're just tubed up and away you go.'

'All my bodily fluids?'

'All.'

'Yech! Sounds messy.'

'I didn't check. But I think they've got it down to a fine art.'

'You didn't check? You mean you know where my Cadaver is?'

'Yes,' I said quietly.

'Why?'

'Why not?' I didn't add that I regularly got reports to check if she was OK, or that I paid an extra sum to keep her at a higher grade of maintenance than the welfare payments would. She'd been previously in a Penitentiary Environment, watched over by prison warders who waited for MIWs to eventually return and face whatever punishment was due to them. It had cost me a great deal for civil rights lawyers to build a case for getting her moved.

'I had a day free so I ran a check to find out where they'd stored you,' I added nonchalantly.

'How'd I look?'

'Bit like you do now . . . a little older. If they ever find a method of getting you back, you'll pass muster as a human being.'

'They'll never find a way.' She suddenly reacted against that dream, knowing that it would always remain a dream. 'Anyway, who wants to go back to the shit-hole up there. Me and Tebor are fine down here.'

'Where is he?'

'He'll be here soon.'

'How is the little script-kiddie? Still hacking into where he isn't wanted?'

She laughed, throwing her head back and it came out, infectious and embracing. 'He thinks he's saving the world. That's not a bad ideal.'

'How?'

'He likes prodding the systems. Says if he breaks them, then someone out there will know they've got a bug and it needs fixing. He's making cyberspace safe for everyone.'

Now was not the time to argue with her. 'Drink?' I asked.

She nodded, then beckoned over to the bar. A beer arrived for her rapidly; this time the barman was grinning at me in a way that said, *you're OK*. I sat back and watched her. She always looked fresh, almost like a brand-new avatar. Unless they were periodically serviced, most avatars became scruffy as they lost parts of their digital make-up. Many MIWs had a slightly dull look overall that came from them never being re-energized by the matrix: they nearly all had the occasional body part, or rectangular small patches on

143

their skin missing, like a faded jigsaw with the odd piece gone astray. That didn't apply to Andi. Always immaculate, sharp, clearly defined as any new expensive avatar would.

'So, how's life in the Web?' I asked.

'Doesn't get easier. They pay us our benefits on time. That's the good news. Otherwise the WebCops grow more eager. There's more cameras sprouting up. SnoopCams everywhere.'

'Sounds like RealWorld.'

'You serious?'

'Yeah, I think you're safer down here.'

'So how're you, yourself? Married yet?'

'What? In the last three weeks?'

'You never will. Too stick-in-the-mud.'

'And you?'

'No point. I'll just be twenty-four for ever.' She giggled. 'I'm dry, you know. Really squeaky clean.'

'Is that the truth?'

'I don't need to lie. Not down here.'

'Good for you.'

'That money helped. From the drug bust.' She'd helped me track down a Siberian drug cartel that operated in the Web. One of my clients had a son who was a smack-head, and I'd used Andi's contacts to source the supplier. It was a successful operation and I made sure she was well paid. 'I got in with a real good shrink. Everyone goes to her. She's been there herself, strung out like catgut. She understands why we need the stuff. I feel good now. Just a fucking shame I can't go anywhere and show off.'

'Rude language doesn't suit you.'

She laughed. 'Just 'cause you're old enough to be my father doesn't give you the right to be my father.'

'Still doesn't suit you.'

'Does it matter?'

'Everything matters.'

She shrugged. 'So what can we do for you?'

I turned just as Tebor pulled up a chair on her other side. I presumed they had both come through a back door. The Huszar was that sort of place. Tebor didn't look as if he'd dried out; instead a cyberpunk with a head full of narco-heat. His clothes, unlike Andi's, were crumpled and ill-fitting. Whereas her jeans were figure tight and crisp, his were torn at the bottom where they dragged on the ground as he walked, the knees were worn through and the colour a faded blue that mixed with all the dirt that attched to it. His hair was punk gone wrong, spiky, tangled, his face unwashed, his eyes bored and untrusting. A child who had seen all the grown-up world had to offer and hadn't been impressed. A real script-kiddie; a tough nut behind a key-board, with mayhem and anarchy in his mind.

I acknowledged him with a curt nod. 'What I have to tell you is for you only. I need your word.'

'You looked after us before. Kept your word. We won't forget that.'

'What about him?' I asked.

'Tebor's fine. He'll do what I do.'

'A very important person has been kidnapped in the Web.'

'Kidnapped?'

'Switched off his JetPax.'

'That's good,' said Tebor. 'A fucking VIP that's MIW.' He chuckled to himself.

I ignored him. 'We have about ten hours to find this person. He can't afford to be MIW.'

'Why not?' asked Andi.

'Because . . .' *what the hell* '. . . he's the President of the United States.'

Andi giggled.

'Now that's a great game,' said Tebor, blowing a shrill whistle through his teeth. His eyes lit up at the opportunity of new sport. 'Gonna stir some fast action round here.'

I was pleased by their responses. They weren't fazed by

the fact it was the President; it just raised the stakes in the game. That meant they would try harder to win, and not carry any political or anarchist baggage with them.

I took them through the events that led to the President's kidnap.

When I'd finished, Tebor reacted first. 'Ten hours. To chase the whole Web. Wow, that's some bender. Pretty damn impossible, too.'

'Didn't take you for a zipperhead.' I moved easily into hackerspeak, attacking Tebor as someone with a closed mind.

'I'm no fucking zipperhead. Didn't say it couldn't be done.' He became defiant. 'Foo to you.' He stuck his second finger up at me. 'Foo to you,' he repeated.

'We're going to need luck and a lot more help.' Andi came to Tebor's rescue.

'Other people might be out there looking for him, but our team is just the three of us.' I decided not to mention my secret weapon the Datakeeper at this stage.

'What can we do? I mean, where do we start?'

'RTFM,' said Tebor, using hackerspeak for 'Read The Fucking Manual', a response for brushing aside trivial questions. 'Let's hack. Conor's got the codes. We blow through the net and just follow our minds. The harder we push, the luckier we'll get. Come on, Andi, it's how we've always done it.'

'You going to give us those codes, Conor?'

I had no reason not to. The choice was simple. Either release all the security codes or don't save the President. The codes were short term anyway; they'd be changed once this was over. And I'd already hacked them anyway. 'I'll give them to you. As and when required. Only don't pass them on to anyone else.'

'OK,' agreed Tebor, too quickly for my liking.

'I'll make sure we don't,' confirmed Andi.

'I'm going out on a limb by sharing all this with you,' I

146

warned them. 'If it gets beyond the three of us I'll pull the switch when I get back to RealWorld. It's really that big.'

They both knew what I meant. And they both needed their Cadavers, even in a catatonic state, to survive in Second World.

'I told you, we won't split.' She turned to Tebor. 'I want your promise.'

'Sure, sure,' he answered sullenly.

'Tebor?'

'OK, I promise.'

She turned back to me. 'Any credits in it for us?'

I knew the codes would be safe as long as she partnered Tebor. 'Plenty, if you're successful. I need you to chase up all your friends who might know if someone's cracked the JetPax security code. Any rumours, anything at all.'

'I'll get on with that. I think Tebor should get into the Brick and pick up some gossip. He's got links everywhere – not all friendly types, but they'll know what's going on. If there's anything out there, he'll sniff it out.' She thought for a moment before continuing. 'Have you pulled in anyone else on this?'

'Why?'

'Just so we don't cross paths and waste time.'

'A Russian colleague. I trust him totally and he's the best.'

'A GameMaster?'

I smiled but didn't compromise Mikoyan. Alex Mikoyan was a great net programer, the best mathematician and theorist. But whilst he was positive in his work, he was totally lacking in confidence in every other sphere of his life. Decisive as a programer, a great risk-taker in his profession, he was incapable of making the simplest decision when it came to his day-to-day activities. He lived alone, had never married and wouldn't even answer the phone in case someone he didn't know demanded a simple answer from him. An old aunt lived with him and made sure he was looked after, as a mother would her son. He trusted me, though we communicated only through email. I'd met him once at a restaurant in the Brick, and we never managed to eat there because Mikoyan couldn't make up his mind as to what to order.

'Even better,' I replied, 'don't expect him on the Brick. He'll log in from home, and I'll keep him updated as we go along.'

'As long as we're not at risk.'

'Not from him. Let's get going. Just don't leave too many trails leading back to us. With all this extra activity about to start on the net, it won't be long before someone gets interested in what we're doing.'

Right then the people with a primary interest in what Conor was up to had another, more pressing problem. The Vice President had called Meisner and Marlin to her office. There the two were surprised to find Will Wilkin, the Speaker from the House of Representatives, accompanied by the Attorney General, Sarah Gilchrist.

'I decided we needed some additional input. Will and Sarah, with their vast experience, were the obvious choices.' Nancy Sumner signalled the two men to sit down at the oak conference table. 'I don't want to appear to be jumping the gun, but we would appear to have a unique constitutional crisis . . . if the President continues missing.'

Meisner was annoyed, because he didn't want others involved. He believed the President would return soon, that he had simply got carried away; that he was merely lost in Second World and would soon find his way out. 'I thought we had an agreement', he protested, 'to give the Security Services as much time as possible.'

'I couldn't agree more, but I don't see the Speaker and the Attorney General as outsiders. I would remind you that our first responsibility is to run the country, and we can't do that with Teddy Dixon absent from the White House.'

Nancy Sumner was not a genuine Dixon supporter. She'd taken the ticket only because it helped her up the ladder. Her latest 'politically correct' stance was that all pets should be accorded family rights, in fact that any animal needing to be put down should have the right to be protected by a visit to a vet and then to an animal court. Five years ago that would have been unthinkable, but now anything and everything had its rights. It had been Sumner who fought through the rights of gays to have their cloned DNA passed to surrogate mothers, thus ensuring the children born would be gay as well. That's why Second World had become so popular. While the thought police and others controlled people's lives rigorously in RealWorld, Second World not only allowed players to live out their weird fantasies, but for many provided the great escape back to basics. One of the reasons Meisner was now surprised to see the Speaker was because it was well known that the widower, whose wife had died ten years earlier, visited his Second World ranch where he lived at weekends with an avatar of his wife. He hadn't gone for a younger model, simply wanted to continue to grow old with the same woman.

Meisner realized the VP had already begun to lay her claim to the throne. 'Nobody knows he's missing,' he argued. 'The world thinks he's just in bed, asleep.' He threw his hands in the air. 'Hell, even presidents go to bed with headaches. That's not a problem.'

'At what stage *does* it become a problem?'

'Only if we don't manage to find the President.'

'Things ain't that simple,' cut in Wilkin. 'Trouble is, Joe, that we all have a responsibility to the country. If the President is ineffectual – '

'He's not ineffectual.'

' – and not capable of carrying out his presidential duties, then we've got to consider the options,' continued Wilkin. 'The truth is, we have no idea where he is.' He turned to Marlin. 'Do we?'

'No,' came the reply.

'Then, to me, this country isn't being governed right now,' Sumner joined in.

'Look, he's only been gone three hours,' said Meisner, 'and you know what he's like. He's off adventuring in Second World, having fun. He could walk through that door at any minute.' He turned to the Attorney General. 'Sarah, at what stage is he deemed incompetent?'

Gilchrist shrugged. 'Tough call. Normally, he'd have to have medical tests, and their expert opinion would be passed on to Congress. Based on that information, they'd make the decision. But, technically, he's still alive – nobody can deny that – but what we don't have is information on his state of mind, his mental faculties. We do know that people in Second World maintain their intellectual power for at least six hours, so, I suppose, legally he's still capable of making rational decisions. And, you're right . . . he could walk into this room at any moment. '

'That's my point,' said Meisner.

'Any precedent we can refer to?' inquired the VP.

Gilchrist pondered for a moment. 'The most famous was President Woodrow Wilson. In the 1920s.'

'What happened?' asked Wilkin.

'Just after the First World War, during the League of Nations conferences. He got pretty sick, couldn't move out of bed, was catatonic most of the time. His wife and members of the Cabinet hid it from everyone, but then Congress got suspicious that something was up. They sent down a delegation, who actually saw the President. They were appalled by his condition. He was definitely incompetent at that stage. They went back to Congress and, in the end, Congress just stuck their heads in the sand and pretended it wasn't really happening. Luckily, he recovered.'

'We do not want to involve Congress,' clucked Meisner. 'Not yet.'

'That would only happen after medical opinion had deemed him incompetent. Then it has to be their decision. If that decision presumed him lost, or dead, then they'd have to swear in the Vice President.'

'Swear in?'

'Sure. You can't take over the reins of government without being sworn in.'

'How long would all this take?'

'It wouldn't be ten minutes. I mean, we have to prove he's not coming back or, if he is, that he's incompetent to govern.'

'You could be talking days.'

'At least. We'd have to get expert advice on whether he's succumbed to WebFever. And that's not going to happen in the next few hours.'

'And then, when they swear Nancy in as the new President, back comes Teddy Dixon. And he's OK. What happens then?'

'I have no idea. I'd have to take advice from constitutional experts. There is no automatic mechanism for that eventuality.'

'Gut feeling?'

'I don't know. The Vice President would constitutionally now be President, although there's an argument that says they're both still Presidents. I guess you'd have to either impeach Teddy Dixon, or say he was the elected President and his position prevails.'

'Messy.'

'You'd probably have to impeach him anyway, if you were declaring him incompetent.'

'Nobody's going to impeach a missing President in just forty-eight hours.'

'Unlikely, yes. They'd want pretty good proof that he was gone, even MIW. Thinking further about it, a smart lawyer could make a pretty convincing case that he could govern effectively from Second World.'

'Impossible,' cut in the VP.

'In this day and age, anything's possible. Let's face it, he's just held a convention in Second World, yet also in the White House. He could easily prove he still has access to the whole machinery of government. He's got easy availability to the Cabinet and Chiefs of Staff. Remember, these days every Congressman's got his own Web office. He can even meet world leaders in the Annex. In fact, he's probably more secure down there.'

'*Was* more secure,' commented Wilkin.

'Sure, but that can be rectified. In law, meanwhile, and under the Constitution, he can be removed from office only when he clearly can't fulfil his duties. I mean, Roosevelt ran the last world war from a wheelchair, yet the same argument, especially in those days, could have applied to him. But that was just an exceptional mind trapped in a useless body, so the President could be deemed to be as effective operating from Second World as he could from up here.' Sarah Gilchrist leant back in her chair. 'In fact, it would be a lawyer's paradise.'

Meisner turned to the others, sensing his opportunity. 'We're only three hours into this, but in another nine we'll have a pretty good idea of where we're at. Why not leave it until tomorrow, Saturday morning? I think that's when we should give serious consideration to alerting Congress.'

'What're our chances of finding him in time?' Sumner asked Marlin.

'We're running fast in every direction. Everything that could be remotely connected to this business is being sifted like spaghetti through a strainer.' Marlin leant forward confidently. 'If there's anything out there linked to the President, in even the smallest way, we're going to find it.'

'Unless you don't know about it.'

'Pardon me?'

'Whoever took him has managed to jump every security system we use. I think, therefore, we should be using the WebCops and SnoopCams.' Sumner clearly wanted to keep the pressure on.

'We can do that. But then there's more chance of it getting out.'

'This situation warrants a few risks.' Sumner knew she had time. If Dixon was gone, then just a few more hours between her and the Presidency she felt was rightfully hers didn't matter. She believed it unlikely that Congress would let Dixon govern from the Web. But, if such an argument could be presented to them, then it would take more than a few days for Dixon to be impeached. She decided to revisit the situation at a more opportune time. 'What about all those guests in the Convention Hall?'

'They believed the story about the President having a bad migraine. They were disappointed, but they bought it.'

'And the media?'

'Went along with it, too. I reminded them they had a big press conference scheduled in the morning and they'd see him then.'

Paul Gallagher knocked and came into the room.

'Ma'am,' he said. 'You said to interrupt if anything came up.'

'What's happened?'

'We've found Marilyn Monroe. In Second World.'

'And the President?'

Gallagher shook his head. 'Nothing, ma'am. Still missing.'

Tebor got up, unzipped and peed against the wall of the cafe. The urine evaporated as soon as it hit the Brickwork. He stared defiantly at me as he did so.

'Why's he doing that?' I asked Andi.

'Just showing how much he likes you,' she joked. 'And 'cause he doesn't know better. Just being a kid.'

'They'd jail him for that in RealWorld.'

'He sees pictures of kids doing it when he surfs Real-World TV.'

'Crazy way of making a statement.'

We all went back to our keyboards.

I concentrated on scanning the NSA and White House networks, trying to follow their angles. It didn't take long to realize that, for all their sophistication, they were swimming ponderously against a fast-flowing tide. What surprised me was the amount of information the Puzzle Palace could access. They were dipping into files that Congress had barred all the Security Services from intercepting: personal emails, local medical records, private bank accounts, even school records. I knew where the Security Services stored most of their data, had hacked into them myself years before, but the scale of what they were intercepting shook me.

They were even going through the First Lady's company files. I presumed she wasn't a suspect but their investigation into her affairs was considerable, including checking her private diary and personal expenditure. I wondered if she'd authorized those searches.

Everyone was trawling out there, all still bringing up empty nets.

Andi spent her time contacting the technical experts and hackers she knew. She worked under the guise that she was considering returning to RealWorld. Yes, she understood the problems – *don't worry about me, I'm only thinking about it* – but it got her into discussions on JetPax and its workings. After twenty minutes she was still drawing blanks.

Tebor was mixing with his friends. He was impressive. He surfed at remarkable speeds, contacting other hackers, MIWs and petty criminals, picking up the buzz on the Brick. He had the ability to ask questions about drugs and other UnderWeb activities without raising suspicion. He was also getting nowhere, albeit faster than the rest of us.

The White House came up with the first breakthrough, while they were monitoring As-Good-As-it-Gets Inc. The company had contacted the police, because one of their Monroe puppets had thrown up a signal reporting that it was destroyed. That was standard procedure on the Web. All leased equipment was barcoded, whether it was a racing car being run at Daytona or an umbrella shielding someone as they walked under the Victoria Falls; a system devised so that any theft and destruction was instantly monitored. The signal had come from a small hotel on the Brick.

A second message was from the WebCops to the White House, reporting they were now on their way to investigate. As requested to by As-Good-As-It-Gets Inc.

Quick decision time. 'I'm going back onto the Brick,' I announced. 'Stay with it, and call me if you get anywhere. I'll be in touch if anything happens.'

'Time to move,' the Voice broke the dull silence.

'Where to?' Dixon was startled to hear the Voice after what had seemed an eternity of silence.

'Interesting places, Mr President.'

Dixon stood up. He'd been snoozing, trying to save energy. Although never a Webbie, he knew about the twelve-hour warning. He recalled an old magazine article about the only way to extend it was to switch off your mind and sleep within the Web. For a while he'd walked around, tried to find if there was any light he could follow or any sounds he might pick up, but everything remained silent and pitch black. He'd stumbled around for about twenty minutes before he settled down in his current location. He'd become warm and clammy in the oppressive confines of the darkness, and soon dozed off.

'Our pursuers are smart, picking up the clues right on schedule,' continued the Voice. 'We need to spread a few more around, make them feel they're getting somewhere. A little bit of encouragement goes a long way.'

'Who the hell are you?'

'That information is on a need-to-know basis, and *you* don't need to know. I bet you say that to all your staff,' he added camply.

'They'll be doing everything possible to find me.'

'Of course.'

'And when they do?'

'They won't.'

'How can you be sure of that?'

'You presume they're hunting me.' The Voice roared with laughter, the sound reverberating through the darkness. But its tone was humourless. 'Could be I'm after them, chasing them, stalking them all the way, tiptoeing behind, creeping up on them.'

Dixon felt air waft across his face. Although he still couldn't see, he sensed he was being moved. 'Where're we going?'

'There's no such thing as real democracy, you know,' continued the Voice. 'You people destroy that, just intrude in our lives all the time. So what's it feel like, when someone intrudes in yours?'

It got lighter; Dixon still couldn't see shapes, but was aware that the blackness was easing. He looked at his watch. He could see the dial, but the watch had stopped, at the time he'd been kidnapped.

'You won't get away with this. My people will – '

The air was suddenly forced out of Dixon's lungs and he crashed to the floor, gasping for breath. The sharp pain once again tightened across his chest.

'Wrong,' said the Voice with reason and calm. 'Remember that when we get outside. One wrong move and I'll crush the air out of you, snap you like a twig. Both here and in RealWorld. Just keep remembering the pain. Know that I can kill you.'

There was one last stab of pain and finally the air was released back into Dixon's lungs. He staggered up, his breathing slowly returning to normal.

What the hell is going on?

His eyes watered as bright sunlight hit him. The first thing he saw was a great big pink old Cadillac, its wings flared behind, its rear lights resembling rocket motors ready to blast it hurtling along the freeway.

Then Gladys said, 'Hi, there. Don't you just love my new automobile?'

The Brick was crawling with WebCops, both on the pavements and on the street itself in their blue KatchVagens topped with flashing lights and sirens. It wasn't busy yet; the Weekenders hadn't hit Second World in force, but a substantial crowd had already gathered outside 6M278K3303.

The place looked under siege as I approached one of the WebCops. He had the number 754 displayed large above his badge. It was the only way you could tell them apart. All WebCops had identical faces, wore the same uniforms, had the same hair colour and haircuts, and were IdentiClones with square jaws, great smiles and matinée-idol features, the only variance being the colour of their skin. This one was Japanese yellow without the tapered eyes.

'Excuse me, Officer 754, but could you tell me what's going on?'

'You'd better move along. We're trying to keep this area clear.' The voice was the same for every WebCop; deep and resonant and very Marlboro man.

'I was expecting to meet a friend here, in the Gallipoli. I'd like to get up there.'

'What's your friend's name?'

He could imagine the RealCop who was running this graphic driven puppet sit up, suddenly interested. One operative usually ran a team of WebCops from a bank of monitors. It used to be they controlled five WebCops each, but budgets had got tighter and now it was eight. Most

159

WebCop answers were programed in, set answers to the usual 'How do I get to . . .' They were robots, pure and simple: programed cyberrobots who moved round the Web and dealt with simple problems in a predetermined manner.

I held up my ID card so the WebCop could read it clearly. 'I'm a GameMaster. Conor Smith.' I waited for a reaction. It wasn't every day that you ran up against a GameMaster.

'Who are you meeting?' asked the WebCop eventually.

'One of my clients.'

'Name?'

'Marilyn Monroe.'

'Wait here.'

The WebCop then went into a tough, don't-mess-with-me stance, but I knew his operator was frantically connecting to a superior.

'Hey, what's going on here?' I acted *I'm pissed*. There was no response from the WebCop, who had now been switched into GUARD and RESTRAIN IF SUSPECT ESCAPES mode. 'Can you direct me to WorldDisney, please?' That should throw it into AutoResponse mode.

'Catch the transporter to MetroPort 698, then go up to 3M428K1123. Stay onto the Brick for about six blocks. It's easy to walk there, take a right at – '

A new voice cut in over the automated response. 'Please stop the humour, Mr Smith.' The operator clearly didn't share my sense of ridicule. 'Just wait, will you? Please don't walk away as Officer 754 has been put on alert should you leave his presence. I would not like there to be an accident.'

Yeah, yeah. GameMasters had important megacorp employers and were insured to the hilt. No WebCop operator would risk hurting a GameMaster. I recognized the Indian accent, so the host was probably sitting in one of the many command centres that proliferated on the Indian sub-continent. Like the old call centres, it had become one of that country's biggest industries.

'Where are you?' I asked genially. 'Mysore or Mumbai?'

No response. I noticed the crowd continued to build, and then another two KatchVagens arrived, disgorging more WebCops. Things were getting serious.

'You can go up, Mr Smith,' said the WebCop after another minute. 'Eighty-first floor, but report to Reception. Somebody will escort you to the eighty-fourth floor, room fifty-eight. Thank you for your patience.'

Yeah. Missing you already.

'I'm actually in Mumbai, sir. How did you . . . ?'

I shrugged and entered the building. The lobby was a Sheraton, a five-star luxury roomer. I ignored Reception and jumped the lift to the eighty-first floor, where I found Paul Gallagher and Don Clancy waiting.

'How'd you pick up on this?' asked a clearly irritated Clancy.

'CNN.'

'Lay off, Don,' cut in Gallagher, stepping between us. 'I told you, getting information is what he's about. Don't ask him where he got it.'

'When this is over . . .' Clancy threatened.

I could do without the empty threats. 'You – and I mean *you* – shouldn't have lost him in the first place.'

'I said, both of you, cut it out,' reiterated Gallagher. 'Come on, I want to show you what happened here.'

He turned and led me up the stairs, Clancy bringing up the rear.

'We have a statement from a receptionist who saw her enter and go up here,' continued Gallagher. 'Didn't speak to her. Said the room was on a seven-day booking . . . some guy came in and paid in advance. We checked the cameras; they weren't working. That's what you expect in a shit-hole like this. We're running the tapes from the SnoopCams on the Brick and those in the Sheraton downstairs. In the last few days there've been thousands heading in and out of these elevators. When the booking was made, last Saturday, this place was packed with Weekenders. He chose a good time to get lost in the crowd.'

'How'd he pay?'

'Stolen credit card.'

'Not reported?'

'The owner died a few days ago. Suicide.'

'Name?'

'Jim Nelson. Washington, DC address. Nothing suspicious yet. Wasn't reported because no one knew it was missing. As soon as Marilyn was killed an alarm was triggered at the company who traded her out. They called the cops and we picked up the call.'

'You sure it was her?'

'Yeah, same barcode.'

'Who hired her before the White House did?'

'A group of golf nuts playing Pebble Beach in Golf-o-Rama. They wanted her programed so she could play golf like a pro. They had her dressed up in that . . . that white dress that flares up when the subway train goes underneath.'

'*Seven Year Itch*,' I said, remembering the film.

'That's the one. I think they got it to flare up every time she sank a putt.' Gallagher grinned. 'But that's all they did . . . they said.'

'What about the actor working the avatar? Her host.'

'Still looking for him.'

'You got his name?'

'Yes.'

'Give it to me – and his address. Most of these guys live off the Web. They don't just run the avatars. They come down here and meet people who like the quirky things they do. A lot of them are into real hard sex. They pick up someone in Second World who likes something different and carry the fantasy back into RealWorld, because it pays better up there. And less chance of being caught – not unless you catch something nasty.'

I chuckled when I saw the distaste on Clancy's face. 'Not everyone lives in the soft comfort of the White House.'

'Simon Que,' Gallagher interjected, not giving Clancy the chance to react angrily. 'That was the actor's name.'

'Que? Where's that? Some Chinese call centre?'

'American. Works as an independent for As-Good-As-It-Gets Inc. Que's his stage name.'

'Who else does he work for and what other puppets does he front?'

When I had the answers I stepped away from the others, and called Andi. I asked her or Tebor to trace anything they could on Que, including places he used for assignations. Andi said they'd made little progress, but Tebor would enjoy chasing the Que lead, as it was right up his street. She said Tebor would punch Que's name into the hackers' and MIWs' group. If he was well known they'd soon respond. There were thousands of them in the group, all permanently switched on for contact from the others. It was their protection, to be in constant contact and to help each other.

'Who was that?' Clancy asked me suspiciously.

'The cavalry.'

We went on into room 58. Inside there were three forensic men checking for clues. The wine glass containing the remains of the drug had been taken to CyberForensics at the nearest police station on the Brick. The clues were minimal, but it was obvious she'd OD'd. They had a pretty good idea how. The glass would reveal the truth in digital DNA, because, unlike RealWorld, there were no fingerprints in Second World. That was something Amnesty International had introduced as a protection against abuse of freedom. That was a waste of space. Who needs fingerprints when you've got digital DNA?

'I didn't notice it, but one of our guys is a Monroe buff.' Gallagher walked round the bed. 'He said this room is laid out just like her real death was.'

'Why did she drink it? Surely she's been around? So's Que.' I knelt down and looked into her face, not peaceful, just full of pain and torment. Sad way to go, even for an avatar. I felt a sudden rush. Maybe Que himself was also heading for the same graveyard.

'I guess she must have trusted the person who gave her the spiked drink,' said Gallagher behind me.

'Absolutely. So does Que.'

'Meaning?'

'By now he knows he could be in danger. We need to find him fast.'

Gallagher turned to Clancy. 'That's your beat. If he's in RealWorld and we go after him, that'll bring in the FBI. And we can't risk that. If Que's involved, if he gets scared off, then we'll never find the President.'

'I'll get on to it.' Clancy urgently opened his Compu-Phone and turned away.

I stood up. 'I wonder if the real Monroe looked that bad when she died.'

Gallagher shrugged, dismissing my remark. 'What've you got?'

'A bunch of negatives so far. But this could be the foot in the door. I suppose the NSA are involved in this?'

'Of course.'

'They're into everyone's private files, Paul. They must have data on every person on this planet stashed some-where.'

'That's against the law, Conor.'

'Shit. I'm telling you, these guys are up everybody's ass.'

'You hacked into their files or something?' asked Gallagher, surprised.

'Just accept that I just know they're into bank accounts, employers' records, *everything*. And it's indiscriminate.'

'I'm not surprised. We all know they're a law unto themselves. But we're not here for that reason. We're here to find the President.'

'I could certainly do with some of their information, but Que's currently our only lead. I need to know everything about him – and get to him before someone else does.'

'I can't ask them for that information. Such knowledge could put you at risk. And maybe I don't really want to know what they get up to.'

'Then you're risking the life of your President.'

Gallagher shrugged. 'Nobody fights the NSA.'

He lowered his voice. 'They don't like snoopers, especially GameMasters, so don't make them your enemy. Back off. If they come after you, I won't be able to help. The last thing I want, after I enlisted your help, is for you to end up like *her*.'

After the photographs were taken, the cleaners moved in with the bodydisks, downloaded Marilyn Monroe from the matrix and then took her away. The CREEPs were unleashed to clean up the mess.

Thirty minutes later, room 58 was ready again for the first of the Weekenders.

Gladys Presley, the King's mother, smiled at Teddy Dixon.

'I said, don't you just love my car?' She proudly pointed at the big pink Cadillac on a rostrum behind him. 'My boy bought me that, just after his first big hit.'

'You're lucky to have such a wonderful son,' said the Voice, next to him.

Dixon, now aware that he was wearing a tight-fitting mask shaped to suit his face, was startled by the sudden brightness. It was the same Voice but through the eyes of his mask he now recognized that the Voice was also wearing a mask, that of Abraham Lincoln.

'I sure am,' said Gladys. 'I sure am.'

As she went to welcome the next visitors, Dixon asked his kidnapper. 'Who are you?'

'Abraham Lincoln,' said the bearded figure in the stovepipe hat and long black dress coat. 'You should know your history.'

'What's happening here?'

'This.'

Dixon felt the pressure on his chest again, felt the air in his lungs being forced out.

'I said I'd keep quiet,' he said quickly.

'Good. You know he was a great President, Mr Lincoln. Took this country right into the Civil War. That's what made us great. I like being reminded of a great President.

166

Anyway, if anyone's out there looking for you, they're sure not going to expect you to be with Honest Abe. I bet there's fifty Nixons and Kennedys and Clintons out on the Brick right now. Probably a thousand Napoleons and hundreds of Lincolns and George Washingtons. They might be looking for a real Teddy Dixon, but not associating with Abe Lincoln. Just need to confuse them for a little while, till we get ourselves a new hidey-hole.'

He led Dixon towards Gracelands, the home Presley had bought and lived in for all his life as a star. The tourist crowds weren't at their peak yet; that would happen when the Weekenders arrived.

'Success is shit,' said the Voice as they walked into the mansion, through that large pillared entrance that was recognized around the world. 'Monroe, Presley, James Dean, both Kennedys – all dead before their time. Was it worth it, Teddy Boy? What do you think? Would you like to go before your time? Become a legend and miss the rest of your life?'

They walked though the building, just as any other tourists would, and entered the room that Presley had designed himself. It was a dark, brooding place full of heavy African wooden furniture. Low, oblong windows kept the room in semi-darkness, made more sombre by the dark wood panelling that lined the four walls. In one corner there was a huge circular chair topped with an ugly wood face carving. Next to it, on the floor, were figures of monkeys in various positions. One was masturbating.

'Great musician, but screwed up,' commented the Voice. He tapped his forehead with his index finger. 'Badly screwed up.'

They walked out through the rear of the house and up the garden towards the memorial graves and fountains. The shrine was a mosaic of roses and lilies, backed up by a huge flowered guitar that looked down on the graves.

'Never could understand why they don't have an avatar

of Elvis around here. I mean, they got everybody else: his mom, Vernon, everyone he knew. But not the King. They keep him dead.' The Voice pointed at the guitar. 'They've got a SnoopCam in there, right by the bass string.' He turned to Dixon and lifted the President's mask. 'Just smile at it, Teddy Boy. Then wave. Come on ... wave. Good, that's enough for now.'

He slipped the Lincoln mask back onto Dixon's head and led him away from the shrine.

'You *wanted* them to see me? To see where I was.'

Abraham Lincoln smiled back. 'You're right. They'll be here within minutes. Only they'll never find you. When they lose you this time, they'll know they're up against the best.' They walked on. 'You're going to go away again, to a weird place, but very safe.' The Voice laughed shrilly. 'Very safe. Just don't waste energy. You'll live longer that way. Just remember I'm plugged into you. Don't draw any attention to yourself or I'll cut off your lungs.'

Then the blackness came again and Dixon felt the earth open under him, sucking him down. He lay flat on his back, in an entombed space. He tried to raise himself but hit his head on something solid, no more than a foot above his head. He tried to swivel, to turn over, but he was totally boxed in. The silence he remembered from before had returned. But now he could see his hand in front of his face.

There was something else next to him, lying in this confined space. He turned his head to see what it was. It was the King lying next to him, dressed as though he were about to go on stage in Las Vegas. Except this time he was dead.

Dixon screamed.

The King swivelled round on him and bared his teeth, deep vampire teeth, and moved in to bite him on the neck, encircling Dixon with his arms, pinning him still.

Don't draw any attention to yourself. He remembered the Voice's warning, pulled himself together and lay very still.

His heart banged loudly but he managed to keep his terror under control. He now also discovered you could sweat profusely in Second World. The King relaxed his grip, then, once he was certain that Dixon wouldn't move, he turned away, crossed his arms over his chest and lay still again.

The President waited quietly for the Voice to return, waited deep under the Gracelands shrine, inside Elvis Presley's coffin. He realized he was only part of a game. He started to pray. It was something he did regularly, and publicly. Only this time he prayed because he meant it, and because it was all he had left.

Things were starting to happen.

'A recognition imager threw up an exact likeness of the President,' relayed the NSA to Gallagher. 'I'm transferring the file to you right now. It's marked NSA/White House File RC EPW3RW.'

'Where's that?' Gallagher responded, whilst signalling one of his men to intercept and download the file.

'Elvis Presley World.'

'Where?'

'You heard me right.'

'You still got him under observation?'

'No. He was only on for a few seconds. Damnedest thing, though.'

'What?'

'He waved at the surveillance camera, looked like he was enjoying himself.'

'Who was he with?'

'Abraham Lincoln.'

'Are you . . . ?'

'No, I'm not. It was Lincoln. There are other people around him, too. We're running their pictures through our IdentiFiles, so should know who they are pretty soon.'

The monitor flickered to life in front of Gallagher. It was definitely the President. And he was waving at the camera.

'Is that SnoopCam fixed in an open position?' he asked the NSA, as Clancy headed towards the monitors.

'No. It's hidden behind a floral display. But they knew it was there, just looked straight at it and waved.'

Gallagher saw Marlin enter the room, along with Meisner. 'OK, thanks for your help.'

'You've seen the pictures?' asked Marlin as he also strode over to the bank of monitors.

'Yes.'

'Does that mean whoever's running this show would have the President's cooperation?'

'Why?'

'It's too fucking obvious – like they want to be identified.'

'Or someone's playing a game.'

'I thought avatars impersonating the serving President are illegal.'

'They are.'

'How do we prevent that?'

'As soon as there's a likeness seen, the CREEPS move in and obliterate the data. That way, nobody can copy the President's visage for more than two seconds.'

'That quick?'

'That quick.'

'But he was waving at us for a lot longer.'

'I know. The only avatar that's coded not to be wiped out by the CREEPs is . . .'

' . . . the President himself,' replied Meisner. 'Just check he's physically OK.'

Gallagher nodded, and spoke to one of his operatives. 'Go check on the President.' He turned to another one. 'Run that tape through the image enhancer. Find whatever's there that we can't see with the naked eye. Get someone to help you, and double track it. You work one half, let them work the other. Priority. While you're doing that, get someone else to inspect all the roads leading away from the scene. NSA have probably already done that, but double-check. You're looking for a pair of Abraham Lincolns.'

'Already done,' came the quick response. 'Nothing found.

A big zero from the SnoopCams on the Brick. And all we got on Monroe was her going into the hotel, on her own.'

'How did she get there?'

'No idea. We've watched all the other cameras on both sides of the street for nearly ten blocks. No sign of her at all until she walks round the corner and just enters the building.'

'There's a church next door. Did she come out of there?'

'No. They don't have cameras in there but I checked all the approaches. Nothing. I spoke to the churchwarden, he keeps an eye on the place. He says there was no one inside. Certainly no one who looked like Marilyn Monroe.'

'Is the warden automatic or an avatar?'

'Linked to a host: a genuine pastor in RealWorld; genuine. They checked his tapes of the church. It backs up what he says. Nobody inside. They're getting ready for a busy weekend.'

'Who isn't? Tell me, what lies between the church and the hotel complex?'

'Just a Dark Area.'

'That all?'

'Yes, sir. That's all.'

A quizzical Gallagher nodded, then turned and swiftly followed the others into the Presidential Transfer Suite, past the guards who were now positioned there. The officer he'd dispatched to check on the President was just coming out of the Suite.

'Still there,' he reported.

Teddy Dixon's body lay exactly as they last saw it, still in his WebSuit in the SensoChair. Annie Dixon sat next to him, watching over him.

He looked peacefully asleep.

'Is there news?' she asked.

'No,' replied Meisner. 'Just making sure everything's OK.'

Clancy glanced over the life-support monitors. Nothing had changed; Dixon was deep in WebSleep.

'Something's up, for you all to come in here, together,' added the First Lady.

'We picked up an IdentiLikeness of Teddy,' volunteered Meisner. 'At Elvis Presley World.'

'He's OK?'

'We think it was a doctored tape. To mislead us.'

'Or tell us he's still alive?'

Meisner looked at Gallagher as he entered. 'Now what?'

'There's more than one person involved,' stated Gallagher.

'Why do you say that?'

'Somebody's tampering with the SnoopCams. People don't normally just keep disappearing from sight, yet nothing picks up Monroe till she walks in the front door of the hotel. Then they just disappear from Graceland after he's waving at the camera. This is not one guy at work. With this size of operation, there's got to be a big organization behind it.'

'Or someone with access to a big organization's equipment,' cut in Clancy

'Like who?' asked Meisner.

Clancy shrugged 'We've pulled in some pretty dangerous and wacky people to help. That means we're releasing sensitive information that could come back and hurt us. We're risking all our security operations.'

'We have little time and no alternative,' retorted Gallagher.

'Maybe now we'll get somewhere?' Annie Dixon said hopefully.

Gallagher smiled reassuringly.

Clancy noticed his smile didn't match the deep concern in his eyes.

I was back at the Huszar, where the other two had made little progress. Maybe my approach was wrong; maybe I needed to call more help in. Risky, though, with all that security on the loose.

I was head down, busily monitoring the White House security system, which was linked to all the other governmental agencies, including the NSA. The advantage was that I could ignore the NSA directly; as the fewer the number of links I accessed, the less chance there was of my being traced.

Andi slid her chair over to my table and watched me scan the security service.

'Where'd you get to with Que?' I asked her.

She'd been chasing the RealWorld travel and hotel groups, trying to find the missing actor. He was a regular amongst the Gay Brigade, someone very actively involved in computer dating for those with less conventional tastes. He was a favourite amongst the transsexuals and ran a 'no questions asked' database for those of a mixed – I called it confused – gender. She said that some of Que's clients were frantically searching for him to make arrangements for their Weekend, but no one had, as yet, found him. 'Apart from that, not very far,' she admitted. 'Just thought I'd switch off for a minute. Maybe I'm rushing at this too much. Maybe I need to back off, get a clearer view.'

'How's the boy wonder?'

'He's doing good. Catching up with his friends, in the Web and in RealWorld. Most of them have been hit by a recent CERT attack.' The Computer Emergency Response Team was run from Pittsburgh's Carnegie Mellon University and had been formed thirty years earlier to investigate hacker attacks on networks. 'All they've got is the usual corpro-gossip. No, this job's very small and very private.'

I waved to the barman for more coffee all around.

'Tell me about Tebor,' I said as I watched the auto-search run through the intelligence files.

'Like what?'

'How come he can't dry out?'

'You think he's a real sleazo, don't you?' she said defensively.

'No,' I lied. 'With these kids, it's all image.' I'd met all types and shades of cyberpunks over the years, and they'd never impressed me, not with their Sex Pistols ReBorn music and constant anarchic search for excitement. Tebor was just another geek who couldn't hack it in RealWorld.

'Do you come from family, Conor?'

'Yes.' I was surprised by her change of tack. 'I come from family.' That made me pretty unusual when more than half the western world's children were born into single-parent families, surrogated or adopted and brought up by an eclectic mix of parents. *The fruits of democracy.* Yeah, coming from a complete family unit was pretty rare in the twenty-first century.

'So did I, which you know anyway, but Tebor wasn't so lucky. His dad abandoned them when he was just six, and his mum didn't give a shit. From then on, she just shacked up with anyone who'd look after them. No way to bring a kid up. So he got mixed up with the cyberpunks. His dad was a programer and taught him about computers from when he could first walk. Playing games on screens, that's all Tebor knew. He's a natch. We've been together eight years now. He was here four years before I met him. That's thirteen years in Second World, thirteen years MIW. In Out Time that makes him twenty-seven, a man in a child's body. And he's grown up in a world where anything goes.'

She suddenly banged the table furiously. 'Those fucking Weekenders. Goody-goodies up there, then they come down here and live out their vile little fantasies. I'm disgusted by what I'm sometimes asked to do. It's time someone brought some fucking morals into this world. People down here are just as alive as up there. It's total meltdown. Do you have any idea how many MIWs there are, Conor? Hundreds of thousands, all living down here, just the same as they always were. And our cadavers are getting older, getting ready to die. And when we do, what happens, Conor? Do we go on living down here? I mean, is this eternity?'

'No, but that's why they keep the cadavers alive and under such strict environmental controls. The Web's not old enough yet for an MIW to die of old age. Sure, some have, of course. But nobody knows who's alive or dead down here. They can't even monitor the welfare system. It's being scammed all the time. It's another big fiddle, drawing credits for those already dead.'

'It's time for an amnesty.'

'Amnesty International's been after that for years, but the governments won't push it. Otherwise they'll have to try and get you all back into your cadavers. And that's not technically possible, not yet. Time'll bring a solution. It always does.'

'Guess that won't make any difference to me,' she said, as she remembered her plight. 'My police records, they'll always be after me.' She changed tack again. 'But you know why I dried out? Because I'm from family. They taught me right from wrong. Not Tebor, though. He's got no values, except to look after himself and me. He's always in the barfogenic zone.' That was a condition brought about by continual VR, a form of motion sickness. 'He's got persistent

176

headaches, feeling disorientated, nauseous. The drugs he takes, especially acid, help him through that.'

'At least you stayed dry,'

'I had no choice. I want to go home one day. I have no idea to what exactly, but it must be better than this shit. Even prison, I guess. It's like being stuck on an island here ... no, a giant warehouse with no doors. You know there's things going on outside, right the other side of the walls. You can hear it, but you can't see it and you can't be part of it. And you get more frustrated as you see the Weekenders come and go. The newbies are worse. They arrive with their eyes open and then, once they get the hang of life down here, they really push all the boundaries. But it's only make-believe. Christ, I just want to get out to the other side.' She sat motionless, lost in her own despair. 'I mean ... if I do ever get out ... do you think they'll still put me on trial?' she said eventually.

'Who knows? But we've got good lawyers up there. I think we could make a good case as to why you did it.'

'But no guarantees, huh?'

'Nothing's for certain. You know that.'

'I don't know if my mum could take it a second time.'

I smiled, remembering my dad's words when I first got arrested, his disapproval of what I'd done, but still being supportive. 'I think most parents are a bit more resilient than their kids give them credit for.'

'You always talk about me, never you. Tell me about *your* parents.'

'Not a lot to tell. They worked hard. Dad was an engineer, nothing fancy, just for a TV delivery company. Mum worked part-time in a variety of jobs.' I grinned as I remembered, then told Andi how they'd saved up to buy my first Apple computer when I was only five. 'They saw the new world coming and they wanted me to be part of it. They were old for parents, both in their late forties when I was born. Mum died first, when I was about twenty. She liked her food, loved it, and was very overweight. Had a heart attack and that was it.'

I explained how my dad had died only five short weeks later. 'Missed her terribly, just didn't eat, had a stroke, and then I was on my own.'

'You feel really bad about that?'

'About being left alone? No. They loved each other very much. Lived in a make-believe world of their own. And they'd given me everything they could.'

I didn't show the real sadness, it was something I rarely thought about. I just always loved them, but had gone in a different direction to what they wanted. If Dad was around now, he'd never believe how much money I made just playing those silly old games.

'What was the last thing he said to you?' she persevered.

'That he was sorry he never came up to my expectations.' I grunted, because that memory stung. 'That's what sons are usually meant to say to their fathers.'

'And?'

'I wish he hadn't thought that, because he was the best father I could have had. I really used to look forward to going home after school. I was a lucky, and happy, kid.'

She glanced towards Tebor. 'He's got nothing to go home to. This is it. And he takes so much stuff, that even if I took him with me, his mind would be totally frazzled. He doesn't know the difference between what's real and what's not. Forget about just right and wrong.'

The barman brought the coffees over and we sat in silence as he put the mugs on the table. *Crown Doulton*, observed Conor.

'There's no particular difference between reality and illusion,' I said eventually. 'You can live in either. They're all up there, trying to get down here for the weekend; and there's a bunch of people here desperate to escape up there. I guess the solution is to make the best of what you have.' I watched as she sipped her coffee. I loved the way everything, even the coffee, was always the right temperature in Second World.

'That's good,' she said, noisily gulping the coffee.

'Why don't you let me contact your family?'

'You always say that.'

'To tell them you're OK?'

'It's better they think I'm dead.'

'They could visit you here.'

'I'd get so homesick for them, and it's bad enough, already.'

'It would matter to them just to know you're alive.'

'No. Why cut them up? Bring all that shit back into their heads? They're probably living normal lives again, and the past is just a nasty blur. Let's leave it like that.' Her imagination took over. 'What if they're not together any more? What if my kid brother, Wayne . . . No. Let's leave things alone.'

'I can find out. Just check how they are.'

'If you want to.'

'Which means?'

'I don't want any bad news. I've got enough of that.' She looked up at him, questioningly. 'I've never worked you out.'

'Why?'

'You're a GameMaster. You've got everything. Nobody comes any higher. Not in ComputerSpeak. You earn more than anybody, probably even more than the boss man of the corporation that runs you. Certainly more than that arsehole Dixon you're meant to be finding. So, why do you bother with me?'

'You make me feel good.'

'Do I? Or are you just slumming? Seeing the seedy side. Does that turn you on, Conor?'

I was stung by her words, but knew it was her way of protecting her sense of not belonging. 'I don't have that much. My house, a couple of friends, and the money really doesn't matter. Never did. If you love computers, then you can be like Tebor. You just need a keyboard and enough for the odd meal and buying network time.'

'Your sob story designed to impress me?'

I shook my head, embarrassed by her brusqueness. 'Of course. You're just a big softie, for all your cockiness.'

She shook her head, too. 'Yeah, yeah.'

'But I mean it when I say we connect. At least *I* feel we do.'

'Then don't say any more. I hear you, but I don't want to.'

'Why?

'Think about it. You can go back up. I'm always stuck here. However nice it seems, Conor, you'd always go home. And, one day, maybe you wouldn't come back. You might meet someone else, I could never check up on you, maybe never find out what happened to you. No. I don't want that.'

She stood up, the mug still in her hand.

'I should've kept quiet,' I muttered.

'I'd rather know. You once described that cottage where you live. It sounds fantastic. You know where we go, Conor? When we want to get away from the lights on the Brick. We go into the Dark Areas.' Her anger flared suddenly. 'That's about it. Nothing. Just a fucking black hole where you can't even see your hands in front of your face. Zero.'

'You go into the Dark Areas?' That was news to me.

'Yeah, Tebor worked out how. Don't worry, it's nothing special. Just somewhere to hide.'

She returned to her own table, started tapping out on the keyboard, chasing more clues. I wanted to continue talking, couldn't believe they'd broken into the Dark Areas. Even I'd never considered that possibility.

Tebor, who had heard her final outburst, stared at me accusingly, then he got up and went to put his arm over

Andi's shoulder. Tears swelled her eyes but she managed to hold them back

'It's OK,' said Tebor. 'We're together.'

She lifted her arm and patted his hand. 'Come on, let's get back to work.'

'Why?'

'Work to do. Need to find Que.'

'Piece of cake. Lots of credits. I'll look after you now we're on Easy Street.'

I double-taked. I saw the triumphant glint in his eyes. *That kid had done the impossible.*

'We've found Que,' said Andi, staring at Tebor's monitor. 'Dammit, we've got him.'

'Where?' asked Conor.

'Some hotel in Baltimore. RealWorld.'

'You sure?'

'Of course I'm sure,' she snapped angrily. Then she calmed down. 'If Tebor says we've got him, then we've got him. One of his clients, a guy I know, left a VoiceMail for Que, saying he would pay him fifteen thousand US for a specific tryst. Only it had to be for tomorrow. This guy'd got some like-minded friends with him. He's the only one who managed to get through to Que. Fifteen thousand dollars is a big come-on.'

'That's an expensive game.'

'Probably some transsexual death or mutilation game. That's top of the charts right now.'

'Absolution of the Dead,' added Tebor. 'It makes 'em feel like God.'

'They use MIWs. That way they really get to kill someone.'

'I thought I knew everything.' I'd heard of these games, but never actually come across one before. This was real cutting edge. Compared to these, my games were for kids.

'You know jack shit,' said Tebor. 'The knack is getting

181

out before they wipe you out. That way they get what they paid for – think you're kaput – and you get easy money.'

'And if you don't . . . get out?'

'No more MIW. Then it's the EndGame. Forever.'

Andi continued, ignoring Tebor's outburst. 'Que answered the VoiceMail. Tried to get the date changed. My friend couldn't agree that, so Que said he'd see what he could do. He hasn't come back yet. During the conversation he let it drop he was stuck in Baltimore.'

'In a hotel?'

'I checked all the hotels,' Tebor cut in. 'No Que registered. So I ran a list of names he might use, something connected with Simon or Que. I found a Simeon "Pron". That's Russian for "who", which in Spanish is "Que". Got to be him. He registered three days ago. Piece of cake to hack into the hotel system. It's old, scratchy security software. From his check I'd say he was living on room service. High phone usage, but no contact with anyone. He's permadialled into the same number all the time, which means he's in the Web. And he's alone. This guy does not want to be found.'

'You're the best,' yelled Andi.

Tebor turned on me. 'And you're fucking lucky she didn't walk on you. I would've, for all that shit you give.'

I ignored him. 'What hotel?'

'Bentine Hotel.'

'You're the best,' repeated Andi.

'I also have a room number.'

I smiled, letting him know he was better than me. 'I thought you might.'

'Room two three seven. Second floor.'

'Well done.'

'Is the GameMaster happy? Do I go to the top of the class?'

'Yeah.' He knew I meant it. I then called Gallagher and told him where he'd find Que.

'What'll they do now?' Andi asked when I came off the phone.

'Send in a local FBI unit. He says he wants them in to set up a video link and secure the area. Then wait for a Secret Service team.'

'Did you tell him an MIW found Que?'

'Did you want me to?'

She shrugged, then went back to work.

We all knew it was only the first step, but the door had just opened a little more.

The hotel was one of those 1920s brownstones that have ended up squashed between two larger structures on many American midtown streets. It had somehow escaped being demolished into another empty parking lot that one day would be redeveloped into a likeness of the steel and glass monstrosities it had adjourned.

But, at the turn of the millennium, the heritage groups set out to defend what was left of their nation's history. The Bentine, as an example of an earlier age, had a protection order slapped on it and was to be preserved for the future. Except nobody told the owners how they could afford preserving it, and the hotel fell into a long, slow decline. Musty and decrepit, as were its clientele, the Bentine's sheer shabbiness became its only permanent reminder of America's architectural heritage because nothing could be done to improve it without some form of major expenditure. The once proud hotel was left to die slowly.

The local FBI unit arrived on the scene within fifteen minutes of being alerted. The White House had informed them there was an ex-con in Room 237 who was causing havoc in Second World with his avatar. They didn't want him disturbed until the Secret Service arrived, because they were currently tracking his avatar on the Brick. The FBI's sole function meanwhile was to set up video links and make sure there was no danger to any other residents.

The Federal Senior Agent took two men upstairs with

him, after questioning the receptionist to confirm that Que was still in his room.

'He had room service take some champagne up about two hours ago,' the clerk had acknowledged nervously, being not used to the Feds. The Bentine was not somewhere the police normally concerned themselves with.

'You say he received champagne?' the Senior Agent had repeated him.

'One bottle, but it was delivered for him from outside.'

'When?'

'About three hours ago. Special order, UPS, and they said it had to be delivered at a certain time. So I did that. Sent up the bottle and also some cheese sandwiches.'

'He order them, too?'

'No, but the instruction, from whoever booked the room, was to send up some food along with the bottle. All that guy eats since he's been staying here is cheese sandwiches.' The clerk searched amongst the papers littered on his desk, and he pulled one out. 'Here's the UPS instruction.' He pointed at it dramatically, as if to clear himself. 'See, that's exactly what it says.'

The Senior Agent took the form. 'Did you take delivery of this bottle? Sign for it?'

'I was in the john. When I got back that note was on the reception desk. I guess UPS must have left it. The weekend's nearly here and I guess he wanted to get home. Wife and kids, you know?'

'That mean you knew him?'

'No.'

'How'd you know he had a wife and kids, then?'

'No, no, no, figuratively speaking. You know what I mean?'

The FBI man sighed. 'Stick to the facts. So you got no idea who delivered it.'

'Yeah.' He pointed again at the sheet in the agent's hand. 'UPS did. It says so.'

The agent looked round the lobby and noticed a camera. 'Your digitals working?'

'Camera's broke.'

'Don't they always.' He knew well that most of these cheap hotels had customers who didn't want to be identified.

'Yeah, it's a bitch. We're still waiting for the repair man.' He watched the agent purse his lips. 'There's no StreetCam out back, and that's where most of the deliveries arrive.' The clerk shrugged. 'Guess you'll have to ring UPS.'

'How do you know he came in through the back?'

'It's no parking out front. Stop for a few seconds in front of those StreetCams and they send you a ticket. All our deliveries are signposted to the back alley.' He changed tack. 'This a bad guy?' he asked, but the look he got convinced him not to probe any further. He turned and unhooked the spare room key, passed it over. 'Room two three seven.' He held onto the key a moment longer. 'Can I see that ID again?' When he was satisfied with the agent's shield, he released the key.

'Any bolts on the inside of the room doors?'

The clerk shook his head. Then he watched the agents bring in the small, palm-held cameras that would create the video link. He went back to his chair. He'd done everything he'd been asked for, including giving them a register of all the guests, and he had confirmed there were no residents staying in the adjoining rooms.

He pretended to read his book but, all the time, he wondered what the Feds wanted with the occupant of Room 237. He felt safe, though, as he'd done exactly as he'd been asked. The champagne bottle itself and the supporting documentation had been delivered two days earlier. He'd kept the documents in the safe, not folded in his pocket, which thus made them appear as though they had just arrived. The champagne went into the cooler, but away from the other bottles stashed behind the white wine. He'd marked his so that he could tell the difference and he had checked every day. The client had insisted on that. It had to be *that* bottle or else he didn't get paid the handsome tip he was promised.

From the corner of his eye he watched the Feds go purposefully about their business.

A view of the hotel lobby came up on the monitor. The FBI operative panned it across the entire lobby and reception. It showed the clerk reading his book.

'He's trying very hard not to seem nosy,' commented Clancy.

'Wouldn't you?' answered Gallagher. He turned to one of his men. 'Run that guy through the files, see what we've got on him.'

The second camera flicked on, showing the corridor outside Room 237. It was a dark, narrow passage with faded red carpets and cheap hanging chandeliers with every second bulb removed, an effort to keep the costs down. Room 237 was the last one in the corridor and was highlighted by a whitish glow that came from the window at the end of the corridor.

Gallagher stepped back just as Meisner joined the group. 'We're close to going in.'

'Where's your team?' Meisner asked.

'A couple of minutes away.' Gallagher knew the Secret Service unit helicopter had already landed at a point nearby. The roads into the centre would be empty as most people, having finished work at noon, were now readying themselves for the weekend sports fixtures or for a visit to Second World. 'Both pictures are being piped through to the VP's office.'

'Good. Let's hope we get somewhere this time.' *Sarcastic comments like that really helped boost moral.*

Gallagher turned his attention back to the screen.

'We contacted UPS, Baltimore,' said a screen operative. 'No deliveries today to the Bentine. Last drop-off was nearly two weeks ago. Just a small package for a resident. Nothing for anyone called Pron.'

Gallagher nodded. 'Run all the local StreetCams' records on those dates. See what you can pick up. And make comparison checks between the people hanging round Elvis Presley World and those present in Convention Hall. See if anything matches on the IdentiFiles.'

'That's a very long shot,' whispered Clancy.

'Long shots and desperation, that's what I'm selling. You got anything better?'

Clancy backed off. 'Maybe you will pick something up.'

'Don't count on it.' Gallagher could feel time starting to run out. 'What gets me is how no one's tried to come through with a ransom, or anything, so far. Why no attempt to contact?'

Behind them, in another corner of the Security Control Complex, two operators worked away steadily, eyes focused on their screens, impervious to the tension that was building in the Control Room. They were breaking down the images of the President waving in Elvis Presley World, their body language was obvious. They were totally wrapped up in their own tension as they stripped away layers of pixels to find their unknown targets.

'I've got something hidden in here,' said the one operating the right-hand screen.

'Keep going,' replied the other. 'Let's find something for certain before we involve everyone.' He looked over his shoulder at those watching the Bentine Hotel screens. 'There's enough guys in here already with their heads up their asses.'

They had two workstations converted to screens tapped directly into the White House Control room.

Tebor, whilst keeping an eye on the other two screens, continued to chase his own contacts.

'How do you get into the Dark Areas?' I asked, as we waited.

'That's Tebor's game,' Andi said. 'You should ask *him*.'

The boy picked up the mention of his name. 'What's he want?'

'Wants to know how to get into the Dark Areas.'

Tebor laughed and shook his head. 'And he's a Game-Master.'

'I didn't think it was possible,' I answered.

'Everything's possible down here and maybe you should know that. It's only RealWorld has restrictions.' Tebor giggled. 'Dark Areas are only places with no light.'

'The network's not been opened up there. It's just nothing.'

'Then why ask? If you're so sure there's nowhere to go.'

'Look,' interrupted Andi, bored with the contest being played out between the two of us. 'They're getting ready to go in.

Tebor leant over and joined the other two sitting in front

of the screens linked to the White House. They watched as the lobby camera followed a unit of five Secret Service agents up the stairs. The corridor camera picked them up next.

They finalized their strategy with hand signals. The FBI was told to stay back and support only if required. Both teams unholstered their weapons. They presumably didn't know what to expect. One of the Secret Service team, with the spare key in his hand, approached the door to Room 237. He knelt down and peered through the lock. Most hotel doors now opened to palm prints and other modern security locks, but the Bentine still had old-fashioned key locks going back thirty years.

I saw the agent indicate there was no key obstructing the lock on the other side. That meant there would be no need to smash the door down to gain entry. The monitor then switched to the agent's CapCam. Through the keyhole it was clear that the room beyond was in darkness, the curtains were drawn, and it took a while for the camera to switch from grey mode to infrared night vision. The picture lightened and it was easy to identify a bed in one corner; someone seemed to be lying on it.

The monitors cut back to the corridor, as the agent stood up, signalling the others to be quiet. Then he slipped the key slowly and deliberately into the lock; I'd seen him spray it with oil to insulate the sound. He checked once more that the team was ready. Satisfied, he quickly snapped the lock open with one hand and turned the handle with the other, pushing the door sharply ajar as it came free from the jamb. He stepped back as the others rushed the door, and entered the room, their weapons kept cocked and at the ready.

Tebor giggled again. 'They like making lots of noise,' he commented as the shouting Secret Service agents made their entrance.

The monitor jumped back to the palm camera; it wavered a moment, then followed the other agents into the drab and

dingy hotel suite. All the monitor showed was the agents'
backs as they stared at Simon Que.

'Jesus,' somebody swore.

Then the agents stepped aside. I looked at my two
companions. It clearly wasn't what anyone expected.

'Who's that going to?' asked Dwight Swilkin when he saw the White House had patched pictures from the Bentine to Conor Smith.

'The receiving computer's registered to a Conor Smith.' The NSA operative began to track the signal. 'The signal's going to a portable keyboard. In Second World.'

'Find out who he is.' Swilkin picked up a phone and dialled the National Security Adviser's screened mobile. 'Can you talk, sir?' When he received an affirmative, he continued. 'The White House is sending a signal directly from the Bentine to a Conor Smith. Do they have clearance to do that?'

'They're using some privateers.'

'What kind?'

'Crackers, that kind.'

'Dangerous that. If we're all hooked into the same network, we could get hacked. Who is Conor Smith?'

'A GameMaster.'

'Then he'll have equipment that can match ours. Maybe better.'

'Don't we have defensive screens?'

'We do, sir, but I'm just stating that there's a good possibility of our being compromised.'

There was a long pause before Marlin replied, 'I can't change that now. The VP supported it, and I believe these privateers have trusted and proven track records.'

'Can I investigate them?'

'Only if what they're up to seems likely to compromise our security.' Marlin didn't need to remind Swilkin that Congress specifically forbade US security services from spying on each other, unless they believed they were at risk.

'I understand, sir. Do we have any other names we can run a check on?'

'No.'

The signal disconnected. Swilkin went back to his operative. 'Scan the White House, and see who else they're tied in to.' He turned to one of his assistants. 'Run a list of crackers who work for the White House, also for the Feds and CIA.' He thought for a moment, then added, 'In fact find this Conor Smith character, let's see what he's made of.'

The bed was unmade, they realized that as soon as they snapped the lights on.

Simon Que, or the person they presumed to be Simon Que, lay stretched on the bed, his body twisted as though he had been trying to frantically escape from some awful apparition. He wore a silver dress, skin-tight but lumpy on his body. A woman's blonde wig had slipped off his head, and now covered his face. The agent with the door key came forward and lifted the wig from Que's face. He had a few days' stubble growth and his eyes wide open, staring upwards.

A champagne bottle stood on the bedside table, uncorked and still half full. The glass Que had drunk from was on the floor beside the bed. The phone he'd been using lay next to it, presumably having been dropped suddenly to the floor. Que's right hand gripped his left wrist, all over which was blood that had seeped through the clenching fingers.

One foot still had a silver high-heel shoe dangling from it; the other shoe had been hurled across the room and now lay under the closed curtain.

His face was a study in acute pain, the final grimace of a man who knew he was dying in agony and dying alone. A half-eaten sandwich, slightly curled at the edges, lay on a plate resting on the end of the bed. It was the last meal he never had.

The palm camera recorded it all for those who were watching elsewhere, and it didn't take long for some to recognize the tableau. It was a scene they had all witnessed not too long before.

'It's the Monroe death all over again,' observed Gallagher grimly.

'Fucking unbelievable,' swore Meisner. 'What the fuck's going on.'

Gallagher ignored him. 'Your call, Don,' he said to Clancy.

Clancy moved past him to the microphone. 'Stanley?'

On the screen the agent holding the door key turned to the palm camera. 'I hear you, Mister Clancy.'

'I'm getting a forensic team over there straight away, so don't touch the champagne bottle or any other items, particularly don't let anyone else into the room. Continue your search of the room by visual means only.'

'OK.' He didn't need to tell the other team members, since they were all patched together. 'You tell us where to direct the camera.' That way the White House team at base could also see everything they examined.

'OK, start by the door, then pan left and just take in everything slowly.'

They watched as the camera started its methodical journey round the dingy room. Que had hung his clothes in the wardrobe, and both doors were still slewed open. The outfit hanging on the rail was garish: a bright yellow shirt with red slacks. It was a typical ultra-gay outfit, with a sharp multicoloured tie draped loosely around the shirt on its hanger. The black, patent leather shoes on the rack below were shiny and very new.

'Get a close-up on all the makes,' said Clancy.

The camera nosed in on the apparel and revealed where the various barcodes had originally been stamped. They had been cut out, unfortunately, so it would take a lot longer to trace the merchandiser who had sold Que his finery. A small sports bag sat next to the shoes. The camera was manoeuvred inside, but it was empty.

'He used that for the dress,' suggested Gallagher. 'I don't see any suit carrier.'

'Looks more like Miss Piggy than Monroe,' muttered Meisner dismissively.

The camera continued round the room, across the bed where Que lay, and eventually back to the door. Apart from the wardrobe, there were no new clues, nothing that hadn't been spotted in the first few minutes.

'OK, Stanley, the forensic team'll be there soon,' finished Clancy.

He looked up as the phone rang, and Gallagher answered it, and could tell from his expression that something interesting had surfaced. 'Well?' he asked.

'Our pals at the NSA,' replied Gallagher, and shrugged as Meisner joined them. 'We traced the call Que was making when he died. It was connected to the Hotel Gallipoli, room fifty-eight.'

'That's where . . .' reacted Meisner.

'Marilyn Monroe was.'

'At what time?' asked Clancy.

'They died at the same time. Whoever they were talking to got them drinking together. Same drugged champagne: one for Second World and one for RealWorld. He must've linked the calls together, speak to one, speak to them both. Clever bastard, laying parallel trails to confuse us.'

'We need analysis on the contents of that bottle and the glass.'

'Have we got a breakdown on the Monroe contents?' Meisner asked Clancy.

'Yes, a psychostimulant called AcidIce. A methamphetamine and phencyclidine cocktail. It's an electronic spike that affects the avatars' senses in the same way real drugs do in RealWorlds. It provides a mindblowing rush of psychedelic and speed together. That's why it's so dangerous. You overdose on it, only one result. Lethal. One trip you'll never come back from.'

'To the avatar?'

'Yes – I mean, the mind takes over but, as far as our experts say, you feel that something comes into you, fills you up, starts to eat you. Then, when you feel full of whatever you see, you just die. Your systems just stop, pushed flat out by speed and also hyped up by the acid.'

'And the person operating the avatar?'

'Well, they rely on the JetPax usually . . .' Clancy cursed himself. He pulled up a chair and sat down. 'Shit!'

'What have I missed?' asked Meisner.

'Whoever we're dealing with . . . knows how to overcome the Jetpax,' said Gallagher quietly. 'That's why Que's left wrist's all bloody. Looks like he was trying to rip off Marilyn's JetPax, only he was ripping at his own wrist instead.'

'I still don't get it.'

'Without an escape mechanism, Marilyn's hallucinations would have been seen and felt by Que. He didn't need to take a drug to overdose. She did it for him. She just blew his mind. And he couldn't stop her. Whatever he tried. Once he couldn't escape Second World, he was a goner. Their minds were one. He just lay there and bled to death. Even if he hadn't done that, he would've ended up in a catatonic state.'

'The champagne in that bottle was simply loaded with stimulants, a real mindblower to help him along,' added Clancy. 'I bet that's what the autopsy will show.'

'We don't have the luxury of waiting for the result,' said Meisner, looking at the clock. 'You've now got under seven hours, and you're just wasting time. It took an outsider to trace Que. This whole thing should've been handed over to the FBI when I first suggested it. They've got the organization and facilities to handle kidnapping. You're all out of your league here. We're talking murder, we're talking major crime. Maybe it's time to hand it all over. I'm going to see the VP because it's time to re-evaluate our situation.'

They watched him leave the room.

Clancy stood up. 'Someone should put him down!'

'Don't get paranoid,' Gallagher cautioned.

'It pays to be paranoid.' Clancy stomped away from the screen. 'Why the fuck hasn't anybody picked anything up yet?' He was shouting at everybody and nobody in particular.

The two operatives who had been working on the Elvis Presley World tape looked at each other, then one nodded.

'We may have something here, Mister Gallagher,' said the other.

Clancy and Gallagher moved over to look. Both screens displayed a broken-tiled effect, where each individual pixel represented a space of more than two inches square. It was the top layer of one of the live pictures from Elvis Presley World. For each frozen picture the magnification was more than five thousandfold.

'I've never seen this architecture before. I'd heard there'd been experiments, but didn't really think it possible.' The operative pointed at one of the pixels. The edges were blurred, giving a shadowed effect. 'I thought this fuzz was down to aliasing.'

'What's that?' asked Clancy.

Gallagher explained. 'Aliasing means it's a jagged edge on a three-dimensional rendering on any bitmapped display. There are jaggies – that's what we call them – along the side of the objects. It causes a flickering effect. You've seen it, if tapes on Second World aren't quite perfect, when images flicker along their sides. You sometimes even see it on normal TV.'

Clancy nodded. Gallagher signalled his operative to continue.

'But this isn't fuzzy because of aliasing.' The agent pointed at the screen, running his finger down the side of the magnified pixel. 'There's a secondary layer of images behind this, and it's really well done. I mean, it's like each secondary pixel has shaped itself to the primary one. These pixels are *intelligent*. They're hiding behind the primary picture, shaping themselves to fit in.'

'Explain that slowly,' said Gallagher, primarily for Clancy's benefit.

'OK. Imagine you've got two separate photos, both in negative. You put one on top of the other. Now, you'll see the second one under the first. Because both images are different, the top one, the primary, doesn't mask the secondary. Well, that's what we've got here. The technology's been around for a while, and it helps move data quickly. Stick two pictures together, send them in the same time frame in tandem, then unglue them when they come out at the other end. We can always identify those pictures because once you start to blow the images up, bang, you see the secondary picture very quickly.' He pointed at the screen. 'See that aliasing, on the side of the pixel. That's another image, behind the primary. But it's trying to hide itself. It's changed its shape to replicate the one in front.'

'How do you separate them?'

'I'm not sure, but we're going to run a download program. I think it might just unstuff the data and produce two separate pictures, just like you would when you download any images in tandem.'

The other operative started the download. Each screen took one set of images. The first screen showed the President at Elvis Presley World, just as they had seen him before.

'Whoever set this up is damned smart,' remarked the first operative. 'I mean, it's like they laid the trap for us, wanted us to find it.'

'Why?' queried Clancy.

'I don't know. We would've unearthed it by running our normal checks. He wanted us to find it, but not right away.'

'Then he was stalling for time?'

'Maybe. Clever fella, this.'

The second screen came alive. It showed the President still waving, then he turned and left. The picture dissolved to a caption.

'Now we know what they want,' said a tight-lipped Clancy as he read the words on the screen. 'Download it to the VP's office.' He turned to Gallagher. 'Then let's go see her.'

The notice on the monitor read:

IN A FEW HOURS YOUR PRESIDENT IS A DEAD MAN
THE JETPAX IS NO LIFELINE
LOOK FOR THE VIRUS
I AM THE VIRUS
YOU ARE THE DRAGON
SAVE THE VIRUS
&
KILL THE DRAGON
MASTER OF THE WEB
THE RANSOM IS . . . HAVEN'T DECIDED YET
I WILL CONTACT
HAVE A GOOD DAY

CONDOR

We watched the discovery of Que's body at the Bentine. No one said much; I realized this was the first time either Andi or Tebor had seen a RealWorld corpse. Not that I'd seen many; just Mum and Dad when they'd died. The scene obviously shocked them, held a morbid fascination for them as they saw the reality of the *other* place.

'Same things happen up there that go on down here,' I said, when Andi looked at me for reassurance.

'I wasn't thinking that. I just wondered what our bodies look like now, wherever they are.' She couldn't hide the concern in her eyes, wanting to know they were safe in RealWorld.

'They're safe. Well protected.'

'They're in the Catacombs.'

'Don't worry,' I tried to reassure her.

'Have you ever been in the Catacombs?'

'I've seen pictures.' That was a lie. I didn't want her to know that I knew well where she was safeguarded. In the early days there had been rows and rows of what looked liked dark grey coffins, in vast grey rooms each stretching for more than two hundred yards. There'd been a Sunday supplement article, written to force the authorities to increase the effort in bringing back the MIWs. It had been the start of the media pressure and its eventual success meant they were now well looked after. 'All I know is . . .' I continued so as not to alarm her, 'they're making every effort to make sure you all come back.'

She turned back to the screen as the camera started to pan once more round the hotel room. Neither she nor Tebor, who watched just like a child, thumb in mouth, said anything until the grisly slow camera pan was complete.

'Foo,' swore Tebor. 'OK,' he turned to me. 'That's one of our leads knocked off. Deader than an MIW in RealWorld. Who else do we chase?'

'His friends. Find out if anyone hated him. Who was his best friend? Who used his services more than most?'

'Who else do we get zapped?' he accused me.

'Walk any time you want, Tebor. Either do this because you want to, or stop wasting my time.'

'We could be hurting our biz groups. We got to follow netiquette.' Tebor wanted to protect his friends, observe the protocol of the Web where those on the same side always protected each other.

'None of your biz groups are into kidnapping. They might hack and phreak, drop in the odd time bomb or trojan, but they're not kidnappers and murderers. Or are they?'

'He's right.' Andi came to my support. She knew the same people Tebor did, not just the MIWs, but also those who sent their avatars into Second World. Yes, they did set off logic bombs that were triggered at pre-set times, or unleashed security-breaking programs that were hidden behind benign simple games. But they were not murderers. They were just people who liked to break the bounds of technology while they lived on the edge of the protocol. Mischievous people, not hardened vicious criminals. They were innocents who didn't understand the constraint and hypocrisy of modern society; they certainly didn't kill those who lived in that society.

She continued to encourage Tebor. 'We don't know where this could all lead. Every hour, something changes.

JetPax failure could leave millions stranded down here. Specially with the weekend about to start. The same could happen in RealWorld. Isn't that why Simon Que died, because he couldn't get his avatar out? His wetware blew up on him.' She was referring to the human nervous system, as opposed to computer hardware and software. 'At least we're alive up there. One day we'll get out of here. What we don't want is for some zipperhead to blow us all away.' She crossed over to Tebor and put her arm round his shoulder. She pointed at me. 'He's only a GameMaster, but you're the WizardPrince.'

Tebor giggled. 'No prince. I'm the WizardKing.'

'And the WizardKing can save us.'

I saw Tebor's shoulders pick up. She was right. He was a wizard on the keyboards. One of those top hackers who knew how the most complex systems of hardware and software worked. He was like me; preferred the old-fashioned keyboard to the thought and speech modes.

'OK,' agreed Tebor and slowly swaggered back to his keyboard, after throwing me one final disdainful glance.

Andi looked at me triumphantly, but before I could respond I glimpsed something happening on the White House monitor.

'Christ Almighty,' I swore.

Andi turned round. The ransom note had appeared. She read it and swung back to me. 'What's wrong?'

'Nothing. I think we need to get out of here.'

'Why?'

'Because they're probably tracking us.'

'You said we were helping them?'

'We are – but the White House people aren't the only ones involved. There are others who could be a lot more hostile.' I switched off my keyboard. The image on the screen went blank.

'You've disconnected, so how will they keep in touch?'

I looked hard at her, felt my voice tight with the tension.

'Contact me through my CompuPhone. Right now, I need to get out of here. So do you two. Please, trust me.'

'OK, OK.' She was confused, but she had no choice. She called Tebor. 'Pack up. Let's go.'

They both took their keyboards and followed me out into the park.

'Will the barman in that cafe keep quiet?' I asked.

'He'll admit we were there. To protect himself and his job. But he doesn't know where we're going.' She ran after me as I kept up a brisk pace. Tebor followed at a short distance.

'Have you a safe house somewhere?' I shouted at her.

'Yes. Just off the Brick.'

I stopped suddenly, so she nearly ran into me. 'Give me the nearest MetroPort number. To your safe house.'

'Nine one two.'

'OK. You go there. Don't use your keyboards. Otherwise they might get tracked. Get out on the Brick and ask questions. The Weekenders are coming, so you'll have plenty of cover. Keep checking in. I'll message you when I'm coming down.'

'How?'

'The message board outside Metro nine one two.' Each MetroPort and various points along the Brick had visual message boards. Users simply punched in a message to their mobile phones or on their keyboards, and the recipient was bleeped immediately. They went to the nearest message board, logged in their PIN and the screen flashed them the message. 'What's your PIN number?'

'AndiGirl 1602.'

'OK. I'll use the call sign TeborFive. That way I'll avoid confusion with any other contacts of his own who want to call him. If either of you get a call, and it's not from me, make sure you know who it is. And you two stay together because, when I come back, I'll need you fast.'

'When's that gonna be?'

'Not too long. We've only six hours left.'

'What's suddenly happened, Conor?' She appeared genuinely concerned.

I smiled, warm and reassuring. 'I don't know. Something's not right.'

She wasn't convinced, but decided not to press me. 'Where're you going?'

'Running away already?' jibed a grinning Tebor.

'RealWorld.' I grinned back at Tebor. 'I'm going shopping.'

'Shopping?'

'Yeah. As they say, when the going gets tough, the tough go shopping.' Don't ask why, but I stuck my tongue out at Tebor. The boy shrugged and turned away. I reached over and ruffled his spiky hair. Tebor pulled away, embarrassed at the close and familiar contact. It was a start, knowing the boy trusted no one. 'I need to sort something out,' I told Andi. 'My host might be in danger. If I protect myself, then I protect you.' I turned back to Tebor. 'Both of you.'

'Be careful, Conor.' She reached over and touched my arm. Sweet.

I nodded, pleased with her consideration. 'I always am.' *Tough guy.* I wished I'd said something more meaningful. 'Keep an eye on her, WizardKing.'

Then I hit my JetPax and dissolved in front of them.

Another strained meeting was under way; politicians as always talking, talking, confusing.

The Vice President saw the kidnapping of Teddy Dixon growing into a squalid tabloid front-pager by the minute. Her first priority was to silence the FBI agents who had gone to the Bentine. To do that, she now involved the FBI Director, John Small. She had a ten-minute meeting with him and briefed him as much as she dare. Then she asked for his silence. Small, an experienced and dapper political operator in the mould of the Bureau's founder, Edgar Hoover, soon agreed. By then, he had his concessions in place. If the President returned, the VP would support Small's requirements for his department. On the other hand, if she were to assume the presidential role, then he would be her trusted adviser in all security matters.

It was an easy discussion; both recognizing each other's flagrant ambitions.

The White House still felt the President was on their turf. Small argued that it was a matter of kidnapping, a federal crime that came under his jurisdiction. Sumner retorted that the body had not been kidnapped and therefore was still out of his area of control. He said he was prepared to accept her views, as long as it was accepted this conversation had never taken place. She agreed. They then agreed it was wise that he not attend the meeting with the NSA, the

Attorney General and the Chief of Staff. It would only complicate matters. Especially in view of the ransom note, which affected a President whose body had not been kidnapped. She promised she would keep him up to speed on all matters.

Small returned to his office and immediately set about monitoring all the White House security systems. He was determined to be ready when the walls, as he believed must happen, finally caved in.

When the others had settled in Sumner's office, including Clancy and Gallagher, she opened the meeting with a brief report from each participant. She then asked for their individual comments and opinions.

'So nobody's any the wiser,' she said, when she had been round the table.

'Not quite that bad,' replied Marlin. 'I feel that my people are making some headway. I just wish we had more time.'

'Don't we all,' snapped Meisner. He turned his venom on Clancy. 'On your suggestion, we have kept the other Security Services out of this. And we've only just found out there was a ransom note. Why did it take so long?'

Gallagher intervened. 'We got to the ransom note pretty fast. Even the NSA, with their advanced equipment, didn't pick up on that.'

'We weren't looking for it specifically, that's why,' protested Marlin.

'Neither were we, but we kept looking until we found something.'

'Let's slow down.' Sumner took charge of the meeting before it degenerated into an all-out I'm-not-to-blame brawl. She turned to Marlin. 'Are you getting all the support you need?'

'No. We asked for the names of the privateers the White House were going to use. We haven't had that list yet.'

'Why not?'

'Because these people work outside the Security Services.'

Gallagher knew he had a fight on his hands. 'They're in there, helping us. I don't want them compromised. Why put them in unnecessary danger?'

'These guys are loose cannons,' said Meisner. 'For all we know they could even be behind the President's disappearance.'

'They're computer freaks, not murderers. They're not with the Mafia or some crazy terrorist group. These are just people who enjoy stretching their capabilities as programers. They live under the kiss principle.'

'What's that?' asked Sumner.

'K.I.S.S.' Gallagher spoke each letter individually. 'Keep It Simple, Stupid. That's the kind of language they talk. This kidnapping is too messy for them. The computer is their means of power, not guns. They don't kill people.'

'We agreed to share information, and that your informers would be checked.'

'Yes, ma'am. But as soon as someone tries to check on them, to cut across their lines of enquiry, they fold up and just disappear. They're good people, and if there's anything to be found, they're the ones who'll do it. Out on the street, where this thing started.'

The Vice President pondered for a moment. 'I would like you to give the list to the NSA.'

'Under protest, ma'am.'

'That's understood. But immediately after this meeting.'

'How many are there?' asked Marlin.

'Just one,' Gallagher admitted softly.

'One guy? Is that all?' snapped an incredulous Meisner. 'One guy looking for the President? For Christ sake, what can one guy do?'

'I felt . . .' Gallagher looked at the VP and realized he wouldn't get support from that angle, 'I felt that my man was the best, and that we didn't want all these guys out on the Brick tripping over each other. With the aid of modern computers, one guy, with a little help, can cover almost as much as ten of them. It's not how much you cover, but how you go after that information.'

'We have all our national security departments on this and you still think one guy's enough?' Meisner went on. He turned to Clancy. 'Did you go along with this?'

'I was kept informed at all times.' Clancy's stoic answer disguised his true feelings.

'I just wonder how seriously you're all taking this?'

'I object to that.' Clancy suddenly found himself defending Conor. 'Let's not forget who traced Que.'

'Enough now.' Sumner turned to Marlin. 'Just make sure this contact, whoever he is, isn't compromised. Run checks, but at a discreet distance. Don't forget, he found Que. I don't want to see doors closed which he might be opening. This Simon Que . . . are we sure he wasn't behind this whole mess?'

'I can't see it,' replied Marlin.

'Don?' She turned her attention to Clancy.

'I agree, ma'am. He was a good actor, but a pretty unsavoury character who led a strange low life and, I'm sure, pimped for well-paying customers. He arranged deals for some real obscene and degenerate people.'

'He was also extremely successful,' interrupted Marlin. 'Had over six million dollars in his bank account.'

Nobody asked how Marlin knew that, but they all presumed the Puzzle Palace had hacked Que's bank account. Gallagher caught Clancy's eye. Clancy shrugged. *Illegal but necessary.*

'It's still unlikely he was behind it,' continued Clancy. 'Our research shows he knew nothing about programing. Whoever's organizing this is an expert. Que was into heavy sex – having a good time and getting paid for it. There's no history of him ever being involved in anything else. As you know, it's too early for forensic to come up with anything yet. But we've a pretty good idea that the drink was spiked, an LSD-based drug with high amphetamine content. When his brain mixed with that cocktail as well as what was going on with his Marilyn avatar, he was ready for the funny farm. We're running DNA checks on the dress he was wearing, on his day clothes, on everything. Nothing's showing yet.'

'They did find fingerprints on the champagne bottle, ma'am,' added Gallagher.

'That might produce something. But, overall, there's nothing to suggest that Que had any involvement other than he was hired to run the Monroe avatar.'

'What ransom demands can you expect?' the Attorney General asked Marlin.

'No idea. Probably money. In some offshore account with funds being moved electronically.' Marlin wasn't being drawn.

'Who's Condor?' joined in Meisner.

'We're running checks on all who've used Condor as a WebName.'

'Well, I suggest you both get back to Control.' Sumner dismissed Clancy and Gallagher. 'Bring me up to speed as soon as something breaks.' As they left the room she continued talking to the others. 'Time's running short. If there's no improvement in the next three hours, we should focus on how this country continues to be governed. We'll need medical opinions on whether the President is incompetent, or not. I'd like us to consider how we prepare for those eventualities.'

'I just can't believe how lucky we've been that the media hasn't picked it up,' said Meisner.

'That won't last for ever,' chimed in Marlin.

Clancy and Gallagher walked back towards the Control Centre. They had been so involved in their pursuit of the President that they had forgotten the consequences should they fail.

'I could do with some fresh air,' said Clancy. 'I don't think a few minutes away from Control is going to make much difference.'

Gallagher followed Clancy till they reached the South Portico. The walked onto the balcony, looking out over the South Lawn, towards the Ellipse. They sheltered under the overhang, the perma-rain drizzling down beyond.

'Fucking weather,' cursed Clancy. 'When I was a kid you got six months' sun, six months' rain, even snow. I thought we were getting this global warming and pollution arriving from the rest of the world under control. Now it's five months' sun and seven months' rain. And they tell us pollution's only a small part of the problem. Apparently the global warming's seasonal, all down to rotation round the sun and its hotspots. I wonder what theory they'll crap up with tomorrow.'

'What's wrong, Don?' Gallagher asked.

Clancy watched a group of tourists on East Street, all in pac-a-macs, hunched against the inevitable rain. 'We lose touch, you know.'

'Explain.'

Clancy took out a pack of cigarettes, offered one to

Gallagher, who declined, then lit one with an antique Zippo. He took a deep puff. *No smoking* was a dictate of Secret Service rules, both for marijuana and tobacco. Lung cancer had been eradicated with tobacco additives, but smoking could still cause respiratory problems. The Service insisted its staffers were superfit, and out-of-breath agents didn't fit the image.

Clancy cupped the cigarette in his hand, so the security cameras wouldn't pick him up.

'Those folks down there.' Clancy pointed at the tourists. 'They don't know what's going on. Just visiting Washington for a few days. Go up and see the White House. Might even see the President. He just might wave at us out of the Oval Office.' He snorted. 'Fat chance. He's missing and the world's just going about doing what it always does. We're really out of touch, Paul. So engrossed in our little world, we forget the knock-on of our actions. If we fuck up, everybody fucks up.'

'Some people would say having a conscience affects how we do our jobs.'

Clancy shrugged. His eyes followed the Washington skyline. 'World's changed. Used to be, once, you could see what was going on. People were right out there, in front of you. Now, you can't see the enemy. They disappear into cyberspace, they hide in phone lines. Nothing's real any more. I'm third generation Secret Service. I was raised on its exploits. My granddaddy was there when they took a shot at Reagan. Real people. Real bullets. Now it's all just electronic spikes. Hell, I'm committed to protect him with my life. And I'm chasing Marilyn Monroe down a phone line. When I do find her she leads me to some guy in a dress and a wig, who is real, but whose only connection is down a fucking modem. Some way to do a job.'

'Easy to understand, Don. It's not supernatural . . . no ghosts.'

Clancy took another lungful, then spat out a laugh.

'GhostBusters've got more chance of solving this than we have.'

'Organizations like the Puzzle Palace understand this game. You're a beginner compared to them, Don.'

'But your guy Smith got to Que before they did.'

'He's one of them. He just works alone.'

'I know I don't like him, but I'm sorry, for your sake, that he got compromised.'

'He'll live. Until they use it for their own ends.'

'How?'

'If they fail they'll shift the blame to him. It's in their nature '

'You're paranoid.'

Gallagher laughed. 'Yeah. Like I recall you saying you *had* to be.'

Clancy chuckled, tossed the cigarette to the floor and ground it with his shoe.

'The problem with cigarettes is they're not dangerous any more. I mean, why smoke when it can't kill you. The risk was half of the fun.'

'You miss the old days, Don?'

'I do. I really do.' He shook his head ruefully. 'And they'll never come back. Not the way it used to be. Now it's all smokescreens and mirrors. I'm an old-fashioned guy, maybe losing touch.'

'An old-fashioned, paranoid guy.'

'That, too. That too.'

ROOM 4201
BLETCHLEY SUITES
GCHQ
BENHALL
NR CHELTENHAM
REAL TIME: ZERO MINUS 6 HRS AND 21 MINS

GCHQ, or to give it its full title of Government Communications Headquarters, had been Britain's primary electronic intelligence-gathering service since the Second World War. During that period it cracked the notorious Nazi military code, Enigma, which shortened the war and saved millions of Allied lives. In conjunction with the American intelligence services it was in the front line of the Cold War and the various Middle East battles before settling down to become, with the NSA, the most powerful eavesdropping network in the world.

Based in Benhall, well away from the Sprawl, it was hard to imagine the immense size and sheer power of its super-computing architecture. All the information it collected was stored on D-RAID architecture and it had, next to the NSA, the largest long-term bulk near line storage system in the world. It was also the most secure network in the world.

Room 4201 didn't officially exist. It was linked directly to the Telephone Exchange at the NSA. It dealt only in the most secret information, that which was only relevant to the two agencies. Often, although never admitted, much of what was passed between the two agencies wasn't made available to their own governments and other Security Services.

The room was larger than the visitor would expect from the single door that serviced it. It was home to one hundred and twelve operatives, each responsible for a bank of twelve monitors. These included cameras on the Dollarsat satellites that could transmit high-resolution pictures immediately from any part of the earth direct to Room 4201. These images, most from low-orbiting craft, could image down to a resolution of one metre, whether with a moving tape image or a single still picture.

These banks of monitors were linked into some of the most sensitive and secure electronic areas in the world. Each monitor was linked to over twenty input sources. All monitors were interactive and any picture lifted anywhere in the world could be seen on any one of the one thousand three hundred and forty-four screens.

As soon as any unusual or suspicious information was received by one of these inputs, they were flagged up on the screens. Information was continually being downloaded and checked by search engines for items that could interest GCHQ in matters of European security.

Room 4201 was linked to the NSA's Echelon system, which was capable of scanning emails, faxes, telexes and telephone calls, searching for specific words. Echelon was driven by a dictionary of suspicious and hostile words; if 'heroin' or 'assassin' or 'Downing Street' were used in a message, the system would register the word and its source to GCHQ.

When any such interesting item was flagged, the operative made a decision as to whether the information should be further highlighted, ignored or tracked. If he decided to investigate, he shuttled it down to the general search rooms elsewhere in the building. If the information was highly sensitive or classified for Room 4201 knowledge only, he would track it himself.

The request from the NSA came through to the Room 4201 supervisor. His department head, Neville Harbour-Smythe was in a staff union meeting, but Room 4201 ran itself. Outside influences rarely disturbed the pace and direction of those who worked there. It was with pride that a visit by Royalty was once ignored in Room 4201 because the team were watching the Epsom Derby from a satellite directly above the course and refused to open the doors until the race had finished. One of the technicians, when that specific member of the Royal Family finally entered, took great delight in telling the Royal that her horse had lost by a nose, even before the photo finish was declared.

So when the Telephone Exchange asked for information, with or without government approval, there was no hesitation in searching and providing what was required.

'He's a GameMaster,' was the first comment the operative made.

The supervisor then asked another operative to reposition two of the Dollarsat cameras over Norfolk, especially in the region of East Harling and the roads to the capital. One camera would scan the roads, looking for red multi-purpose vehicles, while the second would start to lay down a grid of smaller pictures looking for a red vehicle that was parked, or semi-hidden, within a ten-mile-square zone, whose centre point was East Harling.

The supervisor crossed to the back of the room. He pulled up a loose chair, swivelled it round and swung his leg over it, so that he was leaning over its back and looking into the room.

The first operative was already into files on Conor Smith, educational ones, going back to his early schooldays. That's how GCHQ trained their staff to start all searches. From the beginning. Steady, systematic, overlook nothing that you might regret missing later.

Every small piece of information is a road that leads to another.

'Hey,' exclaimed the operative, 'he was a bright student. Passed all his exams, exceptional grades. No wonder the police took him on.'

The supervisor's eyes flicked to the other screen. The cameras on the Dollarsat were already responding, already starting to identify the codes the second operative had tapped in. *Not like the old days*, he thought, *not like when it took hours to get the smallest response from a satellite.* The supervisor was in his last year at GCHQ. He'd been at the old headquarters at Cheltenham, the last of the analysts to leave and come to the new purpose-built, round centre at Benhall. *So many changes, so much improvement.* But it was no different now, just faster, more efficient.

He looked across to another set of screens which was sending other, unrelated data to the NSA. The world's largest spy station, Menwith Hill Signals Intelligence Base in Yorkshire, had been in existence for over fifty years. The section he checked was the one linked to it. Echelon was the major part of Menwith Hill's reason for existence. He watched his number two finally prepare the list for cross-checking. These days it took longer to type the list than get the results.

    Voters' register
    Regional tax files
    Property records
    Credit information
    Drivers' records
    Lawsuit information, civil and criminal
    Employment screening
    Criminal records
    Asset identification
    Police, Special Branch, MI5, MI6, FBI, US Secret Service
      and CIA files
    Investigative information
    Check all newscasts and newspapers
    Find IRS tax returns, vehicle ownership and many other
      public records
    Business records
    Check on doctors', lawyers' or other professionals' files
      on the suspect

Use the Post Office to determine the address behind a
  PO Box
Information and listings to Government-provided public
  records
Searchable Government databases and useful
  Government publications
Legal databases
Court documents
Bank and Building Society databases

'Never been married,' said the first operative. 'No convic-
tions, nothing. Good, clean-living boy, keeps to himself.
Lives in Norfolk.'

'Don't yap,' growled the supervisor. 'Concentrate.'

It didn't matter to him that Conor Smith was a European
citizen, even English like himself.

Neither did it matter that it was illegal to gather such
private information on a private citizen unless national
security was threatened. They'd always crossed that line.
That's how this country, and now Europe, stayed defended
behind the Great Islamic Wall. God knows what would
happen if that came down.

Stay secure.

All that mattered was that Room 4201 fulfilled its duty as
efficiently and as quickly as possible. To him, Conor Smith
was a name printed on a sheet of paper. No more. No less.

Honour amongst thieves is how the Voice put it as he
watched the probing questions scatter across cyberspace, as
it searched for the information that would lead to the
identity of the man known as Conor Smith.

Mahogany Row, on the ninth floor, housed the executive offices of the NSA. It was the hub from which the agency operated, the brain of the most advanced data-collection force in the world.

Dwight Swilkin sat quietly in his office on Mahogany Row, his feet up on the grey steel desk in front of him. He liked steel, it was an uncomplicated metal and echoed the simplicity that he demanded.

He'd taken to the sanctuary of his office ten minutes earlier, getting away from the urgency of the Tracking Room where his team monitored and tracked all the leads, including any on the GameMaster that Gallagher had brought in. He laid out, on one side of a large sheet of white paper, all the clues they had gathered up to then. Then he listed, on the opposite side, in chronological order, the sequence of events that had led to the present situation.

He liked to work on paper. Its simplicity created clarity in his own mind. He started, with a pencil, to link the events to the clues. When something didn't work out, he'd erase and start again. After a while, the sheet looked like a plan of a battlefield, with heavy lines and arrows crisscrossing the words in the columns that faced each other.

Dwight Swilkin firmly believed he could unravel the answer to any question. It was his training that gave him comfort within his arrogance. The training at the NSA's

National Cryptologic School had been of an unbelievably high standard. The magnitude of the students' mental capacity and education seemed overwhelming to those who crossed their paths. Picked from the highest stream of PhDs, the students became the final metamorphosis of the NSA Training School.

Those who topped their classes then went on to the Intensive Study program in General Analysis. This eighteen-week course is designed for the top analyst. Limited to twelve select students, the course involves over sixty books and specialist documents, group discussions and lectures, and more than four hundred practical exercises in code protocol. The reward, for those exceptional enough, was that they became part of the NSA's most secret and elite organization, a fraternity known as the Dundee Society. The Society dated back to the 1960s and was so super secret that only members knew who the others were.

The society was symbolized by a Dundee marmalade jar containing four sharpened pencils, to represent the world's first code-breaking machines. The motto of the society was 'You break jar, you eat marmalade.' The final exam was when the students deciphered the maddening codes of the mystical kingdom of Zendia and attempted to read the info-traffic of its ruler, Salvio Salasio. It was the ultimate cerebral game, the definitive intellectual test.

Dwight Swilkin was one of the great stars of the Dundee Society. Now at forty-three, he controlled the most secret of all the NSA departments. He loved the Agency passionately and, like so many similar young men, he had never married, just got on with his career. It gave him more satisfaction than he would get from sex or any involvement with women. *Things're different now*, his lawyer father had warned him the day he graduated from Princeton. *Women, they've grown balls like men. Ain't worth the hassle. Ain't worth the fight. Personally, I prefer chocolate to sex, anyway. Just don't tell your mother I said that.* The younger Swilkin could have earned much more, leading a highly privileged life as a lawyer or a Game-Master with one of the megacorps. But that, he felt, would have wasted his obvious talents. GameMasters achieved no real result: when the game was over, they went home, then started all over again. But, in his vocation, and that is how he viewed it, he achieved results that had real conclusions. He'd been Team Leader to the group who traced the Chicago nukers that resulted in the bombings of Iran and Syria. *That was a great result.*

He lived in RealWorld, while GameMasters, for all their fame and adulation, merely imitated life in Second World.

The graph he had drawn now irritated him. The facts didn't match the clues. To Swilkin, the clue to any situation was that first act which triggered the events that led to his desk. In this way, the code-breaker could determine whether the actions were structured or irrational. It set in motion a path that the code-breaker could clearly trace, once he understood the motive for the primary action.

The difference in this case was that everything was deliberately designed to confuse, yet to somehow lead to a predetermined and finite conclusion. He had little doubt that someone was manipulating the course of events, that they had a probable exit-route already worked out.

That was fine until he got to the ransom note. That's when it got confusing. It was as though the perp wanted them to follow certain approaches and, while they were doing that, ignore the motive. Which meant: the motive was not what a new ransom note might say, but had a deeper more hidden meaning that would be declared at a later stage.

It had to be an inside job. There were too many small details, especially in the electronic break-ins to the White House and Second World systems, which confirmed involvement from either the White House itself or one of the Intelligence Services.

He quickly reached four decisions. He wrote them down.

1 THE PERP IS A SHOWMAN AND LIKES TO HIGHLIGHT HIS CLEVERNESS

That's why he'd used Marilyn Monroe, made a big statement to show how clever he was.

That would help when they started to identify possible suspects.

2 HE'S AN OUTSTANDING TECHNOLOGICAL EXPERT

His method of hiding the President in Elvis Presley World and masking the ransom note proved that.

Why the hell didn't we find the ransom note before the White House? He would address that failing with his staff once this operation was finished.

The other technological moves were all standard to a good programer. The suspect was obviously a vastly experienced technician and Web architect. Someone who regularly visited the Web, was thoroughly at home in it. Probably worked with MIWs. Could even be using them. That would have helped keep the whole deal quiet until he kidnapped the President. He was a loner in RealWorld, a razor-sharp technological genius used to working with MIWs in Second World.

3 HE WORKS, OR PREVIOUSLY WORKED, ON THE INSIDE, OR HAD A MAJOR CONTACT IN THE SECURITY SERVICES, PROBABLY THE WHITE HOUSE

Swilkin didn't believe the JetPax code had been broken. But, if someone on the inside had deliberately damaged or deactivated Dixon's device, that would explain why the President couldn't return from Second World. Using the First Lady's choice of Monroe was clever. Shifted the emphasis away from the White House. Yet the perp had known about the secret exit route out of the Oval Office. An exit route that didn't go anywhere, except into the matrix. That confirmed the previous two points.

4 HE IS UTTERLY RUTHLESS

The death of Simon Que proved that. It also emphasized the serious danger the President was in.

Was he a she? He doubted that, not in the male-preserve world of the Security Services, albeit there were the usual nominal female staffers. No, there'd been too much sexual aggression towards women on this one. The way Monroe was killed off, the way Que was cross-dressed when his time was up.

There was little else of significance. All the other clues led in no particular direction and his team would, with their banks of supercomputers, chase them to their eventual conclusions. Their time was running short, but once again, he didn't feel that a major factor consideration. The perp felt he had plenty of time; after all, holding the President was the ace up his sleeve. That meant that, when he made his move and showed himself, Swilkin's trackers would have a short, but reasonable, time to trace him.

He could now only wait until the perp made the next move. Unlike some on his team Swilkin didn't accept that a foreign power, or a criminal organization, was behind it. If so, they would have made their demands known by now. To safely arrange a drop-off point for cash or a political prisoner would take considerable time. And, even for the President of the US, most people knew the government was unlikely to stump up a ransom. He reached over to the phone and buttoned the Telephone Exchange.

'Run enquiries on all senior personnel in the White House Control Room. And also the agents on the Presidential protection roster. Highlight those on duty when he was kidnapped. I need to know who's close to the First Lady, someone who knew about the Monroe avatar before it was ordered.' He paused for a moment, then, 'Bank accounts, everything. Especially those who frequent Second World. I expect them to spend a great deal of time in games areas. Technological games. Someone with a high degree of digital experience and ability. I want a deep trench investigation. I'll be up in a minute.'

He hung up and swung his legs off the desk. He walked along the corridor, past the Director's blue-doored office and called one of the twelve express lifts that served the building. He recalled the conversation earlier, with his boss, who was now visiting a new satellite installation in New Zealand.

'You'll be flying solo,' the Director had informed him. 'I can't get back in time. Call me if you get a breakthrough or you need some heads banging together. Just get that fella back into the White House.'

Swilkin respected his Director; he didn't interfere too much, but always protected the agency.

'We had a heavy user in the Hungarian Zone pushing for information on Que.' Mike Tyrrell told him as he entered the main sector. Tyrrell was Head of the WebSearch section.

'When?'

'For a couple of hours. It stopped about fifteen minutes ago.'

'Why wasn't I informed?'

'You were in thinking time,' came the smiling reply. They all knew how he hated being disturbed. 'We got an agent out there.'

'What's the place?'

'Small cybercafe in Budapest. Full of hackers.'

Swilkin showed a sudden interest. 'Anyone we know?'

'Not sure. The signals were to various cybercafes on the Brick. All asking about Que. We're having some difficulty getting full transcripts. It's mostly trashcoded stuff.'

'What host computer?'

'Couldn't trace it. Probably stolen. Could be MIW.'

'I thought they'd be involved.' Swilkin was pleased that part of his theory seemed true.

'They started transmitting about Que a short time after Monroe was found in the Gallipoli.'

'OK. What else?'

'Conor Smith. English. We're downloading right now from GCHQ.' Tyrrell turned to watch the screen that was linked to the Benhall spy centre. 'He's quite a guy, you know. A GameMaster. Started as a hacker, then turned cracker when he was a kid. For the Brit police. After that, and then a long time with the cops, he went back to school and became a GameMaster.'

'Who with?'

'ThemeCorp.'

'Track his CompuPhone, find out where he is.'

'He's blocked it out. I think he was with the hackers who traced Que. MIWs. I mean, the stuff was going out on Que from the cafe and it stopped just before Smith reported where they'd find him.'

'I never even heard of him. I thought all GameMasters were famous.'

'Some keep to themselves. Smith's psycho about his privacy.'

'What's he hiding?'

Tyrrell shrugged. 'He just turns up to work and keeps testing ThemeCorp's games to the limit. He usually cracks them before anyone else does. I read about him once. Doesn't hang around with the fame crowd, doesn't expect something for nothing. Doesn't flash his money or arrive on

Second World in a big car or with his own aircraft transport. You wouldn't recognize this guy if he walked right up and punched you in the eye.'

'But he's good?'

'The best. The White House pulled him in because Gallagher knew him'

'Chase that link between Gallagher and Smith. Now, take me through how he tracked down Que.' Swilkin pulled up a chair and sat down in front of the monitor. He watched the information coming through from GCHQ. The depth of their information didn't surprise him; both agencies shared all their resources and used the same storage station for confidential data, which no other service could access, or even knew existed.

'One of the transmissions reported Que was into a sex deal. That he was in Baltimore. So Smith ran a check on all the hotels, cross-referencing them with the name Que in different languages. Found the Russian translation matched, so he passed it on to Gallagher.'

'Neat. Where's he live?'

'In England. Hides away . . . far away from the JunkBelt.'

Swilkin watched the data on Conor's life unfold in front of him. The latest picture of the Englishman came up, taken a few days earlier on a SnoopCam near Dragon Park. Swilkin froze the picture, studied his face before letting the data continue.

Tyrrell looked over his shoulder at the screen. 'Looks older than forty-nine. I mean, this guy's had no recon-surgery, wears no face jewellery, has no record of tattoos, apart from two small ones.'

'What are they?'

'One says 'Hey'. The other says 'Baby'. 'Seems he's just not interested in himself. What sort of guy has so little self-respect that he doesn't care about his image?'

'Or doesn't need to because he's so sure of himself?'

Swilkin let out a low whistle. 'He's a very rich boy,' he

continued. 'Doesn't spend much . . . just leaves the cash in the bank, ticking away, making interest. No expenditure, apart from buying antique Nintendo and PlayStation games. He sure loves using eBay. Christ, he's been paying over the odds for those.' He leant back in the chair as the data streamed across the screen. Shopping visits, fuel used and paid for by eurocredits, tapes of Conor Smith being picked up by RealCams in the streets of Norwich. 'He likes driving his car around. Places he's fuelled up at show a wide spread . . . mostly looking at landmarks in the rural areas. Clearly doesn't like the JunkBelt. Medical records coming up. Did you know he went to the doctor only a few hours ago?'

'No. Why?'

'Says he's got pains. Doctor told him to take a hike. Literally. *Get some exercise and don't bother me.* Told him to get a dog. What sort of medical advice is that? Run a check on some of the doctor's other patients. See if he's as rough with them as he is with Smith. That'll tell us if they're colluding on anything. Hey, now that's interesting . . . he always sign off as Conor Smith?' asked Swilkin, suddenly leaning forward.

'I guess so.'

'Did you know what his WebName was in the old days? He last used it in 2014.'

'No.'

Swilkin pointed at the screen as the information rolled past. 'Condor.'

'What?'

Swilkin stood up. 'Wow! Is that for real, or is he being set up? If he's that clever, why would he allow his name to end up on the bottom of the ransom note? Doesn't make sense.' Swilkin was even more confident now that they were being nudged in certain directions by person, or persons, unknown. *Was it Smith? Bluff, or double bluff?* 'Don't tell the White House yet. Keep this just with us. Send that picture of Smith to the agent covering the Hungarian cybercafe. Then get hold of GCHQ in England. Ask them to arrange for someone to go to his house. I want his cadaver where I can see it. When he comes out of the Web be there and make sure he doesn't run.'

'Guys like Smith don't leave easy and obvious clues.'

'I agree, but whoever's leading this chase wants us to go down that road. So, that's what we'll do. That . . . and just wait.'

At the Cafe Huszar, the Weekenders were rolling in. Cyber-cafe buffs. Having spent most of their spare time in Real-World communicating with friends and strangers on the net, they now visited Second World and would do exactly the same. They used the cybercafes to enter chatrooms under their alter egos, to communicate with others who had the same interests.

The chatrooms were the great dating agencies of the Web. Let your avatar talk dirty, then, if you clicked, arrange an immediate meet somewhere on the Brick. Those who preferred the cafes of the poorer zones liked them because of their anonymity and their cheapness. A dollar or euro-credit went further in a poorer economy. With their portable keyboards and their cheap money, they bagged the tables, bought a coffee or a beer, and plugged into the chatrooms. It was an exciting start to the weekend.

The NSA operative who had been dispatched to the Cafe Huszar found the place much busier than when Conor had been there. He spoke to the barman, who wasn't interested until two hundred dollarcredits were flashed across the counter. 'Yeah,' he remembered, 'some kids and an older guy.'

'What did they do?' continued the operative.

The barman pointed to a corner and told him they just drank coffees and used the screens with their own

231

keyboards. 'They didn't say much. Then the girl appeared to get excited, like she'd discovered something and after that they all left.'

'Together?'

The barman nodded.

'You seen them before?'

The barman nodded again. 'The two kids, you know – MIWs,' he said.

'You sure?'

The barman shrugged an I-know-an-MIW-when-I-see-one shrug, then went to fill up someone's coffee cup.

The operative mobiled the Puzzle Palace and reported to Tyrrell. When he had finished, he turned his phone round so he could look at its small screen. Conor's face stared back at him. He went back to the barman and showed him the picture. 'This the guy who was here?'

The barman nodded.

'OK, describe the kids to me.'

'I'm busy.'

'Where do you live in RealWorld?'

The barman grinned. 'Out of your shitty Yankee jurisdiction. Any more information, you pay.'

The operative took out another two hundred dollar-credits. 'Don't even think about any more. Now describe the kids.'

Four minutes later the operative was back on the phone. 'The barman recognizes Smith. He was here with two kids. I'm playing back the phone recording of the witness identification as we speak. Definitely MIWs.'

He listened to Tyrrell before finally answering. 'The way the barman saw it, something scared the older fella. I think he's gone to ground. And he's taken his team with him.

BOOK THREE

ROLLING THE DICE

It was getting busy everywhere. The Weekenders were hitting the Brick, pouring out of the MetroPorts. Exciting, rambunctious, bawdy, happy, vulgar, narcissistic, selfish, bullying, throbbing, rushing, explosive, nervous, jealous, envious, bitter, uncontrollable, bitchy, dismissive, angry, brutal, loving, hopeful, destructive; you could bounce any adjective onto the Brick and it glued itself to someone.

Each network provider paid to link into the MetroPorts, the exit stations that lined the Brick. Thus it was easy to go to anywhere you wanted in Second World. You looked up your directory, dialled the nearest MetroPort into your computer and were transmitted there, along the quantum network, in a matter of nanoseconds. Once there, wherever *there* was, the user got on the Brick and plugged into a central transporter. It looked like a local bus, but was in effect a high-speed graphics transporter that whisked you to your destination immediately. If you had time to spare, or were just cruising, you ran at Real Time speed and sat back and enjoyed the scenery as it whisked past just as it did in RealWorld. You found the world as you wanted it. From then on you walked, or surfed, the street and buildings. That's how the system worked for the millions of Real-Worlders who visited Second World.

The SkyBoards had come to life, as moving images, vast billboards floating overhead in the night sky. Some were over two hundred feet high and equally wide, selling their wares in a moving kaleidoscope of colour and shimmering images, surrounded by limitless buildings and Web monuments that surged upwards along the high-sided canyon that was the Brick.

COCA COLA and PEPSI still slugged it out, their billboards opposite each other, each trying to better the other.

MERCEDES HONDA – *Drive the vehicle of your choice in Fantasy RaceWorld* – floated over the FORD GM dealership opposite the Smithsonian.

INTERCONTINENTAL HILTON HOTELS.

UNIVERSALDISNEY THEME PARKS. They were everywhere and the lines were already forming. Queues in Second World didn't last long, only a matter of minutes. But the semblance of reality was a necessity and queues were a part of RealWorld Disney. Always had been, always would be.

FUJICANON CAMERAS AND OFFICE EQUIPMENT.

LUCKY STRIKE WEB CIGARETTES – *as safe as houses.* Smoking on the Brick caused you no harm; you could be Bogey and take a deep draw as you moodily eyed up the Lauren Bacall look-alike at the next table. *I'm tough, honey, have a gulp from my dirty glass.* No-smell tobacco was the latest craze.

THEMECORP'S 'THE DRAGON PARK'. The Dragon Park was, and had been for four years, the greatest of the games. Most people lasted no more than the primary level, scary stuff for the everyday dragon hunter before they went off to Disney's SPACE MOUNTAIN or ThemeCorp's SHOOT THE NIAGARA FALLS where you went over the rapids in a barrel and lived to tell the tale. The real aficionados fought their way up in Dragon Park, hoping one day to meet the Golden Dragon and enter the Enchanted Castle.

VIAGRAVILLE HOTELS *for the elder citizen.* The Brick's first and longest-lasting offering.

THEMECORP'S LITTLE LAS VEGAS. It was one of the first casinos on the Brick, slightly faded now, a palace that had earned ThemeCorp a fortune but had been overtaken by the new gambling dens which proliferated in Second World.

JACKIE'S MARTIAL ARTS CENTER.

THE GREAT SIXTIES ROCK CONCERT WITH THE BEATLES AND THE ROLLING STONES. *Watch John Lennon sing 'Imagine'.*

MOONSCAPE WALKS.

THE ROARING TWENTIES. BECOME A G-MAN WITH ELLIOTT NESS AND TAKE ON AL CAPONE. There you were shot at, but you could move in DreamMotion, the ultimate SlowMo wired into your JetPax, and thus dodge the bullets as they came at you. Then, while they reloaded, you took out your snub-nosed and blew them away.

RECON SURGERY. IF YOU DON'T LIKE IT, CHANGE BACK. A billboard advertising a RealWorld address.

VISIT ELVIS PRESLEY WORLD. *Meet Elvis and his twin brother, his dad Vernon and mom, Gladys. Meet the whole family. This week's special song is 'HeartBreak Hotel'. Be Elvis' Teddy Bear and he'll sing just to you. Only $40 and you get a KeepMe video.*

Friday night. It was when corporations and the little men who had invested in the Brick made or lost their fortunes. It was a consumer's world. Once the crowd lost interest in their products, once they turned to the latest offerings, businesses collapsed as quickly as they had been launched.

Capital was king on the Brick.

The whole place reverberated with music; a constant carnival. There were no language barriers, since all avatar translators immediately turned their host languages into English. It didn't matter whether you spoke Swahili or Dutch, it always came out as English, and the reply was translated back into your own speak.

The Weekenders hid behind their images. Clerks from Clerkenwell disguised themselves as rich playboys; married mothers from Margate and Maine were single again and on the lookout for their past. It was impossible to find the truth behind any avatar. That is, until they had to dip into their pockets and produce their debit cards. The Brick worked on credits; as they paid, so their credits were changed into dollars, or dollars into yen or rupees, by an automatic, Real Time, currency converter.

The shops were all open now. Versace, Chanel, Polo, Woolworths – everything for a dollar only. The old and famous names still commanded the high prices and exclusivity for those who could afford it. The jewellery and clothing bought on the Brick could only be worn on the Brick, but it showed the manner of man, the value of the person behind the puppet. The great shops filled the great boulevards. New Bond Street, Worth Avenue, the Champs-Élysées, all in their own national zones, whole streets paid for by the shops in RealWorld who didn't miss out on anything in Second World. The jewellery, the special clothes, no more than individualized software, were stored in bank safes and special secure storehouses that were found on most blocks.

There were also the knock-off areas, where shops, usually on short tenancies, pretended to be what they were not. In there the same Versace, Chanel and Polo items were on sale at much lower, almost give-away prices – cheap software imitations often picked up by the WebCops who recognized such counterfeit items because they lacked the original copyright codes. But, for many avatars, it was worth the risk; the ability to wear a St Laurent outfit for even one night for only a few dollars, it was irresistible.

'This is a crazy place,' said the Voice, as he walked along the Brick, watching the crowds. His arm was linked through the President's; two old friends sauntering expectantly through the swarm of Weekenders. 'Crazy, crazy, crazy. You know, I just love it. We're all descending into madness . . . silly, but I really do feel quite at home here.'

Teddy Dixon turned and eyed him through the slits in his mask. He saw Andy Warhol's face looking back at him.

'You like my mask?' said the Voice. 'I bet you'd like to know who you now look like.'

Dixon turned away and watched the crowd. He wasn't tempted to suddenly tear the mask from his face and shout for help. He knew the breath would be instantly crushed from his lungs, that he would be spirited away from this busy place before he got out more than a few words. He realized how bold his kidnapper was to bring him out into such a public place. Only minutes before he'd been still snoozing, in Elvis's coffin, saving his energy. Suddenly, with no warning, the Voice had been next to him, urging him awake, dragging him up through the damp ground until he was under the lights of the Brick, with a mask strapped to his face, being led past the SnoopCams and WebCops who, for all their supposed efficiency, couldn't help save him.

As he walked, he wondered again what the White House was doing to trace him. He was sure that Annie knew by now. He wondered if she'd seen any of the tapes. He hoped she hadn't seen the ones of him with Marilyn in the Oval Office. He broke into a cold sweat at the very thought. She'd been faced with this predicament before, knew his weaknesses better than he did, had so far always forgiven him, but each time the deeper hurt in her eyes ate away at him. He suddenly cursed his weakness, which had got him into this mess, and had probably hurt her once again.

He turned his mind away from her and back to the White House. Don Clancy would be running the search for him. He was Senior Agent right now, with his boss away in New Zealand. And the NSA, too: they'd be involved, with all their tracking equipment. They were probably looking at him right now, their image-identifiers scanning the crowds all along the Brick. If only he could take off this mask, just for a full minute, without the Voice finding out.

'Hey, see that,' said the Voice next to him. 'Now that's fancy marketing.'

He looked across the road to where Princess Diana, the

British Royal fashion icon from the last century, sat outside Versace, surrounded by young men. They chatted away, laughed, shared their jokes, tilted their champagne glasses as they sat on the pavement chairs outside the fashion store. After a few moments, Gianni Versace, the founder of the fashion empire who had been gunned down by a spree killer in Miami, came out and joined them. It was a scene that the avatars would replay frequently throughout the weekend, playing out the same scenario for each new group of Weekenders who passed by.

'Crazy. They must've paid some cash for that little number. Hey, how about her instead of Marilyn?' The Voice giggled. 'No, not your style. Too classy for you, Teddy Boy.'

Dixon wondered again why they were out there on the Brick. The Dark Areas had been the best hiding place. The coffin had been equally effective. It showed the Voice had immense programing skills. So why walk about where they could be discovered? It suddenly hit him. The bastard wanted everyone to know he didn't care, that he controlled the situation.

'How's your energy, Teddy Boy?' The Voice continued. 'I hope you slept well. Don't want you beat and worn out.'

'What's the ransom?' asked Dixon.

'Why?'

'They won't pay.'

'Depends what I want.'

'That's the order. Whoever it is, you don't pay.'

'Maybe I've got other ways of getting my reward. Maybe you're just part of a bigger picture.'

'Like what?'

The Voice shrugged. 'Time'll answer that one. Say, do you think the NSA are in on this?'

'No doubt.'

'With all that super equipment they've not been very successful. Hey, if you get back, you better ask them what they're doing with that big budget of theirs.'

'Why're we out here, where we can be seen?'

'We're one of fifty million, all out enjoying ourselves. Your boys think they can see. Truth is, they're blind.' They walked for a while, past two WebCops giving street directions before the Voice spoke again. 'You ever considered how little freedom we have these days?'

'People are pretty free.'

'Bullshit. I'm talking about the freedom to do what they want to do. Without any interference; without being watched all the time.'

'That's how we protect.'

'Protect who?'

'The people.'

'Like hell. The only thing you're doing is protecting yourselves – from the people. Do you think they have any idea of how much you've infiltrated their lives? Do you think they'd stand for it if they knew?'

Dixon shook his head sharply. 'We've got laws protecting the public from snoopers. Including our own Security Services.'

'Some laws,' came the dismissive answer.

'I'll protect that freedom with everything I've got.'

'Cut the party political bullshit. It's only me listening. But you have no idea about real freedom, about what's going on around you. You're as blinkered as the rest of us. Why? Because you've got your head stuck so far up women's pussies that you've no idea what's going on.'

'So tell me.'

'Not yet. The time'll come. And when it does, I hope to hell I'm wrong and you turn out to be as decent as you say.'

Dixon looked into the eyes of the man who was now Andy Warhol. They were angry. And for a moment, for an instant, he felt he recognized the man in the mask.

The Voice pushed Dixon onto a high-speed transporter and they found neighbouring seats in a crowded carriage.

The Voice slid his debit card through the swipe and the transporter moved off.

'You won't trace me through the card,' he told Dixon. 'That's if you ever get back.'

Dixon made no comment. He knew there was a healthy market in stolen and forged debit cards. He looked round the transporter. Nobody seemed concerned that he and his companion were wearing masks. This was Second World and many would see stranger sights before they all returned to their homes, ready for a Monday morning back at the desk. He wondered how many fellow passengers were Americans, how many would come to his defence if he declared himself. *Not many*, he thought wryly. Nobody trusted politicians any more. Anyway, if he did show himself, they'd probably disbelieve him, just think he was another nutty avatar on the loose. He turned his attention to the pavements and shops that sped past on the Brick. They were going into the cheaper rental areas, more rundown and squalid than the haute couture shops and Weekenders he was used to. He recalled the various trips he'd made to the Brick, sometimes with Annie, but always surrounded by a Secret Service squad, always in an avatar form that no one recognized. Two stops later, and deeper into a collection of ramshackle buildings, they finally disembarked.

'This is one of the first areas opened in Second World,' said the Voice, as the transporter pulled away. 'I don't suppose you've ever been down this way before.'

He wondered what awful contrivance the Voice had in store for him. The area seemed vaguely familiar, somewhere he'd been in the past. He turned to his keeper and shook his head.

'Wrong again, Mr President,' the Voice continued. 'This was the second community shopping mall constructed on the Brick. The first in the American Zone. You opened it, the young senator from Alabama.' He pointed at a shop on the corner, a general amenities store which had seen better days. 'Right on that corner. You cut the tape and went in and bought a guide map for the Brick. Hell, it was all really small then. Nobody imagined it could get this big.'

Dixon remembered. This had been a bright place then. He remembered the shopkeeper's bright, freshly washed face, so proud of his new business. There'd been a crowd of about two hundred: all avatars, all pleased to be in the new world. But, in the intervening years, time had not been kind to this small corner of the Brick.

'Sunshine and Hope Mall' said the sign over the entrance. There wasn't much sunshine and hope here. It was like any small, dilapidated and ignored shopping mall in the US. All that was missing were the drunks with their paper-bagged bottles who littered the pavements elsewhere. Buildings on the Brick, just as in Second World, needed constant maintenance. Otherwise, without regular software updates, they lost their newness, the Brickwork developing holes as cubits were lost in the protocol of the whole massive network. As software improved, it discarded the older software, left it standing dark and alone in the newness of an ever-expanding Second World. There was no need to change things, however. The Brick was simply so large that the developers rolled on, past the old, taking their new junk into the next Dark Area. One day, maybe in a hundred years or so, they'd be back here when they'd run out of space. Then they'd rip down this old stuff and start all over again. Just like in RealWorld. *Create the ghetto, rip it up and build it again.* He suddenly felt very sad, not because of his own plight, but because of lost ambitions and forgotten dreams. He hoped the shiny-faced shopkeeper had survived, gone from strength to strength.

So long ago, so much water under the bridge.

'Damn you,' he swore at the Voice. 'I don't give a fuck what you do.'

The Voice laughed at him. 'You will if I turn off your lungs again.'

'I'm getting so I don't care any more.'

The Voice continued to laugh, and walked into the same corner shop. Dixon paused, but as he recalled the pain, his resolve disintegrated. He stood there, angry and ashamed of himself. It was his own weakness that betrayed him, that not only put him in this position, but now imprisoned him there.

He followed his jailer into the shop.

There was no response to the policeman's first knock. PC Giles Renreth was a plodder who had left the InnerSprawl MetPol fifteen years earlier to await his retirement in the rural peace of Norfolk. At fifty-nine he was just eleven years off his gold watch, and the one thing Renreth had no intention of doing was jeopardizing that eventuality.

He'd been parked in the country lanes near Long Stratton, had another three hours till he finished his shift, and was enjoying a quiet soft-narco smoke when his radio suddenly crackled. It was the Superintendent in Norwich ordering him to go to Rose Cottage, some seven miles away. The Super, a known nine-to-fiver, was in a bad mood, no doubt at being wakened early in the morning by someone important enough to drag him out of bed. Renreth realized something important was up; it had been a long time since the Super had gone into HQ at seven in the morning.

'See if Conor Smith's in,' instructed the Super. They all knew Conor – or of him. He was one of eight British GameMasters and the only one who lived in Norfolk. 'If he's there, tell him you've been ordered to keep him there. Nicely, mind. Some Yanks are on their way from London – they want to interview him. You give them every possible assistance you can.'

He knocked louder the second time, then shouted Conor's name. When there was still no response, he walked round the house, peering in through all the windows. There was definitely no sign of the GameMaster. Renreth checked the garage and found the car was there. He'd seen that car often; it was an old, well-preserved PeugeotFiat four-wheel drive EconoCruiser.

He went back to the front door and called Norwich. After he reported his findings, or lack of them, he was told to wait for the Americans. Before he switched off he heard the Super calling for the traffic cops to keep an eye out for Conor Smith, probably on foot or a bicycle. Renreth returned to the prowlcar and waited.

The people he was supposed to give full assistance arrived ten minutes later, the *chupchupchup* of the helicopter coming from the west. Renreth watched the lights of the chopper as it circled the house before descending to the field in front. When the rotor died, two men jumped out and came over to him. He watched them approach through the morning gloom, guided by the torch he pointed.

'Philip Neville, EI5,' said the first man on reaching him. He held up his ID card.

Renreth recognized the EuroIntelligence insignia. He nodded at Neville. 'I was told to expect Americans.'

'That's me,' said the other man. 'You sure he's not inside?'

'I banged loud enough to wake the dead. Couldn't see nothing, either.'

'Could be in the Web.' The American walked past him to the front door and examined it. 'And the car's still here, huh?'

'In the garage.'

'OK. Let's break this door down.'

'I need a warrant.'

'Tell him,' the American instructed Neville.

'We don't have one,' admitted the EI5 man. 'But this is a matter of national security.'

'I'll have to call my Super . . .' Renreth paused when he saw the American pick up a large stone. 'I wouldn't do that, sir,' he warned.

The American ignored him and broke the window. As he reached inside and unlatched it, Neville shot a polite but firm warning at the policeman, who had no idea what to do next. These were top security officials who were breaking and entering private property. But he'd been told by the Super to give every possible assistance. He decided not to risk his pension, so shrugged his non-committal assent to Neville.

'You stay here and keep an eye out for Smith,' barked Neville. 'We'll be inside – and if anyone turns up, apart from Smith, tell us but don't let them in. And don't come in yourself unless we ask you to. Understood?'

Every possible assistance. 'I'll stay here and keep watch, sir.'

The American had opened the window and climbed into the house. A minute later the hall light went on, then the front door was opened. Neville entered, closing it behind him.

Renreth settled down, relieved that he hadn't been forced to compromise himself further by illegally going into Rose Cottage. He let out a loud sigh. This was the first major incident he'd been involved in since he left the InnerSprawl, and he was glad he'd escaped to the country. Neither did he like the two men who'd arrived by helicopter. They had disturbed his patch. And that definitely didn't please PC Giles Renreth.

'OK,' said Swilkin as he viewed the big central plasma screen that dominated the bank of monitors. 'Go find him.'

The Telephone Exchange was now linked, through GCHQ, to the small camera that Neville and the American from London, Jim Piercello, had taken into Rose Cottage with them. The house was plainly furnished, the hallway's stone-paved floor and white-painted walls providing the first glimpses of Conor's simple lifestyle.

Swilkin and Tyrrell both stood, while Marlin sat in a chair to their right.

'Did you attempt to get into his Second World house?' asked Marlin.

'Yes. I think it's a copy of what we're looking at,' replied Swilkin, his eyes never moving from the screen. 'We tried to crack it, but he's good. It'll take hours, maybe days for us to hack in. He's got one of the best security systems I've ever seen. Designed it himself, I guess. Every time you get in one door, another code comes up and you start all over again. It's a PGP for quantums I've not come across before, and he'd make a fortune if he marketed it. But, then, he's already worth a fortune.' He considered the transmitted images for a while. 'What I see goes with what I expected.'

The camera, carried by Neville, showed a view of the bedroom. It was the first room on the right of the hall. There was a monastic look about it. A single bed, a loose-standing wardrobe, a small farm table serving as a dressing table with a stool in front of it, and a small mirror on the wall were the only furniture there was. A pile of books lay on the floor by the bed.

'I broke a window to get in,' explained Piercello's voice as the camera showed the broken panes.

'What're the books?' asked Swilkin, not much concerned with the agent's actions to gain entry.

'*Oliver Twist. Bleak House. A Programmer's Guide to Quantums. A Gift of Wings . . .*'

'What's that?' asked Marlin.

'Writer called Richard Bach. Fanciful book about flying.' Swilkin tried not to show his annoyance at the interruption.

'A couple of Stephen King books, two paperback westerns, a Webster's dictionary,' continued Piercello. 'Google-Pages for various zones on the Brick.'

'No new writers?'

'No. Pretty much all from the last century.'

'What zones do the GooglePages cover?'

'US, England, Hungary and New Developments.'

'OK. Let's go next door.' Swilkin turned to one of his assistants. 'Run those GooglePage zones and see if you can get anything on his phone bills where he contacts people or organizations on a regular basis.'

'Wasn't the cybercafe in the Hungarian zone?' asked Marlin.

Swilkin nodded. *How the hell did someone so slow witted get to be National Security Adviser?*

The camera pictures continued back into the hall and then crossed to the room opposite. It was also a bedroom, very similar to the other. In one corner there was a group of computers laid out on tables. The camera showed them to be a varied selection of machines going back many years. 'Most of this stuff is pretty ancient,' said Piercello. 'Collector's items. But it looks like it's all wired up and in working order.'

'Cupboard's full of old software as well,' added Neville. 'Classic material. Beats anything I've ever seen, even in a museum.'

They watched the camera leave the room and enter a small area next to the sitting room. It was packed with the latest quantum hardware. There was a leather chair in the middle, an old sea captain's chair, facing a big screen that dominated the wall between the two main computers. Swilkin heard one of the agents whistle, confirming what he already knew. Conor Smith certainly enjoyed the luxury of the latest cutting-edge technology, and he had equipment at his disposal matching anything to be found in the Telephone Exchange. *That's what happens when you blur the line between security and commerce.*

'Next room,' he called.

They walked into the sitting room, more comfortable than the starkness of the bedrooms, but the furniture was dated. The large sofa faced a second plasma screen that hung on the wall. Someone had left a message on the screen: THE CONDOR IS SOARING UP HIGH, WAY ABOVE YOUR CLOUDS, TO FIND YOUR PRESIDENT.

'Shit,' swore Swilkin. 'He knew we were coming.'

'How the hell . . . ? joined in Tyrrell.

The two men looked at each other.

'Find him,' yelled Swilkin into the microphone. 'Find Smith. Get that English flatfoot to help you. Dammit, find him.' He swung round on Tyrrell. 'Get GCHQ to dig deeper. Pull every favour we've got. Then put an extra team in here. Find out if he's hacked us. Check the White House as well.'

'What makes you think he's intercepted us?' asked Marlin, alarmed at what may have been unleashed. At least he himself hadn't made the decision to involve the privateer. That had been the VP's choice.

'Because the White House specifically cut off all external signals before they deciphered that ransom note. We were the only two organizations who read the note. And as far as

Condor being his WebName ... only we knew that. We didn't even tell the White House.'

Marlin was startled by Swilkin's admission. 'That's not what we agreed,' he protested.

'I took the decision, sir. I didn't want anyone warning him.'

Marlin was thoughtful for a moment. He glanced at the Telephone Exchange plasma screen. The camera had shifted off the message in Rose Cottage and was now roaming the rest of the sitting room. 'It wasn't our investigation,' he said eventually. 'The understanding was that it came under Secret Service jurisdiction.'

'I'll inform them right away,' was Swilkin's sarcastic reply.

'The VP ordered that specifically. Dammit, he could be anywhere in Europe now.'

'Then the President's dead. That's if it is Condor and he's disappeared into RealWorld.' Swilkin didn't show his irritation that Marlin had missed the obvious. 'But I don't think he's dead, any more than Condor's gone walkabout. No, he's more likely moved to a new location, then gone back into Second World.'

'He's probably got an accomplice,' suggested Tyrrell. A warning look from Swilkin didn't encourage him to continue.

'I don't think so. He'll want to be close to his man when he sends the second demand.' He turned away from the plasma screen and shouted across the large room. 'Phil, I need satellite time.

'The Brits are already using Dollersat. Want me to link in?'

'No, use our own. Get something focused on this East Harling place. Scan at least thirty miles all around, especially the roads heading towards London. This boy came from down there and he could still have friends there.'

Swilkin watched as the camera continued its investigation. He realized there would be few clues there as the

GameMaster would have covered his tracks. He spoke quietly to Tyrrell, 'Get me a list of Smith's friends and contacts. Break his past down and see if there's someone from his younger days who lives up there, a close friend who'd go out on a limb to help him. Get his movement habits, for shopping trips, everything, and set the Snoop-Cams to pick up his image. I don't believe he's taken a runner. I'm convinced he's still in Second World.'

'Why?'

Swilkin grinned. 'Because he likes this game. It's for real, and he's going to do his damnedest to win.'

'There's a lot at stake.'

'There is, but I'm not convinced he's got the President. Even if he has, he'll do his best and lead us to him. That's what the game's about.'

I took the UpScalator out of MetroPort 913 with a raft of Weekenders. They disgorged themselves onto the Brick, joining the shifting mass that flowed in all directions. The crowds were denser than normal, and all the signs pointed to a busy weekend. That gave me more cover, an easier ride in avoiding the SnoopCams and WebCops. It was only a matter of time before they'd get my picture out on the image-identifier system. I mixed with the crowds, keeping low, letting myself be sucked along in the swirl. When I arrived at the message board, and was satisfied nobody was following me, I punched in Andi's PIN: AndiGirl 1602. I leant forward and covered the screen so no one else could read the message.

Her reply was instant: SEE YOU AT PUNKS R US. 6M432K5733. THERE ARE NO SNOOPCAMS FOR AT LEAST TWO BLOCKS EITHER SIDE OF IT. WE HAVE NEWS.

I deleted the message instantly and headed upnumber, past 913 and kept going for another seven blocks. I was surprised at her choice; it was a well-known and popular cafe, although I'd never personally used it. The trip took over ten minutes. I didn't take a transporter as it was almost impossible to avoid the macro SnoopCams in them. Within two blocks of 6M432K5733, I started to run, remembering her message that there was no street surveillance. I kept my eyes peeled meanwhile for any WebCops or KatchVagens that were patrolling the Brick.

I knew this area. The Valley of the Dragons was only a few blocks away where I'd been only ten hours earlier. The thought shook me: I'd been so busy chasing the President that I'd forgotten my time spent in the Web. I felt OK, no tiredness, no blurring, no sudden loss of concentration or lack of direction. I'd be fine for a few more hours – six or seven at the least.

PunkS R Us was a side street cybercafe. Its usual clientele, going by the signs over the door, were skaters, bikers and other racers. The large windows on each side of the wooden door were covered in old newspapers to keep passers-by from peering in. Surprisingly, considering its upmarket location, there were hints of decay and missing cubits on the outer structure. I guessed being shabby was part of its tradition, and that it was really a well-maintained, well-used and profitable establishment. Its clientele were probably well-heeled business people living their own peculiar vision of an underground life; they probably rode Harley Davidsons, wearing skull helmets, in RealWorld. A sign over the door, MEMBERS ONLY, confirmed that.

The interior was just as simple and extended the deliberately decaying look. Ten wooden tables took up the middle area, each with four chairs and with two computer flat screens engineered into their work surfaces. A bar, serving alcohol and soft drinks, encompassed half the wall directly facing the entrance. To the left and right were private booths, similar to those found in old-style bars. Each booth had a long table with simple benches on either side. Similar booths lined the remaining wall space next to the bar, and there was a small door to one side that said DINING ROOM.

PunkS R Us was already busy and all the computer stations were occupied. Nobody took much notice of me as they were all engrossed in their screens. But I knew that because I wasn't a regular, I was being carefully watched. The fact I wasn't intercepted meant someone had OKed my entrance. Most of the screens had games running on them, the contestants playing others in the same room, at separate monitors. Such places had a gambling reputation: high rollers, illegally wagering on their ability to trounce each other in top-quality video games. The Brick had only certain areas set aside for gamblers; since all gambling had been brought under control many years before, after Weekenders had lost fortunes and found themselves bankrupt on returning to RealWorld. The various international Mafiosi had then controlled the gambling, just as they did prostitution and other illegal sexual activities. It had resulted in governments slapping down severe restrictions in Second World aimed at safeguarding its visitors.

Andi and Tebor both sat in a corner booth. Tebor was working a keyboard and he made a point of ignoring me. She, however, gave me a big warm smile. In spite of the sense of danger it still made me feel good. I slid in next to her, noticing there were mini-scramblers positioned over each booth. That showed how important the customers here considered their privacy. It meant nobody could pick up what was being said in each booth, not even by those who sat at the next table.

'I thought I asked him not to use his keyboard,' I complained to Andi across the table. 'They'll trace it easily.'

Tebor shook his head, kept his eyes firmly fixed on his screen and went on pounding the keys.

'Don't worry,' she said. 'He's borrowed someone else's. Why such a rush to get away earlier?'

I explained why, on seeing the ransom note was signed 'Condor', I had to protect myself as well as both of them. I told her where I'd gone.

'Will you be safe now? Up there?' *Up there* was somewhere she no longer knew anything about.

I nodded, thinking. *As safe as I can be with half the world looking for me.* 'Any luck while I've been gone?'

'Tebor's discovered a lot more about Que.'

'How?' I didn't tell her the NSA and GCHQ would be running Echelon and looking out for keywords like 'Que'.

She frowned, slightly irritated. 'He didn't use his keyboard, not for that. Just like we agreed. No, he asked people direct.' She waved her hand toward the room. 'This was Que's usual hunting ground, and that's why we came here. This is where he hung out. His favourite place on the Brick.'

'I've never been in here before. How come I wasn't stopped at the door?'

'You're no Gamemaster, you're a kluge,' chuckled Tebor, using a term usually reserved for Heath Robinson devices. 'I thought you dudes knew everything.' He dismissed Conor's lack of importance with a wave of his hand. 'I told them you were OK.'

'We've been coming here for years. MIWs usually get well looked after,' explained Andi. 'Actually, the clients like us. Especially if we're good at accessing the net.'

'And no WebCops sniffing at the door either. Trouble with those robots is you can't pay them off. I mean, how do you bribe a cubit zombie? With android sex?' Tebor giggled at his own joke. 'Hey,' he said in a deeper, throatier voice, 'come here, zombie, and I'll firewire you through your back door.'

Andi laughed with him, then hushed when she noticed my firm-set expression. 'He means . . .'

'I know what he means,' In hacker's terms, *back door* was a hole deliberately left in a piece of software through which service technicians could enter without disturbing the system's security shields. Hackers always looked for the back door before anything else. 'Listen, I don't want to be a killjoy . . .'

'Yes, you do,' interrupted Tebor.

'But, we're running out of time.'

'Why're you still chasing the kidnapper?' asked Andi.

'Because I said I would.'

'But that's changed now. They think you're part of the snatch.'

'Not all of them.'

'I don't understand you. I mean, they could hurt you, really hurt you, if they found you there in RealWorld.'

'And that's the best reason I have for cleaning this mess up.'

She leaned away from him, examined him carefully before she spoke. 'Tebor thinks you might have set all this up. As a game. That you're in it up to your neck.'

'Why should I do that?'

'He says because you're a GameMaster.'

'He's wrong. There're certain games you don't play.'

'But you could've done it.'

I nodded. 'Probably. But I didn't.'

'You have the access codes to the White House. To all those secure areas.'

'You're right. And, if I was that devious, do you think I would've shared them with you. You know how vital those codes are. Even if I'd let *you* have them, do you think he – '. I pointed my thumb in Tebor's direction. ' – would've got them? Being a GameMaster is more than being clued-up on computer protocols. They take you through psychological tests; emotional and subliminal assessments that last for hours over a matter of weeks.'

'But you've done all you can. You could just stop now.'

'Trouble is, I don't know how to back off.'

'So much for the emotional and subliminal assessments.'

She'd got me there. I grinned, then knuckled down. 'So tell me about Que,' I said seriously.

'I want you to win,' she said. 'And I want you safe. You're the only outsider I trust. We MIWs don't hurt each other. We're all trapped in here together, so we need each other. It's the outsiders who hurt us. They take what they come for, and their loyalty is zilch. You're different. You helped me off the drugs, never demanded anything, even asked or suggested. You're my lifeline to the world I've lost. And that's why I'm going to tell you these things.'

She then told me about the NetRunner Odyssey.

In some respects, it wasn't a story I particularly wanted to hear.

The hard reality of finding himself implicated in a serious criminal act was now foremost in the receptionist's mind.

When the Feds turned up, he assumed the guy in Room 237 was some sort of minor crook, just some dickhead stupid enough to get caught.

Jesus, all he'd been asked to do was deliver a bottle of champagne.

After keeping him hanging around for a long time, the Feds had taken him upstairs to Room 237. They made him wait all over again in the hall, away from the door that accessed the room. There were people in and out all the time, frantic movement, all rushing, all urgent, all ignoring him. But he sensed he was being watched, that they wanted to see how he reacted while he waited.

When the paramedics then arrived he presumed the guy was hurt, or maybe he'd taken some drugs.

He looked a fucking weirdo, anyway.

'Am I expected to stand here all day?' he complained to a passing Fed. 'Or can I go back to the desk?'

The officer ignored him, didn't even bother acknowledging that he'd heard. The receptionist stayed where he was, his unease growing. He tried not to show it.

What the hell was going on in that room? He tried to move closer to the door and peek inside, but a Fed came straight out and stopped him, sent him back to where he'd been told to wait. That was when he realized for certain that they were watching him. *How else did they know I was trying to get a look?* Another ten minutes went past before they finally came to get him.

'OK,' said the Senior Officer who stuck his head round the door. 'You want to come in now?'

He approached the door tentatively. The one thing he'd picked up whilst waiting was that, in spite of the urgent movement in and out of the room, there had been no audible protest from the guest in Room 237.

It didn't take long to register that the guy on the bed was dead. Even if he was wearing a dress and high heels. He'd seen plenty of those before, as you did in hotels like the Bentine. But a dead man, that was something he'd never experienced before. He was ushered up to the bedhead, so he could look down closely at the dead man's face. The look of frozen horror and pain repulsed him. He suddenly lurched backwards as the stench of death hit him.

They led him out as he choked down the Cajun chicken sandwich he'd eaten for breakfast. He looked back once as he reached the door. He noticed the champagne bottle on one side and a Fed examining the glass the dead man must've drunk from. That's when he knew he was in real trouble. In the shock of it all, he dropped suddenly to his knees and started to vomit over the carpet and his own clothing. Through it all he was constantly aware that the Feds still watched him closely. When he started to recover, one of them led him into the next bedroom. On entering, they let him sit down. There were two of them, though he didn't know they were White House staff. It had been Don Clancy's idea to run that game.

'That the same guy who booked in?' asked the man who appeared to be in charge.

'I never got that good a look at him,' answered the receptionist. 'Not dressed like that, anyway.'

'You want to go back in there and make sure?'

'No.' The receptionist almost shrieked. 'You guys enjoying this, or something?'

'Yeah, we do this all day, every day.'

'Look, he registered like normal. It's in the book. Like I showed you. And he had no visitors. Nothing.'

'We want to know about the champagne.'

'I told you. It was a UPS delivery.'

'They have no record of any deliveries to the Bentine. Not for more than two weeks.'

'I showed you the delivery note.'

The second Fed moved to the window and slid it open. The chilly February air rushed into the room. 'I can't stand the stink in here,' he said. 'You know, we think you're lying. We think you were given that note with the bottle and told to deliver it to Room 237.'

'If I did that, then I'd tell you.'

'Not if you're going to be charged with murder.'

'Hey, come on.' The receptionist held his hands up. 'The guy's dead, but who says he was knocked off?'

'The bottle with the drugs in it says,' cut in the first Fed. 'And you delivered it. You said that yourself. You took it up and the guy drank from it and then he died. That does more than just involve you. That gives you opportunity. All we have to do now is find the motive.'

'And when he says *we*, he means Uncle Sam.' The second man now closed in. 'That's the whole of the FBI, the White House Secret Service, the local police, the IRS, the National Guard – anybody else we want to pull in. We can have ten thousand law officers with nothing to do except concentrate on you for twenty-four hours a day, seven days a week. Don't tell me we won't find something that's going to drag you down.'

The first Fed spoke again over his colleague's shoulder. 'Scum like you always have something to hide. Do you really want us to find out all your little secrets? Huh?'

'Just tell us, who gave you the bottle?'

The receptionist was shivering, partly from the clammy cold that followed his vomiting, and partly because he now knew he was deeply involved. However much he protested, he was involved because he'd delivered the poisoned bottle. 'I said, I only got the note,' he said feebly.

'Come on, you got to do better than that. We checked every StreetCam for miles. Nothing came near that back alley for over two hours before we arrived. And the nearest UPS delivery was made three streets away. We ran the tapes and tracked the vehicle, and it didn't get any closer. That was four hours earlier.'

'You tell me how it got there then.'

'No,' shouted the first Fed. 'You fucking tell me.'

'Listen,' intervened his colleague consolingly. 'The guy up there ... he's part of something really big. We can't tell you what, but this is fucking ginormous. There's no way a nobody dirtbag like you could be involved in something this important. But if you don't help us now, you'll get sucked in. And you'll soon be in so deep that when you finally come out with the truth, it'll be too late. Nobody'll believe you. If you think you're in trouble now, you wait till that happens.'

'Just tell us then. Save yourself.'

The second Fed, Mister Softee, knelt down in front of the seated receptionist. 'Listen.' He leant forward conspiratorially, having difficulty keeping his composure in the stench of vomit. 'You didn't do anything wrong by taking that bottle up. I believe you when you say you didn't know what was in it, but, don't lie about anything, because that's where you're breaking the law. Perverting the course of justice is what it'll say on the charge sheet. That's behind bars stuff. Tell us, and you're clear. Then you've done nothing wrong.'

'Except he did fucking lie,' yelled the first Fed.

'So he was scared. Everyone gets scared.' The second man

smiled encouragingly at their suspect. 'Come on, help us. That way you help yourself.'

'How can I trust you?' The receptionist was weakening, looking for any door to jump through.

'Because you have no alternative. We're not after *you*. Do you think we're all here just because of you? No. I told you, this is big, very big. Just tell us what happened and then you're out of here.'

'What if someone says that because I took the bottle up, I killed him?'

'We know you just delivered the champagne. You didn't know what was in it. We believe that. Just don't go on hiding things from us.' He leant even closer, spoke quietly yet firmly. 'This is important. So much so, that if you don't tell me soon, I'm going to leave the room and my colleague here will get to work on you. With a lot of help from some of his friends. Now, they don't care if they kill you, because this is about national security. It's important, it really doesn't get any bigger. Why do you think we've all come down from Washington? Just to say hello to you?' The agent leant as close as he could get. 'Do yourself a favour, and get on side.'

He then stood up.

Behind him, the first man moved threateningly closer.

Three minutes later they had the complete story.

With a full description of the man who had delivered the bottle, they set up a direct link with an artist at the White House, and she spoke directly to the shaking receptionist. Then she sketched a primary image. Her drawing pad was linked to a graphics imager that took her simple pencil sketch and started to fill out the features. The sketch was supplemented by information fed in by the agents as they continued asking questions. The supercomputer-generated IdentiPic started to take shape. It then connected to all the databases it was linked to, and began to auto-search for the nearest human face it could identify.

When they finally stopped asking him questions, the receptionist only hoped they wouldn't demand the money he'd been paid to deliver the champagne. *Fuckit, I didn't know what was in it. It's just my tip for doing my job.*

But by then everyone in Washington had lost interest in the receptionist. Suddenly they had a clear, identifiable picture. Finally they could put a face to the man who might have kidnapped the President.

Swilkin paced angrily back and forth in front of the screens. He was furious with Marlin, who had made Swilkin ring Gallagher at the White House and apologize for not passing on the discovery of Conor Smith's WebName. Apologies were not part of Swilkin's portfolio. He had suffered a further indignity even whilst Marlin contacted the VP and explained there had been a problem over information not being passed between the services.

'I have Mister Swilkin with me,' he'd explained, looking sniffily across the room at his subordinate. 'I have just given him a direct order to ensure it won't happen again. Marlin listened for a moment. 'Thank you, Madam Vice President.' He hung up and leant on his desk, in what he considered a masterful pose as he fixed his gaze on Swilkin. 'Don't make me look bad again. The Director tells me you are one of our brightest people, but you've got to play with the team.'

'Yes, sir.' Swilkin had contained his fury. *This was such a waste of time. The President's missing and I'm down here being canned.* 'May I go back to the investigation?'

Marlin shook his head and waved his hand, dismissing Swilkin, who turned and left the room, catching the elevator to the Telephone Exchange.

'Picture's coming through,' said Tyrrell, as Swilkin entered. He could tell immediately his boss wasn't in a good mood.

Tyrrell stood still while Swilkin continued pacing up and down. On the screen a picture, still being focused by IdentiPic, was slowly appearing in front of them.

'Enhance it as it comes through,' Tyrrell told the operative in front of the screen. He turned to Swilkin. 'Want me to transmit this to GCHQ?'

Swilkin nodded. 'Ask them to get any match they can.'

Tyrrell signalled the operative to link the picture to their British partners. The picture, once it was fully received, would be sent to the Imaging section. There they would then scan it, enhance it further, and send it through a system that would automatically start matching it with the identicards and files held on almost every citizen in the US. And in England, where GCHQ would do the same. And Canada. And France. And most other countries who were linked to the Web.

The trouble was that, apart from England, none of the other countries knew they would be taking part in a search for the US President. The reason was given that their man was a potential terrorist that they wanted to pull in for InterNetPol. Neither would they know that their citizens were being scanned by the two largest and most sophisticated security networks in the world.

Swilkin watched closely as the picture began to take final shape. It showed a middle-aged white man with fair hair and sharp features.

Swilkin shook his head. 'That's probably just like ten per cent of the men in the United States. Hell, this thing doesn't get any easier.'

Four storeys below, the computer scanners whirred as they began their search. The machines began to systematically enter areas that officially didn't exist. They began to indiscriminately break the laws that man had created. The same law these machines had been designed and built to defend.

Dixon didn't remember the interior of the shop at all. That didn't surprise him, as it had probably been through several ownerships since then. The old corner store was now simply a small gift and utility shop, selling everything from maps to transporter passes to basic avatar repair software. One man stood at the counter, an unwelcoming expression on his face.

The Voice crossed over to the counter. 'I'm looking for some action,' he said.

'Hey, man,' came the startled reply. 'This is a utility store, and the only action you get here is blowing bubbles.' He reached down and pulled a pack of bubble gum from under the counter. 'We got plenty of that, though.'

The Voice took a quantum SmartPass from his pocket and showed it to the shopkeeper. 'I got a pass from the NetRunner. You want to argue with that?' The Voice put his thumb over the ID pad, then offered the card across the counter.

Dixon watched as the man shrugged, leant over and accepted the card. The President was alarmed to recognize a quantum card. They were brand-new, the latest ID cards used by the military to access the White House and other top security establishments. It worked through the polarization of photons, with each card containing thirty light-traps or cells, minute devices that captured and retained individual photons. By having each cell reflect the light in a different way, the sequence of thirty light-traps, the card's ID number and the user's photograph and name, it was impossible to make forgeries.

The shopkeeper held the card up and examined it in the light. 'You guys cops? Trying to lay something on me, huh?'

'Would I be giving you that card if I was?' The Voice seemed unruffled. 'Come on, run it through and let us in.'

The shop door suddenly opened and a scruffy, unshaven man burst in. He pushed past Dixon and the Voice. 'Hey,' he demanded. 'Give me a lottery ticket.' He passed a debit card over the counter and stared threateningly at the other two men. 'You don't mind me jumping to the front, do you, Georgie Washington?' he asked aggressively, more a statement than a request.

Dixon saw the Voice shake his head. This was the seamy side of the Brick, where polite guys came down to Second World and behaved like arseholes. *The guy's probably a priest.* Queues meant little in the Web. 'No problem,' he heard the Voice say.

They waited while he bought his lottery ticket, then watched him depart, throwing one final menacing look at them before he left the store.

'Shit from the sewer,' commented the shopkeeper. 'Even MIWs have got better manners.' He held up the card again. 'Like I said, who says you're not WebCops.'

'Swipe the card,' urged the Voice. 'If it don't work, then throw me out.'

'I've never seen you before. And you're both hiding behind masks.'

'Just swipe it. It's got my thumb prints all over it.'

The shopkeeper shrugged, then leant under the counter and swiped the card. Nothing happened for a moment, then a green light came up on the till. The shopkeeper suddenly smiled and passed the card back to the Voice. 'Just got to stay careful. Those WebCops get more real every day.'

He turned and flicked a light switch behind him. An

opening appeared in the wall at the back of the store. 'Hurry up,' he urged, 'before someone else comes in.'

'Thanks.' Dixon felt the Voice take his arm and guide him into a small corridor beyond. The opening closed as they passed through and a light suddenly switched on in the darkness. Dixon saw a closed door at the far end. The Voice held him under his elbow and propelled him towards it.

'You're going to enjoy this, Teddy Boy,' the Voice chuckled. 'Just your style. This is an experience you'll never forget.'

They went through the door and entered a small sitting area. Its design was turn-of-the-century Americana, low wooden coffee tables and well-upholstered, leather-buttoned club chairs. The Voice signalled Dixon to sit down, and then pulled up a chair opposite him. As he sat, the door leading out of the parlour opened and a waiter, dressed in white shirt, bow tie and black trousers, walked in.

'Can I get you gentlemen a drink?' he asked.

'I'll have a beer,' said the Voice. 'You got Japanese?'

'Yes, sir. We got Sapporo, Aroma of Yufuin, and Golden Ale.'

'Golden Ale sounds good. What about you, Teddy Boy.'

"I'm fine,' replied Dixon.

'No, you want a drink.' This time it was a command. 'I hate drinking alone.'

'A Coke. That'll do.'

'A Golden Ale and a Coke,' the Voice ordered from the waiter.

'Wet or powder, sir?' The waiter asked.

'Which do you want, Teddy Boy? Up your nose or down your throat.'

'Wet. Please.'

The waiter nodded and left them alone.

'That's what I love about these anything-goes-for-the-right-price joints. They cater for your every wish. Did you ever take real coke, Teddy Boy?'

'No.' Dixon's answer was terse, tight-lipped. After his recent humiliations he was now fully prepared for the totally unexpected, at its worst.

'Not even stuck it up your nose, but didn't sniff?' The Voice laughed cruelly. 'Like smoking cannabis before it was legalized. Smoking but not inhaling. I remember reading one of your predecessors admitted to that.'

'I never tried it.'

'Don't know why. It's a fuck-you world, and you can do anything you want down here. Be as disgusting, as immoral as you want. You can kill, maim, fuck a kid up the arse, eat shit and drink piss, try every drug going, anything. All you need is enough cash in the bank to pay for it. Yet, back up there, when you've gone home to RealWorld, nobody even exceeds the speed limit. They just go about their business, being polite, upsetting no one, nice as pie. Then, if you want to smack someone, clatter them round the head with a baseball bat, you just slip back down here and whack someone. Boom! And never get arrested. Even crime pays down here, Teddy Boy.'

The Voice sighed. 'Makes you wonder what really goes on in people's minds, when attitude is what you wear and your place in society is only as high as your bank balance.' He paused, his eyes now fixed, steadily through the Andy Warhol mask, on Teddy Dixon. 'I come down a lot, you know. Not to places like this, admittedly. I come down to escape, from my job, my friends, my family – just to get some rest. I go to the theme parks. They're great. I play the games, and I'm good. Then I walk the Brick, where nobody fucking cares. Nobody fucking cares.' He leant towards Dixon. 'I'm good at what I do. I'm one of the best progra-mers there is, came out of UCLA with the highest honours. Decided not to just go out and make money. I had some scruples.' He mocked himself as he said it. 'All I ended up doing was watching arseholes like you make a fool of us. Feeding us the illusions you think we want. Making us choke on our own dreams. And how do you do that? By knowing everything there is about us, through our telephones, our credit cards, our movements on street cameras. We even get tracked by satellite. And why?' he shouted at Dixon. 'What the hell do you need all that information for? What the hell can you do with it?'

'To protect you.'

'From whom? From ourselves?'

The door opened and the waiter re-entered, carrying a tray. He put the bottles of Coke and Golden Ale on the table, both with straws in them. 'Would you like your guests to come in now, sir?'

'No,' answered the Voice brusquely. 'I'll call you.' He waved the waiter away.

'Guests?' asked Dixon.

The Voice nodded. 'We'll come to that in a minute. First I'll tell you about watching us, then you tell me how you call that protecting us.' He leant forward and took a sip. 'I was, still probably am, your model citizen. I work hard, don't abuse the system, only take what's due to me. A safe pair of hands, that's me, Mister Average. I got rich, but I was still Mister Average.' He flicked his hand at Dixon. 'Have a drink, and at least look as though you're interested.'

'I am.' Dixon picked up the glass and took a long suck through the straw. It tasted good, fresh and icy. He suddenly realized how thirsty he was. He took another long draw.

'I used to be married. Real women's mag stuff. Childhood sweethearts, great future, two kids. Best love on the planet. Jenny worked, too. Like all modern women, they feel there's something missing if they don't go out and work. It's how it is now: people are mass-produced. If you're a woman and you don't work, then there's something wrong with you. She'd rather have stayed home, and she said so. She liked being with the kids. But, because she felt that was wrong, wasn't as other women – her friends – would expect, she denied herself and did a nine-to-five every day. We had two kids. Girl and boy, thirteen months between them, almost to the day. Funny how you remember those things. Yeah, almost to the day.'

The Voice sipped from his glass. 'They were average, nothing special, just good kids with all the normal hang-ups of good kids. But our boy, Tom, started to drift. He was fourteen, played football – in fact, I think that's where he would've excelled. Great sportsman in the making, just so much natural ability. He didn't get that from me. Anyway, he didn't like coming home to an empty house after school, so he got to hanging round with older kids. Some were on drugs, some pushing drugs. But he kept cool, didn't get sidetracked by them, didn't touch the stuff. They liked him because he was good at sport. Afterwards someone said they protected him from the stuff because they wanted him to succeed, wanted him to win. For them, I guess, it was reflected glory.' The Voice shrugged. 'Who knows? I'm no analyst. Anyway, they looked after him.' He stopped, suddenly lost in his own thoughts.

Dixon, for all the danger he faced, was still a politician, a man who had, by nature, became involved in other's problems. For all his weaknesses, for all his frailties, Teddy Dixon couldn't help but be drawn in by the emotions of his constituents. 'Go on,' he urged.

The Voice looked at him angrily, clearly irritated by the interruption. Then he calmed down. 'Police called round one day, came right into my office. You can't believe how arrogant they were. And they enjoyed coming into one of the most secure places in the country and treating me like dirt. *"We want to talk to you about your son. We have good cause to believe he's selling drugs."* Wham! Just like that. I asked what evidence they had and they produced this SmartDisk. I played it on my machine. He was being tracked by the street cameras, from location to location. There was nothing to tie him in with those others. Hell, he mixed with them, but he never once took anything, or passed on anything to anybody. It was guilt by association. I saw others selling drugs, saw them using them. All types. On every StreetCam that followed them. Christ, I didn't realize just how much we're watched by them, how pervasive they've become. Even though I . . .'

He stopped sharply. 'Doesn't matter, it's not about me. The cops said they were going to pull the gang in. They were no gang. Just kids, individuals, with time on their hands and no one to guide them. I said there was no proof against my kid, but it didn't make any difference. That afternoon, before Jenny got home, they arrested all of them. I went to the precinct house and found other parents there. Some expected it, most were as shocked as I was. Ours was a good neighbourhood. Hell, the kids had just been allowed to grow a little wild. Shit, we're out working hard to give them a better life and they're out of control because we're not there to help them grow up. That was a bad night with Jenny. She took it all on herself, like it was her fault. I said that wasn't so. She didn't listen, just cried all night, blaming herself for what had happened. You know, the real trouble was she didn't know how to cope. We've all been so protected, for so long, nobody knows how to handle things any more. Not ordinary people, not burb people. We don't understand real crisis. We go to work, we get paid well, we enjoy ourselves, spend time on holidays, or in the Web or watching TV. It's a perfect life and it's as boring as hell. And then you get slapped in the mouth when something like this happens . . . and you don't know what the hell to do.'

The Voice finished his beer in a final swig. 'He went to court the next day. Got convicted. Twelve months with three suspended. No real proof. Even though all his friends quite clearly stated that he was innocent, that he had never taken or carried drugs for them. You know what hung him? A record of a phone call and an email. The phone call because someone rang him at home, my home, and asked where one of the other kids was. Said he needed a fix and told my boy what he wanted. My son . . . gave him that phone number. That's all. Just passed on a phone number. My lawyer asked the judge whether or not they'd got a phone-tap court order. The judge said it didn't matter because the police informed him that I used a foreign carrier for my phone, because it's cheaper in today's global network. They said, can you believe this, that the call had left US soil and therefore I was as open to being tapped as any foreign citizen.'

He shook his head furiously. 'Now, how the hell did they find out I used an offshore carrier? Same happened with the email. One of my boy's friends was in the house and sent an email from my son's computer to someone who also needed a fix. They had a copy of the email, chapter and verse, as court's evidence. Once more, because we used that foreign phone carrier, it was admissible evidence without the need for a warrant. The guy who sent the email explained it was him and that my boy wasn't even in the room when he sent it. Didn't sway the judge, or the police.' He leant back and stared at the President. 'Is that what you call protecting us?'

'There are appeal courts. There are . . .'

'Sure there are. All following a zero tolerance line that you politicians instigated. Why'd you do that?'

'To meet targets. Law officials had got sloppy.'

'Targets designed solely to make you look better than the other political parties. It's a fucking sham, the way you people behave.'

'The appeal courts will – '

'Do nothing. They tossed it out. He spent seven months in juvenile detention. When he came out he'd changed, hardened up, couldn't give a damn about anything. Just went up to his room and stayed there. Came down for his meals, never said much. Finished school, then just upped and left one day. Disappeared into the JunkBelt. New York, Los Angeles, who knows?'

'When was that?'

'Nearly sixteen years ago. It didn't finish there. Jenny stopped working, just stayed at home, waiting for him to come back. My daughter couldn't take it, not seeing her mom like that. She married the first guy who came along and she's living – if you can call it that – in Virginia. He's a real creep, disappears into the Web every weekend. I dread to think what he gets up to.'

'Your wife OK now?'

'I don't know. I told you, she couldn't hack it. Didn't know how to. Too protected by society all her life. Went to counsellors, they just sympathized so much that they played to her problems. They drown you in your own pity.' He spat out the next few words. 'How the hell do they know what's going on? They're nine-to-fivers, fucking advisers who get paid to make people cry. She almost sobbed herself to death. Then, about four years ago, she got dressed up one night, hooked into the Web and went out. Does that three, four nights a week. I have no idea what she gets up to. Whatever it is, it doesn't make her any happier. So, a year ago, I left home. No point in staying. I mean, we're all dead now. The whole family's fucked.'

'I'm sorry.'

'Maybe you are. Maybe you aren't.'

The Voice slammed his empty beer bottle down on the table. 'You know what really shook me up? When the cops, when it was all over, came to see me again, I listened and still said they had no proof. I lost my temper because one of them said, "They're *all* guilty. You don't need to be holding the stuff in your hand. They're just guilty because they're there." I guess I went over the top and one of them got mad, too. He said I thought I was better than him because of where I worked, that I didn't have to shovel shit all day like he did. "You're so clever. But you know fuck." That's what he said. "But you know fuck." And he told me how much research they'd done on me. Christ, they'd gotten into my bank account, my social security records going back to school days, my navy records, data from phone calls I'd made, emails I'd sent. These guys knew everything about me. Everything. Stuff that should never have been picked up, or should've been destroyed. I realized someone had tracked me, the whole family almost since the day we were born.'

'Where'd they get it?'

'The cops thought I was involved, so when they realized I worked for a government agency they got their superior officer to get information on me. One of the guys admitted he was surprised with how much came back.'

'Which agency?'

'Who cares. But it's not just me who's being watched. It's the whole country. Someone, somewhere, is watching and recording everything.'

'No.' Dixon was adamant. 'No, we have laws to stop that.'

'But you know *fuck*. You think they tell *you*?'

The Voice's dismissive reply stunned Dixon. 'They probably checked up on you because you were in an important job,' the President cautiously continued.

'I did some homework. It had become easier for me over the years. I was in a senior position, head of my section. What I found was that everyone was being watched. From you, yeah, the fucking President, right down to the lowlife in the JunkBelt.'

'I would not allow that.'

'I told you. You know nothing. What I do know is this information's all got to be stored somewhere.'

'Believe me. I really don't know.'

'There *is* a place.'

Dixon noticed the Voice's breathing was suddenly becoming laboured. 'If there is such a place – '

'There . . . is.' He struggled just to get the two words out
'Where?'
'I . . . can't . . . tell . . . impossible.'
'Why?'
'Fuck offff,' shouted The Voice. 'Leave me alone. I can't
say any more.' He leant forward and rang the small bell
under the table.

'Don't take this any further,' pleaded Dixon. 'Let's get out
now. Let me help put this right. I promise I'll protect you.'

'Too late. It won't bring my family back. It's too late for
some of us now.'

The waiter entered the parlour. 'Are you ready for your
guests now?' he asked the Voice.

'Yes, but not in here. We'll go straight to the room.' The
Voice stood up and signalled Dixon to follow him. Suddenly
his authority had returned.

As Dixon stood, he felt his legs go weak. He put his hand
out and steadied himself against the arm of the chair. There
was a wooziness in his head; he was suddenly light-headed
and it took a moment for him to recover his balance. He
wasn't a techno-freak, but he knew avatars rarely suffered
from loss of balance or illness unless they had been programed to. 'What've you done to me?' he asked.

'I want you to be open-minded,' replied the Voice, as he
held out his arm to help Dixon along. The waiter took his
other arm.

'You spiked my drink.' Dixon's voice was husky, throaty.
He felt blurred, yet everything seemed clear, a world slowing
to dream-speed and effortless motion. He allowed himself
to be led from the room. He'd never experienced narco-
sensation before. Like everyone else he smoked cannabis
occasionally to calm himself during times of intense pressure, or to simply relax, but this emotion was distinct, sharp,
pixel-clear and endless.

What started out as a gentle ebbing of sensation now
grew into a tidal wave of anticipation and energy. Colours

sharpened, the men who held his arms became irritations to his greater presence. He shook them off, arrogant in his dismissal, and strode down the corridor towards the door at the end. He would've walked right through it if the waiter hadn't raced ahead and opened it for him.

He felt the blood surge through his veins, felt the sheer excitement and passion of his being rise to a great crescendo of emotion. He wanted to cry. He wanted to shout and laugh. *Hallelujah. Rock and Roll. Twist and Shout.* He had never felt so alive before.

Everything was beautiful.

Everything had meaning.

Teddy Dixon, the President of the United States, was experiencing his first full rush, had reached that same conclusion that every narco-junkie in RealWorld and Second World lived for and sometimes died for.

The bedroom he entered was a simple room. Pretty, with chintzy wallpaper, a small golden chandelier hanging from the ceiling and good old-fashioned farm furniture. The bed stood out: it was a large four-poster with the duvet folded back.

His opiate memory recalled this long-forgotten room.

Claire stood at the foot of the bed.

Sweet Claire. Sweet sixteen.

Golden hair cropped short, grey eyes, a round face, always full of wonder. She was tall, almost an inch more than him. Even so, he always liked her wearing high-heeled shoes; they showed off her wondrous legs that somehow travelled right up to her neck. And her marvellous breasts. Firm and just a bit on the heavy side. Always inviting, always begging to be touched or brushed against as they pushed out against her tight blouse.

'I always loved your breasts,' he said. He tried to take off the mask, but it wouldn't move, seemed glued to his head. He tore at it, but to no avail.

'Leave it,' she said. 'I know what you look like.' She

smiled that wonderful smile he remembered. 'You've been gone a long time, Teddy.'

'You're not angry.' He suddenly remembered how badly he'd behaved towards the end, how he'd suddenly left with no warning for the big smoke, a big university campus and the world he wanted to conquer. He felt the tears well behind his eyelids and the colour of the wallpaper obligingly changed blue to match his mood. 'I'm so sorry.' She'd not wanted to go with him, wanted them to be married so he could take over her father's farm. That would never have been enough for him. They had then argued incessantly, each chasing their own dreams. One day he upped and left, never wrote to her, let his parents explain to the small town where he'd gone. 'I'm so sorry,' he repeated and the room got even darker as it reflected his sorrow.

'It turned out OK,' she said. 'In the end we both got what we wanted.' She gave him a big smile and the sun came out again; the room exploded with light. 'I married Harry Fletcher. Do you remember him?'

He nodded. The high school football star. Another farmer's boy. 'Sure, I do.'

'We had three kids and a pretty good life.'

The Voice spoke from behind, but a distant out-of-sight voice. 'First loves should sometimes be left alone, Teddy Boy. It's something you never replace, and you can never take with you.'

'He's right,' Claire agreed. 'It was so sweet. So special. Wouldn't it be something if we could go back? Feel the same things. You never get that first love again, honey. However much you fall in love.' She came over to him and touched his arm.

He went back all those years, over-eager and youthful sensation coursing through him. He wanted to touch her, crush her to him, feel those breasts against him, do all the things they had learnt so innocently with each other so long ago.

She wrapped her arms round him and crushed his lips with hers. He wasn't aware of the mask, it was all so real, so perfect, so alive.

Sweet petals. Sweet rose petals.

'I missed you terribly,' she said eventually. 'For years, Teddy.' She clung to him. 'I'm so proud of what you achieved. I always knew you were special. So different from everyone else.'

I am different. He felt a rush of pride. *I'm the fucking President.*

'Why'd you marry her?' she asked.

He couldn't tell her it was because Annie came from one of the oldest and richest political families in America, that she'd opened doors for him that made his ambitions so much easier to achieve. 'It was a long time after us,' he replied weakly.

'I don't suppose it had anything to do with her being a Walker-Smith?' she replied mockingly. She knew why he'd married Annie. Were there no secrets down here?

'I loved you so much,' he said. 'I just didn't want to farm.'

She smiled. 'Truth is I didn't want to go to the city either.' Then she kissed him again, her tongue probing his mouth as their sexual senses ignited.

As he kissed her he worked her towards the bed. Then he started to undress her. The breasts first, as luscious and full as he'd always remembered. He nuzzled them as they fell free of the blouse, bit her nipples, heard her groan. Then he stepped back and tore his shirt off. As he looked down he realized his body wasn't middle-aged any longer, was hard and firm and flat-stomached as it had been when he was seventeen. He pulled her towards him again, rubbed her breasts against his chest as he hugged her, felt their firmness as they entwined and clung together to become one. Then they took off their lower garments and were suddenly naked, lying on the bed where they had first consummated their puppy love all those years ago.

It was the first time, all over again.

He rolled on top of her, felt her part her legs and then wrap them round him. He felt her quiver, knew the excitement was just as it had been back then. Wow. That first entry, that first moment when you became a man. Just as he was about to enter her, a hand touched him on his shoulder.

He swung round, startled.

A beautiful woman, with dark bobbed hair, short and about thirty-five, knelt on the bed beside him. She was naked, apart from high heels, stockings and a suspender belt. She smiled an obvious come-and-fuck-me smile. She took her hand away from his shoulder and began stroking her breasts, exciting her own nipples.

'This is my friend Jackie,' explained Claire.

Dixon felt his emotions split. Right inside him, as if he was two people. Part of him wanted to keep the purity he was now remembering with Claire, the other side wanted to enjoy them both. He was back where he always was, living on the edge. The excitement made him shudder as another surge of opiate-passion coursed through him. He gave in immediately to his weakness. He turned round and grabbed Jackie, pulled her down on to the bed, pushing her alongside Claire.

Claire smiled a knowing smile, understanding his weakness.

'Is this what you wanted?' he asked her.

'It's what you wanted.' She pulled him back down on her and started to kiss him.

Jackie, not wanting to be left out, slid down the bed and put him into her mouth, massaged him with her tongue. They continued in this fashion for a while before she rolled over on her knees and pushed herself towards him, offering herself.

'Fuck her first,' said Claire.

'I want to fuck *you*.'

'No. I want to see how you do it with other people. I want to see how experienced you've become.'

He rolled off her, pushed her legs aside and knelt behind Jackie. He pushed into her and they both came alive. It was a tremendous sensation. He had never experienced sex like it, his body fired by the drug, his emotions scattered and then frighteningly focused through the hallucinations in his mind, his senses electrified as he touched her inside.

'Don't come yet,' he heard Claire say from behind. She reached over and stroked him as he fucked Jackie. 'Don't come. Just don't come, my little baby. My little Teddy.'

He knew he wouldn't. The drug had taken him beyond that. It would keep him going as long as it lasted, each stroke, each push a fireball of sensation.

'Fuck *me* now,' he heard Claire shout as she flipped over onto her back.

But he couldn't stop his efforts with Jackie, just kept pumping.

'Fuck her, fuck her now,' yelled Jackie.

'I can't stop,' he replied, pushing harder.

Jackie suddenly pulled away, twisting onto the bed so he was out of her. 'It's her turn. Fuck her,' she demanded.

He swung round to Claire and straddled her.

'I love you,' she cried. 'I always loved only you. Give me what you just gave Jackie. Please. Please.'

He tried, was desperate, but couldn't find her entry. He pushed harder, there was no softness, no slit, nothing. He put his hand down to guide it in. He felt the penis. He felt the softness of the balls. They weren't attached to him. He looked down sharply.

Claire, still beautiful and soft under him, still with the breasts and hair and mouth he loved so much, had become a man where it really mattered.

'Don't you still love me?' she purred. Then she laughed, coarse and hard, and pushed him off.

Behind him he heard Jackie start to shriek at him. 'I told you to do her,' she screamed. 'Do her. Do her.'

He rolled off the bed and fell backwards onto the floor. The two girls hugged each other, then Jackie knelt down and slipped Claire's new penis into her mouth. Claire groaned and lay back as Jackie worked her expertly.

Dixon scrambled to his feet, his eyes still fixed on the couple of women, fascinated by what he saw. As he watched he burst into tears. *Lost youth. Lost dreams. Lost in cyberspace.*

He sobbed. He wrapped his arms around himself and just sobbed uncontrollably. The opiate heightened his anguish, turned his shame and helplessness into tumbling depression. The sobs racked him, he felt them burbling up inside, uncontrollable, wave after wave after wave of despair. The room got darker, the sounds from the bed louder.

Then the drug wore off as quickly as it had taken hold. The light returned. He was still in the room, but there was no Jackie, only sweet Claire. She lay naked on the rumpled bed, her head snapped sideways at ninety degrees to her body, a thin trickle of blood winding its way from her left eye across her cheek. The bed started to fill with blood, a deep red staining and spreading across the sheet.

He stood up, his face blotchy, his eyes stinging from the tears.

'I'd get dressed if I were you,' said the Voice coldly, matter-of-factly. He stood by the door.

Dixon reached for his clothes, dragged them across the floor and hurriedly started to dress. He was deeply ashamed to be seen this way. When he was finally dressed he went to the door. 'Why did you do that?' he asked.

'I only unlocked your mind. Actually, the drug did that. All you did was see your own perversion.'

'Why did she have to die?'

'Why not? Not pleasant, eh, seeing yourself as you really are, Teddy Boy.'

'I haven't thought about her for years.'

The door opened and the waiter came in. 'Will that be all, sir?' he asked the Voice.

The Voice nodded.

'Nine hundred and sixty-two dollars, sir,' said the waiter, holding up the bill. He could clearly see what had happened in the room but he chose to ignore it.

'Have you got your debit card?' The Voice asked Dixon. When the President nodded, he held out his hand. 'Please give it to the waiter, to pay the bill.'

Dixon took out his debit card and handed it over. *Why? They'll trace the card. They'll find me. He must know that.*

'I'll get it authorized, sir,' said the waiter and left the room.

'Pretty good, huh, going back to your first love. That's a pretty common thing, down here on the Brick.' The Voice leant against the door while he waited for the waiter to return.

'Where'd you get her picture? How the hell did you know about her? About this room?'

The Voice shrugged. 'The information's all there: everything about everybody. All I did was look it up.'

'Only Claire knew about us. I mean, no one else did.'

'Don't believe it. Nothing is sacred, nothing is protected. Even the sex you had with Annie's aunt.' The Voice watched Dixon's mouth drop. *Nobody* knew that. 'Or the hit-and-run you never reported. Luckily young Nick Murray lived, but he's in a wheelchair now. Bright young man, too. He now works with handicapped people. Isn't that what politicians do? Change people's lives? You certainly changed his life.'

'Where the hell . . . ?'

'Maybe you should start to take a good hard look around you, Teddy Boy. If you ever get back.'

The door opened and the waiter returned. He handed the card to Dixon. 'Do you need a receipt, sir?'

Dixon shook his head.

'Thank you, gentlemen. Please call us if you need our services again.' He smiled at Dixon. 'It's good to see you, Mr President, whatever the circumstances.' He turned and left the room.

'Where do I look?' Dixon asked.

'If anyone has the power to find the key, you do. Seek and ye shall find. Just remember, you're not the only one who gets touched by those who watch us.'

'Meaning?'

'Did you like Jackie?'

'Some hooker you employed.'

'Sure is.'

'You know some weird and wonderful people.' Dixon's sarcasm wasn't lost on the Voice.

'Both avatars were hookers. The one who played Claire, she's an actress who plays any part. Jackie, well she goes out the same all the time. That's how she looks in RealWorld. She's a great favourite. Anything you want, she'll do. But always with her own identity.'

'You sound as though you know her in RealWorld.'

'I do.' The Voice sighed. 'She was once my wife.'

He shook his head, gave Dixon time to digest that information. 'That's what happens', he continued, 'when you let others rule the roost, Teddy Boy. That's what happens when you lose control. It's the ordinary people who end up losers.' He looked round the room. 'Time to go.'

He grabbed Dixon and led him to the only mirror in the room, a small one by the window. Dixon stared, now seeing the mask. It was a likeness of himself, an illegal one sold in Second World. No wonder the waiter recognized him.

Then Dixon saw the mask lose its brittleness as his own face melted through, saw his own tormented eyes and the blank, expressionless face of the man who was supposed to be the most powerful man on earth staring emptily back at him.

Through the still open door the waiter saw this happen, and gasped when he recognized the President behind the President's mask.

Nothing hurts like the truth. Because you can't change it, can't hide from it.

I know it goes on, and I stopped being surprised by what went on in the Brick a long time ago. It's a place of excess. That's how it was designed. To let people live out their weird, wired and wonderful fantasies in one world whilst being upright and uptight citizens in the other. What the eye missed, the heart couldn't grieve for.

But it's people like Andi who suffer in the end. People for whom the Web is just too big, too overpowering. Not just MIWs, either, but ordinary people who couldn't get their fulfilment in RealWorld, who desperately needed the kicks of the Web. As addictive as any drug, the Web was legal and actively encouraged by those in power. The masses had got their regular opium, and every day millions more hooked in and got their kicks on a habit that couldn't be kicked.

I'm part of it, too, but I know it's going wrong: fantasy and reality slowly merging into one. Suddenly the kicks aren't enough for many. How long before they go for the same thrills in RealWorld? Then what? How do the authorities react then?

Easy, they'll just switch the juice on and take over our minds. Invade us, just control us from their megacorp desks and government offices. Christ, they could wipe out half of the world's population by just switching this place off. Close this

287

environment down and spawn a new one, do the whole thing all over again.

I watched Andi as she waited at the counter to order them a drink. I felt even more protective towards her now. That wasn't an emotion I was familiar with. I shook my head and grinned, remembering the old adage: *there's no fool like an old fool.* And only I would get involved with a spirit, even if I could touch her and ask her to go get me a soft drink.

I went over what she'd just told me. PunkS R Us had started way back when everyone was opening a cybercafe on the Brick. Most had since folded, especially after the bigger companies moved in. Only they had the resources to develop the Brick, to spend money on cutting-edge software that gave them the most modern-designed buildings, the most accessible locations next to the MetroPorts and theme parks, and the latest furnishings and computer-links for their customers. If they met competition from the smaller operators, they used their financial muscle to slash their own prices and force their way into controlling the market. It was therefore Wall Street and the Square Mile banking the Brick. The result, as always when the bankers got their snouts in the trough, was a sell-out to the highest bidder. Some of the cafes moved to lower-rental zones and took a few of their customers with them, usually those with the lowest incomes but the most exciting ideas. In time, the smaller companies withered and died from lack of support. The few good cafes left went after the niche markets. They developed their own styles and were usually ahead of the market, testing new ideas and retaining their individuality, which in time developed into exclusivity. It was a successful cocktail, and some became icons for individuality and freedom from Big Brother's influence.

PunkS R Us had been one of the first. Now it catered to a fashionable membership who paid vast fees so as to keep it out of range of the everyday Brick visitor. The diversity and wealth of its members meant other pursuits had developed over the years. The clients needed their own thrills satisfied, but in the security of a location where they couldn't be identified. It became a meeting place for those with other interests: sex, drugs, gambling, Real Life game boards. Apart from gambling, none of these activities took place on the premises, but it was a clearing house, a meeting place for those who went beyond the rules of the Brick. PunkS R Us had such a developed and sophisticated supercomputer network that no outsider had ever hacked it, in fact as good as any top international security service.

This wealth and cybersecurity brought in carpetbaggers like Simon Que, the pimps who could provide anything. They masqueraded as programers, as rich members of the cafes. They paid the high fees because it was their office. It was where they came to satisfy the members' needs in the Dantean inferno of the Brick.

They were the NetRunner Odyssey: a group that provided everything for anyone who had the ability to pay. On the Brick it was bigger than the Mafia or any other band of criminals. It didn't concern itself with cheap prostitution or furtive narco-deals in back alleyways. It dealt exclusively with those who had access to power or money. In that way, because of its list of powerful contacts in RealWorld, it easily protected the environment in which it flourished.

The owners and managers knew what Que and his sort provided to their members, but they deliberately kept their eyes closed and mouths sealed.

Que's friendship with Andi and the rest of the MIWs was based on earning them credits whilst they helped fulfil the members' dreams. It was an easy relationship; both sides offered something the other needed. The boy needed the credits for his narco-habit. Andi had the same requirement until recently.

'It doesn't matter,' she'd said earlier. 'I mean, I'm only an avatar.'

'That's dangerous,' I'd replied. 'You could catch something.' I referred to various sexual viruses that had been introduced into the Web years earlier by obsessive hackers, which could destroy avatars slowly and painfully like AIV: the Avatar Internal Vortex. 'And if you did, you'd just get eaten up. The worm inside would fill you, then you'll *never* get back.' I remembered Marilyn's dead body sprawled on the bed.

She shrugged. 'I said, it doesn't matter. Now I'm clean I don't need to go that route.' She'd changed the subject. 'Que was top dog here. He helped start NetRunner. He knew top people, I mean, really important guys, with plenty of credits. They loved him because he always got them what they wanted.'

I gathered that the clientele here were all rich individuals, many of them household names. They were merely thrill-seekers, not serious or committed enough to kidnap the President. Some were obvious serial-typos, killers, rapists, molesters, muggers and all the other crimes that thrilled people and kept psychoanalysts in full employment.

'You don't think it's one of them, do you?' asked Andi when she had gone through most of the people she had associated with.

'Who knows?'

'They're bad people.'

'Sure. But they're serial-typos, all acting out the same stereotype crimes. This guy's different. He's a pro. Probably very straight.'

Tebor broke away from the screen and leant across the table. 'Straight, like Jim?'

'What's he talking about now?'

'Jim's good. Like you said, straight. Not like the rest of the weirdos.'

She took over. 'There's this friend of ours, called Jim. He and Que got very close. They used to sit in a huddle, always whispering. I mean, no one can hear at these tables, anyway.

That's why they put the scramblers up. You just can't break into conversations, but, whatever they talked about, it was pretty secretive. I mean, for them to huddle together and whisper when they know nobody can hear anyway.'

'How long ago was that?'

'They started meeting . . .' she looked to Tebor for confirmation '. . . about a year ago, maybe longer.' When he nodded agreement, she turned back to me. 'Last time I saw them together was two weeks ago.'

'Here?'

'Yeah, always here. It's safe.' She paused and thought for a minute. 'You know, Que went missing about then. I mean that was the last time I saw him.'

'Careful, he might think it's Jim,' warned Tebor.

'No way. Not Jim,' she reacted to the suggestion strongly.

'Why not?' I asked.

'Not his style. Like Tebor said, he's straight. He used to be with the US government.' She turned to Tebor. 'Didn't he give Que the key?'

Tebor shook his head. 'Only to me. Que didn't know about the key.'

'What key? Suddenly I felt another door opening; that same shiver down the back of my neck I always got when I was near to cracking a game.

'To the Dark Areas,' she replied. 'I told you we could get there.'

My breath stopped. This was a whole new level. Something I'd never even thought about before. 'Que gave you the key?'

'No, he didn't have one. Jim gave one to Tebor.'

'Why?'

'He wanted me to be safe,' said Tebor. 'Gave me the key and said then I'd always be safe.'

'Why you?' I spoke too sharply. I then lost the boy.

'Why do you think? Because he liked me.' Tebor shrugged dismissively and went back to his keyboard.

'Did Jim ever say anything about what he did?' I turned to Andi.

'No. Tebor tells me everything. We share everything. That way we both know what's going on. But he never said what he did. Just that he worked, or used to work, for the government.'

'And the key. How did *he* get it?'

'Never said.' She turned to Tebor. 'Did he?'

'No.' Tebor concentrated on the screen in front of him, never even turned to them. 'Only that he got it from the department that looks after the Brick.'

'Have *you* got the key?' asked Conor.

'Sure.' He slid it out of his pocket and pushed it across the table.

Conor picked it up and examined it. A white quantum SmartCard. Printed on the card were the words GOVERN-MENT SECURITY COPY. DARK AREAS. NUMBER 07WH. 'How's it work?'

'You just go to one of those billboards advertising space to let, find the slot, swipe the card and go in.'

'That easy?'

'Sure.'

'Did he ever say why he had the key?'

'No.'

'What's it like? When you get in?'

'It's nothing.'

'What do you mean, nothing?'

'Nothing. It's black. Zero. No light. You just feel your way around. We always stay near to the entrance, otherwise we'd get lost. For ever. That's what Jim said.'

I held up the card to Andi. 'That's a low serial number. 07WH. This guy's got to be a top official.'

'Why?' she asked.

'There can't be many of these about. And any quantum card is impossible to counterfeit. This is an original. And he had two of them. One for himself and one for Tebor. When did you last see him?' I asked Tebor.

'The same day he saw Que. Only for a few minutes. Said he was going away for a while.'

'And he never told you what he discussed with Que?'

'No. When he was with me he was interested in other things. I may be a hacker, but I'm not going to fry a friend.'

Andi cut in. 'You're way off track if you think it's Jim.'

'I'm just looking at all the angles.' My view was simple here. Most of Que's contacts were interested only in their own nefarious activities, but this one had shared deeper secrets with the pimp. 'Jim the only name he had?'

Tebor answered without looking up. 'Most people use one name only down here. He was OK, a straight guy. I don't know what he got up to with Que, but he was OK with me. Didn't get up to things the other clients did. Used to tell me I was like his son. We talked a lot. About anything, really, mostly about what it was like up there. I can't see him – you know – planning something so big.' Tebor suddenly got excited. 'Hey, things are moving.'

'What's happening?' asked Andi, leaning over.

'I'm tapping the White House' – he indicated me with a tilt of his head – 'with his codes. The President's debit card's been used on the Brick. Somewhere called the Sunshine and Hope Mall.'

'Got a number?' I asked.

'Yeah, 812K1129.'

'That's one of the early sites.'

'He spent nine hundred and sixty-two dollars.'

'On what?'

'Restaurant services and room hire.'

'Let's go.' I stood up.

'They'll be looking for you,' Andi warned me. She pulled a mask from the bench next to her. 'You'll have to wear this.'

Tebor burst out laughing.

It was a likeness of BigMacKnife, one of the biggest stars of CyberBeat. It was the music I most hated, a solitary thump-thump-thumping that was the brutal background to words I couldn't understand. Me, I'm a Guns N' Roses man, from a time when melody was still foremost in rock. 'OK,' I agreed.

'You'll have to put it on before we leave,' she added. 'We don't want the SnoopCams picking you up, do we?'

Tebor hooted even louder. None of the other inhabitants even looked up; there was no sound to be heard because of the mini-scramblers. I grabbed the mask and yanked it on as we left PunkS R Us.

I stood apart from them as we waited for the transporter, rearranging my thoughts after what Tebor had just told me. The Dark Areas were either zones waiting to be developed, or ones which had fallen into such decay that they were closed down. Technically the UN monitored the Dark Areas. They released entry cards only to developers who were building on the Brick. These cards were very limited, usually only to the zones in which developments were currently taking place. Once the developments were complete the cards were automatically terminated.

Two years earlier the US government had been accused of having its own entry cards. The official answer was they needed them for security, and the matter had died when the journos moved on to graze on newer pastures.

The WH-designated number on the card could be the White House. They'd probably worked out they could use the Dark Areas as escape routes in case of a presidential assassination attempt in Second World. But it seemed too obvious. But then, so was the whole thing. Que's death could eventually have led the investigators back to Tebor. There were enough witnesses in PunkS R Us who must have seen them together, enough to have told the Security Services what they wanted to know. Tebor would have been tracked down eventually.

That's what confused me. Everything so far had been only partially hidden, as if the President's trackers were being led down a predetermined route. It was all too neat, too pat for my naturally suspicious nature.

We got on the next transporter, where I kept apart from the other two. The snoopers would be looking for three people and there was little point in making it too easy for them. I slumped back against the seat and closed my eyes as the transporter raced along the Brick. I was getting tired now as a result of my continual sojourn in the Web, and my concentration was starting to lose its focus. I then switched off thinking about the kidnapping and went into my memory banks of how the Brick used to be.

In the early days, when the Brick first opened, I loved racing in the latest car of my choice along its empty streets. Avatars, unlike their human counterparts, were no problem and the cars simply passed through them. It's how they were programed; as soon as they stepped over the kerb of one sidewalk they became invisible until they reached the other side. It had been so simple back then: just walk into a SoftShop in RealWorld, buy a disk that represented the car you wanted to race, take it home and load up the software onto your computer. Then you slipped into Second World, sat in your Ferrari or Aston, punched the ignition button and you were on your way. Yes, it had all been so easy then. Just go out and find someone else looking for a race. Line up next to each other, helmets down, blip the accelerator, count down from five and *off*. Vroom, wheelskid, and away, blow through the avatars and down the empty Yellow Brick Road. One hundred, one fifty, right up to two hundred. Through the few bends, watching the road, anticipating the skids – just like the old Nintendo 'Road Racers'. Except there was no paddle in your hand. This was for real. The crashes came if you hit the buildings. You couldn't go through those walls. They were private property, paid for by the megacorps and companies who were building on the Brick at breakneck speed. Sometimes it was another car that caused a smash. You didn't drive through those. You just felt a sharp searing pain as you crashed, then you were back in your WebSuit in RealWorld, suffering from aches and a soreness that lasted for days.

Good thoughts.

Happy thoughts.

Focus on them.

Rest your mind.

Release yourself into your karma.

I'd been good then, one of the best. It was the early days, the conquering of a new frontier. When I first went on the Brick, you didn't disappear into an invisible form once you stopped on the roadway. I'd wait mischievously on the pavement until a car approached. Then I'd step out suddenly and, if it was a novice driver, enjoy watching them swerve to avoid me. In those days, a lot of people couldn't get to grips with the fact they could drive through an avatar. Kids still deliberately jumped out in the street but the drivers were sophisticated and knew they'd disappear once they crossed the kerbstone. Nowadays you shot your rocks in FerrariMania or at one of the many RaceDomes that copied Indianapolis or Daytona or Imola.

I enjoyed my short relax period because I knew things were speeding up. My moment of rest would be short lived.

'I still think that receptionist guy knew more.' Gallagher referred to the Bentine Hotel.

'I had my best people interview him how they ran every interrogation test. Body language, eye movement, hand vibration, even monitored his pulse, heartbeat and body temperature variations from a portable machine hidden in a briefcase. It's as good as any micro-lie detector. What he told us was the truth. He'd have to be really exceptional to beat all those tests.'

'And the description he gave us?'

'My people believe it's genuine.'

An operative called from across the room. 'We've got something here.'

Gallagher and Clancy hurried across the room.

The message on the screen was clear.

THEY DON'T DEMAND RANSOMS LIKE THEY DID
IN THE GOOD OLD DAYS

NO MONEY. NO HOLIDAYS. NO TERRORIST RELEASES.
IF YOU WANT YOUR PRESIDENT BACK ALL YOU GOT TO
DO IS

WIPE OUT THE INFOCALYPSE
FROM THE ALPHA TO THE OMEGA

'What the hell's the Infocalypse?' asked Clancy.

'Punk jargon.'

'Like apocalypse?'

'Yeah, the four horseman of the Infocalypse. From the early days in the Web, it used to be internationally shared information on organized crime, fraud, drug dealers and terrorists. Then the UN said it violated human rights charters, so from then on that information was only available on convicted felons in the country of their activities, to be kept on local files by local forces. It became a nightmare for the police, especially where terrorism is concerned. Even Interpol got so it couldn't keep cross-border criminal records.'

'That was a long time ago.'

'Rumour is the information never got wiped out. That it's stored somewhere still. And that it grew to include information on literally everyone. Not just on felons. I mean, on everyone. Bank accounts, personal information, anything and everything about everyone.'

'More fucking rumours. Hell, we couldn't do it if we wanted to. Those UN human rights people watch every move we make.'

'Don't mean it don't exist.'

'Why wipe it out anyway?'

Gallagher shrugged. 'Because it's information of the wrong sort.'

'Alpha to Omega?'

'A to Z. This character wants *all* those records destroyed.' Gallagher then turned and instructed the operative to pass the new information on to the NSA.

'They've already picked it up,' was the quick reply.

'Surprise, surprise. Inform the VP that Agent Clancy and I'll be coming up to see her. Get me a printout of that ransom note . . . if that's what it is. And I guess you better call the Chief of Staff and the National Security Adviser. Tell them where we'll be.' Gallagher rocked back on his heels while he waited for the printout.

Don Clancy ignored him and brooded again about how he could have protected the President.

'I don't want your White House contact to know about Jim,' she said firmly.

'Don't worry. Just because Jim's got access to restricted areas doesn't mean he's guilty,' I assured Andi.

We'd disembarked the transporter and were milling with the crowd outside the Sunshine and Hope Mall. The entrance was sealed off by a team of WebCops and it didn't take long to notice the stiff coolness of one couple who stood awkwardly, scanning the crowd rather than showing an interest in the frenetic comings and goings of others. Typical Secret Service agents.

'Let's get a Coke,' I said, turning away. Tebor meanwhile broke away and mixed with the crowd, looking for friends and contacts.

We walked a block south and entered a small Starbucks cybercafe. Andi tapped Tebor's code and told him where to meet us. We were the only customers and, after ordering our drinks, sat at a corner booth.

'Any ideas yet?' she asked.

'Nope, my brain's as flat as Alpha World.'

She giggled. While most Second World terrains included mountains and forests and hills, Alpha World had always maintained its flat undemanding terrain. 'You been there?'

'In the early days, when it was real cutting edge. I bought a place there. Still got it.'

'You're kidding. I thought only hippies and punks lived there now.'

300

'You're not far wrong.' That was exactly what Alpha World had become. Bypassed by an upgraded future, the area had become a vast run-down district, its once proud homes falling into disrepair. The newcomers to the Web moved into the new exclusive gated communities, leaving behind the original techies and punks who didn't want their version of cyberworld to change. The neighbourhood I'd lived in had deteriorated badly, and some areas looked just like Kabul after the Taliban had finally been ejected.

'Do you still go there?'

'Not too often. Mostly just to see if it's still standing.'

'Where?'

'Near Ground Zero. Big grey building, no windows. Looks like a concrete shoebox. With about five acres of woodland. You should use it, when you've nowhere else to go.'

'Sure. How do I get in?'

'Easy. There's one door. Just knock five times and call "Conor says Open Sesame".'

She laughed. 'I'd expect better from a GameMaster.'

'Simplest is best. Anyway, it's still there because . . . it was my first venture into Second World. A sliver from my past.'

'What was it like in those early days?'

'Exciting, at the time. Pretty Mickey Mouse now. There was no sensation; I mean you just walked right through walls and trees. They had about two hundred avatar shapes you could choose from . . . you rented or bought one of those shapes. General landscape was flat and dull, so the houses people built were the imaginative bits. They had lakes and woodlands and pretty gardens. It was like being in a chatroom with the Sims Family.'

'Who?'

'It was a big game at the turn of the century, with simulated people. That was the real thrill in Alpha World. You all played arcade games with your avatars. There was no Marilyn Monroe, and if there was, you'd certainly get no satisfaction from screwing her.'

The small line screen I'd linked into came alive and I read it. 'Here we go again.'

Andi watched as I switched it to her table monitor.

THEY DON'T DEMAND RANSOMS LIKE THEY DID
IN THE GOOD OLD DAYS

NO MONEY. NO HOLIDAYS. NO TERRORIST RELEASES.
IF YOU WANT YOUR PRESIDENT BACK ALL YOU GOT TO
DO IS

WIPE OUT THE INFOCALYPSE
FROM THE ALPHA TO THE OMEGA

I'LL KNOW WHEN IT'S DONE
OTHERWISE YOU JUST KILLED YOUR PRESIDENT
ONLY 2 HOURS AND 29 MINS TO GO

'He's making his move,' I said.

'Him?'

'Whoever. This one's personal. No big groups, no terror-ist activity, this is someone who's got something to cover up. Something he wants taken care of.'

'You seem very sure.'

'Instinct. That's all. Big groups want ransoms or prisoners released. They're protecting their own organizations. This guy is after information – probably about him.'

'Isn't InfoCalypse only punk rumour?'

'Who knows? The UN resolutions say all personal infor-mation belongs to the individual. But then, who really cares about human rights down here? Anyway, it doesn't matter right now. What matters is that the kidnapper *thinks* there's an InfoCalypse, and he's the guy waiting to be satisfied.'

Tebor came in, sat down and said the gossip out there was that a woman, an MIW, had been found murdered. 'I mean, that sort of thing happens in these places all the time, and they're usually more gruesome than this one. Only this time they reckon the perp was the President of the USA.' He added that the murderer was wearing one of those fix-on face-masks of Dixon that were unlawful – as were masks of any national leaders.

'That could be anybody,' said Andi.

'The guy settled with his credit card. Buzz is ... it was ... the President's ... credit card.' Tebor smiled at me as he slowly and tantalizingly released this latest information.

'Who said?'

'The waiter. He knew the girl, had even helped her get ready for the assignation. He's also MIW who works the black economy. He's fucked now because he lived with the girl. There's no way back for her. I mean she's gone. Her cadaver'll keep going until it dies. He said it was awful, her head snapped right back. Anyway, he's scared the cops'll ground him and that's the end of his existence.' Tebor didn't need to add that most WebCops let MIWs go when they were discovered in the Web, but the importance of this crime made that unlikely, as they'd need all the witnesses they could get. 'He also saw them leave. Says he saw Dixon with his mask off, and it was definitely him.'

'Do the cops know if it's *really* him?' I broke in.

'I don't know, but I guess they'll find out. Right now the MIWs are working out how to get the waiter away from the cops. I mean, he needs to go underground for a while.'

'How well do you know him?'

'Not much.'

'He was pretty open with you.'

'I never said I spoke to him,' Tebor flashed back angrily. 'I only said that's what he said.'

'To whom?'

'Jim. He spoke to Jim. I saw Jim in the crowd, and he was the one who told me.'

My phone rang. 'Yeah.'

'Is this a bad time?' It was Gallagher. Maybe he'd got something for me.

'No. How's it going?'

'Deteriorating by the minute. You heard about this murder at the Sunshine Mall?'

'Yes, just. Who was she?' Maybe Gallagher had something else for me.

'An old girlfriend.'

'How old?'

'First love.'

'Why?'

'We're tracing her host. Hope we don't find someone as dead as Que.'

'I'm led to believe she could be MIW instead.'

'That'll save time. Anything else?'

'I don't think this is a group, more of an individual action. Don't ask why, just a hunch. It's someone who knows me. I don't believe that the use of Condor was just a coincidence. I might be wrong, but if it was a group, terrorist or otherwise, they'd be asking for more.' I paused before continuing, unsure how much Gallagher was holding back. 'Whose credit card paid the bill?'

There was a sharp intake of breath before Gallagher replied. 'You already heard?'

'I thought that's why I was down here.' So they *were* keeping things from me. "What happened to sharing info?'

'They're looking for your host. Is it somewhere safe?'

'Very.' I wasn't about to tell him where I'd moved to when I'd gone back to Rose Cottage. I grinned, thinking I'd need a good bath when I finally went home.

'They're chasing every bit of information they can get on you,' continued Gallagher.

'It'll take time.'

'They think you're involved.'

'I know, they've already linked me with Condor.'

'We're thin on leads. The PictureFit they got from the

304

hotel clerk didn't come up with anything. They showed it to the waiter and he didn't recognize him either.'

'Why would I kidnap the President? What about you?'

'Don't be crazy, Conor. I'm the one who called you in on this.'

'That's what I mean. You could also be a prime suspect.'

There was a pause while Gallagher munched on that. 'I guess everyone's a suspect,' he said eventually. 'You take care, and I'll call if I get anything. Meanwhile check your bank account, even your medical records. I know they're digging deep, and they'll be glued to everything you do.'

'Teflon coated, that's me.'

'I'm sorry I got you involved.'

I chuckled. You know what's good, Paul? To be playing a real game. That feels good. And this game matters. That's why I'll see it through.'

They were all instructed to attend, even Swilkin. He was linked through a VideoPhone that projected his image into one of the conference seats. The Speaker, Will Wilkin, sat next to Sarah Gilchrist, the Attorney General, and slightly apart from the rest.

The screen at the far end of the room was illuminated with Condor's last message.

> THEY DON'T DEMAND RANSOMS LIKE THEY DID
> IN THE GOOD OLD DAYS
>
> NO MONEY. NO HOLIDAYS. NO TERRORIST RELEASES.
> IF YOU WANT YOUR PRESIDENT BACK ALL YOU GOT TO
> DO IS
>
> WIPE OUT THE INFOCALYPSE
> FROM THE ALPHA TO THE OMEGA
>
> I'LL KNOW WHEN IT'S DONE
> OTHERWISE YOU JUST KILLED YOUR PRESIDENT
> ONLY 2 HOURS AND 29 MINS TO GO

The Vice President was sitting at the head of the table as Gallagher walked in. She flicked her index finger at him, signalling him to sit down, next to Clancy.

'Any further news from the Sunshine Mall?' she asked.

'No, ma'am,' he replied, sliding into the chair. 'It was definitely his credit card, no fake. The dead girl was, we believe, MIW.'

'How'd you know that?' cut in Swilkin's hologramed image.

Gallagher ignored him. 'So just don't expect there to be a dead host this time. Not like Que. The waiter's pretty scared, and I think he's told us all he can. He's MIW also – been like that for eight years. If we send him back, he'll fry. No way he'll survive.'

'Are you suggesting we let him go?' asked Marlin.

'No, sir. I just wanted to make you aware of the situation.'

'These people are dead anyway. Probably do them good to get some final rest.'

'Let's stick to the topic,' insisted the VP. 'We're not here to break UN resolutions regarding Web refugees.'

'I'd still like to know how the Secret Service found out the girl wasn't a live avatar, but MIW,' repeated Swilkin. 'I think that's a vital factor.'

They all turned and looked at Gallagher.

'I got that from one of my contacts,' he replied.

'Smith? A-K-A Condor?'

'Yes.'

Nobody spoke for a while.

'I guess he also knows about the credit card,' asked Swilkin eventually.

'Yes. He already knew.'

'Don't make me extract teeth here,' complained an exasperated Swilkin. 'What else does your old GameMaster know?'

'He's fully up to speed on everything, getting this stuff from MIWs. They're a close community: if one gets threatened, they all feel threatened. He also believes that the kidnap is not run by a group, but by an individual or very small team.'

'I agree, small, definitely. But a team, not an individual.'

'Why?' asked the VP.

'Because the Que and Monroe murders took place in different worlds. If it's MIWs, like your man Smith says, then they can't escape into RealWorld. So it's got to be someone with access from here into Second World. Or someone controlling the MIWs. You add to that their knowledge about the workings of the White House and it pans out as an inside job, or a major hacker.'

'Like Condor, obviously,' observed Marlin. 'What about the message? I mean, this InfoCalypse stuff. That's a fairy tale. No such thing.'

'The public don't think so,' said Meisner. 'Most think there *is* a batch of secret information locked away.'

Marlin snorted. 'Don't you think I'd know? Don't you think the agency would know? Hell, the President would certainly know ... and that means *you'd* know.' He stared accusingly at Meisner.

'Is there something I should now be made aware of?' the VP asked pointedly of Meisner.

'No. All I said was the public believes there is a secret databank somewhere. You all know it's just the same old rumour.' Meisner decided to kill the subject there and then. 'To my knowledge, and to the best of my belief, there's no such secret data.'

'Then how do we wipe out something we haven't got?'

'Maybe he's trying to mislead us?' Meisner turned to Clancy. 'Anything on the Convention Hall guests?'

'Everybody appears clean and those security staff that weren't on duty have all been alibi checked,' replied Clancy.

'Then there's little point in you boys staying.' The VP leant back in her chair and slowly cast a meaningful look over the three security chiefs. 'We've got less than two hours left. Better get to it. I just can't believe, after the billions of dollars we've invested in your departments, that all you can report is a big zero.'

'We could still send in thousands of agents, Secret Service Counter Assault teams – just go in and search,' blurted out Clancy. 'We've got all the support we need, including two hundred thousand WebCops. Add that to an open protocol with the SnoopCams, and we've covered just about everything. Maybe we just need good old manpower right now.'

'Then we'd have to go public,' responded Meisner. 'If we're considering that, then we may as well alert the WebSlime.' Meisner deliberately used the popular name for Web journalists, all of whom were controlled by individual media companies. They habitually spent their time wandering the Brick, continuously photographing and filming avatars that were fulfilling their fantasies. 'That way everyone gets to look for him, and everyone gets involved. You go down that road and there's no way you'll keep a lid on it.' He looked directly at the VP. 'Are you prepared to make that call, knowing it'll probably mean Teddy's certain death?'

'Mr Gallagher?' The VP turned to him.

'I agree with that, ma'am,' he shot back quickly, avoiding Clancy's sullen glare.

'I second that,' said Swilkin's video image quietly.

Neither Gallagher nor Swilkin looked towards Marlin for confirmation. They both knew he was out of his depth.

Once the three security men had left the room, the VP stood up and walked round the table towards the screen where the ransom note was still displayed. She stared at the message then turned dramatically to face the others who were left.

Always looking out for the main chance, thought Meisner.

'I need to repeat what I said a few hours ago,' she said. 'This country is not being governed right now.'

Nobody spoke. Apart from Meisner, no one else wanted to take sides. This was not the time to commit allegiances.

'Sarah?' Sumner directed her gaze to the Attorney General.

'Technically we still have a live President. That isn't in dispute. And the government machinery and process is continuing. As far as that's concerned, there is no immediate requirement. We're talking about his capacity to fulfil his duties in the case of a crisis.'

'What do you term a crisis?'

'That'll be defined if – and when – one happens.'

'So you don't consider the kidnapping of the President should be deemed a crisis?'

Nice one, thought Meisner.

'Well, he's not actually been kidnapped yet. His avatar has, but that has no real legal standing, apart from certain UN and WHO bylaws. Avatars have commercial rights, in fact a commercial and intellectual right that belongs to the user and the supplier. There are rules that apply to them . . .'

'Rules or laws?'

'Both. The laws apply to the commercial rights and protection of copyright. The rules are about operational conditions and rights. But those rules apply only in Second World. No avatar, that we know of, has ever made it to RealWorld and therefore come under our jurisdiction. And furthermore that's unlikely to ever happen. The other problem is that from a point of view of territory our laws don't always carry through to Second World. I mean, if we find he's in a decidedly foreign Second World area, let's say an Arab country which won't grant us access, what do we do then? Send troops in? But where? In Second World or RealWorld. The boundaries are blurred. As an avatar he doesn't have any legal rights. He's just a commercial entity. Even the UN's bylaws are designed solely to protect the legal rights of the cadavers in RealWorld rather than MIWs in Second World.'

'Hell, Sarah, we're talking about the President of the United States, not some game avatar.' The Speaker reacted with his usual blunt frustration that always made him look for short-cut solutions.

Marlin shook his head slightly in disgust, aware that the Speaker was also frustrated because he realized he wouldn't now make it back to the ranch for the weekend.

'I'm sorry, Will,' responded the Attorney General, 'but there's nothing that says his avatar's any different to anyone else's. I'm only giving you the legal perspective.'

'And Congress is the only way to deem him as not being capable of carrying out his duties,' reflected Nancy Sumner.

'Yes ... but only after we've got good reason to suggest he's not responsible.' The Attorney General shrugged, all she could do was state the legal position, even if it wasn't what the VP wanted to hear.

'So what's your best advice to us?' came the reply. The VP quickly decided the Attorney General was going to carry the can on this one; was forcing her to make the decision they would all stand by.

The Attorney General, no fool herself, did the old Washington two-step.

Compromise ... create time ... ride the punch ... events usually dictate the pace and result of any situation.

'Wait until we know what's really happened,' was her bureaucratic response, 'or until we pass the deadline Condor has set. Don't forget, it's only six in the morning. Nobody expects to see the President for a few more hours. Only security staff on duty know what's really happened. Yes, there has been a murder in RealWorld, but we still have to prove it's linked to the President. My suggestion is that we continue with our best efforts to find him. And if our view is that we don't want it to go public yet, as a matter of national security, then I don't see how we can be criticized.'

'We're always criticized,' grunted the Speaker. 'Whatever we do.'

'But not legally. There is no comeback on us.'

The phone rang and Sumner picked it up. 'Yes, speaking.' She listened, grave-faced, then put down the receiver slowly.

'Events move on, it seems. The waiter. The one who took the President's credit card. He's been wiped out.'

'Wiped out?' asked Wilkin. 'What's that?'

'It's when an MIW is suddenly destroyed in Second World. They just freeze within the matrix, lock into the system. The world goes on moving round their frozen image. Then, because there is no real life force behind them, they slowly disintegrate and the Web swallows up their cubits. After ten minutes it's as if they never existed.' Sumner took her time explaining this to the Speaker, not one of the most Web-savvy people in the government.

'But their body's still alive?'

'Sure,' was Sumner's abrupt response, fighting back her irritation.

'Then our only witness is gone,' pointed out the Attorney General. She was now coming off the hook the VP had baited her with. Events were indeed dictating the pace of this situation. 'I don't think we have any choice but to continue what we're doing now – at least until we're past the deadline. Hopefully we'll get another message, or a clue, by then.'

'At what point do we decide that the President isn't responsible for the running of the country?' asked the Vice President, her tone steely, leaving no doubt that she disagreed with the Attorney General.

'I suggest you keep your ambition on hold for another two hours, Nancy,' said Meisner. As Dixon's Chief of Staff there would be no future for him anyway in a new Administration. He stood up and moved towards the door.

'Watch your tongue, mister,' came the heated reply. 'It's not about ambition. It's about the safeguarding of our country.'

'I'm sorry, Nancy,' was Meisner's unrepentant response, 'but if we were to come under attack, or any similar crisis, the armed forces and government would react immediately. With you at their head. But right now we don't have any such crisis and, God willing, we'll get the President back. I suggest we follow the Attorney General's suggestions and wait until the deadline.' Meisner turned to Will Wilkin. 'Mr Speaker?'

Wilkin nodded slowly but positively. 'I guess, it wouldn't be right to go public yet. But Nancy's correct. We really should be preparing ourselves for the worst.'

Meisner turned and wordlessly left the room, not wanting to show his disgust with them all.

Where are you, Teddy? I can't hold back the tide forever.

PC Giles Renreth was also pretty fed up. He'd been told by his Super to stay on past the end of his shift, and to give all assistance to the team from London. He rang his wife and said he'd be late, got an earful for the privilege by being informed his breakfast was cold, she was out of eggs, and what time *did* he expect to be home so they could visit the Scottish medieval history tour in Second World as planned. She put the phone down angrily on his apologies. 'I'll give your breakfast to the dog,' was her icy comment as she replaced the receiver.

Renreth had spent the last three hours with the American and the man from EI5, thoroughly searching Conor Smith's house and grounds. They'd ordered him to join them once they realized Smith wasn't in the house, but they didn't tell him what they were looking for apart from the GameMaster's host body. That meant Smith was still somewhere in the Web, obviously causing the authorities some concern.

The American, obviously the technically superior of the two, had tried everything to break into Conor Smith's bank of computers, but the systems were security firewalled. 'It'll take weeks to get into this, even with all our sophisticated auto-equipment. He's got passwords that change, that seem to think for themselves. Christ, as soon as you go down one line, the computer changes the parameters – almost sees you

314

coming. It's playing chess with us but it's making up its own rules and moves. It's an intelligent password and, Christ, the best I've ever seen.'

They finally left the cottage and the grounds two hours later. There was little point trying to move the computer as it stood on a balancing table that would trigger off a software self-destruct mechanism if it were disturbed. The American had found that out when he lifted the first computer and a recording announced: 'PLEASE PUT THE COMPUTER BACK ON THE TABLE WITHIN FIFTEEN SEC-ONDS OTHERWISE ALL THE SOFTWARE WILL CRASH AND BE ERASED IMMEDIATELY. A SMALL DETONATION DEVICE WILL ALSO DESTROY THE HARD DRIVE, AND POSSIBLY YOUR HANDS. DATA LOST WILL NOT BE RECOVERABLE AND THEN YOU'VE JUST MANAGED TO STEAL A WORTHLESS TIN AND PLASTIC BOX. YOU HAVE TEN SECONDS LEFT, NINE, EIGHT, SEVEN . . .' The Ameri-can hurriedly replaced the computer, which then added 'THANK YOU. YOUR MOVE. IF YOU BREAK THE ENTRY CODE YOU WILL WIN ONE FREE TRIP TO THE CASTLE OF THE DRAGONS. OTHERWISE PREPARE TO GIVE UP, GO HOME AND WASTE SOMEONE ELSE'S TIME.'

The Super had sent along a second prowlcar to support them. Neville went in the second car and the American with Renreth. They searched the small side roads and fields for any sign of Smith but they all knew it was a waste of time. The two agents knew they were stuck there until they got further orders. As they walked the ditches and hedges or drove from field to field, the helicopter, with its lone spot-light searching ahead of it, stayed above them.

'He must've done something pretty bad,' said Renreth.

'You drive and I'll look,' was the only comment the American made.

They spent the last hour in silence before the American's mobile rang.

'OK, I understand . . . Yeah, I've got that, Much Hidden

Farm. We'll call from there.' He buttoned the phone off then finally spoke to Renreth. 'Do you know a farmer called John Mathews? Much Hidden Farm in Long Stratton. Widge Lane.'

'Yes.'

'OK, let's go there, fast, but don't use your siren.' As the prowlcar sped along, the agent called Neville on his mobile, gave him the address and then said, 'They've run the sat pics. It shows that a small truck went from this Much Hidden Farm to Rose Cottage about an hour ago and then returned after staying for only about five minutes. I guess that was while we were out searching the fields. The truck is registered to a local farmer called John Mathews. Lives on his own according to Scotland Yard. Could be our break, Phil.'

'They're friends,' interrupted Renreth.

'Good friends?'

'As good as any.' Renreth now regretted offering that information. Those were good people, unlike this Yank who was giving him a tough time.

'They're friends,' the Yank confirmed to Neville. 'See you there. We'll go in the front. You two cover the back.'

Much Hidden Farm was a traditional working farm and the small truck referred to was obviously Mathews's old open-backed Land Rover that was parked outside the front door.

Mathews answered the door within moments of Renreth knocking on it.

'Hello, John, not too early, is it?'

'Been up since half three. Remember, I don't have the comfort of working shifts like you do.'

'Mr Mathews?' the American cut in.

'I am. Who're you?'

The agent showed him his ID card.

'Bit out of your jurisdiction, aren't you?'

'My colleague from EI5 is on his way here. We're working together.'

'His credentials are OK, John,' added Renreth. 'We've been asked to help as well.'

'They must be desperate,' joked Mathews. 'National security, is it? Something big in Norfolk. Not much happens out here in the sticks.'

'Do you know a Conor Smith?' asked the American.

'I do. Good man.'

'Any idea where he is?'

'No more than usual. He's his own master. I wouldn't know where he was any more than he'd know where I was.'

'We believe you visited him, earlier this morning.'

Mathews nodded. 'I did. You been watching me through those satellites, have you?' He turned to Renreth. 'They've not had *you* following me, have they?' He laughed and shook his head. 'No, you're no James Bond.'

'Why would you believe you're being watched by satellite?

'How else would you know where I was? You people watch everybody.'

'Why did you go to Rose Cottage?'

'Pick up my groceries.'

'At five in the morning?'

'Bit before that, I think. He goes to Sainsbury's – '

'Where?'

'Local supermarket,' said Renreth.

' – and does my shopping along with his own. Sometimes he does it on the net, sometimes he visits there. Says he likes to see real people. The last thing I want to see is a room full of real people, all pushing and shoving against each other. So he does my shopping for me. He leaves it in a dustbin outside his back door. I take an empty bin down with me and swap them. I leave the money in an envelope inside. He doesn't much like money, but then I don't have any credit cards. He moans he has to go to the bank to cash it in. I always tell him to do the shopping at Sainsbury's. We've done that for years.' Mathews laughed again. 'He's not been stealing from Sainsbury's, has he? You're not here to do me for stolen fruit and veg.'

'This is no joke, Mr Mathews,' replied the American. 'I'm surprised you didn't see us there.'

'At Sainsbury's?'

'At Rose Cottage.'

Mathews smiled slyly. 'I was quiet so as not to wake him. Don't even know where you lot were. But I never know whether he's in or not. I didn't see him, if that's what you mean.'

'The satellite imaging shows you parked up for about ten minutes before driving on to Rose Cottage. Were you checking up on whether we were there or not?'

'Weak bladder. You get like that at my age ... when you work outdoors.'

'Ten minutes?'

'Big weak bladder. It dribbles ... real slow.' He grinned. 'Like I said, it's an age thing.'

'Can you show me what he left for you?'

'Why? Isn't my word good enough?'

'I'd just like to see it.'

'And if I said no?'

'Then I'd think you had something to hide.'

Mathews considered for a moment. 'Doesn't matter what I say to that, does it?' he asked Renreth.

At that moment PC Renreth wished he'd stayed in the InnerSprawl. Yet you developed good community relationships in the country, not like the Sprawl where everyone ignored everyone else, especially the police. He shook his head. 'Nothing I can do, John. We're all jumping to their tune.'

Mathews shrugged. 'You'd best come in,' he said, surly, making them aware he didn't welcome the intrusion.

He led them through to the old farmhouse kitchen, a relic from the previous century, with a wide old Aga burning at one end, the smell of newly baked bread coming from its ovens. He pointed to the dustbin to one side of the kitchen table. 'It's in there. With the receipt. And you'll see it was delivered late last night. To Conor.'

The American rummaged through the black plastic bin, pulling out the receipt and delivery note, while Mathews went to answer a knock on the back door. Neville came in, introducing himself and showing his ID card. The American explained to him where they were up to and the importance of the trash, as he put it. Throughout it Mathews looked vaguely bored with the whole situation, appearing restless, wanting to get back to farmwork.

'Why haven't you emptied the bin?' asked Neville eventually, after both men had sifted through its contents.

''Cause I haven't. I'll do it later. It's all packet or tinned stuff. I do my own milk and meat and perishables on my farm. I'm self-sufficient. You can see, it's sugar and coffee and biscuits, stuff like that.'

'Doesn't make sense. This is a tidy kitchen. You're not the sort to leave things unfinished.'

'What am I? A bloody housewife? What's all this got to do with Conor, anyway?

'You could've left the bin untouched just to prove that's why you'd gone round there.'

'But that's why I was there. Where do you think that shopping came from?'

'And you didn't see him?'

'I've told your mate already. No.'

'Or moved him?'

'Why should I move him?'

'So he could be safe and go back into the Web.'

'But he's safe in his own house, when he's in the Web. Why would I need to move him?'

'Because he was worried we'd come after him.'

'Why're you after him?'

'That's official business. Not for you to know.'

Mathews shrugged. 'I still don't understand why I should move him.'

'Would you mind if we looked round the place?'

'Do you have a warrant?

'No.'

'Didn't think so.'

'We can get one. Pretty quick.'

'Probably. But I've nothing to hide. And I've a farm to run.' He thought for a moment, then nodded. 'Be quick, so you don't waste too much more of my time.'

'If you'd just wait here.' There was no attempt at politeness. 'Where's your computer?

'Don't have one.'

'Everyone's got a computer.'

'You won't find any computer here. Hate them. Destroying mankind. Which is why Conor orders things for me.'

'If it's as you say, we shouldn't be long.'

'Mind if I unpack the bin now. Seeing, as you said, I'm such a tidy-minded person.'

Neville ignored the jibe and they began to search the farmhouse.

Mathews made himself a cup of tea while he waited. He grinned to himself. He liked this game. Conor Smith and him taking on the world. They'd never find him, or the small computer Conor had brought with him as he slid into the passenger well of the old Land Rover. And to think Conor had connected to the Web through Mathews's old answerphone.

No, he felt good. If Conor said they wouldn't trace him, that was good enough for Mathews. He sat back and enjoyed his cup of freshly brewed tea, while he heard the elephants stumbling about in the farm that was his home.

We left Starbucks and found the nearest unregistered cyber-cafe to the Sunshine and Hope Mall. It was called the Nuclear Shaman Cafe, and was an unlikely place for us to be traced.

Andi flipped a screen and was soon accessing her contacts.

'Tell me about Jim,' I asked Tebor.

'What do you want to know?' Tebor clearly saw no link between our present odyssey and his friend.

'I know you like him.'

'He's OK. We talk. He understands what it's like down here. Andi'll tell you. Most MIWs just scratch around for a living and to keep some shelter over their heads. They get boring because that's all they talk about – apart from moaning about not being able to go home. The visitors are different, as they come down here to use you. Sex, drugs, whatever. Even the religious freaks only want to convert you so, they'll get paid more by their sponsors. I've been converted by every church and temple on the Brick. Great way of raising credits. Cheap fucking labour, that's all we are.'

'And Jim?'

'He just ... listens most of the time. He's good, never tried anything weird with me or Andi. Or anyone else that I know of. Just a straight, caring guy.'

'Is he the one who keeps you sharp?' It suddenly fell into place. It was Jim who kept Tebor and Andi in such excellent avatar form, why they had not deteriorated like most MIWs without constant avatar refreshing. So that explained why they didn't have the frayed, frazzled look that was de rigueur of all MIWs.

To do that Jim needed access into the matrix.

'He looks after us,' said Tebor defensively.

'What's he do in RealWorld?'

'Why?' Tebor became aggressive again.

I smiled my *hey, trust me* smile. 'I just want to know what makes him so different with MIWs. Don't forget, I've known MIWs for a long time and I've got a straight reputation too. I guess it's interesting to see what motivates someone who has the same values I have.'

Tebor looked across at Andi for a moment, eyed her with her head still buried in the monitor.

'If Andi trusts me, so should you.' I pushed the point. 'I'm really not out to hurt either of you. I just want to bottom this thing out. And, if I am being set up, I want to get myself off the hook.'

Tebor weighed up what I said. 'Works, or worked, for the US government,' he said finally. 'I don't know what, but he's pretty senior and pretty hush-hush.'

'How old is he?'

'In RealWorld, I think he said something about celebrating his eightieth birthday not long ago. I know he lives in Washington.'

'How?'

'He told me. But said he'd no real, caring family to share his birthday with. Said that his true friends were all down here.'

'You celebrated it?'

'Yeah. Andi came, too. He paid for it all. Took over PunkS R Us for the day. That wasn't cheap.'

'Is that the only name he's got? Jim?'

Tebor nodded. 'The only name I know.'

We sat in silence and waited for Andi. A police car

shrieked past on the Brick. Andi suddenly got up and came over.

'I think that's on its way to the Sunshine and Hope,' she said, her face flushed with excitement.

'What's happened?' asked Tebor.

'The waiter who reported the credit card, he's been wiped out. I just picked up the police call.'

The two of them locked their eyes together in silent sympathy; it was the nightmare all MIWs dreaded. To dissolve out of the matrix and never have the opportunity to return to your cadaver one day.

'You ever see an MIW wiped out, Conor?' asked Tebor eventually.

'Yes.' I'd actually been passing by when an MIW froze: totally motionless while everyone else on the Web just moved about naturally. I tried to help him, but there was nothing I could do. The MIW had OD'd on the latest narco and just died in front of me. I saw the colour leave the MIW to be replaced by black and white cubits; like a black and white still photo superimposed on a full-blooded colour moving picture. Then even the photo faded and the MIW disappeared into the background, still motionless at the moment of death. Except for the eyes. The eyes still looked at me, locked on, still alive, desperately pleading, then all hope dying as he faded away. It was only then I realized that the MIWs were as real in their emotions as anyone in RealWorld. It was the nearest I ever came to believing in a man's soul.

'I'm sorry.' It was inadequate, but all I could say to the two of them.

'The CREEPs are on their way,' reported Andi. 'If they get to him in time they might get an electroDNA and identify his cadaver.'

The CREEPs were the computer regenerating electronic engineering personnel, the automatic matrix and data fixers who continually monitored the web for breakdowns. An

MIW wipe-out usually created a hole in the matrix and the CREEPs moved fast to plug it before any serious damage could result. They were fully automatic cubit robots and could interrogate and identify matrix problems without human help. They were the nearest form of robot to intelligent life, as they could think for themselves but only within certain engineering parameters. Although each CREEP was a single unit, they usually linked together to determine the necessary application for each technical breakdown in the web. It was biocomputing at the cutting edge, the very same that was used in medicine to defend people against cancer, AIS and other diseases.

'Jim told me how he used to work with the CREEPs,' announced Tebor.

'Wow,' I said. 'Now that's a job – setting up the Web. I guess that's how he got to enter the Dark Areas.'

'You would, wouldn't you? If you set it up.'

'Sure. You still going to take me into the Dark Areas?'

'Maybe.'

'Of course he is,' joined in Andi, sliding her chair away from the table. 'Not much activity right now. It's like everyone's just waiting for something to happen.'

'Have you run all the protocols?' I asked.

'All the ones you gave me: the White House, NSA, FBI, local police. It's like waiting for a race to start. I can feel them revving up but there's nowhere for them to go.'

'Tell me more about Jim,' I said to Andi.

'Don't tell him too much,' Tebor warned as he moved over to the monitor and started running the protocols all over again.

'He seems very protective towards Jim,' I murmured.

'Why not?' she said. 'Why put Jim in the firing line?'

'You know me. Instinctively nosy.' I tapped my nose. 'That's why I'm always in trouble.'

'Like *never*. GameMasters never get in trouble.'

'We do. That's why they make us GameMasters. To turn us respectable and keep us *out* of trouble.'

She laughed and moved closer to me. 'What'll happen if they don't find him?'

'Dixon? I guess they'll get a new President. I mean he wasn't that special anyway, from what I've read.'

'I thought he was putting together this great deal with the Islamic countries.'

'Just looking for his place in history. Like all of them.'

'It could be someone's trying to kill those talks.'

'Maybe, but there'd be easier ways of doing it. Just go on bombing Jerusalem, for instance. I mean, that's worked for over two thousand years. Seriously, I don't think anyone from out there has got the technology to pull off this kidnap. And they keep going on about the InfoCalypse. It's like someone's trying to tell us something we don't know.'

'A revolutionary?' Andi suggested.

'Maybe. But someone with a lot of technical clout.'

'That's not Jim Nelson.'

'That his name?'

She game me a Mona Lisa smile. 'I didn't slip up. I *wanted* you to know.'

'I gathered that, but are you sure? Tebor said he only knew him as Jim.'

'He told me himself once. Probably told Tebor, but he only remembers what he wants to. Yes, I'm sure. He helped set up the security on Second World, for the UN. I think he'd worked for the US government before that. He's a techie, a government man. But he's no Che Guevara.'

'He still work for them?'

'I think he retired – got out a few years back. Often speaks about his family. Doesn't get on with his wife. Two kids, boy and a girl, but he had some trouble with them, won't say what. I guess they've grown up, left home, and that's why he hangs around us here. Maybe we make him feel needed. He's always telling us to quit what we do and he'd buy a place and look after us.' She prodded me with her elbow. 'Maybe even one of those old homes in Alpha World or Second Life.'

I returned the dig. I was coming over all playful. 'And he worked with the CREEPs?'

'That's what he said. I remember him once saying that you couldn't have a reliable matrix until you'd learnt how to maintain it. Otherwise avatars would get wiped out all the time. The whole thing would be too unstable.'

'Obvious, makes sense.' I trod carefully. 'Can I run a check on him? Without upsetting you or Tebor.'

'He wouldn't be involved in something like that. Not Jim.'

'Probably not. But I'd be happier if I could just eliminate him from the suspects.'

'Why not meet him?' Andi said guardedly. 'I could arrange that.'

'Why worry him? Look . . .' I tried to sound reassuring, though my head was banging with excitement. 'I can run a quick check. I'm sure he's clear. If you believe in him so much, then he'll have nothing to worry about.'

She nodded reluctantly, 'Do it outside, away from Tebor,' she whispered.

I stood up with a '*I need to pay a visit*' comment and went to the men's room. My keyboard was open before I entered the toilet and I leant against the sink, quickly tapping out an encrypted message to Gallagher.

GET INFO ON A JIM NELSON — MAY NOT BE ACTUAL NAME — LATE SEVENTIES — EARLY EIGHTIES — BLACK MALE — GREY HAIR — 6 FEET TALL — EXPERT ON CREEPS — WAS UN — SET UP WEB RULES AND CREEP MAINTENANCE PROTOCOLS — EX US GOVT EMPLOYEE — COULD BE EX SECURITY SERVICE — POSSIBLE WHITE HOUSE — KNOWS MOST SECURITY ACCESS CODES IN SECOND WORLD.

I decided not to mention the fact that Nelson had access to the Dark Areas.

I clacked on: DIVORCED OR SEPARATED — TWO KIDS — BOY GIRL — BOTH LEFT HOME — RUN SNOOPCAMS OUTSIDE SUNSHINE & HOPE MALL — SUSPECT IS IN CROWD WITH A YOUNG MIW, SPIKY HAIR — CYBERPUNK — URGENT — SEND RESPONSE ON THIS ENCRYPTED CHANNEL.

I folded and slid the keyboard back into my watch and went back into the main area of the cafe.

Gallagher took his two best men-on-duty into his own office, situated on the floor above the Control Complex. He had decided not to inform any of the others about Conor's transcription. He merely explained to them what he was after, and the three of them immediately set about tracing Jim Nelson.

His first operative hunted through files of ex-US government employees, their searches specifying retired, with possible security or White House clearances, and also divorced with two kids. The second trawled the United Nations records looking for similar information.

Gallagher went after the Web program files that included personnel who had helped build Second World and subsequently been involved in the maintenance and security of the matrix.

They traced one hundred and eighty-three Jim Nelsons who fitted that age band and had worked for the US government. The match included postmen, social workers and filing clerks. Forty-two were black. One hundred and ten had two children. Sixty-four of those had a boy and a girl. More than a hundred of them had divorced or separated from their partners. Twelve were registered as gays and one a transsexual. Twenty-six had retired prematurely. Sixteen had worked at some time or other for the UN, either on secondment or on a full transfer. Six had been in the security agencies, three in the FBI, two in the CIA, and one in the NSA. None of these had risen to any meaningful rank. But they all had access to at least some security codes.

Nineteen Jim Nelsons had worked on the nascent Web, most of them technicians involved with the building of the early matrix, and usually employed by the corporations who were rapidly expanding their empires.

But, after sifting through all that information, there was only one Jim Nelson who fitted all the necessary criteria.

'Got him,' said Gallagher. 'What's his current address?'

'Last known here in DC,' confirmed the second operative. 'Lives no more than fifteen minutes away.'

Then they checked his social security records. Jim Nelson had died eighteen days earlier. His will showed he left over fifty-three million dollars to his children. Most of this came from shares in ThemeCorp, which he'd bought at the start-up of the company. The will itself wasn't yet in the public domain, but Gallagher managed to get hold of Nelson's lawyer and eventually, after some official pressure, got the details released to him on a confidential basis.

The following reports and press clippings described how Jim Nelson, a good, quiet, clean-living man, with a substantial government pension and neighbours who valued his friendship, got out of bed at two in the morning, went into the garage, put a loaded shotgun into his mouth and blew his brains out.

The coroner's verdict was suicide with no apparent motive.

What surprised his old colleagues attending the funeral and the wake afterwards was that Jim Nelson, one of the pioneers of Second World, didn't have even a small personal computer anywhere in his small but comfortable three-bedroom house.

His neighbours then confirmed that he used to visit them in order to send emails to his son and daughter who lived out of state.

Twenty-five minutes after receiving the signal, Gallagher returned his answer to Conor Smith:

ALL DESCRIPTIONS FIT. LOG IN TO CODE WHPer-NELS8934. FULL DESCRIPTION THERE INCLUDING PIX. ONLY ONE COMPLICATION. OUR MAN IS WHITE — REPEAT — WHITE. OTHERWISE THE ONLY ONE WHO FITS ALL YOUR CRITERIA. NONE OF THE OTHERS COME CLOSE ON ALL COUNTS. DIED SUICIDE 18 DAYS AGO. DC POLICE REPORT SAYS NO FOUL PLAY AND NO MOTIVE. ALL PIX ON WHPerNELS8934. THAT SITE WILL EXPIRE TWELVE MINUTES FROM NOW.

'They're working things out,' said the Voice with a hint of satisfaction. 'They think they're getting closer.'

The flat words uttered in the blackness woke Dixon up. 'I'm tired,' he pleaded once he'd recovered his bearings. 'How long have I been down here?'

'Almost too long, Teddy. I'd hate to see you lose your mind,' the Voice cackled. 'Not yet anyway.'

'I still don't understand what this is all about.'

'I already told you. About spying on people, about idiots like you controlling our lives.'

'But we only spy on our enemies. Only those who would harm us.'

'You politicians think everyone's out to harm you,' came the dismissive reply. 'You're a bunch of psychopaths; inflated egos fucked up by massive inferiority complexes. No wonder you're all so screwed up.'

'We do our best,' came the plaintive reply in the darkness. 'It doesn't warrant this.'

'If you got out of here, Teddy Boy, what do you think you've learnt?'

'God knows, I still don't see what you're trying to tell me.'

'Find the InfoCalypse and save yourself, Mr President.'

'That's hogwash. There's no such thing.' The pain in his chest came again, the air being sucked out of his lungs. 'Kill me if you want, but I don't know that even exists,' he gasped, his voice getting weaker as he forced the words out. 'I could lie, just to save myself but I feel sure it doesn't exist. For God's sake, don't you think I'd know?'

The air flooded back into his lungs and he started to cough, startled by the ferocity of his capacity to breathe again.

'You really that out of touch?' asked The Voice.

'I would know,' Dixon gasped. 'I would know,' he repeated, weak with fear.

'Maybe your friends are not your friends, Mister President. If you don't know, then someone else is lying to you,' came the measured response.

'That's one thing I aim to find out.'

'If you ever get back?'

Dixon suddenly, instinctively, felt safe. 'How else will I find out? I can't do it from down here.'

He heard the laughter again in the darkness, heard it build and resonate in the stillness of the Dark Areas where there was nothing.

'You're a smart man, Teddy Boy,' said the Voice eventually. 'But then you're the President. Whatever happens, just remember you made me a promise. You break that promise, don't ever think about coming back into Second World. Either you or your family. I'll crush you all like empty tin cans.'

And then silence returned into the blackness.

Dixon knew he was on his own again. But, for the first time, he felt some hope. His instinct told him he would be remembered as a great President if he could find and destroy the InfoCalypse. The real saviour of the people, of democracy. He started to formulate the speeches he would make, the gestures he would adopt as he traced the secrets of the InfoCalypse. The monster which he had always believed was just a fallacy, a rumour spread by his enemies. His role-playing spurred him on, lifted him with hope that he would survive and become the great saviour.

But what if there *was* an InfoCalypse? And what if it was run by his own Security Services? And what if it was their policy not to admit it to him; that it was too secret for even the President to know about? History showed that type of deception had happened many times before. There was even the rumour that JFK had been killed not by the Mafia but by the CIA. And there was that thing between Clinton and Monica What's-her-name. An awful lot of those in the know were convinced at the time that the FBI had set her up to admit what had happened. In moments of darkness since he'd been kidnapped the President had even considered whether his own closest people were involved. What if there was an InfoCalypse, designed to protect the national interest, and the last thing they would want him to find out was that it existed?

He broke out into a sweat, his forehead suddenly clammy and cold in the dead air of the Dark Areas. God! If only he could see.

His renewed confidence vanished as quickly as it had come. He didn't cry this time, just huddled himself in his arms and waited fearfully for whatever might happen next. The Voice was now the sole arbitrator who would decide what would become of the most powerful person on earth.

The information on Jim Nelson came through on my phone. I made sure the others weren't watching me before I opened Gallagher's message. I was more surprised that he'd traced Nelson so quickly than by the fact that Nelson was really white; that was if he was even the right man. Just like before, it seemed too easy, as if the information was left in place, ready to be found. The colour bit made sense, since avatars often displayed some difference from their RealWorld hosts; white becoming black or vice versa was common in Second World.

I tapped back into the White House personal emails and keyed in the identifier that Gallagher had passed to me. WHPerNELS8934. It followed a standard code for White House staff and was listed as in any other digital notice board. I scrolled down until I found the one I was looking for. There were one hundred and eighty-three random thumbnail pictures, and Gallagher had obviously decided to send them all. If somebody stumbled on to these emails by chance, the information would be meaningless, so there was no security risk. The first one was the only one I needed to register. It was the man who Gallagher thought was Jim Nelson. Yes, he was white this time, but I also recognized the features of the man I'd seen with Tebor. No doubt: one and the same.

I tapped BINGO! into the keyboard and sent it to Gallagher through the encrypted channel. As an afterthought

I added: DON'T SEND IN THE TROOPS – I'VE STILL GOT TO
FIND HIM – DON'T WANT TO SCARE OFF MY CONTACT –
STAY COOL.

I came off-line and studied Tebor. The boy was still
chasing leads on Que, while Andi was trying to pick up any
buzz on the Sunshine and Hope Mall. My watch told me we
had less than an hour to go.

'I need to talk to you both,' I said quietly. 'Now.'

They came off their computers and slid their chairs over.

'I need to meet Jim,' I said in a matter-of-fact tone.

'I said he wasn't involved,' snapped back Tebor.

'Let's keep it down. I didn't say I don't believe you, but
he's an expert on CREEPs. That means he's an expert on
the Web. He also knows about the Dark Areas. I mean,
we've got less than an hour to find our missing man. Jim
might just know all the shortcuts, might know where he
could be hidden.'

'I know as much as he does,' countered Tebor, his pride
taking over. 'Shit, I live here all the time.'

'I appreciate that. But you don't have access to CREEPs
and other Web equipment.'

'No.'

'What if the President's hidden in the Dark Areas? You
said Jim could get us into them.'

'So can I. He gave me my own card. I showed it to you.'

'Sure you did. But you also said you never moved far
from the entrances, in case you got lost. He, however,
knows how the Dark Areas work, how they're controlled.
Maybe, with the CREEPs, he can determine if there's been
any unusual activity in them, anything different happening.'

Tebor shook his head, confused. 'I don't know. He trusts
me, always said I was never to mention him to anyone.' He
stared furiously at Conor. 'I shouldn't have shown you the
card. And you shouldn't bring it up . . . ever, ever again.'
He turned to Andi. 'I thought you said he was OK.'

'He is,' she said soothingly. 'He's just trying to save someone.'

'No one we know, just a President in RealWorld. He's not like someone who cares about us down here. He doesn't give a damn about us. Not like Jim does.'

She reached over and put her arm round Tebor's shoulders. 'He may not be our President, but he is Jim's. So maybe Jim would like to help save him?'

That rattled the boy and he stared into her face for assurance. 'I don't know. I don't want to get Jim into trouble. What if he's not meant to have a card for getting into the Dark Areas?'

'That secret stays with me,' I said.

'Maybe we should ask Jim himself,' Andi suggested. 'Talk to him, just the two of us, and let him decide.'

'Just us?' asked Tebor.

'Just us,' she confirmed.

He nodded, reluctantly. Then he slid his chair back to the table and reconnected with the monitor.

I guessed he was contacting Jim. 'Thank you,' I said to Andi.

'Don't fuck us up,' she replied. 'Please. We don't have many real friends down here. Don't scare this one away.'

Swilkin was jumping crazy by the time he arrived at the Control Complex. 'It's taken me fifteen minutes to drive over here,' he complained. 'What's so damn important that we can't deal with it over a secure line?'

'If we've been hacked, as circumstances seem to suggest, the last thing we need is our latest information getting straight back to the kidnapper.' Gallagher wasn't fazed by Swilkin's rage. He knew he could probably have safely passed the data over to the Telephone Exchange, but he was buying time for Conor. He didn't want Swilkin's men blocking any moves the GameMaster might now make.

'So what's so fucking important?' Swilkin demanded.

'Want a coffee?'

'No, I do not want a coffee. Just get on with it.'

Gallagher hid a smile. He knew the coffee offer was stupid but it ate away a few more valuable seconds for Conor. 'Pull up a chair,' he said as he walked him over to an unused monitor. 'I think we may have something here.' Gallagher then took Swilkin through the whole Jim Nelson episode, including both messages from Conor and all the pictures.

'Did this guy have any record of mental instability?' asked Swilkin.

'No.'

'Any known antagonism towards the President?'

'No.'

337

'Any political ambitions or general dislike of politicians?'

'No.'

'And no known links with terrorist, criminal or other wacko outfits?'

'None whatsoever.'

'So you're saying that a guy who blew his own brains out, is already six feet under, and who had no obvious motive, may have kidnapped the President.'

'Put like that it sounds far-fetched.'

'Fucking A it does.' Swilkin suddenly changed tack. 'But your man Smith thinks it's a hot lead?' As Gallagher nodded, Swilkin leant back in his chair and sighed. 'Any chance somebody could have taken Nelson's identity? Or someone taken his? Was it Nelson who committed suicide? You don't leave much for matching identity when you blow your head away. Fingerprints, that's about it.'

'And DNA.'

'I see no mention of either in the coroner's report,' said Swilkin as he scanned the screen. 'They just accepted it was him.'

'There was never any suggestion of foul play. He left the neighbour's house and five minutes later they heard the gunshot. Still in the same clothes he'd been wearing, so everything pointed to it being Nelson. The lab boys at the morgue were probably up to their neck in work. For them just another suicide. Tick the box and move on.'

'Alternatively your boy Smith could be covering his own tracks.'

'With a dead man as his prime suspect. I'd expect a better story from him.'

Swilkin laughed. 'Or he's fucked our heads by making it unbelievable.' He looked at his watch. 'Only half an hour left. This whole mess, the more we learn, the more mystifying it gets. Somebody's running us in circles.'

'I'll call you if anything comes up.' Gallagher rose to his feet.

'No point. So little time left, I'll stay here. If Smith comes across with anything it's you he's going to contact.' Swilkin stretched his legs. 'At this rate we could soon have a new President, and be very interesting to see how they handle it. I mean, technically he's not dead, and his body's next door. Yeah, I'd like to hang around and see what happens next. Could be this is only the start of things.'

'Sure. I'll let you know if something breaks.' He turned to go back to his team.

'I'll have that coffee now,' he heard Swilkin say behind him.

'OK,' he heard himself reply, but his mind was on something else. Maybe Swilkin was right. Maybe the game was only starting now.

He heard Swilkin pick up the phone and connect to the Telephone Exchange. He started to give details of Nelson so they could run their own search.

Across the room, Gallagher saw Nancy Sumner enter, the rest of the gang with her. *Vulture closing in, already probing the carcass.* He then saw the First Lady escorted by Meisner, and Dan Clancy brought up the rear. It was like an Agatha Christie novel with her little Belgian detective, Hercule Poirot, gathering everyone for the denouement. The gathering of the suspects. The corpse lying in the next room. There was only one problem. The corpse was still alive and well and sound asleep. The murder was yet to happen.

MetroPort 956 was situated seven blocks north of the Hotel Gallipoli. I rode with Andi and Tebor to meet Jim Nelson outside the MetroPort. Tebor had already contacted Nelson on his mobile, shielding it from me as he dialled. He'd spoken quietly, not wanting to be overheard. I got the impression that Nelson had been amenable to the meeting; that Tebor had not had much convincing to do.

'OK, he'll meet,' Tebor had confirmed, 'but he wants *us* there.' He indicated himself and Andi. 'No one else must come, just the three of us.'

'That's cool,' I replied. 'Where?'

'MetroPort 956. At the entrance.'

'How many entrances are there?'

'Just the one. He also said you mustn't get mad if he won't answer some of your questions.'

'Sure.' I wanted to get going as time was running out. But I contrived to stay relaxed, not wanting to spook Tebor.

'Please don't tell him I said anything to you about the Dark Areas.'

'I won't tell him.' There was no reason to betray Tebor; I might need the boy at some stage. 'I think we should get up there and meet him.'

A troubled Tebor brought up the rear as we headed for the nearest MetroPort. Nobody spoke on our two-minute trip. Andi sat next to Tebor, putting her arm round his shoulders to comfort him. We disembarked at MetroPort 956 and waited.

The digital clock above the entrance, its seconds visibly ticking away, seemed to pass time in slow-mo. I tried to keep my eyes away from it; the more I watched, the more time stood still.

Where the hell was Nelson?

All around us the Weekenders were flooding onto the Brick. The fancy cars raced up and down and the neons popped and flashed and zigzagged crazily as the Brick painted its face for the party and came to life. The crowds snaked past in both directions, a sea of eager smiling laughing faces all come to worship at their individual churches, well away from the Sprawl where they lived their *who-gives-a-shit* everyday lives.

I checked the clock again, my cool ruffled by my own impatience. It didn't appear to have moved. There were only fourteen minutes left.

I began to realize the hopelessness of it all.

The VP stood apart from the rest, who were grouped in a huddle around Gallagher's desk. Everyone noticed she'd changed her outfit. She didn't care about that; the black, pin-striped suit and pale blue open-necked shirt was what a President might wear when called upon to lead the nation in its hour of mourning. She knew that events would rapidly move her way once the deadline for Dixon's return had passed. They couldn't keep the situation concealed much past that moment.

Will Wilkin, the Speaker, knew that, too; he'd already discussed it with her quietly away from the others, as they had walked from her office to the Control Complex. She felt secure in the knowledge they would all be getting ready now to protect their individual positions.

'Ten minutes to deadline,' she heard Gallagher call out to his operatives across the room. 'Come on . . . something. There's got to be *something* out there for us to chase.'

It was a hopeless cry for help, because there was nothing left to try – not in the short time available. Their machines needed hours more to identify all possible suspects, to sift through the mountains of data about personnel and terrorists and immigration lists and every possible lead they could think up.

Swilkin came off the phone and informed Gallagher, 'Nothing new from the British.'

The clock clicked: nine minutes to go.

'Look's like Smith's out of time,' commented Swilkin to no one in particular.

The First Lady now sat on her own, a jittery Don Clancy just behind her, wanting to reassure her, knowing there was little he could do.

Wilkin and the Attorney General approached Nancy Sumner. 'Sarah and I've been talking,' he said. 'I think we need to give it another half-hour beyond the deadline before we go public.'

'Fine,' said the VP. She already knew it would appear too pushy if she didn't agree to such a short extension. Going any further beyond the deadline meant Dixon's brain would be fried anyway, if it wasn't already. That is, if he wasn't dead already.

The time for compromise would soon be over.

She remembered Lyndon Johnson being sworn in on Air Force One after the shooting of John F. Kennedy. It recalled images that had lived almost as long as those of Kennedy himself being assassinated. She started to work out where she should be when she was sworn in; somewhere dramatic, somewhere always to be remembered. 'And the fact we don't have a dead body?' she asked indifferently. She knew Sarah Gilchrist would be more accommodating now, knowing that Sumner could soon be President.

'We can overcome that,' replied the Attorney General. 'Once we have expert proof that he would probably be suffering from WebFever, even if he did come back.'

'How long would that take?'

'Not long. We've plenty of experts in the field. Maybe an hour, tops.'

'Poor Teddy,' said Wilkin.

'Yes,' answered Gilchrist. 'A real tragedy.'

'Poor Teddy,' echoed Sumner. 'And let's not forget the First Lady. She's suffered quietly and without complaining through all this. She's going to need all our support if it turns out as bad as we fear.'

And the Vice President walked over to the First Lady of the President that she never thought was a good President anyway, and was now about to depose.

That's how Washington worked. Warm smiles and cold deceit. It was the one rule everyone in the room played by.

Hope dwindled, resurrected, and then dwindled again.

'He's not coming,' I said with a trace of annoyance.

Tebor turned to Andi nervously. They both knew Jim, and he wasn't the sort who didn't keep his word. That was a rare quality in Second World.

'Something's held him up,' was Tebor's protective comment.

'Maybe. But we're almost out of time.' My panic and persistent obstinacy took over; there was always time for a last roll of the dice. 'Can we go into the Dark Areas?'

'How will that help?'

'Because the President's got to be around somewhere. Somewhere nobody would expect him to be, somewhere which is the most unlikely place you could imagine. I mean, we're wired into every WebCop, every SnoopCam. We've scanned every avatar's digicode, chased every entrance gate to hotels, theme parks, everything. We've picked up anything unusual that's happened. He can't just disappear with no clues whatsoever. He's somewhere ... where nobody knows to look.'

'There's plenty of places like that. Especially in the old areas of the Brick,' said Andi.

'The Dark Areas are not just a small cupboard you walk into. They go on forever.' Tebor's response sounded more positive, now that he was back on firm ground. 'They're three times bigger than the Brick itself. And there's nothing there: no sound, no light, nothing. Even if he was there, we'd never find him in just five minutes.'

'Did you really speak to Jim?' I found myself yelling at him. 'Did he really say he was coming?'

'Why should I lie? If he didn't want to meet you, he would've said so.' He pouted, withdrew into his sulkiness. 'I've done everything you wanted up to now. I'm not lying.'

'If Tebor said Jim was coming' – broke in Andi – 'then he was telling the truth.'

'I still think we should try the one area no one's looked in,' I urged, a last appeal to them.

'No,' said Andi, firmly. 'I agree with Tebor. On top of which he needs Jim's permission to go into the Dark Areas. I don't think he should jeopardize his friendship. Not now. Not when it's too late anyway.'

'I'm getting out of here.' It was done. I looked at the clock. Only three minutes to run.

'Does that mean we won't see you again for a long time?' asked Andi. 'Now that we're no further use to you.'

'No, of course not.' Even in the muddle of my frustration I was stung that she should think it. 'I just need to sort out some things back home. Some people there will believe I was involved.'

'Why?'

'Because I'm the only stone left to turn over.'

'I'll find Jim, and see if you can go into the Dark Areas sometime in the future. Would you like that?'

'Sure, I'd like that. I'll contact you very soon.'

She smiled back at me, but with uncertainty.

'See you, Tebor,' I added. 'You've been interesting. But thanks, and I mean it, both of you.'

The boy shrugged and turned away. I know how he felt. *The one predictable thing about RealWorlders was their unpredictability.* They were totally undependable.

Andi smiled a last smile of reassurance.

I acknowledged it and JetPaxed myself back into Real-

World, the taste of disappointment and failure at the back of my throat.

The clock above the entrance to MetroPort 956 showed there was just one minute to run before the President of the USA would be stuck in Second World, and possibly forced to continue his life as an MIW.

The President of the United States of America sat, hunched, in the blackness.

There had been no contact with his captor for nearly an hour. It was cold and now and then he had stood up and stamped his feet to keep the circulation going. He'd shouted occasionally to attract attention from anyone, including his tormentor. His voice had fallen on stony ground, there being no hint of resonance or projection to it. He soon realized he was totally alone, that his voice probably didn't even carry any further than he could see. And that meant to nowhere.

His body grew colder and he started to shiver. His mind became vacant, normal thought and logic seeming to fade away. His instinct was to stand up and run about in the darkness, to find warmth and light and maybe a way home. His reason told him to stay put, to conserve his energy, to wait where he had been told to wait, as that was his last point of contact with anyone else.

He didn't think about death. Somehow that happened to normal people. How could he possibly be left here to die? He was kidnapped because he was the President, and to kill the President would be wasteful. He had to be worth more alive than dead. He imagined icicles were forming on his body; one even appeared to be hanging on the end of his nose. He wiped his nostrils, but there was nothing there. He tried not to think of the past, of the good and bad things of his life. That served no purpose.

Remain focused, listen for the sounds of someone coming, for anything that might tell him he wasn't alone in this awful dark that had become his solitary world.

At least he could breathe. His chest and lungs were unobstructed, but the air going into them got colder, icy, long frosty fingers with even longer sharp curved nails reaching into him every time he drew breath, raking at his throat and his lungs. He tried to control his breathing, to make it slower than his normal rate.

Just when the cold in his chest became unbearable, he suddenly felt a blast of hot air from above him, as if someone had opened the door of a furnace. And with that surge came a scattering of light, like stars displaying themselves in the night as the cloud breaks. The light grew, the cold retreated, and suddenly he felt free of the pain and the fear and the unknown.

He gasped for more air, for the warmth of it. He realized he was now sitting in a deep constraint of some kind. He turned his head sideways to look. He couldn't acclimatize fast enough; he still didn't understand where he was.

What game is he tormenting me with now?

His mind focused. It refused to believe what he saw. He turned away, shut his eyes to the new hope he had suddenly been promised. When his breathing was regular and steady again, when the last rime of cold had left his body, he turned onto his side and once more took in his surroundings.

I know it's just another game.

He pushed himself up and swung his legs onto the floor. His body felt different, heavier than it had been. Maybe that was WebFever starting to spread; they said it affected the body first. Or was it the brain? He was confused. He no longer felt cold. WebFever was always cold. But he felt warm, almost too hot.

He was suddenly smothered in a light cobweb and he slashed at it, tearing at it with his hands. It engulfed him, constrained him. Then it fell to the floor. He looked down at it. He recognized the WebSuit, the lightweight kimono wraparound he'd put on so as to enter the Web.

He pushed himself to his feet, staggering, his limbs weak after hours of inactivity. He became light-headed as the blood rushed around, pumping furiously and suddenly through his heart. He tottered and fell against the deep leather seat he had been lying on; blackness swamped him again.

Please, please don't let me die. Not now. Not now. Dear Father, forgive me, for I have sinned.

He didn't faint, just lay there, gathering his breath. Then he stood up again. He now realized he was in the Presidential Transfer Suite. He swore, knowing this was a cruel game being played on him. He took off his WebShades and the fluorescent brightness of the room startled him. He knew he wasn't where he hoped to be, because it was all too bright, much more intense than he remembered. He walked to the door and put his hand on the handle.

Turn it. Whatever happens from now on is intended to happen.

He forced himself to turn the handle. It opened into an ante-room containing a group of SensoBeds. Beyond them he could see the Security Control Complex. He walked unsteadily past the beds and into the main control area. There he saw Annie. He saw Joe Meisner, Will Wilkin, Sarah Gilchrist, Deke Marlin and the Vice President. There were others in the room he didn't recognize – lots of them.

Nancy Sumner saw him first and her mouth dropped open in shock. As the others picked up on her expression, they all turned round, and seemed to imitate her stunned surprise.

Obviously it was a game. *The bastard is playing a game. Any minute now he'll yank me back into the blackness and squeeze the breath from my lungs.*

Teddy Dixon fell to his knees, his head bowed and his

hands clasped in front of him, as if suppliant in some great Mass to an unknown God. He steeled himself for a sudden return to the Dark Areas. After a moment, he looked up suspiciously, winced when he realized someone had crossed the room to stand in front of him. It was Annie.

She slapped him across the face, a wild haymaker with as much force as her twisted emotions of anger and relief could muster. The power of the blow sent him reeling sideways, toppling over onto the carpeted floor.

'How could you do this to me?' she shrieked. 'You and that fucking Marilyn Monroe.'

His eyes watered; his chest was heaving. He knew he was home; it wasn't a game any more.

BOOK FOUR

··

A BUSTED FLUSH

'Neville,' he introduced himself, holding up his warrant card. 'EI6.'

I looked at the ID card and nodded indifferently, like I was the big dog sniffing and dismissing the smaller dog.

I was glad to be home. Gallagher had messaged me as soon as the President returned from Second World. He seemed OK, but I sensed it was not over yet. I'd decided to take a rest before looking for the answers. I was probably still Suspect Number One so it wasn't over for me yet.

I turned to PC Renreth. 'Don't often see you out here this early.'

Renreth smiled apologetically. He didn't particularly want to be out here either. They were all standing outside Rose Cottage where John Mathews had just dropped me off in his Land Rover.

'Don't forget your bacon, Conor,' John Mathews shouted.

I went back to the vehicle to take the packet Mathews handed me.

The EI6 man came up behind me. 'I thought you had no idea where he was?' he remarked sarcastically to Mathews.

'I didn't. He rang and told me to come and fetch him.'

'Where?'

'That's not your business,' I snapped, wheeling round to face the agent. 'Unless you have a warrant or official reason for asking these questions.'

'We'd appreciate your assistance, Mr Smith.'

'Why?'

'You're well aware why.'

'OK, but it's got nothing to do with John. I rang him from the OuterSprawl, I needed a lift and he came and collected me. He now needs to get back to his farm.'

'That's fine,' said Neville. Whatever crisis had prompted HQ to send him to Norfolk now seemed over. He was still here because they'd ordered him to stay and run through a few questions with the GameMaster. Keeping the local farmer around wasn't necessary any longer.

'See you, John. Thanks for the bacon, and the lift.'

Mathews mock-saluted me and drove off, a big smile smeared across his face. I know what he was thinking. *A pigpen.* Who would've thought that Conor Smith, the famous GameMaster, had spent the night wrapped in protective sheeting in a pigpen. It'd take a long time for me to live that one down. I'd been linked to the only computer on Mathews's farm, a small personal quantum machine that I'd given him months earlier and that he'd never even switched on. We powered it up from the pigpen supply, and Mathews had left me all wrapped up, under the straw and swill, in an area nobody would remotely consider even looking in. Finally, when I'd returned from the Web, I had taken a quick shower, changed into fresh clothes I'd already brought from Rose Cottage and set off with him for the InnerSprawl. We stopped where we were clear of all CCTVs at a point we'd agreed he would pick me up.

I saw the broken window. 'Whose handiwork is that?'

'My colleague's,' said Neville.

'The American, I presume? The one John told me about.'

'Yes.'

'And where's he buggered off to?'

'Back in London.'

'Got a bit carried away, didn't he?'

'We'll pay for it to be fixed. I'll contact someone as soon as I've finished here.'

'Don't bother. I'll do it myself.' I switched to the hapless policeman. 'Were you here when they smashed it?'

'They did it before I could stop them.'

'And then they went inside the house?' I enjoyed baiting Renreth, saw the discomfort in his red face. 'I suppose they did that before you could stop them too.'

'The constable was acting under orders from his superior,' said Neville. 'He was instructed, by London, to give us any assistance we required. It was a matter – '

'. . . of national security,' I jumped in. 'I know, I've heard it all before. Now, shall we go in the front door this time or would you prefer to climb through the window?'

'The door's fine,' replied Neville coolly.

I shook my head at Renreth in mock disgust, then opened the front door and led them in. I went straight to the computer room.

'You didn't get very far in here, did you?' I enjoy taunting officialdom.

'You know that already.'

I shrugged and spread myself out in the big armchair. The one thing I trusted was my security system. What they didn't know was that as soon as the house was broken in to, as soon as the silent security alarm kicked in, all data from the computers was instantly downloaded to a secure site in the Sprawl and then wiped off the house workstations. Even if they'd managed to get the machines out of there, there would have been no information, no programs, no records of anything; just blanked-out, useless and fatally damaged irreparable disks.

My meeting with Neville lasted no more than ten minutes, with myself finally pleading tiredness. The EI6 man didn't know what questions to ask, and I said very little. He had only hung around because he'd been ordered to, to ensure that I returned to Rose Cottage, and maybe even to apologize for breaking and entering. When they left, I gave Renreth one last withering glance, implying that would be a favour I'd be calling in one day.

I called Gallagher.

'What state's the President in?' I asked him as soon as he appeared on the wall screen.

'DC,' quipped Gallagher.

'Very funny. Anyway, that's a district, not a state. What do they teach you people in school?'

'How to play video games so we can pay fortunes to people like you.'

'Yeah, yeah. So how is our man?'

Gallagher picked up a report and read from it. 'No excessive motion sickness, OK on interpupillary distance, ditto high- and low-contrast visual acuity and heterophoria. A bit wobbly on near and distance fixation disparity while he's showing some general medium-level reactions on his Simulator Sickness Data Analysis. Balance is good, just a bit of stiffness in the joints. Cardiovascular's fine. Not bad for a guy his age who doesn't spend that much time in Second World. I think everyone's surprised he's come up with such strong results after what he's been through. Doctors say a little rest and then back to work tomorrow.'

'No drug inducement? Nothing suspicious?'

'Nothing the doctors can pick up. It was a quick but thorough examination. Why?'

'Just looking at all the angles. You know me.'

'No suggestion of hypnosis. He's come back very much as himself.'

I stifled a yawn. I needed bed.

'OK, let's talk later. I'm shattered and the sooner I get you off my back, the sooner I can get some sleep. Fancy you not knowing DC wasn't a state.'

'You know you're in a bad place, don't you, Conor?'

'I know.'

'They realize you won't let go . . . that you'll chase it.'

'Who says?'

'Your reputation . . . *Will* you let go?'

He stared at me and saw the answer was in my eyes.

'Then it's not over yet,' Gallagher said. 'Watch your back.'

My final call was to the Datakeeper. There was no answer – which was normal with the Datakeeper.

I left a VideoMessage: *Prez found. Came in unhurt. Will continue chase the game. Going to bed now. Will call later.*

I went to the bedroom, and after closing the curtains, switched off the lights and slept.

The President had tried, but couldn't hold back a deep yawn.

'I think it's time you got some rest,' said Joe Meisner.

'Soon.' Dixon nodded. 'That doctor's report showed I'm in good shape, huh, considering how long I was out there.' It hadn't taken long for his old bravado to bounce back.

He was still high from his adventure, but he realized his body needed time out. He'd insisted on a short debrief once he'd recovered his poise after entering the Control Room. It had taken a while, though, before Annie had gone back to her rooms and the other politicos had left him with the experts. Then Marlin, Meisner, Gallagher, Swilkin and Clancy all listened to his tale; he had already decided to omit such personal details as his time with the two women. Then they gave him a quick rundown of their own efforts.

His entrapment in the Dark Areas caused them most concern, and they'd ended the meeting with an agreement that they would continue to chase any potential leads, while he rested before returning for further dialogue and analysis. No information was to be released, meanwhile, about his disappearance in Second World – in fact it was to be buried and obliterated from all public access.

'Am I in trouble, Joe?' Dixon asked his Chief of Staff once they were alone in the Oval Office.

'No more than on previous occasions,' came the uneasy answer.

'This is different.'

'Only if it gets out. We can ride most of it, but when you put the whole story together, then it won't be so easy.'

'Poor Annie.'

'Nothing she's not used to. Remember, the one thing she'll want to protect is your position as President – and hers as First Lady. You both gave up too much for her to risk throwing that away.'

'Prick happy . . . that's me.' There was no embarrassment in his words; the two of them went back a long way, had set out on the journey towards power together.

'Sumner tried to get agreement to inform the media almost as soon as she knew what had happened.'

'Any support for her?'

'Wilkin buckled, but Sarah stood her ground. For a while, anyway. She just kept everyone aware of the legalities. But Sumner kept pushing and was starting to get through.'

'Fucking bitch. At least I can't run for a third term. Otherwise she'd have my balls if I didn't choose her as running mate.'

'She'll do that anyway. She'll expect you to nominate her.'

Dixon groaned.

'How many people saw you in Second World?'

'Recognized me? Only that waiter.'

'And he's dead, MIW, so he doesn't count. Anyone else?'

'Gladys Presley?'

They both laughed; it was good to share a joke.

'We've got to go on the attack, Teddy,' Meisner said when the President finally settled down. 'We could just ignore it, say you went walkabout, just wandering the Brick. Got tired of all the security. Sorry you caused concern, but you just wanted time to yourself, a new term to face, taking stock of your life and your responsibilities. Remember, nobody can prove anything. You came back of your own volition.'

Dixon remembered sweet Claire and how that had ended.

Maybe someone recorded it. Maybe they'd release it one day.
'Things might've happened down there that got recorded,'
he admitted, not wanting to expand on his recollection. 'I
couldn't live with that every day, waiting for the proof to
blow. We don't know who caused this, Joe – maybe it was
even the WebSlime.'

'Like you said, you've plenty of enemies out there.'

Dixon reflected for a moment, then grinned. 'I know
you, Joe. Where're you coming from now?'

'At first I thought we could say you broke away to test
security. But nobody'll believe that. So it's back to Plan A.'

'Which is?'

'Turn it to our advantage. Let's tell the truth – within
reason. My way, all we have to cover is the Marilyn episode.
I think we could manage that. I mean, no one saw anything
happen for sure. She was just your birthday treat. Even
Sumner would have a tough time proving anything. She'd
have to go to the Supreme Court to get the recordings of
you and Marilyn made public. That would take years, and
it'd make her look bad, too greedy for the Presidency. She'd
never take that risk. By then we'll have erased any record of
what went on in the Web Oval Office. And hell, it wasn't
for real. You were goofing around with a digital sex symbol.
Right now that's happening with millions of others on the
Brick. It's like they caught you watching an old porno
movie. Who cares in the end?

'Except somebody got murdered.'

'Nothing to do with you. You weren't even with Marilyn
by then.'

'So how do we use it to our advantage? By telling
everyone I'm no different to them, that I jerk off over
Marilyn Monroe. What am I, the new JFK?' Dixon snorted
as he shook his head. 'Only difference is he did it with the
real one.'

'Teddy, that's not important. You can bang any movie
star you want. Real ones – they'll queue up on the White

362

House lawn if you tell them to. Though you'll have to wait until your Presidency's over.' Meisner took a deep breath. 'Right now, our only concern is getting you out of this mess.'

'Hit me.'

'We tell the truth.'

'Say again.'

'Stick to the truth, or as near as you can, and you won't get canned. We say that somebody, a group, maybe terrorists, decided that the InfoCalypse was a real database being kept by the US government. Out there they seriously believe in the InfoCalypse, and that this government keeps records on all its citizens. All records, from high-school, through bank and employment records, right up to personal diaries. In the end, you talked them out of holding you hostage, and you've come back to now find out if there really is an InfoCalypse. And you're going to leave no stone unturned until you determine the truth. If there is an InfoCalypse, then you will destroy it, even if it hurts your administration and some of the people who run it.'

The silence hung between them for a long time, as Dixon realized that here was Meisner endorsing the straw he had grasped at in the Dark Areas.

'You're wondering, is there an InfoCalypse?' Meisner asked.

'Tell me the truth, Teddy.'

'I've never hid things from you, and I've never been informed of one.'

'You've asked?'

'Sure. And got the same answer every time, that no such thing exists.'

'Then my advice is we go down that road.'

Dixon sighed. 'I need some rest now. I'll sleep on it. Just give me three hours.' It was well known that Dixon survived on only a few hours' sleep each night. 'Wake me, then get some breakfast brought to the Oval Room, and take me through a more polished presentation of your idea. Then I'll decide.'

'What about the ThemeCorp opening?'

'Is that today?'

'Early evening.'

'I'm nervous about going back on the Brick.'

'You'll be OK. This time those agents will be wrapped round you like a banana skin.'

'I don't like it, Joe. Deep down, I'm shit scared. You don't know the power that guy had over me.'

'It means massive coverage. Billions watching. Cocking-a-snoop at the kidnappers.'

'OK,' was the uneasy response. 'But ease back on every-thing else. For a few days anyway.'

Dixon stood up to leave, and Meisner followed him.

'Three hours,' said the President. 'No longer.' He flicked the intercom switch. 'Want to come in here, Jilly,' he ordered his secretary.

'Jilly's finished for the day, Mr President,' came the metallic answer.

'Is that you, Mary?'

'Yes, sir.'

'I'm going to rest up in the Small Office. Bring your work through there. And leave the phone through to your VoiceMail. I don't want to be disturbed.'

He clicked the switch. 'See you in three hours,' he repeated to Meisner.

Dixon left the Oval Office to go to the Small Office next to it. It was a small suite, with a bedroom and sitting area for when the President was working late.

Meisner walked into the hall outside and noticed the secretary had already left her desk. He heard the lock click on the door that led into the Small Office.

When the President said he didn't want to be disturbed, he meant it. As far as Meisner was concerned sex was only a substitute for boredom.

Meisner enjoyed these moments of panic, of frenzied activity against all the odds – it's what he lived for. He'd been up all night but he wasn't tired, because the adrenalin rush kept him going. He popped a narco juice-drop just in case.

Somehow, as always, he'd make sure Dixon squirmed his way out of the mess.

They were linked by videocam, Swilkin in Washington and Harbour-Smythe in Benhall.

'He's ahead of the game,' said the latter. 'I get the feeling that whatever information we get, from whatever source, is only what Conor Smith wants us to have.'

'Like what?' asked Swilkin.

'Credit information. He doesn't have any, because he pays everything immediately by internet bank transfer. I know he's rich, but he wasn't always. Yet there's no record of him ever borrowing anything. He doesn't even have a credit rating. He owns everything he has, banks through an offshore internet bank which we haven't traced yet and – '

'Neville!' interrupted Swilkin. 'Some bank's got to issue his debit and credit cards.'

'They all do. He's got over thirty accounts with different internet banks. And we're still looking. His firewall is like one of those water fountains you see in the theme parks, you know the ones where the water leaps out of nowhere, crosses overhead then disappears into the ground twenty feet away. Except there's thirty of them doing it at the same time.'

'What else?'

'Asset identification – it's impossible to quantify. No records of what he's bought and what he's sold. When you don't have any credit, no one knows what you own. Mostly bought on the internet under a host of different names. Even his house was bought on eBay. We can't trace the deeds; they're lodged with some company in the Turks and Caicos. I'm sure if pushed he'd prove ownership, but you'll only get that by tapping on his front door with a search warrant and eviction notice.'

'Tax?'

'All paid up, on the dot. Doesn't quibble with assessments, doesn't even claim for allowances. It's like money's something you take for granted, like food or air. In truth, where material things are concerned, he can't be bothered.'

'Taxman must love him.' Swilkin pondered for a moment. 'Don't they wonder if there's more to go at?'

'They gave that up years ago. They tried to investigate whether he was laundering through the Web, or taking undeclared debits for games, anything that involved loose cash. He was totally open with them and they found nothing. So they just took the money offered and decided that's just the way he was.'

'How much does he earn?'

Harbour-Smythe told him.

Swilkin whistled. 'Wow. And they still reckon he's honest.'

'According to my tax contact, it marries with what other GameMasters earn. They make corporations billions. A couple of mill for a few days' work on a security procedure or new game or system test is peanuts in the overall cost structure. Do that a dozen times a year, plus what you earn from your other contacts, and the money just becomes meaningless. Maybe we both took a wrong career path, Dwight.'

Swilkin laughed. He knew they both loved what they did, and that gave him a small understanding of Conor Smith. In that respect he, Neville and Conor were brothers. In a world of materialism, where values had long since flown out of the window, they believed in the professionalism of what they did and nothing got in the way of that.

'We really are digging deep. We've even tried chasing Bounty Hunter resources.' The Web and RealWorld had become a paradise for private detectives who now chased bounties on people who had mostly not paid their debts. 'You've seen the medical stuff. Nothing. We can't even get into his PO Box numbers. The Post Office say they don't exist. Yet, he gets mail, both e- and hard copy through a PO Box in his name. They tried to trace it for us, but once again the information was buried in digital treacle. All we can do is keep going, looking for something that pulls a thread, and then maybe we can unravel Mr Smith's life and habits.'

'I appreciate that, Neville.' Swilkin suddenly changed tack. 'Any other ideas about what really happened over the last day?'

'No.'

'I'm very concerned about the InfoCalypse.'

'We're on Vuephone now, Dwight.' Harbour-Smythe's warning tone was very clear.

'It's secure, trust me. If *I* can't run a secure line, nobody can.' Swilkin laughed again. 'You telling me you're not on a secure line yourself, Neville? I don't believe it.'

Harbour-Smythe laughed. 'We all store information we shouldn't have.'

'The InfoCalypse goes beyond the kind of information you and I hold – even those little titbits only we know about. My instinct is that somebody out there thinks there's a great big government department that does nothing but hold information on every individual, every corporation, every religious order, every ... on everything, I guess.'

'They're talking about us, Dwight. About GCHQ and the National Security Agency. Maybe someone's trying to muzzle us, thinks we're too big for our boots ... possibly too dangerous.'

'The ransom note talks about the alpha and the omega. We don't have anything like that. Do you?'

'No.'

'But that's a specific statement: the alpha to the omega, He says he doesn't want money, no terrorist releases, even threatens to kill our President if we don't wipe out the InfoCalypse.'

'Which he didn't.'

'Or couldn't.'

'Explain.'

'Maybe he just didn't have the will or the means to do it.'

Swilkin stretched his arms over his head, cracking his shoulder blades. 'We both need sleep.'

'Yes. I'm leaving a team trawling through the numbers; see if they come up with anything. A little nap will refresh. Need a fresh mind for this.'

'Let's hope it's just a bloody good hacker playing games. Did the President have any idea where they kept him?'

'From his debrief I'd say in the Dark Areas.'

Harbour-Smythe let out a low whistle. 'Scary.'

'Prime suspect is still Conor Smith.'

'Prime and only. We'll get something on him eventually.'

'Then we'll just sit and see where he leads us. See ya. Love to Henrietta and the kids.'

'Return the compliments to your brood.'

The Visue-link between them snapped off.

Harbour-Smythe leant back in his chair. He wasn't totally convinced that the NSA didn't have some form of Info-Calypse. He was close to Swilkin but they were both professionals. Occasionally in their dealings they had concealed things from each other; it was also in their nature.

Well, Mr Conor Smith. Are you the bait . . . or are you the player? Hare . . . or tortoise?

Whichever, we'll make bloody sure we keep up with you.

I felt good, refreshed. Anyway I never needed long bouts of sleep. There'd been a dream but it hadn't gone on forever like most of my dreams. I'd woken with a start, the dream still fresh.

In it I loaded the Nagan with six bullets; they seemed massive, like squeezing tank shells into the small barrel of the revolver. But they slid in easily. I walked the Brick, trying to break into the Dark Areas, but every time I pushed against the physical extremities of the Brick I was thrown back, bounced back till I fell. Then Andi came, smiling. She slipped her arm through mine, just above where I held the Nagan. And we walked into the Dark Areas. Just like that. Effortlessly easing through the wall in front of it as though it never existed. She vanished as quickly as she had come, and then I knew I was in danger. I crouched, looked round in the darkness, waited for the enemy, whoever that was, to come at me.

It was Tebor who came first, silently out of the blackness, rushing towards me. I fired the gun, but there was no sound, no bullet, not even the empty metallic click of hammer on chamber. I kept firing and still nothing happened. I heard sounds while I pumped the trigger, knew they were all around me, were getting ready to attack, to hurt me. *Why didn't she warn me?* I turned the revolver towards his face and looked down the barrel. There was a small light at the other end of it. I peered closer, in the darkness, until the barrel was against my eye. I pulled the trigger. There was still no sound. But the bullet came, slow-mo, spinning, towards my eye. I tried to get away, snatched my head back in a desperate effort to escape. But it was like the barrel was glued to my eye, so I couldn't shake it off. Behind the bullet, down the barrel, I saw Andi. She smiled and blew me a kiss, and suddenly everything exploded into a brilliant white light.

I awoke, no sweat, no racing heartbeat that follows most nightmares. I smiled, savouring the emotion and the fear, then turned over and went back to sleep.

Later on I showered and changed, toasted three slices of white bread, smeared them with butter and thick-peel marmalade so chunky that it was collapsing off the edges, and devoured them quickly so as to stop the jam falling onto the plate. The jam I did drop was scooped up with my index finger and licked deliciously.

Then I slid the plates and knives into the dishwasher, put the marmalade and butter back into the fridge and headed for the sitting room with a mug of coffee. Mr Domesticity, that was me.

I enjoyed these simple routines; they cleared my mind, stabilized me, gave me the space to reflect over the events of the past few hours from a detached viewpoint. I crashed onto the sofa and called up the emails. There were only three.

The first was from Tajo, my eager student from the day before. He wanted to set up another game session when he, Nomuna and Icarus could once again raise their game and proceed further in the Valley of the Dragons. I decided to let them sweat it out for a couple of days before responding.

The second message was from ThemeCorp. They'd like me to come in as soon as possible. It was not a matter of extreme urgency, but sooner rather than later would be appreciated. It was signed by Malcolm Bonham, Vice President of Defence and Security. Bonham was a main board director and in charge of one of the most important arms of the megacorporation. I'd dealt with him before on a number of occasions, usually when there was a new product launch and it was necessary to make sure the software and systems could not be breached by hackers. This message surprised me, as I'd never met Bonham on a one-to-one before: our meetings had always been at ThemeCorp Web offices with others present. Maybe it had to do with the President's disappearance, as obviously they'd have picked up on it by now. The corporate language was easy to follow, *not a matter of extreme urgency* meant as soon as possible, like *now*. I decided nevertheless to sit that one out until I'd got the rest of my plans together.

The third email was a picvox from Andi. She smiled and said, 'Remember me. We were fighting the world yesterday. Have you forgotten me already?'

I emailed her back. HANG AROUND. CATCH UP WITH U LATER. WHO DID U SAY U WERE? ARE U SURE I KNOW U?

The phone rang. It was John Mathews. 'Your man's on the box. All channels.'

'OK.' What endeared Mathews to me was his obstinate use of forgotten terminology, his Viking shield held high against laser-guided rockets.

It was a news bulletin, and the President of the USA was about to make a broadcast. A caption declared this statement would not be broadcast live in Second World, through the White House Annex. It didn't add that by doing so Teddy Dixon was clearly concerned that he might just outdo Houdini and David Blaine and David Copperfield by disappearing live in front of more than two billion viewers. That was not something the Secret Service was likely to risk.

Dixon looked meaningfully into the camera. 'My fellow Americans, our coalition partners, and all those who believe in a free world. I come to you from a state of shock and distress. What I tell you now is something that many of my advisers urged me should remain a secret. I'm not here to criticize them, though, because they have a very valid point with regard to national and international security, as well as the security of the office I am proud to hold.'

Dixon leant forward in a manner that he considered implied sharing a secret with his audience. *Difficult, that, with billions of viewers.*

'The reason I come before you now is because we must conquer a fear we all have. It is one that I did not take seriously until yesterday, one which must be stood up to, and faced head-on, and defeated once and for all. This is no enemy with weapons of mass destruction, no evil that manifests itself openly before us. This is a silent, insidious weapon, with a power so great that it can destroy the very fabric of the society and democracy that binds us all together.'

I leant forward, the coffee in my hand forgotten. *Surely not?*

'Yesterday,' Dixon continued, slowly and deliberately, to let each word sink in, 'yesterday, I was kidnapped inside the Web. From the White House Annex. Just after I had met there with many of our supporters and colleagues, I wanted to meet with the people there on the Brick. As many of you saw, I was hugely entertained by Marilyn Monroe singing "Happy Birthday" to me. Knowing what a huge admirer I was of John Fitzgerald Kennedy, our thirty-fifth President, my wife, Annie, arranged for Miss Monroe to sing for me just as she had for the great JFK. It was a glorious surprise and one that she had wanted to be shared with all of you.'

He took a sip of water. *Kidnapped? Marilyn Monroe?* He now had two billion people spellbound, hanging on his next few words. He put the glass down.

'I invited Miss Monroe to walk through the Brick with me. I wanted her to sing for you and I wanted to shake the hands of those of you who, like me, believe in the free world we inhabit. It was imprudent and rash of me. I should have spoken first to the Secret Service. But I was carried away by the moment: the emotion of entering a second term, the devotion of my wife, the happiness of my birthday all overcame me. I was injudicious in my actions.

'Somehow, and we are fully investigating how, I got separated from my JetPax and was held prisoner by a person or persons, as yet unknown to me or to our intelligence agencies. It would be wrong of me, at this time, while our Security Services are still investigating all avenues, for me to describe what took place during those hours that my avatar was held captive in Second World. I don't have to remind you of the dangers of being kept away too long from our bodies, or of the WebFever and disorientation that can follow. Fortunately, I was allowed to return to RealWorld before any damage occurred. After a doctor's examination I have been passed completely fit to resume all my Presidential duties. Which I will promptly do. My first duty is later today, with the launching of an exciting new venture for ThemeCorp, another great American institution that is a leader in world business and innovation. So listen, you out there, whoever you are.' Dixon wagged his finger at the screen. 'I will not allow myself to be cowed by these Web terrorists. Freedom is a war that must be fought and won every day as it comes. As Commander-in-Chief I will uphold that freedom at all costs. If going back on the Web today is part of defending our freedom, then I will do exactly what is required of me.'

He reached down and took another sip of water slowly, using the drama of the moment to let his audience absorb what he had just implied. *Freedom Fighter Teddy Dixon.*

'There was no ransom involved, no release of political prisoners stipulated. The only demand made was that we wipe out the InfoCalypse. Now you all know what that's meant to be, this mythical InfoCalypse. Information supposedly stored in a secret place by a government that continuously spies on its people. But I have to tell you, there is – to my honest knowledge – no such thing countenanced by our government. Unless I have been misled, lied to by those who would keep such information from me. I therefore believe it to be no more than rumour.

'But whoever kidnapped me, this ... this *person* genuinely believes there exists an InfoCalypse. And I know that many others in our nation, and throughout the free world, believe this ... organization exists. In view of that, I shall make every endeavour to find out the truth, with every means at my disposal, to once and for all lay this public nightmare to rest. And if by any chance it does exist, then it stands against everything our democracy represents. Of course we watch and monitor those who might harm us. Of course we tap their phones. Of course we open their mail and read it. But all this is done within the framework of our Constitution, of our laws and the United Nation Bill of Human Rights. And always with the sole aim of protecting our citizens.

'As President I cannot tolerate any covert actions, by my government or any other, which would infringe these basic rights.'

He held up his right hand as though taking the oath of allegiance.

'I swear that. And I will not stop until I have discovered the truth, so help me God.'

He smiled his Presidential Teddy Dixon I-love-you smile.

'From Annie, who waited patiently and always believed I would return unharmed, no doubt helped by her prayers and her belief in our God – from both of us – with our deepest love to you, thank you.'

The Presidential emblem then appeared, and I switched off. I took a sip of coffee, which was now lukewarm. I went back to the kitchen and just as I put the mug on the draining board, my phone rang. I flipped it open; it wasn't a number I recognized.

'Smith?' blasted a powerful voice.

'Who's that?'

'Bonham. I thought I instructed you to call me.' The ThemeCorp Security and Defence VP spoke like a fast rat-a-tatting typewriter, a crisply yet softly spoken former British Army colonel who punctuated his rapid speech with occasional repeating of words, like he was giving his mouth time to catch up with his brain.

'You said it wasn't urgent.'

'No. I said it was not a matter of extreme . . .' he hissed and repeated the word, drawing it out this time '. . . extreeeme urgency. I also quite clearly said *sooner* rather than later.'

'I'm sorry. I misunderstood.'

'No, you didn't. You're far too clever for that. Which is why we pay you the ludicrous amounts we do.'

'You can always stop, let me go.'

'Don't be facetious, Smith. You know you're on contract. And you know we're not going to release you, however rude you are to me. But never trust anyone who's continually rude, that's what I say. Now, when can you get in here?'

'Can't we meet in your Web office?'

'Can't do, because I'm not in Hollywood. Arrived in London, overnight flight, to see you – *you*. Top security. Eyeball to eyeball stuff. Very urgent.'

'But not "extremely" urgent.'

'I'll ignore that. How soon can you be here?'

'Four hours, minimum.'

'If you left now you could get here in under three, maybe two. Trains are faster than that antique wreck you call a car.'

'I've things to do. Important things.'

'Get in now!' Bonham spat.

'Sorry. If you don't like it, tear up my contract.'

Bonham hissed, as if exasperated at dealing with a child. 'I'll expect you here in four hours, no longer. Earlier would be appreciated.'

'I'll do my best.' I paused. 'Bonham?'

'Yes.'

'Is this anything to do with the broadcast I've just seen?'

'Don't waste my time and I shan't waste yours. Get *here*.'

The phone went dead and I flipped it shut.

I then pushed Bonham and the President and everything else into background mode while I went to do what I really considered was important.

He sat very still and felt the waves. Small movements, stabs of energy that ran along the matrix and that he absorbed, minute rippling sensations that told him where they were coming from. He waited patiently, a spider deep in the heart of his Web, touching the strands that had become his one life, trusting the many instincts he had inherited. They'd be coming soon. He felt no emotion; he was beyond loss, whatever the outcome.

He ran over the past, recalling how he had got to this point in the infinity of his existence. There was no reminiscing, no tender recollection of warmer and happier times. He only dissected his pasts, examined them in infinitesimal details, tried to learn beyond where he had been taught. He recalled his childhoods, his groups of parents, his schools, his colleges, his careers, and ultimately he always came back to the same point.

He was right. He knew he was tired, but tiredness never came to him. He had become himself, all the sum parts of Jim Nelson and Mike Keebles and Dom Murphy. The men who had no blackness in their souls, yet had passed their anger and bitterness on to him. He would be the Saviour. Not because that's what was expected of him. It's what nobody expected. Jim Nelson and Mike Keebles and Dom Murphy would be proud of him. He himself was incapable of pride. Only confusion, but he wasn't confused; he didn't understand confusion.

I know who I am but who am I?

I know where I came from but where was that?

They put me here but now they are gone, leaving me alone when I don't even recognize loneliness.

Why am I the Saviour?

Am I the Saviour?

The Saviour of . . . what?

Somebody was pulling his strings. He remained still; the spider waiting for the strings of his Web to stir so that he would know they were coming, and could finally fulfil all the things he had been born not to do. That was the only bit that continued to confuse him.

I entered the computer room, and was about to slip in to Second World, when a signal came through from Gallagher. I could do without it, but knew I had to speak to the American. We met in Second World, in a small chat room on the Brick that Gallagher had specially hired.

'We firewalled here?' I asked as he entered the room.

'Of course.' Gallagher sat down in one of the two conference chairs. 'Were you on your way out?'

'Yes, I was. You get some sleep?' I didn't bother sitting, had other things to do.

'Enough. You saw the broadcast?'

'Interesting angle. But not quite how it happened.'

A big grin split Gallagher's face. 'Politicians, always come out of shit smelling of roses.'

'The heat's off now he's back and safe. I've got a couple of errands to run meanwhile, then I'll get down to giving it my full attention. I presume that's what you still want?'

'Yes, but you're on your own. This isn't official.'

'Am I still number-one public suspect?'

'Probably.'

'When can I have something on Jim Nelson?'

'We're working on it. I'll patch anything we get through to you. Unofficially, of course.'

'OK. I'll call when I'm back. So what did you really want?'

Gallagher hesitated. 'Swilkin,' he said eventually.

'Get to it, Paul. I'm short on time.'

'This is not an accusation, but you and I both agreed we'd share all our thoughts.'

'We did.' *Up to a point.* I had decided I would sit on the information about access to the Dark Areas.

'Just before the President returned I got Swilkin to come over. I said I had information about Jim Nelson and I wasn't prepared to pass it through normal channels. We had about half an hour to run to the deadline and I wanted to give you more time while you went to meet Nelson, without the Telephone Exchange chasing you.

'What surprised me, when Swilkin eventually arrived, was that he didn't seem overly concerned about Nelson. In fact he relaxed and just sat back watching us operate. There was no sense of urgency and yet his own team was running out of time. It crossed my mind that Swilkin arrived there because ... maybe he expected Dixon to appear. I know I myself asked him to come over, but it was all too cool, too relaxed.' Gallagher leant back in his chair. 'I just thought you should know that, if you believe there's an insider involved. I mean any InfoCalypse has got to be backed by a big organization, one like Swilkin's, one that's going to benefit from InfoCalypse and know how to use it.'

'Then why would you kidnap the President and draw attention to yourself?'

'There's been a lot of publicity over this recently. This way they can run this investigation and come up with a lot of zeros. It'll ease the pressure from Congress and maybe from the media. It would kill the InfoCalypse dead. Hell, the Telephone Exchange and the NSA will probably handle the investigation themselves. They'll be judge and jury at their own trial.'

'Maybe not so crazy.' It made as much sense as any other theory. 'It's the sort of thing these guys spend billions dreaming up.'

I drove to Norwich station, parked and caught the City-Express into Liverpool Street.

I'd picked up my two shadowers minutes after I left Rose Cottage; a man and woman in a grey General Motors people carrier. Silly choice; that way it was difficult to merge yourself into your surroundings in the narrow empty lanes of Norfolk. So I deliberately took an obtuse and long-winded trip to Norwich and they confirmed my suspicions by staying behind, always at what they thought a safe distance.

I dumped the car in the multi-storey and, having already bought my ticket through the bucket shop, boarded the waiting train. I sat at the back, first class, and watched others on the platform. The woman, in her late forties, not unattractive with her sharp Doberman features, followed me onto the train. She sat at the other end of the carriage, and I thought about introducing myself to her, playing along with the game.

But I'd get bored within minutes. I'd only enjoy the moment of revelation and her stunned surprise. Or maybe not. Maybe they *wanted* me to know I was being followed.

Another passenger, also a woman, climbed in and sat in the adjacent row. She took her GoggleVision out of her handbag, slipped it over her eyes like spectacles, plugged in the earphone and started to watch the news.

'Anything interesting?' I asked her after a couple of minutes, once she took it off.

She shook her head. 'Same old turgid stuff. Nothing much changes, does it?'

'I heard the US President got kidnapped.'

She laughed. 'If you believe that, you believe anything. Anything for publicity. Probably got himself into trouble with some girl. Isn't that what he usually does?'

She slipped the GoggleVision back on her head and settled down to watch a longer programme. Probably a soap, maybe *Coronation Street*. That was created by another of my clients. You didn't just watch it on TV anymore, as you could actually go to Second World, to the *Street* studios, and join in, play out your part as a character.

It was a one-hour trip, so I gradually lost myself in my thoughts.

The train, on electromagnetic rails, slid out into the greenery of rural Norfolk, picked up speed till it was effortlessly gliding at nearly two hundred miles per hour. That wouldn't last long, not once we hit the Outer Conurbation and slowed down for safety reasons.

I loved the countryside; it was cool. It never changed, was always constant. The seasons, the life of the animals and plants and people who lived there, hadn't really changed for centuries. They just did things more efficiently, but the underlying culture never altered. It had its own pace of evolution, in spite of genetic crops and farming techniques. There was still winter, spring, summer and autumn, and rural life had no choice but to simply revolve round those phases.

I'd soon be in the Sprawl, first the Outer, then the Inner. The heart of civilization. *Like hell*. It ran from the south coast all the way up the central spine of England, linking all the old industrial cities into one overcrowded metropolis.

The woman laughed as she watched her GoggleVision programme. At least someone was happy for her; no problems. *Who gives a damn if the President got nicked?*

The heat of the Sprawl developed its own localized global warming, so was usually enveloped in perma-drizzle. I saw the grey damp clouds in the distance as the train rushed towards London. Then came the first strands of the OuterSprawl, the first warm drops of drizzle spray, the last views of the freedom and greenery that I left behind.

The lights in the carriage glowed brighter in the darkness of midday. My watcher pretended not to notice me, while the lady with the GoggleVision was lost to the world.

Twenty minutes to go. The houses that backed up to the line were all similar. We passed through Colchester, then Chelmsford, then Romford. It all looked the same, rows and rows of similar eco-houses, same-sized windows, equal-sized gardens. Each house had a stab at shouting its individuality; different colours, different shrubbery all bought from the same garden centre, different garages for the identi-cars. But in their efforts to be different, all they succeeded in was looking exactly the same.

The CityExpress slowed as it got into the old East End and the heart of where the under-privileged, the latest economic immigrants lived; Whitechapel, Finsbury Park, Old Kent Road. Amid cheap shops and plenty of bargains.

Shit. I hate it here.

We soon passed into the InnerSprawl. Flats, apartments, maisonettes, offices, shops, the debris of human-rat existence, all crammed together, all jammed into their little twelve-by-fifteens, and proud to be sophisticated Londoners.

What a joke!

The rain got heavier as we finally pulled into Liverpool Street.

'You definitely enjoyed whatever you were watching,' I said to the GoggleVision woman as she stood up and gathered up her bag.

'Yeah,' she replied. 'It was OK.'

Satisfied that the art of conversation wasn't dead in London, I followed her off the train. My tracker kept her distance and waited till I was half-way up the platform before disembarking. When she set off after me, I stopped, swung round and waited for her.

'I'm going to ThemeCorp head office,' I said when she was level with me.

'Sorry?' she queried.

'You're not very good at this, are you?'

'I don't understand.' She tried to act bewildered.

'ThemeCorp,' I repeated. 'Wardour Street, Soho.'

I walked towards the taxi rank. As I climbed in to the cab, she waved to someone across the station. I didn't bother looking to see who it was. They knew where I was going. It was a cheap shot but I'd enjoyed what I'd just done. *That's how they do it in the old movies.*

The electro-taxi moved into the stop–start traffic.

Jim was already at the table when Andi and Tebor arrived. He welcomed them with a big smile, kissed Andi on the cheek, and ordered their usual drinks.

'So,' he said as the drinks arrived, 'Exciting times.'

'Who did it, Jim?' asked Andi. 'Something that big.'

'Who knows? But you two were in on it. Right up to the end. Unbelievable.'

'Didn't get anywhere, did we?' commented Tebor. 'They're one step ahead all the time.'

'They'll get him.'

'Him?'

'Whoever. They've got to follow something this big all the way.'

'Does that mean they'll come after us? Ask us what we know?' Andi was clearly concerned. 'We're MIWs, so we could be in trouble.'

Jim smiled reassuringly. 'Relax. They don't send MIWs back. They're not allowed to. It's against the UN resolutions. If they ask questions, just tell them what you know. Then we'll get you away.'

'We?'

'Me. I always said I'd protect the two of you.'

'That's what Conor kept saying,' interrupted Tebor.

'He's a good man, good reputation. They certainly put the best GameMaster onto the case.'

'He asked a lot about . . .' Tebor stopped sharply.

'About what, Tebor?'

'Everything.'

'What did he ask about me, Tebor?' The smile never left Jim's face but his eyes pierced right through the boy.

'Not much.'

'You told him I was your friend?'

Tebor nodded. 'You're my best friend – you and Andi. There's nothing wrong with that.'

'Nothing at all.' Jim turned to Andi.

Still the smile but the chill of his eyes scared her; she leant back in her chair.

'You like him,' he continued. 'He likes you. What did you tell him, Andi?'

'We both helped him, Jim. We were good. He did ask about you, but we told him you were a good friend, that you looked after us. We wouldn't have mentioned you if you'd told us not to,' she reasoned. 'You always said we had to protect each other. If you'd said not to speak to him, we wouldn't. But you never said.'

The warmth came back into Jim's eyes. He turned his attention back to Tebor. 'So why did you tell him about the Dark Areas, Tebor?'

The boy's mouth dropped; he couldn't answer; the fear filled him. He *needed* Jim. He didn't want to upset him.

'Just tell me what happened,' insisted Jim.

Tebor dropped his head and shook it from side to side, small tears began running down his cheek. 'Nooo . . .' he moaned.

'I'm not here to hurt you, but I – '

'He loves you,' cut in Andi. 'He wouldn't hurt you.'

'Then tell me what he told your friend.'

'He told him we could get into the Dark Areas.'

'Anything else?'

'Like what?'

'Like my SmartCard.'

Tebor let out a howl and put his head in his hands, the tears now in full flow.

'Yes,' said Andi. 'He showed him the SmartCard you'd given him.'

'And the number?'

'Yes.'

'What did Smith say?'

'He reckoned it was from the White House. Also noticed that it was a low number, so that made it a senior official's card.'

'Clever. Did Tebor tell him *how* to get into the Dark Areas?'

'Yes. He told him all that.'

'And that I knew Que. That he introduced us.'

'Yes,' she replied. She suddenly realized he knew everything.

Jim leant back, still smiling. 'Good, you see, the truth doesn't hurt.' He put his hand on Tebor's head. 'Time to stop crying. Everything's cool.'

'He didn't mean any harm,' she said, strongly defending Tebor. 'He's just a kid. Just trying to impress.'

'I know. Come on, Tebor, calm down and have a drink. Like I said, I'm cool.'

Tebor lifted his head cautiously. When he saw Jim still smiling, he slid the back of his hand over his cheeks and wiped away his tears. Then, believing he was out of trouble, he sat up and took a sip from his drink.

The three sat in contented silence. All that needed saying had been said.

'Jim,' said Tebor finally.

'Yes, Tebor.'

'How did you know?'

'Know what?'

'That I told him about the Dark Areas and showed him your SmartCard. And all about Que.'

'Smart kid,' smiled Jim.

And he kept smiling as he finished his drink.

He hoped Conor Smith was half as smart as the kid in front of him. He leant forward and ruffled Tebor's spiky hair.

'Smart kid,' he reiterated. 'Smart kid.'

Wardour Street, though surrounded by the glass and steel monoliths that the commercial centre of London had become, had somehow survived through the last century. Like a faded old banged-up tart still looking for an acting part, the street that was once the centre of the British film industry had retained its 1950s style and was now the heart of the major European Second World corporations.

ThemeCorp had moved into the old Warner Bros offices, and recreated them much the way they used to be. Once you entered the main foyer there was little to tell you this was the European headquarters of one of the world's largest corporations. Old and new movie posters lined the wall and the receptionists and security staff looked as though they had stepped out of the 1950s. There was a *Gone with the Wind* poster next to one advertising the latest *Speed Craze*; on the opposite wall was a picture of James Dean in *Rebel Without a Cause* fighting against the new *Titanic* casino that was soon to open in ThemeWorld. The casino was to open next to the 'Valley of the Dragons' park. The *Titanic* liner, which had been constructed in the early days of the Web, had been upgraded with the latest technology and would then be moved from its existing position in the old sector of the Brick to its new home. The move was scheduled for later that day. It was to be quite an event and the media had been full of it. It would be the most expensive premiere ever.

There was no such hyping of the many other ThemeCorp parks or casinos, including the famous 'Little Las Vegas', which had been the first big success and was now tired and rundown. Maybe that's why they had invested so heavily in *Titanic*, because they had a need to reassert themselves in the gambling market.

I hadn't been there for some time but the security chap waved me through to the lifts. He didn't know me, but behind the dated facade was the most sophisticated security and communication technology in the world which would have recognized my face print and cleared me immediately.

I buttoned the third floor, where Bonham kept a permanent office. There was an empty wooden ladderback chair outside the door. It was usually occupied by Biloxie, Bonham's minder. That was a surprise because Biloxie was rarely away from his sentinel post. He was a big ugly brute, nearly seven feet tall, with scars across his forehead and cheek, reminders of the days when he was an underground bare-knuckle fighter. He'd made a small fortune from his exploits and from the heavy betting that followed him from bout to bout. He just as quickly lost his small fortune as soon as he stopped fighting, saving schemes and investments having never been one of Biloxie's earlier preoccupations. Bonham, looking for a big mauler to protect him, had hired him after he found him living rough on the streets of New York. Since then Biloxie followed his master round like a puppy, but one that could, as everyone assumed, turn into a savage killer. To everyone's surprise, his natural fighting ability and cunning had made him a top games player and he, like the GameMasters, had a free run with all the latest ThemeCorp games. Although he rarely understood the programing side of his skills, he was viewed as the most ferocious and unbeatable player in the ThemeCorp stable. Except for me – but you'd expect me to say that. We'd never met in cybercombat and, according to the gamezines, were deliberately prevented from doing so by ThemeCorp.

Because of his link with Bonham, he was given the title of GameMaster. Although the other GameMasters were dismissive of him, rarely did anyone take Biloxie on in competition.

The secretary smiled as I walked through the office suite door.

'Mr Bonham's ready for you, sir,' she cooed.

'You're being followed,' said Bonham, as soon as I entered his inner sanctum.

The office wasn't retro; this was very highest tech. Screens covered the walls, all linked to offices in New York, Hollywood, Rome, Mumbai, Beijing and Tokyo. There was a Real Time link to Second World and one of the screens was currently showing a live battle scene from *The Valley of the Dragons*. It was Level Eleven and I saw two warriors moving through the rocks, totally unaware that they were about to be pounced on by a ferocious FireDragon. If they didn't react fast enough, both hosts would wake up tomorrow with the most awful headaches and tingling skins that would irritate throughout the day. Fantasy merging with Reality.

Bonham sat at an all-glass table that appeared to float, its leg supports invisible because of their mirrored design. There was one keyboard and a phone on the table. In front of the desk was a single grey metallic-framed chair with black leather stretched across its seat. Apart from the screens, the walls were brilliant white, with no other decorations. I recognized it instantly, as this room was an exact copy of Bonham's office in Second World.

On one of the screens, showing Wardour Street, I recognized the woman who had shadowed me from Norfolk.

'I know,' I replied. 'She looks cold and wet. Would you mind if we invited her into reception for a coffee?'

'Yes, I would mind. Let her fr-freeze. Who is she?'

'Don't know. Probably EI6.' I sat. 'They've been snooping around.'

'So I believe. Not good, not good at all. Getting yo-yourself involved in this mess.'

I shrugged my best couldn't-care-less shrug. 'When did you come over?'

'I'll do the questions.'

I did a follow-up shrug. 'Must be important to drag you over here.'

'Shut up, Smith.'

'And where's Biloxie? He's not part of the economy cuts you've been promising shareholders? Or is he out destroying some poor bugger in a head-to-head?'

Bonham shook his head in mock despair, then grinned. It was the first time I'd ever seen him smile. I preferred him serious. 'Behave. Now I know why I never had children. I've enough of you lot at ThemeCorp.' The smile was replaced by his usual scowling features. 'We have a ser-serious problem that needs sorting out.'

'To do with the President?'

'Absolutely. I am up to speed on your involvement. Unfortunately, and this is for your ea-ears only, we are also involved.'

Bonham tapped the keyboard and the wallscreen filled with the picture of Jim Nelson, the same one I'd already seen. 'How much did you find out about him?' he asked.

'Quite a lot. Most of which doesn't make sense.'

'It will.' He tapped again and Mike Keebles's picture fitted next to Nelson's. 'The same applied to Mister Keebles. They were both colleagues of our Chairman, Patrick Murphy.'

'Dom Murphy.'

He nodded. 'The man Jim, who probably kidnapped the President, he was a composite of two men . . .'

'Nelson and Keebles. That is correct. Except that he's not a man.'

'He's an avatar?'

'Wrong.'

That shook me. 'Got to have a host?'

Bonham shook his head. 'When they built the Brick, our Chairman with his close colleagues, Nelson and Keebles, were put in charge of security and maintenance by the American government. They were top men in the field, had tremendous reputations. They were seconded to the UN and given all the facilities and money they required. They decided to use microbiological computers to automatically maintain and secure the Brick. They fed in specific DNA composites that would resolve any situation that arose . . . ar-arose. You know how it works. Each nano-computer, each CREEP, has a single purpose, a specific function. When a particular problem arises, a signal is sent out and picked up by the nearest passing CREEPs whose programs suit that particular function. They form together, in a specific DNA style, to become one big super-computer that resolves the problem. Fixes the hole in the matrix, protects JetPax, whatever. Once they have completed their task, they split up again into their individual micro-parts. They may not be required for the next problem that arises, only for those that require their specific program. They just float around in the matrix waiting for the next call. Trillions and trillions of them.'

'And the system's gone wrong.'

'Please . . . pl-please let me finish. Our Chairman, once the Brick was set up, stopped being a civil . . . civ-civil servant, left the Security Services and raised seed money to invest in a new venture.'

'ThemeCorp.'

'Precisely. Other colleagues joined – after all, who was better placed to understand the Brick than those who had built it?'

'Were you one of those?'

'I was – but GCHQ background. No matter, we weren't

doing anything wrong . . . wr-wrong. We just preferred the private sector.'

'Were Keebles and Nelson also directors of the company?'

'They stayed with the UN and the US Secret Service. But, because of their original involvement, and their undeniable contributions, they were given options that made them very wealthy men. Then they both decided to quit and became recluses . . . re-recluses. Don't ask me why; I have no idea. In my view, you should never trust a man who acts as if he has something to hide. Something rattled them, and they just dropped out.'

'These guys didn't even have computers at home?'

'Didn't need them. The damage was already done.' Bonham pointed at the screen. 'I see your woman's been replaced.' The street camera showed my shadower walking away and a man in a black raincoat taking her place. 'Probably she'll go home now, snuggle up with a hot water bottle, and die of the cold she's just caught. Bloody amateurs . . . am-amateur.'

'But they're both dead.' I steered Bonham back.

'Only in RealWorld. Think about it. They created a robot that lived in the Web. They'd programed a specific DNA structure that only they could trigger. When they did, that structure formed this character, Jim, whom you saw. And who, we now believe, kidnapped the President.'

'Are you telling me that he was kidnapped by CREEPs?'

'We think so.'

'Jesus, that means they can combine themselves into Jim, complete a task . . .'

'Like kidnapping the President.'

'. . . and just drift back into individual cells again. Just melt back into the matrix, without any record of where they've been. I suppose the next time that robot forms for a particular task, it doesn't even need to use the same cells, just any cell passing by that contains the necessary requirements to build a DNA. These CREEPs could be set up for any number of identical, or even completely different, missions.'

'Precise . . . pre-precisely.'

'How do you catch them?'

'That's why you're here. You're the GameMaster. *You* tell us.'

'I'm also a suspect.'

'Actually the prime . . . pr-prime suspect. Clever that; signing off as Condor.'

'Very funny.'

'Just reassure me that you never met Nelson or Keebles before all this.'

'Not that I know of.'

'But they would appear to have locked you in.'

I nodded. 'Maybe they needed a-an experienced Web player.'

'And pulled your name out of a hat?' He snorted. 'You're smarter than to believe that. They'll have used you for a purpose because you can deliver what they want.'

'Maybe.' I didn't need to share the fact that I'd felt manipulated from the start. 'So how do I stop being a suspect?'

'You don't. You're the only concrete lead anyone has. Que's dead, but he was only a pimp. Never trust a man who lives off sex and other people's weaknesses. Anyway, you appeared every time there was a problem, and you knew everything they did. How?'

'Tricks of the trade.' Wrong. Not the moment to be cocky.

'I'll ignore that. You brought Jim into the game. Why?'

'It was Jim brought me into the game. Once contact was made, in my case with the MIWs, he morphed through them and laid down the clues. On reflection, he's probably linked in to a whole gaggle of MIWs. Maybe he was just waiting to see who was the first fish on the hook.'

'Possibly . . . Anyway, it was the Jim contact that's hooked you. The Yanks and GCHQ both have information on Nelson and Keebles, but have no idea how they're involved – or even if they are involved. They're after you because they believe you've got the answers.'

'What about the InfoCalypse?'

'Rubbish. Pure rubbish. Just a silly rumour.'

His answer was too quick, too glib.

'All this information you're giving me – who else knows?' I asked.

'A few of us in ThemeCorp, and yourself, and any trusted person you may need to call in, with our agreement. Not your Web chums, I'm afraid. I do not expect anyone else, including the Security Services, to find out any more. It would cause us great embarrassment. I've never trusted anyone who works for the government.'

'You used to.'

'Different agendas now, different loyalties.'

'Any theories as to why Nelson and Keebles did it?'

'None whatsoever. I presume they didn't have any IT around their homes because they didn't trust anybody, didn't want to be hacked.'

'Which confirms they set this Jim character up while they were still building the Brick.'

'Obviously.' Nobody voiced disdain like Bonham.

'I want to see Patrick Murphy.'

'Out of the question.'

'He was there when they set up Jim. Maybe he saw something, maybe . . .'

'No.' Bonham was adamant. 'He and I have discussed the problem at some length. He cannot recall anything . . . an-anything that he would consider suspicious.' The hiss was louder than usual. 'He's a busy . . . bu-busy man.'

'I'll need help.'

'Whatever you want.'

'A good DataMan, first of all.' DataMen were Game-

Masters who were historians as well as senior programers in the Web. They were essentially theoreticians who rarely ventured into the Brick, professors who lived in a world of hypothesis and supposition. I had already enlisted Alex Mikoyan and now saw this as an opportunity for getting official consent to use the Datakeeper.

'I know you've already used Mikoyan on this one. Let's continue the arrangement.'

That surprised me, but I didn't show it.

'I needed Alex to do some work for me,' Bonham continued. 'He said he was busy, but wouldn't tell me what it was. Knowing your friendship I presumed he was helping you. And why not? He's the best.'

'I needed good support.' I confessed, knowing Theme-Corp were very strict about their employees working together without their agreement.

'I have no problem with that, and that makes it official for you. Shame you didn't come to me earlier. I'm not all ogre, you know.' He grinned frighteningly again.

'Have you also told him about Nelson and the CREEPs?'

'Of course. Only a few minutes before you arrived. He is working on it and expects you to call him when we've finished.'

That was good, Bonham opening doors for me.

He pointed to the small screen again. '*There's* someone else watching you.' He adjusted a switch on the table and the camera zoomed in behind the sallow-faced man who had taken over from the woman. Another watcher, an older man, was watching the watcher. 'Looks like a Yank, as they all still think they should look like Humphrey Bogart. Probably CIA? I never did trust the CIA.'

'Do I have access to the Dark Areas?' I asked.

'No point, as you'd never find your way round them. And Jim'll find you too easily – it's his territory. The matrix would pass him that information within a nanosecond.'

'Don't care. I need every resource I can get.'

Bonham weighed it up. 'OK ... Ok-ay. I'll arrange a secure card for you. You'll have to sign for it.'

'Obviously.'

'These are not Smarties I'm handing out. They are very special. I mean, *very* special. When you get one, it'll be time-coded for a specific period. Just don't get caught in the Dark Areas when the clock runs out. You'll be frozen in there, and you'll never get out.'

'Do *you* have one?

Bonham waved my question aside. 'Not your business. And if you lose it, I'll fine you a fortune.'

'No doubt.'

'But then money doesn't matter to you, does it?'

I grinned; he never let up. 'How much do the Telephone Exchange and the Secret Service know?'

'They may know about Jim Nelson, and Mike Keebles. Even about the Chairman. It's not our responsibility to do their job for them. What they don't know, and I do not expect them to discover, is what Jim really is.'

'A rogue robot. What made those guys do that? Why?'

'That is what we expect you to find out.'

I left a few seconds later; the meeting suddenly terminated by Bonham, who said he didn't want to waste any more time and could I please ... pl-please hurry up and get the thing sorted.

On the way out I noticed Biloxie had still not returned to the chair.

Alex Mikoyan, as always, started right at the beginning. He took his tea and a packet of imported English chocolate digestive biscuits to his workshop in the attic, closed the door and settled down to chase the game.

The dacha, a large house on the edge of the forest, was Mikoyan's hideaway: the centre of his own universe on earth. He had not left this house in fourteen years, and had the money to protect himself with guards, electric fences and the most sophisticated surveillance equipment available. Now in his late fifties, he was a man who lived life on his own terms and was obsessive about guaranteeing his own privacy.

The forest was famous; it was where the last Russian Tsar and his family had been buried after being butchered in nearby Ekaterinburg, more than a hundred years earlier. The burial spot, known as the Four Brothers after four lonely trees that stood by the secret grave, was no more than a few hundred metres from the entrance to the house. Not content with being so close to one historical landmark, Mikoyan had named his dacha after Yuri Gagarin, his great hero who had been the first man in space.

He logged into the ThemeCorp main computer and once again ran through the files Bonham had opened to him. He wasn't surprised by the amount of secret information ThemeCorp had extracted from both the American and

British security files. Not only was ThemeCorp the most technically advanced outfit in the world but it had also been started by men who knew the workings of the Security Services inside out. The same applied to data on the Brick; he was soon downloading SnoopCam recordings of Sunshine and Hope, Elvis Presley World, and every other area the President had visited.

On a second and third computer he downloaded biographies and records on President Dixon, Jim Nelson, Mike Keebles, Andi Whitehorn and Tebor, then Bonham, Gallagher, Swilkin, Nancy Sumner, Joe Meisner, Patrick (Dom) Murphy, Que and all the other people who had found themselves drawn into the kidnapping. Most of this information came from his own memory banks; Datakeepers spent all their time watching, storing and evaluating.

He ran a series of questions on each person: birthplace, political allegiance, criminal records, lists of friends, known vices, financial statements, properties owned, hobbies, and so on.

Then he turned to the Web construction data. He needed to understand exactly how the CREEPs worked. He fed in questions on the original construction sites like Alpha World, Second Life, Disk World and even FurryMUCK, a game based on the role-playing theme of anthropomorphics where the avatars were always furry animals. He didn't type, simply asked questions which were computed through his system and out into the mass of data that floated through cyberspace. His computers automatically locked on to connecting facts and made all the necessary links which were reported back on his screen. The first link was himself – as a young man – playing FurryMUCK. He warmly remembered his early days, when he had represented himself as a sable.

The computers whirred into action as Mikoyan settled back, stretched, crossed his legs, pulled out a chocolate digestive and dunked it in a cup of lemon tea. This was the moment he loved. Release zillions of atoms of knowledge into the ether and watch them seek and interact and ignore and collide, and eventually throw out that small connection of facts that was the answer to all he had searched for. All within minutes or seconds.

He sensed anxiety, something he was not used to. Every problem had a beginning, middle and end – that was the natural order of things. To discover the truth, Mikoyan knew he had to be patient; that was his normal ally, his great strength.

Always start at the beginning; take the first step so you can reach the end of your journey.

But something churned inside; it confused him, made him want to hurry, even though it was not in his nature. As he squeezed the first digestive between his tongue and the roof of his mouth, he allowed himself to jump to the middle.

Had Nelson and Keebles, before they died, created a robot in the Web that was a fusion of their two identities?

Did it have their instincts, their views, their emotions?

Did it have emotions or was it only a program based on their beliefs and instructions?

What motivated Jim?

Did they live on in Jim?

Did they live forever in Jim?

Why else kill themselves?

Was Jim alive: a new species, created by them, for them?

Could there be life for the MIWs after human death? Was this the new afterlife?

Could he do the same, live consciously forever in the Web?

He smiled ruefully. There were no quick answers.

The first responses were already stacking up on the screen.

Andi Whitehorn was a fugitive with a murder charge over her head. He wasn't surprised she'd gone MIW.

He wondered if Conor knew that.

Comrade! He smiled; it was what Conor always called him.

And as an afterthought, as the computers started their massive and painstaking search into the darkest corners of the lives of each potential suspect or witness, he added a further name: Conor Smith.

Conor Smith was already on another list.

Swilkin sat in his office with Tyrrell, his assistant.

'Unreal,' admitted Swilkin. 'Like it never happened.'

'All we can do is go back,' replied Tyrrell. 'And look for the clues there?'

'Why's he backed off? This is not a kidnapper who lost his nerve. Christ, he held all the cards.'

'Unless we were getting close to him and didn't realize it.'

Swilkin shook his head with certainty. 'No, he was always in total control. That's obvious from the President's testimony.'

'We have a full list of people who hold access codes or SmartCards to the Dark Areas.'

'Smith on that list?'

'Nope. Not that we know of. The main technicians dealing with it were Jim Nelson and Mike Keebles.'

'And . . . ?'

'Their SmartCards were never handed back. Number's seven and eight on the White House distribution list.'

'How many cards were released?'

'In the US, about thirty. Ten were White House, six in the CIA and four FBI. The rest were distributed to individual contractors who helped set up the Web, all time-coded, and they've been out of date for years.' Tyrrell looked

404

through a pile of papers he'd brought with him, pulled one out and passed it across to Swilkin. 'That's the total list of SmartCard holders. Those cards are dedicated to the holder, so only he can use it. Any changes have to go through the CardDistributor in Langley. It comes under the UN Resolution on the Web and is site-protected in Langley.'

'And cards held outside the US?'

'Restricted access, with time-codes. It's our technology and we've always controlled it, with certain UN safeguards. Any licence to a contractor, or to an outside government, is strictly controlled and only allows access to Dark Areas which they're still expanding into. Western and allied governments, like the Brits, they're in with their own technology, and we share most things, as long as we agree to total control security in the Web. It's no problem because we're all protecting ourselves.'

'I note' – Swilkin held up the sheet of paper Tyrrell had handed him – 'that ThemeCorp have *two* access cards.'

'More. Their Chairman, Dom Murphy, also had his own SmartCard. Another leftover from the early days.'

'Smith also works for ThemeCorp.'

'Those cards are dedicated to the holder only. They're linked to DNA passwords through palm perspiration and skin prints. In this case, getting your hands on one guarantees it won't work.'

Swilkin sighed. 'I'm split on Smith. He's the obvious first choice. He's been in on every discovery, usually ahead of us. They used his webname, Condor. Why? It's so obvious, so deliberately misleading. The first ransom note, what did it say? "I AM THE VIRUS – MASTER OF THE WEB." Master? GameMaster? That's another strong link. It all points to him, but it's somehow too easy. Or does he just want us to think that? Nobody'd expect him to lay such simple clues.'

'EI6 haven't yet got anywhere.'

'They're useless. All that European security shit, they run it by committee, trying to please everyone in the Republic.

They don't even have a common language. Sure, they followed him, into London, but they found out nothing. I mean, he even told them where he was going.' Swilkin laughed. 'Guy's got some balls.'

'Our London people says it's unusual for him to visit the Sprawl. Even more unusual for him to go to ThemeCorp; he usually just visits their Web offices. Last night, their security director, Malcolm Bonham, flew in from the US and was already at ThemeCorp when Smith got there. It's highly probable therefore that they met, may even be the reason that Bonham went over there.'

'Where are they now?'

'Smith's heading home and Bonham was on his way back to London Heathrow. Company jet, flight planned to Atlantic City.

'Where's Murphy?'

'Head Office. Hollywood.'

'Was Bonham another big shareholder in ThemeCorp?'

'Yes. Joined after it started, but he's top dog after Murphy.'

'So what was so important that he and Smith needed to talk in private? Now that's something I'd like to find out about.'

The Brick had exploded after the US President's TV statement. A human flood swirled down the highway, swollen by the millions of day-trippers who had come to gawk, almost doubling the usual number of Weekenders. Add to that the big parade due to start in a few hours and it was definitely one of the busiest weekends since the Brick had first opened.

The media had filled in the gaps of the President's short statement, and thus the Hotel Gallipoli acquired an instant notoriety, along with the Sunshine and Hope Mall and other places the President had been dragged through. The bizarre death of Marilyn Monroe was the star attraction and the Hotel Gallipoli management had booked out Room 58 on the 84th floor for the next three months, all reservations taken on a no-deposit-returned basis.

Outside, the crowds pushed and shoved and pointed upwards towards the 84th floor. While the gawpers gawped, the next-door Lutheran Church had organized vast protests and banner-waving reformists who urged the Weekenders to give up their squalid, seedy and whoring lives and return to the morals and beliefs of the past. The Lutherans knew that God had given them a heaven-sent opportunity to win over converts and, as the crowds continued to swell, so the Lutherans, in their smart purple-shirted and white-trousered uniforms, passed amongst them, waving their modern simple-to-read bibles and passing out religious literature and video strips on the Life of Christ. The crowds, good-natured, joined in and sang hymns with the Lutherans and pointed to the 84th, and speculated about what would happen next.

Not a lot appeared to be the answer. Whatever the next piece of action, it was unlikely to be at the Hotel Gallipoli.

Andi and Tebor were among the crowd, lost in its anonymity and easily avoiding the SnoopCams and WebCops. They knew that pictures of Jim had been circulated and now the crowds were being scanned extensively for a sign of their friend. But he'd vanished, well aware that the authorities wanted to find and interview him.

'Going to RealWorld,' he'd said. 'Catch you later.'

'Did *you* do it?' asked Tebor as Jim left PunkS R Us.

Jim had smiled his usual friendly smile – he genuinely loved Tebor's honest and straightforward approach – but he had shaken his head. 'I'm not into that sort of heavy stuff. I keep my politics for election day. The only weapon I use is my cross on a ballot paper.'

Jim had disappeared only seconds before his photo started appearing on the giant billboards that floated over the Brick.

'HAVE YOU SEEN THIS MAN?' they shrieked silently across the sky. 'TELL A WEBCOP IF YOU HAVE.' They further warned: 'THIS MAN IS DANGEROUS.'

'Funny,' commented Tebor, 'him disappearing just before that stuff came up. Almost like he was expecting it.'

'No way. Nobody's that close to the matrix.'

Tebor grinned and shuddered. 'Creepy, isn't it?'

'Jim?'

'Everything's seriously creepy. Can't wait for the next instalment.'

They worked their way along the Brick, picking up on the excitement of the hordes.

'Keep moving and stay bunched in the crowd,' advised Andi. 'They're probably looking for us too.'

MIWs couldn't change their appearances; they needed conscious hosts to arrange that but the pair of them were adept at keeping clear of the SnoopCams and WebCops as they mingled with the crowd. Eventually they reached the Hotel Gallipoli. They stopped to watch, but the only action now was in the crowd. The majority of the talk was about JetPax loss. Most passers-by thought it was a virus that was introduced by terrorists, but their curiosity and sense of adventure still overcame their caution. For once there was a degree of real fear on the Brick. This was *real* adventure. If the President himself could be isolated in Second World, then so could the rest of them. Danger was all around them and they waited expectantly, like innocent trembling lambs in a slaughterhouse, for the inevitable to happen. It was the ultimate thrill-seek.

'Tebor,' a voice called from across the pavement. It was a young blond James Dean look-alike who had spent time with Tebor before. He waved, signalling Tebor to come over.

'Who's he?' asked Andi suspiciously.

'Client. Actually he's ninety-four, but he thinks I believe he really looks like that.' Tebor laughed and waved back. 'He's generous with the credits.'

'Be careful. We should stick together.'

'Come with me. He's pretty harmless. Talks a lot, likes me telling him how young and handsome he is.'

'No, I'll beep if I need you. Maybe it's better if we split anyway. They're looking for the two of us and they'll expect us to be together.'

'Meet later?'

'PunkS R Us.'

'Tebor,' yelled the Dean look-alike again.

Tebor turned and pushed through the crowd. Andi watched him for a moment, watched his thin shoulders and straight back get swallowed up in the throng. When she couldn't see him any more she went with the flow, still shielding herself, still absorbing herself into the crowd.

She ignored all the attention from passing strangers that

a beautiful woman automatically attracted. She kept her head tilted downwards and moved along the Brick in a random and irregular pattern, doing nothing that might attract attention from those around her. What appeared to be an aimless pattern was a gradual progression towards MetroPort 911 and the message board that she hoped Conor would use to contact her, as they had arranged.

Where was he? Where had he gone?

She suddenly felt she was being watched. She swung round but no watcher caught her attention. As she continued on she knew there *was* someone there, but she also knew she wouldn't see him.

Come on, Conor. Come on.

They'd followed me back from Wardour Street to Rose Cottage. There were two of them; one obviously EI6 and the other, keeping further back, probably American, probably CIA. It was fun; the EI6 man appearing unconcerned that I was obviously aware of him while he, in turn, was unaware that he was being tailed by the Yank.

This strange procession ducked and dived its way back to Rose Cottage where, in the openness of the country lanes, both security men acted as if each other didn't exist, while they watched the cottage and waited for further orders. It had certainly surprised EI6 when he finally noticed the other guy.

There was no way I could go back to John Mathews's farm. I set the intruder alarms to their highest setting, which included locking myself into the computer room where I'd get time to JetPax home if someone should try to force an entry. I grilled a bacon sandwich, and then munched it while I texted Mikoyan.

'Hi, comrade,' I tapped. In case the phone was bugged I added, 'Call me at Rose Cottage.' He knew my system at home was secure.

I waited for a full minute before Mikoyan appeared on the screen.

'So, Conor, your people fucked up.'

'Looks like it.'

'We're the same here. It's all a mess. Russia, half a century

411

after communism, and still no order in society. Not unless you're an oligarch or a hooker. In those days everyone got fed, everyone had a job, everyone had respect.'

'What do *you* know? You weren't even born then.'

'It's in my blood. My father was a revolutionary who taught me the old ways. My grandfather stood next to Stalin when the world trembled and fell to its knees if the USSR sneezed.'

'Was that before or after he killed sixty million Russians during his pogroms?'

Mikoyan dismissed that with a shake of his head. 'Western propaganda. If we had not become soft and started wanting McDonald's for lunch, we would have become stronger than America. Then I would be telling you that JFK murdered twenty million of his own people.'

'But he didn't.'

'How do you know? The victors always rewrite history. Maybe he murdered forty million, maybe even more.'

'You really believe that crap, comrade?'

Mikoyan smiled slyly. 'I believe anything is possible, and I know how they –' he waved his hand airily upwards, ' – change the truth. We both know it. You and I, Conor Smith, are not so far apart. Trust nobody, because they all have something to hide. In the end, all these governments, these politicians, these bureaucrats in power, have no alternative but to lie. They lie just to survive.' Mikoyan grinned. 'Roll back the years to communism. It is the only solution.' He opened a pack of Rowntrees Fruit Gums and popped a handful into his mouth. 'What is the death of a few million compared to the survival of seven billion?'

'What're you worth, comrade? Twenty million, maybe more? Is that what they call the communist dream?'

'Bah! I'm rich because I have no alternative. Without money you starve in Russia. That is capitalism for you. In the old USSR, I would not have been allowed to starve.' He snorted and waved his hands again to signal the end of the debate. 'So tell me, Conor Smith, why has all this happened?'.

'No idea. I was surprised Bonham knew I'd contacted you.'

Mikoyan shrugged. 'It was difficult for me not to admit it. You know how suspicious he is. This Jim ... he is definitely involved.' It was a very adamant statement.

'I agree. Bonham claims he's a robot.'

'Bonham says only what he wants you to hear. It all depends on whether he wants that robot caught or not.'

'Agreed, but I can't see why they'd set me up.'

'I also can think of no reason. Yet. I mean, stealing the President seems a bit, how do you say, above the top.'

'Over the top.'

'If you only learnt Russian we wouldn't have these problems. Why don't you switch your language translator program on?'

'Why don't *you*?'

Mikoyan laughed. 'For the same reason as you. I like you to hear what I'm really saying.'

'I've always had the feeling that I was being led down a predetermined path. All those clues, they came up too easily.'

'And too obviously. Naming Condor, and also saying the virus is the master...' Mikoyan repeated the word. '... *master* of the Web. Either stupid, or too obvious.'

'Not stupid.'

Mikoyan nodded. 'As is the alpha and the omega.'

'You've traced that?' First Tebor, now Mikoyan. They were all beating me to the finish.

He smirked back at me, his Cheshire cat grin getting wider. 'Easy one. You should've cracked it.'

'It's all right for you Datakeepers, just sit quietly in a room and have all the time in the world to work things out. Not like the rest of us, out there in the field under real pressure.' I enjoyed such repartee with Mikoyan, but I was even more pleased that he was making progress. 'So why was it so easy? If you're right, that is.'

'I *am* right. And I am surprised you missed this.' Mikoyan was suddenly serious. 'I suggest we keep this to ourselves for now, my friend. Or this could turn to your disadvantage.'

'Go on,' I replied, suddenly fearful of what was coming next.

'I went all the way back to the beginning. Right back. And one of the people I checked up on was you. Your early days, even before you were Condor. To the very first property you bought on the Web.'

'Alpha World.'

'Yes. You bought the plot and built a house there in 2017.'

'For three thousand dollars.'

'It's all in the public records. You still own it and your property tax each year is more than you originally paid for the place. But I notice that your property tax is paid by another name.' Mikoyan smirked at that one. 'Who is John Mathews?'

'That's up to you to discover.'

'He's not a neighbour, is he? A farmer.' Mikoyan positively purred with that revelation.

Typical. But it didn't matter; We were as protective towards each other as much as we were to ourselves. That was the great unsaid GameMaster law: protect each other at all times. 'If that's the alpha, from Alpha World, then what's the omega?' I asked.

'You've just answered your own question. You should've worked it out by now. You've become too subjective in this game.'

I shut my eyes, tilted my head down, and concentrated my thoughts.

'Stay in Alpha World,' suggested Mikoyan. 'Stay in the neighbourhood.'

After nearly a minute, click, and I opened my eyes. 'Clever.'

'You understand now?'

'Titanic.'

'Correct.'

'Straight to my door.'

'And that's where they'll nail you. You and I, we know it's too obvious. Somebody is definitely setting you up. Your protection is that they will have to archive some old British records. It takes the Americans time to do that.'

'But not GCHQ.'

'True.'

'So who owns Titanic now? Still Omega?'

'ThemeCorp, bought it years ago. It's a big investment for them'

'Since when?'

'Since they decided to build a new "Titanic Casino" at ThemeWorld. Next to "Valley Of The Dragons".'

I remembered the poster I'd seen in Wardour Street. 'I didn't realize it was the same Titanic.'

'The data's on its way,' said Mikoyan, punching his keyboard. 'It's cheaper for them to refurb an existing project than it is to build from scratch. I suppose they already had the hull and basic ship, so they just had to upgrade it. Cost about four hundred and fifty mill.'

'Dollars?'

'US. It would've cost twice that to build the entire liner to the size they needed – and taken much longer. Omega did a good job and his replica was full size.' Mikoyan picked at his teeth with his fingernail. 'Fruit gums always stick in my teeth. When did you last visit Alpha World?'

'Maybe a year ago. I never get rid of things. The house is . . . just something I own.'

The official form appeared, floating on my screen. I reached out and took it, started to read: *Alpha World. Titanic site. Project 11786. Location 2349N-1917W. A vast,* well-designed replica model of the ill-fated Titanic, with state rooms, cabins and decks. The model extends to a full block and is listed as a private home. Originally built by user 'Omega' in July 1999, the list of its previous owners is below. Now stands unused, in a dry dock, on a four-acre site. Is being refitted by its owners at a cost of $350M before being moved to its new location next to the top ThemeWorld attraction 'Valley Of The Dragons' where it will become a floating casino, one of the largest in the world. There were a variety of WebPictures with the report, most from the Web newsrag called the *Daily Episode*. The Second Life oracle, the *Daily Herald*, also covered the story. The pictures covered the *Titanic* from all angles, a gigantic ship out of water, standing upright on its keel on a huge tract of grassland. A huge iceberg appeared to rise up through the grass, and the ship was impaled on it at the bow; the whole ship rose up at the front as if rearing out of the ground. It was exactly as I last remembered it.

I went through the list of owners, many of whom, like the originator Omega, used their WebNames.

Mikoyan continued when I'd finished reading. 'Eventually the Feds will trace your property in Alpha World. EI6, the Yanks, EuroPolice – somebody will definitely home in and find your name as owner.'

'Condor's name.'

'In their eyes there is no difference.' Mikoyan chuckled. 'Old Web is not a good investment. You should have sold out long ago, although ThemeCorp seems to agree with you. It owns big chunks of Alpha World.'

'I think I'll keep my investment. Maybe ThemeCorp knows something I don't. They buy cheap-land digibanks for future development. How many private landowners?'

'At least fifty per cent of Alpha World. It's basically still an old hippy commune. Suits the dropouts, your capitalist dispossessed.'

'Like me?'

He laughed. 'There's no room in communism for individuals, Conor. If we came back to power, you would be the first we would have to stand up against a wall. Then bang bang.'

'Stop fooling around, Alex.'

'We both know they will trace the alpha to you, and then link it with the omega. You must decide what to do.'

'Run . . . but not hide.'

'Let them find you? On your terms. That's good.'

'Anything else?'

'Not much, yet. I still cannot see why the dragon is important. Why is the kidnapper linking that with the alpha and the omega? I don't understand that. And this robot, Jim. If, like Bonham says, he's made up of these individual cells, then he'll have broken up and gone back into the matrix. Impossible then to trace.'

'Unless we can trigger something that gets all those cells to form the same DNA pattern again.'

'I don't know how you'll do that. But if you are the target, our friend Jim will come after you. What we need to find out is why they've involved you – whoever *they* are. You have become part of their game and you must lead them on and be ready when they come to find you.'

'InfoCalypse?'

'Who knows? You need to return to the Brick now.'

'I agree.'

'Stay in touch. If anything comes up I will contact you immediately.'

I left the WebRoom and went back into the computer room. The news was running on one of the screens. A picture of Jim came up and the newscaster's voiceover asked everyone to be on the lookout for the man who was now the main suspect in the President's kidnapping.

I wondered how long before my own likeness would replace it.

Soon . . . soon.

I punched AndiGirl 1602 and sent a message to her via the notice board at MetroPort 911. I gave her a time to meet later and went back to the Brick.

'He's on the move again,' Tyrrell reported to Swilkin.

'Where to?'

'The Brick. Don't know where, but GCHQ picked up avatar activity around Rose Cottage. Do you want me to get the snoops to go in and check?'

'No. We've broken in once without a search warrant. Twice would give him a legal case against us, and he's one guy who definitely knows how to use the law. It was justifiable when the President was missing, but not now.' He ignored the downloaded Monroe tape found at Rose Cottage. That was the President's decision, and he was here to follow orders. And they were simple: catch somebody, whoever. But find a reason, and an end, to this game.

'I'll get EI6 to check through the windows.'

'OK. Is his profile registered with the SnoopCams and WebCops?'

'Yup. On silent surveillance. Identify and report to us. No action to be taken.'

'Has Clancy got his Secret Service boys out?'

'All over his known haunts. They're watching the girl and the kid Tebor, too. The Feds have stuck their snout in the trough. They've a bunch of agents out there. Someone'll pick him up.' Tyrrell came over as very confident.

'We'll see. Right. Let's rock and roll and see how good these GameMasters really are.'

GROUND ZERO
(0,0)
ALPHA WORLD
THE OLD BRICK
SECOND WORLD
REAL TIME: ZERO PLUS 12 HRS AND 31 MINS

Ground Zero hadn't changed much in fifty years.

It was a red-tiled city square with large advertising bill-boards and ringed by a motley selection of houses, mostly brownstone with square, prison-like windows. The sky was blue, as always, and there were cyber mountains ranged to the south, minimal in detail, as were so many of the early Web locations.

Ground Zero was the very centre of Alpha World. A Cartesian coordinate procedure had been used to mark out the vast area that Alpha World inhabited and the origin and centre point (0,0) of the coordinates was the focal point known as Ground Zero. This was where visitors and residents entered Alpha World.

I stepped out from the MetroPort which served the monorail system, built on stilts with wood-planked walk areas, and which had been the first transport system in the Web back in 1998. There were more than forty monorail stations in Alpha World but many of them had fallen into disrepair over the years.

Little had changed on Ground Zero since my last visit. It looked sparse and devoid of character, lacking the immediacy and authenticity of the Brick. In the latter it was the trivial effects that created a sense of reality, the litter and chocolate wrappers swirling around the streets and the trees waving in the wind that blew over the yellow-bricked thoroughfare. All this was lacking in Alpha World, more like a canvas in primary colours that had been painted by numbers and was as soulless as the wood grain in Formica.

They'd have fun trying to recognize me, as I was now using my first ever avatar. It had been the latest state-of-the-art technology at the time when I first started exploring the Web. In those days I'd worn a full body suit with a helmet and goggles, so my avatar, the first Condor, had a blobby look about it. It wore purple pants, a bright green striped knee-length waistcoat and a yellow shirt, along with high-sided white rubber boots. I also had a shiny bald head, bushy eyebrows and a black Mormon beard.

My first avatar.

I'd forgotten all about it until I scrolled through my old files. I laughed now, but I remember how proud I'd been when I first produced it. It was before there was speech on the Web and communication then was by typed chat notes that appeared in a cartoon bubble next to your face. I'd modernized it to include speech therapy when that was launched, but had kept the same avatar form for a number of years before ditching it for a later model and thus the second Condor.

I decided to use it now because it would stand out in any modern crowd. A lot of early avatars that had gone MIW still retained their original forms. You even saw them every now and then on the Brick, moving along with their awkward jelly-wobble movements, nearly always on their own, and forever painfully lumbering to keep up with the rest of the swarm.

I hurriedly updated it so that it would work with my latest equipment and would, if needed, revert to myself, Conor Smith. I added a selection of weapons; a stun handgun, a sharp matrix-cutting samurai sword and a bullwhip that could cut another avatar in half with its steel-tipped end.

There were few people at Ground Zero and most were

tourists who had simply come to stare at this pioneer site. I walked past the all-glass Dougie's House that had once won awards for its design, past the old library that had never carried any books, past the few empty shops with no stock in their windows, and on for about a half a mile till I reached *Titanic*.

Unlike most of Alpha World, it was totally changed. Once Omega's pride and joy, I expected another now-faded reminder of the early excitement and pioneer spirit of what was then known as the Wild Web. But *Titanic* was not like anything else thereabouts. It was new, its steel hull shone as if it had just been delivered from the Harland & Wolff dockyard in Belfast where she had, in the reality of a distant past, once been built. The fresh paint gleamed on her sides and the wood of her decks was highly polished like the hand-crafted dashboard of a new BMW RollsVagen. I could even smell her newness, that freshness of turpentine and paint and polish – and even the electric excitement of her first voyage.

ThemeCorp had obviously invested heavily in restoring the ship. Few corporations had the resources to create the software and bring the ship to her present outstanding quality. She'd be a star – indeed a White Star, as her original owners were called – in ThemeCorp's portfolio. But it was also not like ThemeCorp, the most profitable and competitive company on Wall Street, to spend unnecessary money on anything that did not promise a huge return.

There were no crowds around it, no queues waiting to board the ship. Only a sign that read: 'NO TRESPASSERS. ALL WILL BE PROSECUTED. NO EXCEPTIONS'. The security cameras that covered all possible entrances to the liner backed that threat up. As did the two security WebCops who patrolled the street, their eyes watching for strangers, their batons slung idly over their shoulders. Not avatars to be messed with, if they hit you with their ZapBatons, the electric ion charge would be felt for days after you returned to RealWorld. Both guards wore ThemeCorp patches on their sleeves.

They carefully watched me pass them, then went back to their routine surveillance. They were used to early avatars in Alpha World; it was part of a passing age and even in modern times the romantics still flourished. Some people drove old cars, some people enjoyed being old avatars.

The people up on the decks, dressed in costume uniforms from the last century, looked as though they were preparing for a long journey.

I was surprised to see that the iceberg that had ripped into *Titanic*'s hull was gone; she sat there, in dry dock, as she must have done all those years ago, ready for her maiden voyage across the Atlantic. The pictures from the public records which Mikoyan had shown me were out of date. That was unlike the Datakeeper. Either the renovation work on the *Titanic* had been kept secret or the public records property offices had got their information wrong. The second was unlikely since public records were automatically updated as soon as there was any change in the matrix. That was a priority for the CREEPs. If it was being deliberately kept under wraps, and the public records had not been informed, then someone really had tied into the CREEPs and the whole matrix system.

Some of the crew were visible on the bridge, so I smiled and waved a greeting, which they returned. Happy days. They were about to sail the vessel straight up the Brick to its new berth. Typical ThemeCorp, always with an eye to maximum publicity.

I walked away towards my old home, making sure the recent images in my eye of *Titanic* were downloaded on to my host computer. Once round the corner and out of range from the cameras and guards, I called his computer and programed these *Titanic* pictures to be emailed directly to Mikoyan.

The house, one of the first in Alpha World, went under

the name of Grey. At a time when all the other Alpha World residents were building more modern and outlandish homes, fulfilling their RealWorld ambitions in the Web, the young me had elected to build a drab uninteresting building that stood out amongst those peacocks.

I called it Grey because it was designed as a simple concrete shoebox, no painted walls or windows, just one simple bunker-like concrete front doorway. There had been plenty of complaints from the neighbours but, as there were no zoning issues in those days, I took great delight in doing what everyone else was against. Set in five acres of woodland, Grey stood in an area that was now a ghost town, long since abandoned by the early pioneers and homesteaders of the Web. Like most of Second World, there were no squatters' rights for MIWs and, without the passwords to get into abandoned buildings, entry was impossible. The house, if it could be called that, stood in a clearing surrounded by black and white conifer trees. That was another one of my jokes. To add insult to injury, the ground was the only colour I'd allowed. It was a deep purple, as was the grass that grew on it.

I'd probably do exactly the same today. It was *my* place and I always felt comfortable there. I knocked hard on its rough frontage. After the fifth knock I said, 'Conor Smith says Open Sesame.' The door swung open easily.

The inside was warmer. Pastel colours filled the walls and there was a plush green carpet that ran throughout the single-storey dwelling. Arched openings stood where doors normally hung and Grey was filled with a soft light that comfortably reflected the pastel walls. The house was sparsely furnished, except for the sitting room, which had a traditional three-piece suite, a large TV and a cluttered computer corner. At first sight it all looked like old technology, but over the years I'd updated it so that within this old grey box lurked the very latest systems and networks.

I sort of blobbily fell into the deep armchair.

'Contact Mikoyan,' I said and the computers came to life. Within seconds the Russian himself was on the TV screen.

'Is that you?' asked Mikoyan in disbelief.

'Of course it is.'

'I'd get another plastic surgeon, if I were you.'

'Crap Russian humour. Did you get the *Titanic* pictures I transmitted?'

'Yes. Mine were the latest published ones – slightly different from what you saw.' Mikoyan rubbed his nose. 'I keep sneezing. That's the trouble with Mother Russia. Too bloody cold.'

'Keep your germs to yourself.'

'I wouldn't waste them on a capitalist.'

'Even if I paid?'

'That's different. That's business. You want I should email you some? COD of course.'

'Buzz off.'

Mikoyan chuckled. 'Are we safe?'

'Yes. I'm firewalled here, just like Rose Cottage.'

'I think there could be something similar to the Info-Calypse out there.'

Conor sat bolt upright. 'Why?'

'Instinct. I've been concentrating on why the President was kidnapped. My bet is that he was never in real danger; that he was always going to come home safely. And, from the files I've been given, there's no doubt it was Jim.'

'Our rogue robot.'

Mikoyan nodded. 'Do you trust Gallagher?'

'Why?'

'He was very forthcoming with you, I reckoned.'

'They were in a jam.'

'With all *their* resources?'

'They were strapped for time. You know the security boys. They're OK when they work the system, but once they're out of it they're useless.'

425

'Even so, they came to you very quickly.'

'Gallagher was a pupil of mine.'

'Not recently.'

'Where're you coming from, comrade?'

'The one constant thing in this has been the InfoCalypse. Mentioned in the ransom note and also, from what Gallagher's told you, the kidnapper spoke to the President about it. That seemed the main concern, the only concern, of the kidnapper.'

'Jim.'

They both sat in silence for a while, lost in their shared thoughts.

'Why did you come back to the old house?' Mikoyan asked eventually.

'I was looking for answers. The alpha, the omega, maybe there was something here. Some sort of clue.'

'I think that was put in as a clue, to pinpoint you. Like Condor was like Master of the Web.'

'Gimmicks.'

'They haven't worked out the alpha and the omega lead?'

'Not yet.'

'They still had to get me involved in the first place. I could've turned them down.'

'True but unlikely.' Mikoyan smiled. 'We all know you cannot resist a challenge.'

'You're saying I was set up before the President got kidnapped?'

'A possibility. But the kidnapper could have had a number of clues set up for any GameMaster the authorities pulled in. Even for me, who knows? It doesn't take long to get a ransom note out. And nothing, I recollect, that was said to the President pointed directly towards you. It was all in the ransom notes and the fact that you knew things just as soon as the security boys did.'

'Contacts.'

'MIWs.'

'So?'

'Maybe they were fed information to point the finger at you.'

I thought about Andi. Not her. Tebor, yes, maybe, but not Andi. Or was I too emotional?

'Robots are programed, remember. They can't think for themselves,' Mikoyan continued. 'If the Telephone Exchange is hiding the InfoCalypse, and they do seem the most probable culprits, then they would want you to become the suspect.' The Russian was reading my mind. 'Maybe Jim is harmless. Maybe he has another role, a simpler one. Maybe the Telephone Exchange is using him to mask their own activities. Maybe they were simply testing the system.'

'By kidnapping the President?'

'Did you know Swilkin was – is – a star of the NSA's Dundee Society?'

'No.'

Mikoyan smirked his self-satisfied smirk. He was extremely pleased with himself. 'That's why, my friend, I am a Datakeeper and you a mere GameMaster.'

'I am not worthy, O Russian Master.' I bowed my head in mock deference.

'Mikoyan got serious again. 'Nelson and Keebles were both members of that same society.'

'I thought the Dundee Society was only NSA.'

'They both started with the NSA, as very young men.'

'What about Dom Murphy?'

'There's hope for you yet. Yes, he was also a member of the society.'

'Malcolm Bonham?'

'No, he is just a foot soldier. But the other three all had links with the NSA. And, whatever you do, you never get out of the Dundee Society. They have a couple of known paedophiles in their ranks, three traitors going back to the USSR days, and a bunch of sexual perverts with a variety of erotic interests.'

'Where do you get all this stuff from?'

'What is it Confucius says? The Master must teach the pupil everything, except how to be the Master.'

'That's exactly what I tell my pupils.'

'Then you will appreciate its meaning.'

I shook my head. He always had a smart comeback. 'What else?'

'The three of them had no known fetishes.'

'Swilkin?'

'As clean as the other three.'

'Have you passed this on to anyone else?'

'To Bonham but I had no choice. He was getting impatient, threatened to cut me off from the network unless I got results. Not a pleasant man.'

'Was Gallagher involved with them?'

Mikoyan shook his head. 'He's good at what he does, but he isn't in the same league. He would never have been accepted into the Dundee Society. That doesn't mean he isn't close to Swilkin, or that he isn't helping out the NSA. Which is why I believe you may have been singled out to join in the search.'

'So tell me about the InfoCalypse?'

'I don't know yet. I haven't discovered the key. But, as I said, my instinct tells me that is what it's all about. One of these government agencies has it: information on *everybody*, right down to the cough-drops you buy when you've got a cold. Whatever it is, it'll break every known UN law. I don't understand where Jim the robot fits in, but there is a common thread starting to run through this. The Dundee Society is definitely one of the strands that tie it together. Nelson and Keebles had an ulterior motive, and then someone forced their hand, which is why they committed suicide.'

'Or were murdered, and made to look like suicide.'

'Maybe. The kidnapping of the President would take everyone's eye off the real motive.' Mikoyan threw his hands up in exasperation. 'Maybe someone is warning us about the InfoCalypse. And that's why people are being killed. To hide the truth. Look to Swilkin. He did the minimum when Dixon was kidnapped, I find it difficult to believe they could not get further with all their resources. And he was even present at the White House when Dixon returned. As if he was expecting it.'

'He had been invited by Gallagher,' replied Conor, and then explained what the Secret Service man had told him. 'But Gallagher said that, too, that Swilkin hung around, almost as if expecting Dixon to suddenly appear. He said Swilkin didn't seem much surprised when the President finally showed up.'

'Maybe Mister Swilkin is in deeper than he'd like us to believe. He may know a lot more than he's admitting.'

Teddy Dixon sat back, his unshod feet resting on the corner of his Oval Office desk. Nancy Sumner, his Vice President, sat opposite him, next to Joe Meisner. She knew he was deliberately baiting her, showing her no respect as he waggled his black nylon-socked toes right in front of her.

'I just wanted to thank you for holding the fort while I was . . . out of touch,' he said with a big smile.

'Thank God you came back safe,' replied Sumner, contriving an equally warm smile.

'I was lucky – no thanks to our Security Services.' There was now more than a hint of irritation in Dixon's voice. 'They really had no idea how to find me, did they?'

'I'm sure it wasn't for lack of trying.'

'Not good enough. The President goes missing from right under their noses and they have no idea where to start. Nancy, that puts all of us at risk: you, me, anybody who's been elected to serve the people. I mean, that's dangerous. That blows the bottom out of our democratic system. Imagine if we couldn't go on the Web any longer. How would we speak to people? On television? Nobody watches it any more. Nowadays you *live* television . . . not sit and watch it. Life and Reality TV have merged into one.'

'I'm not sure exactly where you're coming from, Teddy.'

'It's very simple, Nancy,' interjected Meisner. 'We, as an administration, cannot be seen to be as helpless as we were. I mean, this business could force us to keep out of Second

World. That would be admitting that the USA had lost control of the very technology it invented.'

'I appreciate that, but I'm no techno-guru. I'm a lawyer.' She didn't need to add that Dixon himself would be the butt of the jokes that would follow. If anything, it might even help her come through as the saviour of the country's standing in the world. Even if she didn't find the kidnapper, she would simply say that Dixon had failed and that she would make sure it never happened again. She found it hard not to smirk; she enjoyed watching him on the rack.

'Trouble is', said Dixon swinging his feet off the desk, 'we're both walking the plank on this one.'

'All I did was hold the fort . . . while you were absent.'

'And, like I said, I'm very grateful. Problem is, Nancy, that if I go down on this, so will you.'

She returned his steady gaze. She stared into the eyes of a cold-blooded lizard.

What's he playing at now?

'I think the President will get the sympathy vote on this,' added Meisner. 'That could leave you out in the cold.'

She slowly swung her gaze round to Meisner. 'Why?'

'Because the public already accepts the President has his weaknesses. Guess that's why he's so popular, because he's a pretty straight kind of guy.'

She wanted to slap him as he got that little smirk at the corner of his lips. She leant back and held up her hands in a portrayal of innocence. 'All I did was . . .'

'Hold the fort. Sure. But the press would say, not very well.'

She swung round to Dixon and shook her head. 'No, this is not one you plant on me.'

'I'm trying to protect you, Nancy,' said Dixon smoothly. 'And myself, and the whole damn administration.'

'You're the one who took risks, went missing, and created this mess. That Monroe thing had nothing to do with me.'

'Ouch!' He leant back and put his hands behind his neck, started to tilt back and forth in the rocking chair he'd copied from JFK.

Why was he looking so fucking pleased with himself?

'It's been recorded. I watched it. This whole sordid mess was something I was *not* – I repeat – *not* involved in. For a few hours I just protected everyone, including your reputation.'

'There is no tape,' said Meisner coldly.

'I saw it.'

'Maybe.'

'So did you.'

'All I saw was the President flirting with a Monroe avatar. Harmless stuff. Then the screen went blank.'

'You can't eradicate something like that. Nobody'll believe you.'

'There's nothing to believe. I guess the tape got wiped when the kidnapper broke the President's JetPax. If he could do that, then he could almost certainly destroy a recording. The guy's clearly a techno-genius.' Meisner let this information sink in before continuing. 'The Telephone Exchange, the CIA and the NSA will confirm that. I believe the report's already been prepared.'

Dixon shook his head. 'We could've got some good clues from that tape. Bad break.'

I should've known better. He's Nixoned the tape.

'It won't do us any good if this thing is allowed to go on, to fester.' Dixon stood up and came round the table, stood tall in front of her, to intimidate her. He smiled comfortingly. She saw it as it was: the shark moving in. 'Dammit, Nancy, we're both high and dry on this. Me because I let things get out of hand; you because you could be seen as the VP who couldn't handle pressure during an emergency. I'd be remembered as the President who fooled around – that's while some Public Prosecutor out to make a name for himself tried to get me impeached – and you'd be totally unelectable. There'd be so much dirt flying around that you'd never find out who was throwing the mud, or who was in it. We'd be gone in sixty seconds.'

'There are witnesses who watched that recording.'

Meisner shrugged. 'Just their opinions. Nobody could swear, even on a stack of bibles, that there was any definite impropriety. Maybe a bit of harmless flirtation. Hell, a date with a famous icon for one evening, but they talked most of the time. He asked about her life. And he was delighted she sang for him just like she sang for JFK. We all have our heroes. Even the President.'

'She sat on his lap.'

'So. Maybe you'd like Robert Redford to sit on yours. No crime.'

'Is he dead yet?' asked Dixon.

'Redford. Must be.'

'Don't you people take anything seriously?' she shrieked suddenly.

The two men stared at her.

Then Dixon smiled his vote-catching smile.

'We need to find the guy,' he said. 'Dead or alive. We think we even know who he is.'

'Can you tell me?'

'Sure. If I can't trust you, who can I trust? A Game-Master. English.'

'You mean Conor Smith?' She remembered the name, presumed it was the same person who had been unleashed into the hunt by Gallagher of the Secret Service.

'It's pretty circumstantial, but his profile's starting to fit the bill. What's more important is that we wrap this thing up. We've got to be seen to be in control. Decisive, committed leadership, from both of us. What we can't afford is mass panic in Second World. That could destroy our economy, and both our careers.'

'What if it's not him?'

'By the time we get that far it'll all be forgotten.'

'And when we've destroyed the poor English bastard?'

'Then we get on with our lives. I have four more great years, and you can work out how you're going to become the next President of the United States. Nancy, I have absolutely no intention of letting something like this stand in my way. And, once you've considered it, neither will you.'

He walked back and sat down in the rocker.

'Was there anything else?' he asked her coldly.

'No, Mister President.'

'Good. Then, Madam Vice President, if you'd excuse me, I'd like to get on with my work.'

Brutally – deliberately cruel – the Vice President was dismissed. Dixon looked down and started to read a document on his desk. Nancy Sumner, only one heartbeat away from becoming President of the United States and the most powerful person in the world, rose from her chair and meekly left the room, never looking back.

As she was closing the door she heard the two men start to laugh behind her. She snapped the door shut as quickly as she could, trying to avoid the laughter carrying into the hallway, smiled sweetly at the secretary they all knew Dixon was banging, and walked back to her office.

One day. One day I'll get that arsehole.

The muffled laughter faded in the corridor that led back to her room.

The noise surprised me. It came from the back of the house, from the bedroom zone. The house had nine bedrooms; I'd always wanted a big sprawling mansion when I was younger, and that had been part of my life when fast cars and fancy living was top of the agenda.

The sounds were human, grunts and groans muffled and indistinct, with no rhythm to their pattern. I opened the sitting-room door and tried to catch where it was coming from. There was obviously someone at the furthest corner of the house. I went silently along the long corridors and through the double doors separating my living and entertainment zone from the bedrooms.

The sounds were clearer now: male noises, excited, shouting, animal-like in intensity. The activity came from the last bedroom, the one set apart from the rest – the one I always used when I stayed there. I took a deep breath and pushed the door open slowly. They were lost in their own perverse heat. Tebor was on his knees, his trousers rolled down to his knees, his head forced down by the man who crouched behind him on the bed.

The man – the same one who had met Tebor earlier, while with Jim and Andi – was naked. The Weekender had forced himself into Tebor; their game was rape and Tebor was playing his part. The Weekender thrashed the boy's buttocks as he pumped away at him; the beauty of Second

435

World was that you could make love forever without resorting to one of the wonder erection drugs people used in RealWorld. If you paid for one hour, you got one hour. Sex ran as regular as a Swiss rail timetable down here.

'What the hell are you doing?' I yelled.

The two on the bed sprang apart, Tebor tumbling on to the floor, hurriedly pulling his pants up. The Weekender fell backwards, recovered his balance and watched as I moved towards him. But, before I could get to him, he'd punched his JetPax and disappeared into the matrix and back to RealWorld.

I swung round to Tebor.

'How the hell did you . . . ?'

'Who are you?' shrieked the frightened youth.

'It's me, Conor.' I'd forgotten I was still Blobalong. No wonder they were both terrified. 'It's OK. It's me.'

Tebor looked stunned, then the fear vanished as he realized it really was me. He suddenly got mad. 'He never paid,' he shrieked at me furiously. 'I never got his credits.'

'Fuck that. How did you . . . ?'

'You spoilt it. So you'd better pay me.'

'This is my home.' I was incredulous.

'You cost me credits. He was my friend. You scared him away. You owe me.'

'I owe you nothing.'

Tebor ran at me, his trousers now zipped up. 'Foo. You owe me, two hundred US.'

'Bollocks,' I said, surprised, stepping back to protect myself as he scratched at my face. Then, as I held off the spitting, writhing youth, I got the giggles. This was ridiculous. 'I'm not paying you, you stupid kid.'

'I want two hundred US.' Tebor tried to kick me.

'No way.' I wrapped my arms tightly round the boy, held him still, stifled his movements. 'Stop it. Behave yourself.' I waited until Tebor ceased struggling, then gradually released him. But I held up a warning hand to keep him at a safe distance.

'Two hundred,' yelled a furious Tebor.

'Nothing to do with me.'

'I helped you. And all for nothing. Now you cost me money. So you pay me.'

'That's different. I said I'd give you something.'

'Two hundred. That's what he would've paid.'

'I was going to give you more.'

Tebor appeared slightly mollified. 'You were?'

'I said I would.' He started to calm down. 'How the hell did you get in here?' I finally asked.

Tebor shuffled his feet, then he let out a big sigh. 'I heard you tell Andi how to.'

'So you decided to let yourself in?'

Tebor grinned. 'It was a good idea. No rent, not like a hotel, so more profit. Anyway, you said you never came here.'

'I didn't expect you to claim squatter's rights.'

'MIWs can't do that,' Tebor replied sullenly. 'I suppose you'll change the password now?'

'What gave you that idea?'

'Why you wearing that silly costume?'

I was saved the explanation when I heard a shout from the sitting-room area.

'Christ, what is it? Open Day? Come on, Tebor,' I ordered him as I walked down the corridor, 'Get out of my bedroom. You've caused enough trouble already.'

Andi was in the living area. With Jim.

'Hi,' I said. 'I thought we'd agreed to meet at MetroPort 911.'

She was startled at first, then recognized my voice coming from the strange avatar. 'Wow, you really look different. I came here because Jim said you'd . . .' Andi looked over my shoulder as Tebor then entered. 'What're you doing here?'

she asked sharply. She was obviously shocked to see the boy there, so at least she hadn't knowingly let him in.

Tebor pulled a face, went over to the large armchair and sat down; making a great play that he was ignoring them. She turned to me quizzically.

'Don't ask,' I said. 'And no, he's not my type.' I swung round to Jim. 'You weren't surprised to see Tebor here. But, somehow, that doesn't surprise me.'

Jim sat on the chair arm and ruffled Tebor's spiky locks. 'You OK?' he asked.

The boy nodded, closed his eyes and leant his head against Jim's chest. Andi crossed over to the sofa and sat down opposite the pair of them.

Happy families. I moved next to Andi, so that I was facing Jim.

'You and I need to talk,' I said.

'Sure, whatever you want,' replied Jim.

His perma-smile was beginning to irritate me.

Neville Harbour-Smythe felt on unsure ground. His logic told him to work closely with Dwight Swilkin, to trust him in this matter. After all, they were both members of the Dundee Society. But his instincts told him otherwise.

The Telephone Exchange had shut him out when he asked for their files on Jim. He knew that Nelson and Keebles were involved, but could get nothing more from Swilkin. The two men, now dead by their own hands, had also been Dundee Society members. Swilkin had merely shrugged off his questions, insisted that their suicides were not linked and that they had nothing to do with the President's kidnapping.

Harbour-Smythe knew it didn't need a diploma in intelligence, or even domestic sciences, to appreciate he was being squeezed out of the loop. That had never openly happened before, certainly not as blatantly as now. Yet they still wanted everything he could gather on Conor Smith. He'd exhausted the subject, set his best men on the task, and come up with nothing new.

The GameMaster had built an impenetrable firewall round himself.

'Keep going,' Swilkin had insisted to him. 'Go back to the beginning and start again. There's got to be something there.'

So Harbour-Smythe started again, put his team back

on the keyboards and told them to attack all the data available.

He finally discovered a link. It was all too easy. So easy that they'd missed it the first time. He was convinced that someone was deliberately setting up Conor Smith. The leads were obvious: Condor, the Master of the Web, and now the alpha and the omega. It was missed the first time round because everyone was busy chasing the present, yet all good analysts knew the answers usually hid in the past.

The urgency of the situation had pulled them all away from the routine tracker methods.

They'd checked the early Second World property records, but there had been a shortage of accurate information. Many of the early deals were by barter of techie information or using credit cards which had only vague descriptions attached to their purchase.

By raiding the British American Express archives, one of the GCHQ operatives came up with Condor's purchase of a property in Alpha World. It was something even the Telephone Exchange would not have instant access to: the 2017 UK Amex records. Once GCHQ triggered that link, the connection between alpha and the pioneer house builder Omega was uncovered almost immediately. What he found equally interesting was the acquisition of large swathes of Alpha World by ThemeCorp, including the purchase of the *Titanic*, which was now being refurbished.

Harbour-Smythe realized that all these clues had been laid to point the finger of suspicion at the GameMaster. Clearly, someone wanted him to take the blame. If Smith had really been involved, he certainly would have covered any tracks that eventually might be discovered. He didn't know Conor Smith but his naturally sceptical nature made him pause before passing any such information on. If Smith had kidnapped Teddy Dixon, the last thing he would want was to be identified. There was no possible benefit to him in that. But if the Americans were now setting up Smith, then their motives were just as confusing.

Why kidnap their own President?

Why shift the blame onto Conor Smith?

Why push for a ransom that didn't demand money or some other political or criminal stipulation?

Just a GameMaster. Just a chap who played games and was an expert on the Web. Why him? What were his strengths? What did they want of him? In which direction were they pushing him? Why did the Yanks want him to be guilty? Why was he the only suspect?

What aren't they telling me?

His quandary created a Catch-22. After all, his friendship with Swilkin and his membership of the Dundee Society meant he should be sharing his knowledge with his colleague. Except he was now convinced his colleague wasn't being entirely truthful in response.

The other problem was that Conor Smith was British and probably innocent. He wasn't some traitor who'd threatened national security, so it was Harbour-Smythe's duty to protect him.

The only constant commonality running through the equation was that the President had been kidnapped and the ransom note demanded the end of the InfoCalypse.

Conor Smith had, to the best of his knowledge, never been near the President, had never appeared to contact him prior to the kidnap, and had been under full view of SnoopCams at most times and certainly in touch with the Secret Service after he was called in.

Which left the InfoCalypse as the real threat. Somebody believed in the certainty of the InfoCalypse strongly enough to actually kidnap Teddy Dixon. Nobody had any real idea who that person was. But in protecting the InfoCalypse they had to identify a kidnapper . . . and eventually take him out, permanently.

Conor Smith was the ideal and obvious choice. But he would also lead them all to the real perpetrator.

I wonder if he's any idea as to what danger he's in?

If the game continued, Smith would, almost certainly, be killed at some point.

Suddenly a far more important point occurred. *Dwight Swilkin must know, or believe, that there's an InfoCalypse.*

Harbour-Smythe understood Swilkin's motives, since something that important needed protecting. It was now time to use the special relationship, official and personal, even if Swilkin continued denying all knowledge of the Info-Calypse. In time, if he helped bring in the big fish, and let Swilkin know he had sussed why he had done it, then his friend would have no choice but to grant him access to that all-pervading information. He smiled at his own folly. *Friend?* In the end, there were no true friends in intelligence.

He tapped the keyboard and connected to Swilkin's direct Vue-Link at the Telephone Exchange.

'So who are you, really?' I wanted to know.

Jim smiled benignly. 'I am who you see.'

'No riddles, please.'

'All GameMasters are interested in riddles. How else could you play the game?'

'This is no game.'

'Everything is a game.'

'Who's your host? In RealWorld?'

'You know the answer to that.'

'I don't. How the hell can you be a robot? I mean, if it's true somebody's really pushed the limit of technology on that. Nobody's that far ahead.'

'You're no robot,' said a surprised Tebor, lifting his head from Jim's chest and peering up at him.

'I am what you see,' replied Jim. 'Your friend, and your protector.'

I glanced sideways at Andi but she wasn't even aware of me. She looked straight, with wonderment, into Jim's eyes.

'Jim Nelson,' I said suddenly.

Jim said nothing.

'Mike Keebles.'

Still nothing.

'Dom Murphy.'

I sensed a flicker of fear in Jim's eyes. But it had been too quick, so maybe that's what he wanted me to see.

'Did you kidnap the President?'

'Why should I harm him?'

'I didn't ask if you'd harmed him, only if you'd kidnapped him.'

Jim's smile got bigger. 'I thought you just said no riddles.'

'Malcolm Bonham, how about him?'

Silence again.

'Bonham says you're a robot, created by Nelson, Keebles and Murphy. He says you're made up of trillions of microbiological robotic cells which, under certain conditions and circumstances, come together and DNA themselves into you. Also that you're one helluva supercomputer when you're all connected up.'

Jim started to laugh. Tebor pulled away and looked at him in awe.

Andi's expression hadn't changed.

'So, what's inside you? Some great sleeping giant? You going to turn into the Incredible Hulk if you get mad?'

Jim ignored the jibe. 'Am I any different from any of you down here? MIWs, avatars, we're all somebody's DNA, somebody's dream, living someone else's life down here.'

'So Bonham's right about you.'

'What?' Jim shook his head. 'That I was put together to come down here just to kidnap the President. Impossible! These kids have known me for years.'

'We have,' said Tebor, swinging round on Conor. 'Haven't we, Andi?'

She continued staring at Jim. He returned her gaze for a moment before she finally spoke. 'For years,' she affirmed softly, her smile reflecting his.

'How did you know I was coming back here, to my old place?' I asked.

'My picture is being circulated along the Brick, so Andi very kindly suggested we come here to your safe house. You already said she could use it, and you were simply here when we arrived.'

444

'Andi was surprised when she saw Tebor, but you weren't.'

'Surprised? That he was here? Why? I mean, this is Second World, where everything happens.'

'I said Jim could come here,' confirmed Andi. 'I didn't think you'd mind.'

'You, and Bonham, too, have a pretty ragged theory.' Jim laughed, waved his hand dismissively. 'For me to behave in such a ... with all these microbiological cells hurtling together ... wow, that would be some colossal program. Especially if ... you'd been programed to think.'

There was a long silence.

'No,' continued Jim, shaking his head. 'You can be programed ... or you can think. I don't think you can do both.'

'Is there really an InfoCalypse?'

'Does that concern you?'

'Yes.'

'Why?'

'Because of the way I've been dragged into this mess.' I regretted allowing my sudden irritation to show. 'I have nothing to do with all this. I was called in to help. Now I'm suspect *numero uno*.'

'Do *you* believe there is an InfoCalypse?' asked Jim.

'I have no idea.'

'Then why get involved?'

'Because I am. Why ask me what you already know?'

'Do I?'

'Don't waste time. Tell me about the InfoCalypse.'

'I'm told it's just a rumour.'

'Is it?'

'I can't say. Follow your instincts. The answers lie there.'

'Why did Jim Nelson die?'

Jim looked surprised.

'Jim Nelson is alive,' he stated positively.

'Why did Mike Keebles die?

445

'Mike Keebles is also alive.'

'Where? Living inside you?'

Jim seemed confused. He turned to Tebor, then to Andi. They didn't know how to react to his sudden bewilderment, one of almost childlike innocence.

'They are both dead,' I stated flatly.

'No, *alive.*'

'*Dead.* Within a few days of one another.'

Jim shook his head sharply. 'I would know. I *do* know.' Suddenly the smile came back. 'They *are* alive. Nobody can kill them.'

I spoke slowly and very deliberately. 'They killed themselves. Shot themselves in the head, put the barrel to their mouths and pulled the trigger.' It dawned on me that Jim had genuinely no idea they were dead.

'They can never die.'

'Why not?'

'Because they are the Masters.'

MASTERS OF THE WEB. Those were the words in the first ransom note. I AM THE VIRUS. Maybe they'd all got it wrong. Maybe it was just a hacker's virus. No, it wasn't that simple. Bonham had confirmed Jim was a robot. But Nelson and Keebles were dead. That had been relayed to me by Gallagher, from the Secret Service itself. Yet Jim, supposedly created by them, clearly didn't know that. If *they* were controlling him, he would have known. So who, if anybody, was actually controlling him?

For what purpose did Jim come together? Not just to kidnap the President – not if he was going to let him go. What was the reason for his existence?

Who was he?

Why was he?

'The Masters of what?' I asked Jim.

Jim shrugged. 'The Masters.'

'Who are the Dragons?'

'They will come to you. And you must slay them.'

446

'When?'

'When it is time.'

'What about you?'

'I cannot fight the Dragons. I can only warn you.'

'And if I can't go on, can't achieve what you want me to?'

'I can hide you, protect you by taking you into areas they can't enter.'

'I can do that already,' I replied, taking the SmartCard from my pocket. 'This will get me into anywhere, including the Dark Areas.'

'Where did you get that?' asked Jim suspiciously.

'From Bonham.'

'A frightening man. No soul there. Only efficiency matters to him. You do realize that they're tracking that SmartCard, that they already know exactly where you are.'

'Yes.'

'Did Bonham touch that card?'

'He did.'

'Then it will have his DNA on it – just as it will yours.' Jim's sudden excitement was obvious.

I started to understand. Anything a cyber traveller touched in RealWorld, like a credit card, was DNA'd and automatically transported through the sensory nerves of the fingers into Second World. I had inadvertently carried Bonham's DNA with me on the card.

'I know that. So?'

'May I hold it?'

I didn't see any risk in handing it over. I passed the card across, hoping that Jim wouldn't wipe it clean.

He held it uneasily, rubbing it between his fingers. 'I can feel him,' he said eventually. 'This is good.' He smiled and put both his hands over the card, squeezed it between his palms and then held it still. After a few seconds he opened his hands, looked at the card and silently passed it back to me.

'Don't lose it. It holds our futures. For all of us.'

I closely inspected the SmartCard. It looked just as before. Nothing obvious had changed.

'What have you . . . ?

The TV screen flickered, interrupting me, startling everyone, and then Mikoyan appeared, the camera focused tight on his eyes and nose.

'Conor?' He spoke quietly, almost a whisper, with difficulty.

'What is it, comrade?'

The camera pulled back slow-mo and a revolver appeared, an old-fashioned American Frontier Colt six-shooter with a long army barrel. The barrel was between Mikoyan's lips, pointing inwards and upwards into the roof of his mouth. The hammer had been clicked back. The slightest vibration could shake the trigger loose, snap the hammer down and blow out his brains.

Those in Grey could clearly see the bruising around the Russian's eyes, the swollen lips, the congealed blood under his nose.

'Help,' burbled Mikoyan.

He started to cry. The cries turned into frantic sobs. There was nothing any of us could do but wait, and see what came next.

Swilkin faded in on Gallagher's desk screen.

'Your people need to pull in Smith,' he said. 'I've got the confirmation order right here.' He held up a typed official document for scanning so that Gallagher could then reach out and take it from the printer attached to his monitor. 'From the Vice President herself. Apprehend – at any cost, is how it reads.'

Gallagher read through the detain order. 'Wrong decision,' he said impassively.

'Not yours to make. Just go get him.'

Gallagher swung round. 'Don,' he called and handed Clancy the order. 'We need a Web Force: WebCops and our own avatars. Put them together and get down there immediately. Don't wait for me. I'll be down in the Transporter Room as soon as I can.'

'Grey? Is this Smith's place?' asked Clancy as he read the details.

'That's what it says. Secure it when you get there. Fully armed units.'

He watched Clancy turn and start barking orders, before he himself swivelled back to the screen. 'You tracked him there?'

'Yes,' came Swilkin's impatient response.

'You going to tell me why we're going in there?'

'Sure.' Swilkin then explained the alpha and the omega to him.

'Pretty circumstantial,' said Gallagher, when he'd finished.

'That's more than you guys've come up with. None of the SnoopCams picked him up. so we ran a check on the avatar copyright bureau. What you see on the screen now was his first ever avatar. Pretty basic stuff. Not what we'd expect. We ran recorded tapes and the SnoopCam at Ground Zero identified him, nearly an hour ago. We traced him to the *Titanic* – Omega to you – and then to his own place in Alpha World. It's registered as Grey. That's the image on the screen right now. I guess it's pretty well fire-walled.'

'You can take that as given.'

'The original buildings in Alpha World could be entered through walls, windows, anything. You just walked into your space. So did everybody else. Although Grey was an early property, we believe Smith has updated all the walls and other natural barriers. We couldn't find any zoning applications for building updates, but that's not something our man would worry about.'

'Like I said, he'll have that house wrapped up tight.'

Swilkin disregarded this. 'He's got company, a girl – the same one we saw him with earlier on.'

'Whitehorn?'

'The same. And wanted on a murder rap. Killed her sister's partner. Probably a psychopath, insane jealousy, wanted what her sister had.'

'Maybe *she* was the victim?'

'Aren't they all? Also the kid with spiky hair. He went into the house with some guy, either MIW or a Weekender, before Smith and the girl got there.'

'No one else?'

'No. Why'd you ask?'

'If we're rushing in, we need to know.'

'Flush him out, no escape, no fuck-ups. If he comes back to RealWorld, we'll be ready waiting at his place. I didn't think we could, but all this latest information gives us the right. EI6 are on their way there with support from our people in London, and fully armed response units. I want them inside Rose Cottage, waiting for him. Same rules of engagement apply to you. If he tries to run, take him out. Freeze him in the fucking matrix, I don't care. Just get him before he causes any more problems.'

'Can you hear me?'

Mikoyan moved his head up and down slowly, not wanting to vibrate the revolver and thus release the trigger.

'Are they still there?'

Mikoyan nodded again.

'Can they hear me?'

'Of course we fucking can,' rasped a tinny, digitally disguised voice off-camera. 'You keep asking him questions, keep him nodding his head, and that way he'll blow his own brains out. There's a hair-trigger on that gun. That's the fun, waiting for it to go off. When, Smith? When's it going to blow?'

So they'd linked me with the Russian. How much more did they know? I'd never recognize the voice, not when he was speaking through a VoxMuffler. I moved towards the controls to activate the decoder.

'Stay where you are, Smith,' ordered the voice.

I stopped.

'Don't get up to your old tricks,' it continued. 'I know how you operate. No decoders, nothing. You start to do anything I find even suspiciously suspicious, and your Russkie pal becomes your headless pal.'

'Whatever you say,' I said, stepping back. 'But he's only helping me. I'm the one you're after.'

'Don't worry, your time will come.'

'What do you want?'

'You're becoming a problem. Playing games, that was harmless. Just kids' stuff for which you got paid a fortune.'

'I guess this isn't about me being a GameMaster?'

'Obviously.'

'It's about the President.'

'Who else.'

'Did *you* kidnap him?'

There was a cackle of laughter. Mikoyan closed his eyes, starting to shake. He couldn't handle this sort of intense pressure.

'Take it easy, Alex. Try and control it.'

Mikoyan nodded, but as hard as he tried he couldn't.

'Your pal's just wet himself,' snorted the voice, then he let out another chilling, tinny laugh.

'Try, Alex. Just try.' My tone was calm, trying to strengthen the Datakeeper's resolve.

How did they know about Alex? I hoped the automatic recorder was on. Whatever now happened, I'd be able to replay the voice and decode it to get an accurate voiceprint.

'Conor!' Andi called out urgently.

I turned my head, and she indicated the exterior surveillance screen with a nod of her head.

The garden outside my house was packed with men, many armed with technoM16 carbines. They had the appearance of US security personnel and were supported by WebCops. I counted at least thirty men surrounding the house. They were looking for an entrance into Grey; I knew it was me they'd come after. There was no immediate problem, as they wouldn't crack the entry code that easily. We were secure for the moment.

'They're *all* after you now,' said tinny voice. 'Why, Smith? Why's everyone thinking it's you?'

'You tell me.'

'Conor,' sobbed Alex.

'Control, Alex. Please, deep breaths, try and – '

'Shut up,' shouted tinny voice. 'The trouble with you, Smith, is that you're too fucking full of yourself. But you're just lucky, that's all. Just fucking lucky.'

'Why did you kidnap the President?' I wanted to keep him talking. Maybe he'd let something out, maybe he was another GameMaster. Just keep him talking.

'Not even lukewarm.'

'Then you killed Keebles? And Nelson?'

'If that's what you believe.'

'Nelson and Keebles are not dead,' said Jim.

'Alex Mikoyan's got nothing to do with this,' I pleaded. 'Let him go. I'll meet you, anywhere you want, but let him go.'

Tinny voice started to laugh. 'You're not going anywhere. Not with that lot outside. Why'd you do it, Smith? Why'd you kill Nelson and Keebles.'

Jim turned and stared uncomprehendingly at Conor. 'They are *not* dead,' he said simply, almost childlike.

Over his shoulder Conor watched the Feds and WebCops trying to force an entry into Grey.

'Tell him, Smith,' continued tinny voice. 'Tell him why you killed them both.'

'He's not that stupid.' I realized what the voice was doing, trying desperately to turn Jim against me. I swivelled round to face Jim. 'It's not true. Why should I do that.'

'Kill them in RealWorld and come back down here? Tell him how you did it.'

'Not true,' burbled Mikoyan. He was breathing deeper, fighting to bring his fear under control. 'Not true. The InfoCalypse. From the Alpha to the Omega. To the Dragon's Lair.' His eyes looked straight at Jim. 'Conor is your friend. Trust . . .'

He never finished the sentence. A hand reached across and knocked the revolver.

'No!' I screamed, moving helplessly towards the screen.
Bang.

The sound was louder than the word.

It reverberated across the room as Alex Mikoyan's head exploded upwards and the bullet smashed into the roof of his mouth, through the greyness of his exceptional brain, cracked open the top of his skull and embedded itself in the ceiling of his computer room.

Andi screamed; Tebor leapt up, his eyes wide open with excitement.

'Fucking superlunary,' he shrieked.

Jim just stared, his lips still twisted in that frozen half smile.

Where there had been features — eyes, a nose, a dark hairline — there was now only a red mush of all that had once been Mikoyan. Then the Russian flipped over backwards, almost in slow motion, and disappeared from view.

Some blood, almost purple and very thick, spattered across the screen.

'Goodbye,' said tinny voice. 'You killed him, Smith. You involved him and you killed him. How many more are you going to kill?'

Then the line was lost, the screen went dead.

The room was as silent as outer space. I stepped back and fell into the sofa, staring at the empty screen. This was beyond what I was used to. This was for real.

Jim came up behind me and ran his hand over my head. There was a tingle, a short fizz of static that disappeared as soon as Jim's hand had passed over. 'I'm so sorry,' he said. Then he walked into the wall and faded into the matrix.

'He's JetPaxed,' said Tebor. 'My friend's moved on.' Tebor looked vacant, zapped into overdrive, blown with exhilaration.

'He'll be back. When it's safe.'

'Then he's not a robot. I told you he wasn't.'

Andi still stared at the empty screen, her right hand held up to her mouth, gagging herself from screaming, her eyes full of pain and shock.

'Andi?'

She ignored me.

I got up and crossed over to her, put my arm round her shoulders. Her body was stiff with shock. I stroked her gently, reassuring her. It took some moments before she accepted I was there. As she relaxed her body, as the trauma released, she started to whimper. This was the second time she'd seen a dead person in RealWorld. It shook her; this the same fate that awaited her one day. After all these years in Second World, unlike so many MIWs, she still understood the finite difference between reality and fantasy.

'We need to get out,' I said, still holding her tightly while the tautness unwound and she regularized her systems. Finally, when I felt she was under her own avatarian disciplines, I gently let go. That was the problem with MIWs; there was no conscious reaction from their hosts, and therefore extreme shock often resulted in WebFever and eventual wipe-out.

'OK, now?' I asked.

She nodded and looked round. 'Where's Jim?'

'JetPaxed. Gone. VaVoom,' said Tebor, clicking his fingers. 'Like *we* got to.' He got up close to me. 'You going to JetPax out and leave us here alone again.'

I ignored him and concentrated on the screen. We were still OK, but those outside would eventually break in. It was time for my DoomsDay scenario, though I never thought I'd have to use it. I hoped I'd created a good program because if it didn't work, we could all be wiped out in the matrix.

I crossed over to the main computer and downloaded tinny voice's vocalprint into the portable memory on my watch. Then I initiated a download of all software, programs and data, into the concealed storage bins at John Mathews's farm. I then sent a message to the farmer's phone and answerphone. After three minutes, once the download was completed, I triggered the DiskDestroy command on my computer. It was a shame as it had been a great technological set-up. It would take time to rebuild a new system . . . one day.

Then, with a very sad and pissed-off heart, I activated the countdown that would see the destruction of Grey. I never believed this day would come.

'Did someone really kill your friend?' Andi asked, breaking into my furies.

'I think so. That was no televisual imagery. That was for real.'

She hung her head. 'I'm sorry.'

'Not your fault.'

'How do we get out of here?' asked Tebor.

'I might just leave you behind. You're a nightmare.'

'Can we get out of here?' asked Andi.

'Sure. Just stay close to me, both of you, otherwise I can't protect you. It's going to be quite a ride.'

PC Giles Renreth was on his way to Rose Cottage, once again. He'd had little sleep, another row with his waspish wife, and then answered a call from John Mathews telling him Rose Cottage was being robbed and if he got there he could apprehend the burglars. He was about to tell Mathews to call the police station instead, when the farmer added that he had his shotgun and was on his way there already.

Renreth leapt out of bed, dragged his uniform over his pyjamas, and was now driving furiously towards Rose Cottage. On the way he called Norwich and asked for back-up. Mathews was already there when he arrived. So were some official looking people. Renreth sighed when they showed him their EI6 ID cards. His nightmare had not gone away.

'We're waiting for a warrant,' said one of the agents.

'They were about to force their way in,' insisted Mathews.

'You said burglars,' reminded Renreth.

'That's right. And burglars they are ... until they get a warrant.'

'How'd you know they were here?'

'Cos they were seen and I got called. Just being a good neighbour.'

'You can put that shotgun away now. You shouldn't have it out here.'

'It's not me who's committing murder anyway.'

'Meaning?'

'Conor's in the Web. If this lot go in, and hurt him, try

458

and bring him out of the Web, they'll be committing murder. That's what the UN Charter says. No one's host should be disturbed when they're in the Web. I mean, that's a murder charge, isn't it?'

'I know the law,' Renreth insisted. It was a necessary law. Spouses and family had often died that way in the early days, deliberately disturbed whilst in their trance-like state. Most of those crimes had been committed to secure large insurance pay-outs, although many more were crimes of passion or infidelity.

'We'd like to go in before the warrant arrives,' said the EI6 man.

'Look at that.' Mathews pointed at the broken glass. 'They've already broken in once. You're not going to allow them to do it again, are you?' Mathews was appealing to the policeman. 'I mean, how's that going to look for you?'

Renreth suddenly understood why Mathews had called him specifically. There was no way he, Renreth, could allow unlawful entry twice. But this time, he realized, there was a difference. Not just breaking and entering, but also challenging UN regulations. They'd need more than a search warrant for that.

'Why?' he challenged the intelligence man.

'We need to look round.'

'Your people have already done that, only a few hours ago.' Renreth sensed their uncertainty. 'Your chap before, he said it was a matter of national security. Is that still the case?'

Long pause, then sullenly, 'We'll wait.'

'And I need clearance from UN sources that you have permission to disturb a person who's in the Web.'

The agents looked at each other. Neither of them answered.

'Satisfied?' he asked Mathews.

A farmer's white van drew up and three of Mathews's workers got out; one of them even carried an axe. Mathews waved them over; his support troops had arrived.

'I am now,' the farmer said, with a huge grin on his face.

The plane, one of a fleet of GulfStream Private Scramjets owned by ThemeCorp, was passing through forty-seven thousand feet up to its cruise altitude of seventy-three thousand when the attendant came through to Malcolm Bonham. He'd just settled down with a whiskey and soda as she handed him a FastFax printed on smart paper.

Marked URGENT it was from his secretary in Wardour Street:

CONTACT WITH THE DATAKEEPER LOST AFTER AN EMERGENCY ALARM FROM HIS HOME WAS TRIGGERED. OPENED CRISIS LINK AND HAVE TRANSMITTED PICTURES TO YOU — YOUR AUTHORIZATION ONLY. ALSO TRANSMITTING SATELLITE PICTURES OF HIS AREA. CHAIRMAN IS BEING CONTACTED. NO SIGNAL FROM CONOR SMITH BUT SECURITY SERVICES ARE ATTEMPTING TO FORCE ENTRY TO HIS HOME IN ALPHA WORLD.

AWAIT YOUR INSTRUCTIONS.

Bonham gulped down his drink and swung the video screen in the side panel towards himself.

'No interruptions,' he ordered the attendant. 'I don't want anyone coming back in here, and the only call I'll take is from the Chairman.' He put his thumbprint on the screen, which ID'd and came alive. 'Or from someone called Conor Smith,' he called to the departing attendant.

Somehow, he knew Smith wouldn't be calling him.

Bonham was immediately connected to his database. He tapped in his code and then used both his left and right thumb prints to authorize entry into his personal security signal bin.

All GameMasters and Datakeepers had crisis video links from their computer centres to ThemeCorp. They could only be triggered by ThemeCorp if an emergency alarm was activated. These links had been installed at the insistence of the insurance companies in case of fire or similar emergencies. They had not been installed for the reason Bonham now found himself watching.

There was no one now in the computer room except Alex Mikoyan. Bonham presumed it was Mikoyan because there was no face remaining to identify. The Russian, if it was him, was strapped to a chair which had fallen over backwards, away from the main computer screen. What looked like an old revolver with a long barrel lay on the floor beside the near headless man. Flames lapped round the camera, flickered and then spread across the room. He realized it was the fire that had tripped off the emergency alarm and crisis link to ThemeCorp. He didn't bother waiting to see the flames move across the floor and shrivel Mikoyan.

He immediately switched to the next image. The ThemeCorp satellite picture was clear. There seemed to be an explosion that erupted from beside the dacha, ripped the left half of it apart and then started to burn ferociously in the other half. Bonham realized that side was where Mikoyan would have been. He presumed the man's aunt would have also been somewhere else.

He noticed someone walking through the woodland extending to the east of the house. He zoomed in but couldn't identify the person because of the canopy of trees and smoke drifting from the burning building. Maybe it was just a passer-by, but the cameras would never clearly identify anyone who had by now disappeared into that mass of foliage. Even the thermal imagers would have problems following him, especially once he'd merged with other people.

Bonham fast-forwarded through the recording until he saw the local fire service arrive. There was little they could do; the Yuri Gagarin Dacha was now a roaring blaze that would eventually burn itself out. They'd probably decide it was a gas main or something; the Russians were still deliberately backward when it came to health and safety issues.

A caption, THE CHAIRMAN IS ON VIDEO LINE, came up on the screen. Bonham flicked channels.

'You receiving this stuff?' asked Dom Murphy. He was a tall wiry man, hawk featured with a slightly bulbous veined nose that reflected his love of the hard stuff, usually Japanese single malts.

'Just seen it.'

'Are we in any way implicated?'

'There's no way that ThemeCorp could be dragged into this.'

'Jim and Mike were good men. I know our friendship ended some time ago, but they were still good men.'

'I agree.'

'Can we replace this Datakeeper?'

'Not easily, but we will. In time.'

'Keep me in touch.'

Bonham leant back and rang for the attendant.

'Whiskey and soda,' he ordered when she came through.

When he'd received his fresh drink he tilted the seat back, raised the leg support and lounged back with the glass resting on his chest, clasped between his hands. He felt a glow of satisfaction. Life was getting interesting.

The ball was now with Conor Smith. Bonham wondered how long it would be before the GameMaster fumbled and dropped it.

BOOK FIVE

ACED AND CHASED

Grey became white became blue became red became green.
The first change the security agents noticed was the deep
purple grass turning a brilliant green, as lush as any start-
of-the-season football pitch. The trees then followed; their
black-and-white silhouettes transforming to brown bark and
green leaves. Under them the dull grey shadowed flowers
sprang into the spring of life. The garden that had once
been the scourge of the district was now as bountiful and
beautiful as any avid gardener could wish for.

Clancy called his men to back away from the house. He
had expected the GameMaster to attempt something but
didn't want his team hurt. His decision was right. The house
itself also changed. It developed a brilliant white sheen,
blinding to the eye, making the security men turn away
while their hosts in RealWorld adjusted for brightness.

One of the agents fired a round from his carbine at the
transmuting Grey. The bullets rebounded, coming straight
back at the gunman. He tried to duck but the bullet glanced
his shoulder, sending him spinning to the ground. He
reached for his JetPax and hit the button.

'Hold your fire,' yelled Clancy, as he saw the agent
disappear from Second World. That was one guy who'd
have a sore shoulder for a few days. 'The walls are programed to deflect any missile straight back at you. Just wait
till everything settles down. Meanwhile stay your ground.'

I watched it all on the security screen. Time to go. I held out my right hand.

'Don't lose touch,' I said. 'Hold tight and hang on.'

Andi clasped my left hand and, once Tebor had grabbed her loose arm, I hit the escape function button on my keyboard.

'Goodbye, Grey,' I said sadly.

In the garden Clancy saw the house metamorphose. The rectangular concrete shoebox shape split into four quarters, separating like melted steel as it parted. When it had completed this separation, each huge section was turned into a sharp-edged equal-sided cube. The whiteness was gone, now replaced by clear shiny steel, transparent yet mirrored so that those outside could see their reflections in it. In each cube there was a shadow of a man, a woman and a boy. The shadows crystallized and I saw myself with Andi and Tebor, all linked together, close to each other, almost one person.

An agent sprayed the cube that was nearest me but was too late in ducking when the bullets, deflecting back, hit him in the stomach. As he fell away, shrieking in pain, he managed to hit his JetPax and save himself. In the White House, his host came awake, clutching his stomach and vomiting over the Sensor couch.

'Don't shoot,' screamed Clancy again. 'Stand your ground, but don't fucking shoot.'

The four cubes split again, into smaller identical units.

Once again the three fugitives, ourselves, appeared in each of the sixteen units, just visible behind the mirrored sides.

This time the agents held back. No one fired a shot.

The cubes split again, now down to life size. There were two hundred and fifty-six, this time all with mirrored surfaces, all with the likeness of the three runaways within them. The cubes totally filled the garden.

I started to walk forward. 'Stay close to me or you'll be

sucked out of the cube,' I reiterated firmly. As I walked, so the other mirror images followed. All going in different directions, all pre-programed to follow a variety of routes to confuse my pursuers.

Clancy never had a chance here, just didn't have enough men to cover each cube. The cubes moved fast, flat along the ground as if on skates, first at running speed, then up to the maximum Web speed. They dispersed as quickly as was possible on the Web.

Another agent fired and was downed by the deflection, his leg broken as he JetPaxed out. The SnoopCams would follow each cube, but I knew Clancy and his teams had lost the one easy chance to stop me.

I felt great. The program had worked. It was time to head back to the safety of the Brick, get lost amongst the Week-enders. Finding us there was going to be a nightmare.

My last view of Grey was the garden. It had returned to its natural cyber landscape; flat and monotonous. Then the light dimmed and the colour faded away to black and white. The trees lost their greenery and the flowers were once more only shaded grey outlines.

Clancy once more stood on purple grass.

I could see him yelling, then they all vanished and, I guess, JetPaxed back to the White House.

'Where is he now?' ranted Swilkin

'Back in the White House,' answered Tyrrell.

They both stood in front of Tyrrell's monitor, where they had watched the advance of the Secret Service on Grey, watched as the action unfolded until the house itself unfolded and the GameMaster engineered his escape from his pursuers.

'And?'

'No idea.'

'He was meant to go with them.' Swilkin paced up and down as he spoke, his frustration verging on anger. 'I'm under pressure to conclude this thing but I'm surrounded with incompetents.'

'We're tracking all the cubes,' advised Tyrrell. 'They're heading in every direction, most of them towards escape routes into the Brick.'

'Speed?'

'Top allowable Brick speed. All we can do is monitor. But the SnoopCams will pick them up as they enter the Web.'

Clancy came on the screen, back in the White House Control Center. 'Did you see what – ?'

'Where's Gallagher?' interrupted Swilkin.

'I don't know. I saw him come into the Transporter Room as we shipped out. I thought he was following us.'

468

'Didn't you wonder where he was?'

'I was told to secure Grey and get hold of Smith. That was my prime objective,' snapped Clancy.

'Someone must know where he is?'

'Why's it so important?'

Swilkin ignored that and watched the monitor. He saw Clancy's men returning from the Transporter Room. He also saw Gallagher's team frantically trying to track each cube as they sped out of Alpha World in every direction.

One of the Secret Service team crossed over to Clancy.

'Gallagher's still in the Transporter Room,' he reported. 'Gone Web.'

Clancy swung back to the link with Swilkin. 'You catch that?'

'Don't you guys ever sign out when you use the Transporter Room?' responded Swilkin.

'Wherever he's gone will be after Smith. Probably the Brick.'

'Let's hope he knows what he's doing. More than can be said of you arseholes.'

The phone rang and he picked it up.

'President's just seen what happened,' said Marlin. 'You following this guy?'

'No, sir. Not yet.'

'You people got *anything* under control?'

'Secret Service had the guy cornered. They let him escape.'

'Give me something . . . anything . . . to report back.'

'We're going into Smith's home. In England. We believe his host's in there.'

Swilkin hung up and walked over to Tyrrell. He waited while his assistant finished on the phone. He didn't like the look of disappointment on Tyrrell's face when he finally put the phone down.

'Bad news?' Swilkin asked, preparing for the worst.

'We can't get into Smith's house?'

'Don't tell me that's struck camp and gone too.'

Tyrrell allowed himself a half smile, but wiped it off when he realized Swilkin's anger. 'Some friends of his turned up. With the local constabulary. They're insisting on a search warrant before anyone goes inside.'

'So get one, quick.'

'London doesn't think we can. Can't find a good reason for a local judge to OK it. Especially as we've broken in once already.'

'I want them into that house.'

'They can't.'

'Can't or won't?'

'Won't, I guess.'

'That's great. Jesus, fucking amateurs.'

'These *friends*' – Tyrrell highlighted the word – 'are also insisting they go into the house and protect Smith's body. Have already claimed it would be murder . . . if anyone tried to harm him. Quoted all the usual UN resolutions about Web travel. All we can do is wait outside and make sure he doesn't get away once he does come back.'

'Which leaves Gallagher. What's he know that we don't? If he's on the Brick, we need to find him. He might just lead us to Smith.'

Going back to Rose Cottage was the last thing on my mind.

The answer was down in Second World; it was wherever Jim had gone to.

The three of us had finally reached an Alpha World MetroRail station and boarded a train for the Brick. The cube had dissolved and we boarded the train.

'Do they know it's us?' asked Andi, indicating a Snoop-Cam in the corner of the carriage.

'No.'

I explained how the cubes had been programed to divert to a variety of destinations and that each dissolved at approximately the same time as ours. Out of each cube IdentiClones of Andi, Tebor and me would walk or sit or climb into a train and follow predetermined paths for a matter of minutes.

'Not bad,' acknowledged Tebor grudgingly as the train moved out of Alpha World and onto the Brick.

'When do the IdentiClones vanish?' asked Andi.

'Not long now. We need to be off the train within the next five minutes.' I hesitated before continuing. 'I need to talk to Jim. We're all in trouble, and Jim's probably the only guy who knows the answers. We need him . . . quick.'

A few minutes later we exited the station near Theme-Park. It was the only place I could think of going. We split and mixed quickly with the Weekenders, losing ourselves in the throng. As we walked northwards I morphed from Blobby to my normal self.

'Thank God for that,' Andi said approvingly. 'You were pretty spooky.'

'I used to think I was pretty futuristic.'

She giggled. 'No wonder you never got married. She'd have to be something pretty weird to chase you.'

'HaHa.'

I felt some comfort as she brushed up behind me, trying to keep up with my pace. We bought masks from the next Brick peddler. Tebor paid with credits he had received from his clients; I didn't want to be traced using mine. Tebor's weird sense of humour continued as he handed me a mask of some pop star I'd never heard of.

'RainStorm . . . of the Urban ForeSkins,' Tebor identified the caricature for me. 'He's a great musician.'

I studied the punk face, clamped with so many steel rings and piercings that I couldn't even identify the singer's face underneath, even wondered whether it was a man or woman. I shook my head in mock dismay and put the mask on.

The two kids burst out laughing; Tebor whooped loudly and slapped his sides.

It was good to be on the Brick again.

Swilkin sat with Tyrrell and watched the silvered cubes disappear one by one, followed by their clones of the three fugitives, spreading out in different directions.

Then all two hundred and fifty-six groups of three people – Smith and his two companions – faded out as well. Some just evaporated where they stood, others were swallowed up by the crowds or into trains and buildings before they could be identified.

'He's got to be back on the Brick,' suggested Tyrrell. But not all the clones had arrived at the Brick, many having vanished into other homes in Alpha World.

'With the Weekenders shielding him.'

'Maybe Gallagher's picked him up.'

'And maybe not.' It was Swilkin's nightmare scenario. He was being rushed into a decision, forced along a path he couldn't identify. This was not something his structured mind was comfortable with.

'Put Smith's picture all over the Brick,' he yelled sharply across the room. 'On billboards and anything else we can get our hands on . . . Metro entrances, even hotel booking systems. Blitz the place with his image.'

'Which picture?' asked Tyrrel.

'Both. The early avatar and his real face.'

'And the two kids?'

'Them, too. Let's hunt them down before they cause any

more damage.' Swilkin paused, then he grinned mischievously. 'With a big ransom,' he declared.

'We'll need clearance on that.'

'Don't worry. Take it as read. There's too many frightened people upstairs who want this deal closed.'

'How much ransom?'

Swilkin's grin grew bigger. 'The max. Twenty million credits.'

He picked up the phone and called the NSA. Hearing what Swilkin had done, Marlin was quiet for a moment. 'Is there no other way?' he asked anxiously.

'Not if you want him picked up quickly. We might just get in that one shot if we act now.'

Swilkin heard a deep sigh, then, 'OK. Take it as read that you've got the money. I'll work it somehow through our budgets. Then Marlin suddenly blurted, 'That's a shit thing to force me into.'

'For the best, sir,' said Swilkin and put down the phone before the other man had second thoughts. He moved quickly back to Tyrrell to confirm his order.

"Make sure that twenty million reward hits the Brick *now*,' insisted Swilkin, as he headed off towards the room's exit.

'You leaving?' asked Tyrrell.

'Yup. Into the Brick.'

Tyrrell frowned, because Swilkin rarely ventured from the Telephone Exchange. He wasn't a natural WebTraveller, was also known to suffer from spatial disorientation. 'You want me to come with you?' he said, concerned.

'I'm fine.'

'Where the hell will you start?'

'Where he least expects me.' Swilkin smiled. It was unusual for him to go out in the field to hunt his quarry. He was a desk-General; a planner, not a plodder. He sensed the buzz of excitement as he realized he was going up against a GameMaster. 'Just call me as soon as you find anything.'

'You not going to tell me?' Tyrrell sounded puzzled.

Swilkin shrugged. 'I'm playing a hunch, but I need to be out there, or I've just sat here too long trying to get into his mind.'

Swilkin was starting to put things into place.

'If nothing else, that twenty million credits will get the whole place jumping,' offered Tyrrell.

'You bet. That's what I'm counting on.'

Conor Smith's face lit up the skies all over the Brick.

Through my mask I saw the advertising hoardings and floating billboards broadcast both my face and Blobby's, just as they had done with Jim's earlier. Next to me, Tebor gasped. It was as the reward figure appeared.

'Twenty million credits,' blurted Tebor.

The only bit missing was DEAD OR ALIVE. But they were getting desperate.

'Twenty million US credits,' repeated Tebor. 'For you?' he said, unbelievingly.

Around them people seemed stunned by the message, and then started to search through the crowd for the face that appeared all around and above.

'Split up,' I hissed, when Andi and Tebor's likenesses also appeared.

'They're after us, too,' said Tebor, 'but there's no reward – only for you.' His disappointment was obvious; he wasn't important enough.

'They'll be looking for three,' I said, 'so I'll go with Andi. We'll meet you later.'

'Why can't Andi go with me?' Tebor complained.

'If that's what you want? Just let's split now and meet up later.'

'I'll go with Conor,' confirmed Andi, and put her arm round Tebor. 'I'll catch up with you later. PunkS R Us. Jim might be there. You go find him, and I'll take Conor underground. Nobody's going to trace any of us that way.'

Tebor scratched his head, still unsure.

'Come on, let's go . . . instead of just standing around,' I urged.

'Tebor,' scolded Andi, 'find Jim.'

Tebor shook his head. 'PunkS R Us, later.' He whirled away into the crowd, not a happy soul.

'Is he going to blab his mouth off?' I asked her.

'Of course not,' she snapped. 'He may not like you too much, but he's not going to hurt *me*.'

I took her arm and headed northwards.

The crowds were excited; there was a game on, with a twenty-million-dollar first prize.

WINNER TAKES ALL announced one of the messages in the sky. $20 MILLION US CREDITS IF YOU FIND THIS MAN.

We moved on through the crowd. A fight broke out on the pavement edge, as one man tried to rip the mask off another.

'Stay apart,' I told her, releasing her hand and stepping away. 'Just don't lose sight of me.'

'Where're we going?'

'Let's get to ThemePark. I'm OK there, since it's my patch.'

We continued northwards as the excitement grew around them.

'I feel naked,' she said, moving towards him again. 'As if everyone knows I'm here. I don't see any Weekenders, just you and me. Like they're all staring at us, because they know who we are.'

'Keep walking.' I moved away again. Somebody grabbed at my mask and I brushed him away with my arm. He tried to follow me but got swallowed up in the crowd as it swirled between us.

I crouched lower and speeded up.

'You're leaving me behind,' she shouted, as she caught me up. 'Look, look,' she pointed upwards, panic in her voice.

The picture on all the AdverBoards had changed. It was of my mask.

The mask peddler. It had to be the peddler. He'd bloody recognized us and now he was after his money, all twenty million of it.

I tore off the mask and dropped it to the pavement. I saw her do the same. It gave us some respite; everyone would be looking for that mask now. Most would have forgotten my real face for a while.

I suddenly remembered the SmartCard. It was time to go underground. I grabbed her hand and led her down the next narrow side street. It contained a few small exclusive shops, not many people about. Now clear of the crowds I started to run, almost dragging her along. At the end of the alleyway was a brick wall with a couple of local adverts pasted on it. I didn't know what to expect.

'Let me go first,' she said.

'The card will only work on *my* hand.'

'OK. As long as we are actually touching, we're OK to break through, so we need to go in together,' she explained. 'Once you're in, just take a few steps. Don't turn around, don't change direction. If you keep to the same position, we'll be OK, we won't get lost. Otherwise we'll never find our way out.'

I bowed to her experience. 'Let's go.'

I was relieved no one had followed us. I put the card in my left hand and held hers with my right. I then extended my left arm and pushed it into the wall. There was a slight sizzle of static and I just walked straight into the wall, as if stepping from a heated room into a frosty night. Then there was nothing. Unbelievable: no shadows, no light, no sound, no air movement. I was in a black lifeless vacuum.

I felt the touch of her hand behind me. There were no other sensations, and the warmth of her fingers entwined with mine was all I was aware of. I squeezed and she squeezed back. I took five steps just as she'd told me. Then I stopped and waited, not turning, not moving.

She bumped into me and I stood still while she moved round and was facing me, clutching me. I embraced her. She buried her head in my chest and entwined her arms round my waist. We stood in silence, in safety, in contentment.

'What about Tebor?' I asked eventually.

There was no response. I realized she couldn't hear me.

I put my mouth right over her ear, touched it with my lips, and spoke again. 'What about Tebor?'

She giggled, pulled away, then moved her mouth over my ear. 'If he doesn't want to be found, then . . . he won't be.'

It was as if she was speaking through a long tube. I mouthed into her ear again and repeated the exercise. 'I'm sorry I got you into this.'

'Why? It's the most exciting thing that's happened to me in years. But what about you, Conor? What've you got yourself in to?'

'I don't know.'

'I'm sorry about your friend.'

Mikoyan's death suddenly flooded back. He'd been a fine man, deserved better. I was already racked with guilt. It was I who had involved Mikoyan. But nobody knew that . . . apart from Bonham.

She interrupted my thoughts, changed my focus. She pulled my shirt out of my trousers and ran her hands up my spine.

'Hey,' I said, surprised. Only nobody heard.

'My hands cold?' she giggled as she spoke closely into my ear.

'No.' It came out as a growl. Now was not the time, not with what had just happened, but I was helpless at the first stirrings of excitement; she moved her warm hands over me, stroked me, squeezed me. Very strange. Even though she was up against me I couldn't see her, couldn't even feel the breath from her mouth.

The sensation got stranger. I only felt anything when she touched or pressed against me: blackness and silence mixed with small surprising tingling electric shocks as she moved her hands over me. I shuffled as I grew with excitement, pressing roughly back against her.

'I said not to move,' she said down the tube, her lips pressed against my ear. She slipped against me and I caught her from falling, realized she was on her tiptoes. 'You've got to stay still,' she repeated, 'otherwise you won't remember which way you were facing and we'll never get out of here.'

I froze as she slipped her hand down and unzipped me. A new, unknown sensation raced through me, shivered me. A rush of emotion took over, like a shot of heroin racing through my veins, scorching me in hot pulsating waves. Only I had never had a rush like this before. She moved away suddenly, only for a fractional moment and I stumbled as the pressure against me relaxed. I caught my balance, waited for her in the silent flat blackness. Then she came back out of the nothingness, surprised me as she slipped my trousers down. I couldn't see her, but sensed her nakedness.

I pulled her to me, lifted her so I could find her lips and kiss her. Not just for me but from her response, I knew for both of us it was a kiss neither of us had experienced before. In the blackness it exploded our minds. We locked together and as we kissed, so we made love.

It was all so easy to become one with so little effort, combining bodies and emotions that in no way were strangers to each other. The rhythm of lovers totally at ease with each other, the kiss never parting, our lips sank into each other's softness.

'I love you,' she said and this time I clearly heard her words in the darkness.

'I love you,' I replied and desperately believed these words

I'd never spoken before. I pulled apart from her and spoke more closely to her ear. 'I love you,' I repeated.

'I love you too,' she replied.

'I really do,' I said, once more to the darkness and just her touch. Then the silence returned.

I knew the words weren't enough. I wanted to say more. I was sad there was nothing more I could say.

Is this love? Knowing you can never express what you really feel?

Then, for no reason, I felt her stiffen. She shivered, half stepped away, then fell against me.

'What's wrong?' I said into her ear, concerned.

'Nothing. We should get dressed now.' Factual. Icy.

'OK.'

'*Are* you OK?' I asked when I had composed myself, reached out and found her.

'Yes,' said her voice into my ear. Still sounding cool.

Maybe it was through embarrassment at having shown me her true emotion; or that her memory took her back to the life she now led.

'How much longer, do you think?' I tried changing tack.

'Maybe half an hour. Let everyone move on.'

'Sounds good. You sure you're OK?'

'Why shouldn't I be?'

The silence contained us and our separate thoughts.

'I'm going to sit down,' I said after three minutes.

'Good idea,' she said. 'Just don't forget which way you're now facing.'

'Where're you?' I asked after she pulled away.

'Close enough. I'll reach out for you when it's time to go.'

I slid to the floor and there, in the blackness of the Dark Areas put my mind to work at what I knew best. No way would I be confused by her sudden change in mood. I didn't want it to confuse me in any way. That would sort itself out in time; right now I had other priorities to resolve.

Why was I here and where should I go next? The darkness helped. Enveloped within it, I could almost see into my own mind. I ran over the events of the last twenty-seven hours. I slowly stripped out the peripheries and concentrated on the main events.

It was so much easier in the total silence and dark.

Then, for the first time since I'd set out on this journey, things began to come together.

Swilkin followed the crowd that followed *Titanic*.

It must have cost ThemeCorp a fortune to change the programing on the Brick.

It was an awesome spectacle; this great liner that had once been the ultimate in world technology, serenely steaming down the Brick. For a hundred metres in front and behind the great ship the yellow bricks turned into churning blue waves, breaking across the bows and leaving a white-topped wake behind it.

Swilkin's gamble was that Smith would lose himself in the largest crowds available and the *Titanic* definitely supplied those.

He'd already picked up the mask peddler's report. That put the GameMaster ahead of *Titanic* by about ten minutes. His reasoning told him he was getting close to his prey. There were so few places that Smith could hide without the SnoopCams or the WebCops picking up some clues, at least.

He looked up at the decks, from which partygoers and guests in period costumes waved at the crowds.

'Have we checked all the guests on *Titanic* yet?' he called Tyrrell.

'Still checking. Nothing yet. ThemeCorp are pretty tight on their security. They've got to be where gambling's involved.'

'What about staff and crew?'

'According to ThemeCorp everyone's security-listed and checked.'

483

'Gallagher?'

'Nothing. Only ID was from a SnoopCam that picked him up not far from where you are now, about thirty minutes ago.'

'OK. Keep me in touch.'

He followed the ship, changing direction regularly so that he could cover the crowd for a sign of his prey. Above and around him the reward notices and bulletins had produced the desired effect. There was an additional buzz within the crowd, not just from the excitement of the parade but because there was a real game on with twenty million dollars at stake. Fights broke out, everyone checking on everyone else. He himself was yanked around by a group of men who were intent on inspecting every person in the vast ever-changing crowds. Swilkin knew that this sort of excitement could lead to riots, to crowd anarchy. He didn't care, not if it weeded out Conor Smith and the other two for him to interrogate.

Most people thought it was just a publicity stunt linked with the *Titanic* venture. A few even shouted that it was linked to the President's kidnapping. In the end, the crowd couldn't care less. What mattered was the twenty-million ransom.

'I don't like it. They could easily trace it,' said an uneasy President.

He was right to be concerned; the twenty-million-credit ransom would end up at his feet. Without budgetary approval he would come under extreme pressure from his political enemies.

Meisner shook his head. 'You didn't ask for it,' replied his chief of staff. 'Nothing to do with us. It was an NSA decision. Their responsibility. Their budget.'

'Which I'll have to support, even if I didn't authorize it.'

'Of course, sir, but they did what they did because of the national interest. That includes protecting the President and his administration.'

'At least we got a good media reaction to my broadcast.'

'We had a few cheap-shot jokes about you and Monroe, usual WebSlime stuff, but they all see your decision to go back into the Web as a real statement standing up for our freedom.'

'It was a good speech, Joe. You did well.' One of Dixon's better traits was that he always gave credit where credit was due. 'But I'm still jumpy about going back there.'

'Don't worry. You'll have Secret Service everywhere backed up by WebCops and even National Guard ready to come straight into the Brick ... But only if anything happens.'

'Could be too late by then.' Dixon remembered the Voice and the way it controlled everything in the Dark Areas. He was suddenly clammy, a small line of sweat trickling down the nape of his neck. He wiped it away.

'Crowds will love it. And it'll show you're tough . . . that you don't give a damn . . . that you're there for the people.'

'This guy had me out among the crowds – right out there, for everyone to see – but it didn't worry him. He was always completely in charge.' Rivulets now ran into his collar; he felt sick, suddenly needed fresh air. He got up and walked to the windows and opened one. It was a lovely day; a few tourists waved from the distance. He waved back. The cool air hit his face and revitalized him, dried the dampness around his neck. He gulped in the air, enjoyed its freshness.

'They reckon there'll be over two billion people either watching or on the Brick itself,' said Meisner, who now stood behind him.

'Am I safe?' asked Dixon.

'Yes.'

'OK then,' he agreed uneasily.

Dixon waved at another group of tourists. His stomach was starting to settle. 'When?

'They want us down in about five minutes, to brief us.'

'What about?'

'Just in case. Don't worry, they want to tell us exactly what they're doing, how they're going to run the security.'

Dixon finished waving, closed the bulletproof window and came back into the room.

The expression on his face reflected that he still wasn't very convinced; but then none of them had been there, in the cold dark, breathless with no air in his lungs, buried in the blackness of the Web.

The President started to sweat again.

I sensed him before I heard him.

'Hello, Mr Smith,' said the Voice. It rang clear in the darkness.

'Hello, Jim.' My own voice sounded just as clear. So he *could* manipulate the Dark Areas.

'You don't seem surprised by me.'

'You've left enough clues.'

I heard Jim chuckle. 'And where has that led you?'

'It's amazing how much you can see in the dark. Is Andi still here?'

'I'm here,' she replied.

Everyone remained quiet for a while.

'The President was always safe, wasn't he,' I said.

'Yes.'

'Because you're not programed to hurt . . . or kill.'

'That's man's worst trait.'

'Nelson and Keebles programed you to *protect* something.'

'Yes.'

'Something secret that you couldn't admit to, only lead the way to.'

'Yes.'

'The InfoCalypse.'

Silence.

'You're silent because you can't admit it exists,' I continued.

'Are Jim Nelson and Mike Keebles really dead?' It was a genuine question.

'I'm afraid so. I'm sorry I had to tell you.' I felt I was telling a child about the death of his parents.

'I was not made aware of that.'

'How could you? *This* is your world, and you have no actual contact with RealWorld – only that information which Nelson and Keebles fed you. And they're not around any more.'

'I am a real person, Mister Smith.'

'Yes, you are – here in Second World. But this place is only a set of computer commands. If someone pulls the plug, kills the power, then you don't exist any more.'

'My creators are dead. But I'm still here.'

'I appreciate that.'

'They are in me. They created me in their likeness. Whatever souls they had, those parts which they felt mattered, they passed on to me. I have a function . . . which is based on their goodness.'

'But that isn't why you were first created. You were put here initially to protect the InfoCalypse – which was also created by them. Afterwards, when it all became too much, when they realized what they had built was wrong, this super spy system that monitors our lives, they used you to alert the world about it. The only thing they couldn't overcome was the final firewall, the one that self-destructed you as soon as you tried even to mention the existence of the InfoCalypse.'

'An interesting theory.'

'So they pumped you full of their own finer emotions. They tried to make you human. They tried to create reason and original thought in you. They came at it from a human angle, but they had to turn you into an emotional caring unit first. They programed you to be concerned and to lead us to the InfoCalypse.' I heard my voice get sharper, urging Jim on. 'Where is this secret data? Where is it kept?'

'*You* must find it.' Long pause. 'Everything is vulnerable.'

'Everything I seek?'

'. . . Is exposed. In a weak position. Almost defenceless.'

'Why?'

'*You* must tell me,' Jim replied firmly.

'It's data. It's only data. But masses of it. An enormous amount.'

'Data is knowledge. Knowledge is power. Power kills.'

'Data is only dangerous when it's security systems are open to be hacked . . . or while being transferred? Otherwise it's locked away, stored, firewalled, untouchable.'

I paused to consider Jim's words. 'So why is the data being transferred?'

'Why *would* it be transferred?'

'Because . . . it's in an unsecured place . . . or someone's close to discovering it . . . Or else there's a technical problem.'

'Why a technical problem?'

'Maybe it was somewhere that was under threat . . . or was somewhere that needed upgrading . . . or had run out of storage space.' That last suggestion rammed home, like me being hit over the head with a cricket bat. Now I understood. 'The disk was full.'

'All storage is finite. Very good.' Jim suddenly changed tack. 'How were they killed?'

'Suicide, according to the reports, but I don't believe that. Someone killed them. I don't know who yet. And I won't know until I get back on the Brick so I can interrogate my home computer.'

'He took a voice print,' commented Andi. 'Of the person who killed his Russian friend.'

'You think he also killed Nelson and Keebles?' asked Jim.

'I'm not sure,' I replied.

'Were they all killed because you were getting close to the truth?'

'Mikoyan was.'

'Which puts you in danger?'

'All of us.'

'They're looking for you on the Brick. Do you really want to go back out there?'

He was cleverly directing me back to the Brick.

I think I now had all the information Jim could give. That's how it worked. The original program forbade Jim from giving any information on the InfoCalypse. Nelson and Keebles had re-programed him the best they could, without disturbing the original protocol, which if it had been breached, would definitely have destroyed Jim.

'I need to go. I can't stop anything while I'm sitting here in the dark.'

'At least we can rectify that,' said Jim.

A soft light came up, a yellowish glow spreading across the area nearby. There were no walls, no ceiling, no floor. We were suspended, floating in nothing. The whole phenomenon startled me, yet it felt solid underneath. Jim stood about three feet in front of me, that perma-smile still on his face. Andi was sitting cross-legged just to Jim's right. I met her eyes, but she turned her head away and stared around the emptiness.

'Who killed Norma Jean?' I asked.

'The same man who killed your friend.'

'So tell me?'

He shook his head. 'You're a clever man, Mr Smith. But there's a big organization against you. The biggest.'

'They still couldn't protect the President.'

'They won't be taken by surprise a second time.'

'Why me?'

'That wasn't our decision. You were their chosen bait . . . to try and hunt us down. We were glad it was you. You have a good honest reputation. Others chose you . . . we used you. I laid the clues once I knew who they had chosen. After all, I cannot tell you about the data, but I have access to it all. Now, it seems, you are finally on your own.'

So that was it. I'd been set up just to find Jim. The same person, or organization, that killed Mikoyan was now after me. Jim couldn't defend me, couldn't really help either. He was a pawn in a game he didn't know the rules to.

'Let's get going,' I said.

'OK. But, remember, I cannot change my appearance. I can only help at a distance. I cannot harm or fight any avatar because I'm simply not designed to do that. I can threaten, perhaps, but I have limited powers. I can affect anything that is made of data, including the air that you breathe, yet I cannot kill or even permanently injure an avatar.'

'But I can.' My response was cold, unyielding.

Jim shrugged; I don't think he could comprehend any anger or passion. 'Be wary. Everything is not what it appears.' He beckoned us both to stand up, then walked over to the exact point in the alleyway beyond that Andi and I had entered by.

He swung round just before taking us back on the Brick.

'I *am* a real person, Mr Smith. As real as anyone else you'll find down here. You mentioned souls, earlier on. What is soul? Is it that which makes the man? I am Jim Nelson and Mike Keebles, men of courage and conviction. Men of belief. If that isn't soul, then I don't know what is.'

Jim, the CREEP robot, turned and walked out of the Dark Areas and into the Brick, just as *Titanic* sailed into view.

Clancy waited by the six SensoChairs positioned in the Transfer Suite.

He smiled warmly as the First Lady entered, followed by the President and Joe Meisner.

'Thank you, Don,' she said as he led her to her chair and helped her slip on the kimono-like WebSuit. He handed her her shades and watched as she took her seat. He clipped the JetPax to her arm.

Behind him Smerton tagged the nervous Dixon into his SensoChair.

'We'll be next to you at all times, Mr President,' said Clancy, turning to check him. 'I've assigned four agents to you and three to the First Lady. We've another fourteen agents within thirty feet of us. Nobody moves until you do and we all keep to our assigned distances.' He held up his arm. 'My JetPax, sir, is linked to yours. Should there be any problem, as soon as I hit my escape button, it also triggers yours.'

'What about Annie?' asked Dixon.

'Linked to Agent Smerton. The same procedure.'

'I presume my JetPax also works independent of you.'

'Yes, Mr President.'

'Do you anticipate trouble?'

'None.' Clancy shook his head comfortingly. 'ThemeCorp have got their best security people supporting us. This time we've covered every aspect. We won't let you out of sight.'

'OK, let's go.'

Clancy nodded and turned to see Meisner settling down.

'OK, there?' Clancy asked, not too concerned as he knew the Chief of Staff was a veteran WebTraveller. When Meisner gave him a thumbs up he went through to the anteroom to join the rest of his team.

'This time no mistakes. Anyone steps out of position and I guarantee you can kiss your pension goodbye.' He looked round at his men individually, meeting each one's gaze steadfastly.

'OK,' he said when he was satisfied. 'Let's go to work.'

We followed Jim out of the alleyway and onto the Brick itself.

Although my real face and the mask I'd worn were still being displayed all along the Brick, the crowd's attention was now fully on *Titanic*. She glided majestically northwards, the blue water turning into a giant wake, her bow proud as she passed the millions who stood on the pavement watching her.

'Here comes the President of the United States,' broadcast the announcer's voice from the *Titanic* itself as Teddy Dixon stepped on to the prow with the First Lady by his side.

He held up his arm and waved, then put it round his wife and pointed at her with his other hand. They both were together. They were surrounded by an entire phalanx of Secret Service agents. Nobody was taking any chances this time. Patrick Dom Murphy was standing just behind Dixon. The Chairman of ThemeCorp, though a secretive man by nature, had little chance of avoiding this occasion. I heard Jim gasp and stare upwards in awe. It wasn't the President but Dom Murphy who had the robot's attention.

A voice cut across me as I was about to ask Jim why Murphy had drawn his gaze.

'There you are.'

A hand gripped my shoulder and I swung round, half crouching, ready to defend myself.

'Easy, easy, it's only me,' said Gallagher.

'What're you doing here?' I straightened up.

'Looking for you – like everyone else. Only I'm on your side. I got you into this, remember?'

'I remember.' I felt no malice towards him.

Gallagher looked over my shoulder. 'This must be Jim?'

'Possibly.'

Gallagher laughed. 'I've seen the IDs. Where're you going now?'

'How'd you know I was here, Paul?'

'I guessed you'd be around here somewhere. Near the ship. Camouflaging yourself in the crowd. The only lead you could follow was back here, where the President was going to be. I got lucky.'

'How did your boys find out about Alpha World? About Grey?'

'The alpha and the omega. It was GCHQ dug that up, from studying your old credit cards. They told the NSA who ordered the Secret Service in.' Gallagher walked past me and stuck out his hand in a handshake to Jim. 'You're quite a guy, Jim. I mean, didn't you kidnap our President?'

Jim stepped back and Gallagher lowered his arm.

'It wasn't him, Paul,' I said, then I sensed something was wrong. I looked round, but there was no one acting suspicious.

The crowds pushed against us as the liner started to pass right by. We all moved into a furniture shop doorway to avoid the congestion.

'Then who was it?' asked Gallagher.

'I don't know.' I lied.

Gallagher turned his next question to Jim. 'Who's your host, Jim?'

'Why?' answered Jim.

'Because I don't think you have one.'

'Everyone's got a host, Paul,' I cut in.

'Robots don't.'

'What robot?' Gallagher's demeanour was too cool, almost threatening.

495

'I reckon Jim's an amalgamation of Nelson and Keebles, and maybe your boss Dom Murphy. Two're dead, so either Murphy's hosting him, or he's a web robot put together by two or three of those guys.' Gallagher pointed up at the passing ship. 'I can see Murphy up there, with the President, so he's clearly not the host. Maybe one of his people, though? Maybe even one of you GameMasters? Christ, he employs enough of you.'

'No robots in the Web – that's what the UN demands. Only CREEPs and WebCops allowed.'

Gallagher shook his head. 'These boys helped build this place. They could leave anything behind and no one would ever trace it.'

'So why would he steal the President?'

'That's the sixty-four-thousand-dollar question.'

'We should go,' said Jim, grabbing my arm.

'Where you going to take him?' Gallagher slid himself between Jim and me. 'Where do you have to take him, Jim? What have you got to show him?'

'Back off, Paul,' I warned him. I pushed him back, and held my arm forward to protect Jim.

'You're being fucked,' Gallagher shouted at me. 'He's designed to lead you somewhere. That's what he's all about. He wants *you* to sort out their mess.'

'Whose mess?'

'Nelson and Keebles. The guys who programed him. Probably Murphy as well. They're dangerous men.' Gallagher jabbed at Jim's chest, reaching over my arm. 'Tell us. You can't hide any more. We already know *where* to find you. We'll soon know *how* to find you.' Gallagher stepped back as I pushed him away again. 'We'll get the codes that make you appear. They're out there somewhere. Nelson and Keebles would have kept them somewhere, if only to protect themselves. Wherever you hide, it won't do any good. We'll just click the button, introduce the code into the matrix, and get all those singular cells rushing together to form you Jim.' Gallagher snapped his fingers. 'It'll be that easy.'

'Who *are* you, Paul?' I yelled at him.

'Just protecting my President.'

'That's all?'

'I'm a government man, Conor. Not a privateer like you.'

'Why you doing this?'

'Doesn't matter now. Job's done. They won't believe you and they certainly won't believe him.' Gallagher jabbed his forefinger once again towards Jim.

He then stepped out of the doorway and started to shout. 'I've found him. I claim the reward,' he yelled, waving his arms to attract attention. 'I've got him. He's mine. I claim the reward. It's my prize. Hell, I'm rich. I claim the twenty million.'

The crowd picked it up, saw Gallagher turn and grab me. People rushed towards us, scenting a new excitement, a new chase.

I noticed Jim's face. The smile was gone. Only sadness there.

'I'm sorry,' Jim mouthed. 'Help us,' he shouted to me.

Then he faded away, broke up into a trillion CREEPs and was sucked back into the matrix.

I struggled with Gallagher as the crowd got closer, pushing in to see what was happening. Tebor broke through and pushed Gallagher to the ground. He had a broadsword in his hand and he slashed at Gallagher's left arm, slicing open the flesh. Tebor turned back to the crowd and stood his ground. Someone darted at him and he cut them also with the sword, but it didn't deter the mob, who all moved forward threateningly. Tebor brandished the sword above his head, trying to keep them at bay. As someone shot forward, so he would slash at them. They fell back; those who were struck disappeared back to their hosts, to awake with bruises where they had been cut.

Gallagher struggled to his feet, holding his bleeding arm, determined to stay with his prey. I leant over and pressed the agent's JetPax.

'Fuck yo . . .' screamed Gallagher as he disappeared from Second World.

'Come on,' shouted Tebor, grabbing Andi's hand and pulling her down the alleyway, back towards the wall.

The crowd followed.

'It's my twenty million,' shrieked someone in the crowd, aware that Gallagher had disappeared. 'I saw him first.'

'No, I did,' joined in someone else.

The crowd bayed and roared, and rushed towards the three of us. I reached the wall, scrambled through my pocket to find my SmartCard and then inserted it into the Brickwork. Nothing happened. I tried again. It was useless, now just a worthless piece of cyberplastic.

'Take my hand,' instructed Tebor urgently.

I grabbed it and saw that Andi was already clinging to the boy. Our eyes met, I smiled, warm and comforting. She smiled back, but the lip movement was automatic, her eyes cold.

What the hell's changed?

The crowd were all around us, grabbing, pulling, falling over themselves. Behind them I saw the *Titanic*'s stern now float past. In that moment, in that macrosecond of clarity, I clearly understood all that had happened, as the jigsaw finally came together. Then it was dark again.

'Hang on,' said Tebor. 'Don't let go.'

I grinned. There was no way I was going to let the little punk go. Not now I had solved the puzzle. Poor Jim. Poor Mikoyan. Poor Nelson and Keebles. I would do what they wanted. The GameMaster would finish the game.

Swilkin was standing on the opposite side of the road to the alleyway when Tyrrell called him.

'Gallagher's back,' he reported.

'Where's he been?'

'The Brick. Says he found Smith and the others. He's nursing a pretty badly bruised arm. Said he was cut with a sword.'

'A sword?'

'The spiky-haired kid jumped him.'

'What?'

'Gallagher was grappling with Smith at the time. I'm sending the images through.'

Swilkin studied the images from the SnoopCam as they were beamed down to him. 'I see *Titanic* in the background. Where were they exactly?'

'Two blocks behind you. On the opposite side.'

Swilkin turned and started to run, pushing against the crowd. He jumped into the water to cross the Brick and found himself running on top of it. He raced to the other side and continued running till he found the mouth of the alleyway. There was still a crowd there, but now starting to disperse. He reached the wall they had disappeared into. He pushed against it, found it was as solid as it looked.

'Am I at the right place?' he asked Tyrrell.

'Yeah.'

'And there's nothing behind this wall?'

'The Dark Areas.'

'He must have an Access SmartCard.'

'Looks like it,'

'Even if I got one there's no point going after him. I'd just get lost.' Swilkin walked swiftly back towards the Brick. 'Check the cameras up ahead. They're going to come out further up. I think maybe the *Titanic*'s got something to do with this. Why else would he be here? Also put someone on surveillance at the ship's destination. Maybe that's where this is all heading.'

He went to the nearest MetroPort and caught the first people-mover to ThemeWorld.

'Gallagher's going back into the Web,' reported Tyrrell.

'How's his arm?'

'I didn't ask.'

'Say where he's going?'

'Something about joining the rest of the President's squad.'

The sudden arrival of Gallagher startled Clancy, who had not been informed of any arrivals from the White House. Web security protocols protected the President. No avatars could appear near him unless they had specific clearances. Any avatar without clearance could not break through the firewall, would simply merge into the matrix and be sent back where it had come from.

'Where've you been?' he asked. He noticed that Gallagher's left arm seemed damaged, was hanging loosely by his side.

'Chasing Smith.'

'And . . . ?'

'I got to him, not far from here, but he escaped with those MIWs he's hanging around with.'

'They do that?' Clancy pointed at Gallagher's arm.

Gallagher nodded. 'Everything OK here?'

'On schedule. Where's Smith now, do you reckon?'

'Don't know.'

'Maybe we should get them out of here?' Clancy indicated the President and the First Lady.

'No. How much longer before this engagement's over.'

'Forty minutes max.' He looked to the right where they were passing the entrance to the Valley of the Dragons. 'You said Smith knew our security protocols.'

'Old protocols. Would I allow the President's security to be compromised?'

'Don't you think you should be back in the Control Room?'

'"My team's on top of things. Say, this is some crowd. Never seen it so busy on the Brick.' Gallagher pointed to the Valley of the Dragons. 'You ever been there?' he asked Clancy.

'No.'

'You don't play games, do you, Don?'

'You know that.'

'More the boys-night-out type, huh?'

'What're you getting at?'

'Nothing, Don. Playing games gets you into the habit. I mean, you see *everything* as a game.'

Clancy turned his back on the President and faced Gallagher head on. 'What're you getting at?'

'Nothing. Just making a point.'

'Which is?'

'Swilkin's gone walkabout. He's out on the Brick somewhere. Not like him at all. He never goes out of the Telephone Exchange if he can help it.'

'Get to the point.'

'I don't trust Swilkin. I told you how he turned up almost as if expecting the President to come back from his kidnapping. Now he's out there,' Gallagher waved his hand over the crowds below, 'where you'd least expect him.'

'You saying he's the perp?'

'I'm saying it's not his normal behaviour.'

'Take a look at this, Don,' Smerton suddenly said over Clancy's earpiece. The pictures he transmitted, fresh off a SnoopCam, showed Gallagher claiming the reward, then grappling with Conor Smith and being run through by Tebor. He saw the three of them all vanish into the wall, and probably into the Dark Areas.

'See what I mean,' said Gallagher. 'There's something not right. I'm going to find Swilkin. I'm going to make sure I'm there if things start to blow.'

502

'Keep them all clear of this area,' warned Clancy. 'If there's trouble, I only want *my* agents around the President.'

Gallagher laughed. 'Sure, Don. I understand. You play your game while the rest of us play ours. Sure beats Reality TV, don't it?'

The hotel stood in a forest clearing on the road between the Koptyaki Forest and Ekaterinburg. Its grand name was not reflected in the hotel's actual stature. A simple thirty-bedroom, two-storey building constructed of wood, it was merely the nearest watering hole to the spot where the Romanov family were buried after being murdered by the Bolsheviks.

The hotel's name pulled in the tourists who came to visit the shrine at the Four Brothers, named after the four trees that stood, now very old and very gnarled, near the secret grave the Tsar's family had been thrown into. There were many who believed the original trees had long since fallen down and the Russians, with their usual eye for a quick rouble, had simply moved the grave's location to another group of four trees.

The man who killed Alex Mikoyan had been lucky to find a spare room there at such short notice. Many of the fellow guests were foreigners, so he didn't stick out from the other tourists. The Russian staff all spoke adequate broken English, but would have had difficulty recognizing his country of origin from his accent.

His features were less easy to disguise, far easier to identify. So, whenever emerging from his hotel room, he wrapped a thick scarf round his neck and chin and pulled low on his forehead a woollen bobble hat with Manchester

United Football Club emblazoned across the front, thus merging easily with the others who were equally swaddled against the cold.

Despite his stoop, he could not, however, disguise his height and bulk, all six feet eight of it, and that was what would be eventually remembered when the police came to ask questions. He now sat alone in his hotel room, the curtains drawn and the door locked, a DO NOT DISTURB sign hanging outside to protect his privacy.

The TV played as the *Titanic* was about to berth at her new site on the Brick. As an image of the President and his wife waving at the crowds appeared, he immediately picked up on the edginess of the Secret Service men visible in the background, their eyes constantly darting around, looking for an attack that could come out of nowhere. He smiled, unsurprised by their restless movements; they'd grown soft while all had seemed secure in the Web. Now they finally had to do what they were paid for.

Never trust technology is what the Boss always told him. *Never trust anything that doesn't have a purpose of its own.*

As he watched the TV screen he switched on the shank that was implanted in his neck, thus connecting to the keyboard that lay on the table next to him. He tapped into the telephone line and was through immediately.

'Hi, boss,' he said when the miniature built-in screen in his solar shades flicked alive.

'Not finished yet,' said the face on the screen.

'No. Do you want me to go into the lion's den?'

'We have no other choice. Shame about the Russian. He was a good asset.'

'Smith's fault. He shouldn't have involved him. Not without permission.'

'Smith was always a wild card with no loyalties, except to himself. And to his own ridiculous sense of principles. Never trust anyone who does not want or like money.'

The man who killed Alex Mikoyan allowed himself a

flicker of a smile. It was another of the Boss's *never trust* sayings. But then, in his job, the Boss could never trust anyone.

'Is Smith my only target?' he asked.

'Yes. Unless anyone else gets in the way of protecting our main asset.'

'*Anyone?*'

'I don't care who. Protect us at all costs.'

'Yes, boss.'

'Smith will be a difficult target, so just make sure you succeed . . . succ-seeed.'

She was resplendent in her glory as she sailed to her final resting place under the high entrance arch that seemed to span the sky. The whole entrance area, running directly off the Brick, was azure Mediterranean-blue water surrounded by landing piers and old-fashioned custom sheds copied from her voyage's port of origin in Southampton. Everywhere, the piers, the sheds, the loading ramps, were packed with thousands of onlookers.

The four-funnelled, black-hulled, white-topped ship shuddered as her engines kicked in to reverse and she slowed to docking speed. The massively long superstructure, which was originally designed to carry up to three thousand five hundred people, seemed to be going too fast and sure to crash into the pier.

The crowds reacted with screams and were forced back by those at the front immediately threatened by the looming liner as it juddered to a stop just inches from the walkways they were waiting to climb. She lurched to one side and sent a wave crashing against the pier, its white-flecked tops splashing skywards.

A dark mass, pointed and sharp, totally unexpected, burst upwards through the water and pierced her sides, ripped through the superstructure, lifted her bow thirty feet out of the water. Then the shiny iceberg settled, and finally slid back under the ship and out of sight. The *Titanic*, the gaping hole in her side swallowing itself, was then perfect once again as she settled back on the water and eased the last few feet into the dock.

Behind the crowd, on both sides of the huge dock, the skyline changed to depict her destination; harbour lights shone and the skyscapers lit up and crowded in to look down on her eagerly awaited arrival.

At last, after a journey through two centuries, *Titanic* had finally arrived in New York. The explosions and ticker tape and gigantic firework display erupted and filled the Brick and the sky with noise and ever-changing colours. There had been no danger, since computer-generated optical events were controlled in nanoseconds. But to the crowds there was always the hint of danger as it appeared, for a brief moment, that maybe something had gone wrong, that *Titanic* was about to crash again, after already being hit by the iceberg, and sink right in front of their eyes.

'Now that's what you call a maiden voyage,' shouted the President above the din, keeping his footing. Although the ship had reared upwards, its decks had remained flat so that the many guests could maintain their balance.

'Glad you liked it, Mr President,' said Dom Murphy. 'Hope the ride wasn't room-rough.'

'Hell, no, that was great.' Dixon turned to his wife. 'Long time since we've been on a rollercoaster, Annie. Just like we used to.'

She laughed and suddenly tripped as the ship finally settled, falling against Murphy. She grabbed at his arm and he held her tight until she regained her composure.

'You all right,' he asked softly.

'Just fine,' she replied as she stepped away.

'Hey, just look at all those people,' Dixon exclaimed, gesturing to the First Lady. 'Annie, get over here and look at all these folk.'

Teddy led her to the edge of the Promenade Deck, watched the crowd surge forward again. They waved to those below them on the pier, and a great shout went up as people recognized them. The more the couple waved the louder was the frenzied response of recognition. Celebrity mania was always a priority on the Brick.

The ship locked into its berth, the gangplanks were lowered, and finally the waiting crowds flooded aboard.

'You got enough room for all those people?' Dixon asked Murphy.

'Plenty,' replied the ThemeCorp Chairman. 'We've got nine decks in all, rising as tall as a thirteen-storey building, extending all the way from the Boat Deck and Bridge right down to the crew and machinery areas at the bottom. This ship was originally built for nearly three and a half thousand people, and that was with the storerooms and dining rooms and sleeping accommodation. You get people just walking round, or playing the slot machines, and you'll get ten thousand on board this version, probably more. Originally her second-class cabins were as luxurious as first-class on any other ship. She had so much space that could be redesigned, so that passengers would never run into any crew members – and there were nearly nine hundred of those. We've turned the engine rooms and storage rooms into slot machine salons, designed in such a way that they're built into the engine machinery, which clanks on just like for real while you're playing. Two thousand people can play in front of the slots down there. And that's just on one of the levels. We've got three levels in all in the machinery zone, but we don't want too many tourist visitors, since we're here really for exclusive gamblers. Not like those slot houses and casinos on the Brick that can take fifty thousand gamblers and still run an internet gaming site. And it's good down there, in the engine rooms. Very little obtrusive sound, just a good gentle ship-like movement. We've even got a little rumble in the superstructure so you feel like the ship's moving. Reality at its best. Then we got all those different gambling levels further above, right up to this deck where they can play open-air poker and craps. This deck'll be laid out so it can accommodate a thousand people, some of the highest rollers in the world. It's invitation only on the Promenade Deck.'

'Fantastic, Dom. This is a helluva show.'

'Thank you, sir.'

'We've both come a long way since I was a young senator and you a Secret Service Agent.'

'You've gone a lot further than me.'

'Only for eight years, and I've already used up four of those. How do you rank now, in the top twenty richest men in the world?'

Murphy laughed. 'For what it's worth, Mr President, third.'

'I didn't know that high.'

Murphy looked at Annie, then back at her husband. 'I've been lucky – just like you have in having such a wonderful and charming wife.'

'She is that.'

'Why, thank you, Dom,' said Annie Dixon.

'It's a pleasure, ma'am.'

They both smiled at each other as Dixon went back to waving at the crowds.

Clancy fumed impatiently and thought it was time to tell the President they should be returning to the White House.

Biloxie sat waiting in his hotel room, watching the scenes of jubilation near the *Titanic* as she docked. His mobile rang and he flicked it open.

'He's broken cover,' said Bonham. 'Just crossed the matrix out of the Dark Areas. Right opposite the *Titanic* Berth. Coordinates 6M432K9212, the Brick.' The ThemeCorp Security Chief had linked into the Dark Areas and simply waited for its skin to be penetrated. As soon as Conor Smith stepped back onto the Brick, his position was locked into a relay monitor in the ThemeCorp Control Room, and transmitted instantly to Bonham's office.

'I'll go in,' said Biloxie.

'Keep a watching brief. Act only if he gets near the truth. Otherwise leave him for the security boys. They'll bumble into him eventually,' he added dismissively.

'Have I got assistance on this?'

'One person down there, waiting for you. He's already got a visual on Smith and his support team.'

Swilkin saw Conor and stepped back into the crowd for cover. He'd seen them come out from behind an advertising board on a side street branching off the Brick, obviously emerging from the Dark Areas. Conor was followed by the girl and the punk boy.

They mingled in the crowd and Swilkin realized the fugitives felt safe that close to the *Titanic*; the crowds that had searched for them were now entirely focused on the docking of the giant liner. The explosive fireworks display and rapidly changing skylines mesmerized the throng who now ignored the twenty-million-dollar reward notices that could still be seen floating high above the Brick.

I had a very short time frame before the crowds started to look for us again. So I hurried through the crowd, head down, eager to get on to the *Titanic* itself. It took nearly three minutes to reach the first gangplank. The crowds moved fast, as they always did on the Brick. As I started to climb into the bowels of the ship I felt a tug from behind. I was surprised to see Jim behind me, his smile beaming as always. Tebor was behind him, his hand resting on Jim's shoulder. Andi brought up the rear, clinging to Tebor's waist so as not to be separated.

'Do you know where you're going now?' asked Jim.

'I think so,' I replied, not stopping, moving upwards and stepping into the ship's bulk.

Our motley crew reached the top of the gangway and entered the great engine rooms, now decked out with military rows of slot machines, an army of them primed and ready to pander to the gambler's weaknesses. Between the rows stood waitresses, all Marilyn Monroes, all dolled up to sing to the President and wish him 'Happy Birthday'.

Trust ThemeCorp to use the kidnap situation to highlight their launch.

As we pushed our way through the throng of gamblers and rubber-neckers, I asked, 'Are you coming all the way with me?'

The little half smile, then, 'Only to watch. I cannot help. Not now.'

'But you got us all here?'

Jim shrugged. 'Someone had to.'

'What's this all about, Jim?'

'To protect freedom at all costs.' Jim said it mechanically, emotionlessly, even though that was his very reason for existence.

We climbed on towards the upper decks, towards the public rooms, the restaurants and veranda cafes and palm courts, the Cafe Parisian and the first-class grand staircase that rose sixty feet with solid oak carved panelling running all the way round it.

'What am I looking for?' I asked as we ascended out of the engine-room decks. Jim didn't answer so I kept going forward, constantly searching for a clue, for any hint, any pointer that would lead me to the target I knew was here.

I'd noticed Swilkin just after we entered the *Titanic* superstructure. I didn't then know who it was, just realized that he showed little interest in the activity bustling around him. I took him instantly for a security agent; saw the stiffness and discipline in the watching man's movements. My instinct was that his avatar was merely a duplicate of his RealWorld self, meaning someone not at ease on the Brick.

I caught Andi's eyes momentarily, but she gave no hint of interest in where we were going. She still clung to Tebor, whose eyes were ablaze as he looked round, desperate to join in the celebrations. We climbed through the Lower Deck up to the Bridge and Middle Decks, and to the first layer of gaming tables and private salons. One look back confirmed we were still being followed.

'Do you know who that is?' I asked Jim.

'Swilkin. NSA,' came the reply. Jim didn't even look back to verify his comment.

'Paul Gallagher told me about him.'

'I know.'

'Swilkin's a top man at the Telephone Exchange. That

ties together with everything else about this caper. Why is he on his own?'

'I don't know.'

'But he is?'

'Yes.'

I swung round on him. 'You telling me that he's working without the agency's knowledge?'

Jim smiled and shook his head. 'I merely told you who he was.'

I shook my head, frustrated, and pushed on. There was little of interest on this deck, just rows of croupiers and tables with poker and blackjack and chemin de fer being played for low stakes, the seated gamblers being served by the now familiar Marilyn Monroe hostesses. The higher we climbed, the higher the stakes and the status of the high rollers. Here we were still on the gawper levels with cheap money and cheap gamblers.

My computer database linked through and fed me the facts on the voiceprint I'd downloaded earlier. It surprised me, but then I was getting used to surprises. Everything was starting to fit together.

I moved through the crowd. Someone else had written the script, but I was determined to re-write the ending.

The President kept a careful distance from the other guests as he walked along waving and smiling at those around him. The First Lady walked a few feet behind him, conversing with Dom Murphy, the two of them in a conspiratorial and joky huddle. There had been rumours that Murphy had bankrolled her media technology group but nothing had ever been proved.

Clancy and his team surrounded the small party, politely but firmly keeping well-wishers at bay. They were taking no chances of losing their President a second time. Suddenly Clancy detected a change in Dom Murphy. From Murphy's abrupt change of expression Clancy realized he'd picked up a communication from the small earpiece he wore. The man stopped, his hand held up over his right ear to shield the crowd's noise as he tried to clearly hear the communication.

Annie Dixon didn't realize he'd stopped and walked on for a moment before turning round to see where he'd gone.

Clancy reached Murphy and stopped too, signalling the rest of his team to continue with the President.

'Everything OK?' he asked Murphy.

Murphy held up his hand to silence him. 'Which level?' he asked. After he got a response he continued. 'Don't alarm anyone. And I don't want any pictures broadcast around the ship. Just identify and follow. I'll come back to you.'

'What's up?' asked Clancy again.

'Conor Smith's on board.'

'How the hell . . . ?'

'I don't know.'

'Anything wrong?' asked Annie Dixon, moving back to join Murphy.

'We've got to get you and the President back to the White House straight away,' said Clancy

'Why?'

Murphy ran through the latest development while Clancy called to one of his men to stop the President's progress.

'Let's go join the President, Ma'am,' said Clancy. He offered her his arm and she took it. He then led her, with Murphy following, to where Dixon now waited.

'Don't you have SnoopCams down on the pier or here in the ship?' Dixon asked Murphy nervously when they explained why they had stopped.

'No, sir,' confessed Murphy. 'We only just finished the project in time. Their installation was planned for next week.'

'I think we should go back to the White House,' urged Clancy.

'What do you think, Annie?' Dixon turned to his wife.

'Are we in any danger?' she asked him.

'Are we?' This time the question was directed at Clancy.

'Not immediately, sir.'

'I think it would be wrong to be seen to turn and run,' the First Lady continued.

Dixon nodded. 'You're right. Especially after my broadcast.'

'Then let's go somewhere you're easier to protect.' Clancy was obviously prepared to stand his ground. 'A smaller, more controllable area, so if we see any danger coming, we can JetPax you out immediately.'

'OK.' Dixon turned to his host. 'Dom?'

'I've got just the place, Mr President,' smiled Murphy.

'Good.' Dixon turned back to Clancy. 'Let's not rush. We'll take our time. Just make sure you stay close to us.'

'If you'll follow me,' Murphy indicated.

The group moved along the deck, the President and his First Lady once more waving and smiling at the well-wishers. Murphy was leading the way.

'Where's he now?' Murphy asked Bonham quietly over his AudioLink.

'Still Middle Deck.'

'Can he get any higher?'

'He'll have to show either a pass ... pass or an invitation.'

'No chance of that.'

'Jim Nelson's with him.'

'Goddammit!'

'Which means he'll get through, then. Short of blocking everyone's passes, there's not much we can do. The place would jam up while they were waiting for new ones. Be total chaos. Biloxie's on his way up, with support.'

'OK. I'm taking the President to a safer place. He refuses to go to the White House yet.'

'That could be a mistake.'

'No choice, I'm taking him to – '

'Don't tell ... te-tell me. Nelson might pick it up.'

'Biloxie must take out Smith.'

'That was always the plan. Smith was never going to survive anyway.'

'Now where?' I asked as we reached the Grand Staircase.

'You'll need this,' said Jim. He passed me a gold-edged invitation card. 'This is not the time to get thrown out for gate-crashing.'

'For all of us?' I looked back at Tebor and Andi.

'Of course.'

I held up the card and, after a brief inspection by the guard, was waved through.

'Have a nice time, Mr Pavarotti,' said the guard at the foot of the stairs, next to the Cherub light with the ostentatious carved wood clock behind it.

'Thank you, I will.' I climbed the sixty-foot staircase to the Promenade Deck. Once there, and satisfied the others had kept pace with me, I moved to the outer area.

Jim didn't follow and I pulled up.

'Wrong way, huh?'

No response, still that benign smile. Behind him Tebor giggled. Andi looked apprehensive, like someone knowing exactly where she was going and dreading it.

I saw Swilkin arguing with a guard who refused to let him through. Swilkin was insistent, finally showing him what was no doubt his NSA-ID card. The guard was still reluctant and beckoned one of his colleagues over.

'We should leave Agent Swilkin to his own devices,' urged Jim.

'Sure'. I stared at him briefly, then set off towards the back of the Promenade Deck, following a sign to the First Class Smoking Room.

This time Jim followed.

Most of the guests on this deck wore suits, tuxedos, flowing evening gowns. Our small group stood out in their street dress, but this was Second World where nothing was ever too unusual. We headed to the rear and into the Smoke Room. The room was now empty as all the first class guests were outside on the upper decks, watching the opening procedures. In the distant background the noise banged on, music, shouts, the crowds enjoying themselves. I even heard the far-off sound of a calypso steel band starting up.

The room was large, panelled mahogany inlaid with mother of pearl. The bar was extremely well stocked and ideal for those who required an after-dinner drink or somewhere to drown their sorrows after a bad session at the tables. Painted glass windows, depicting different ports from around the world or other White Star Line ships, covered the walls. Around the room there were bite-size computer terminals, all linked together, all top-end range quantum computers which were there for the use of guests wishing to communicate with RealWorld. Besides these were further computers linked to shopping centres, internet suppliers, other casinos, online gaming centres, even one to Google Pages. It was a surfer's paradise. On the portside I saw a small veranda. I crossed over to investigate and found it led to the small Palm Court area overlooking the aft Promenade Deck. That's where some of the first class guests were standing, watching the boat being linked to the Pier, watching the fireworks start to die out, watching the New York skyline live out its fantasy as it watched over its long-lost new neighbour.

Jim was sitting at a table when I came back, his feet crossed as he gazed at the centrepiece fireplace, which suddenly burst into flame, crackling with burning logs that threw out a cedar aroma into the room. Jim began staring at a painting that hung above the fireplace. His ever-present smile was gone.

The painting, by Norman Wilkinson, was titled *Approach to the New World*. I looked at the banks of computers, then back at the painting. It was the entrance to Plymouth Harbour; the beginning of the journey that had first led to the New World. The significance revealed itself; small hairs stood up on the back of his neck.

Jim finally smiled again. Tebor just stayed excited as before. Andi also stared at the painting, then at me. She too smiled, again. I saw beyond the smile and recognized the pain in her eyes.

I took the SmartCard that Bonham had given him and crossed over to the painting. I tried to insert it into the canvas but it met solid resistance. Jim merely shrugged; he wasn't programed to help in any way. But he still smiled.

Andi came to me and covered my hand with hers. I felt the tingle, the togetherness that came from our touch. Then she leant up and kissed me on the mouth; no passion, yet startling in its surprising intensity.

'Try now,' she said.

I turned and pressed the card back against the canvas. My hand passed through, just as it had into the Dark Areas. The maritime picture changed; the canvas became a spinning tornado of bright white light barrelling down, a long dark tunnel narrowing into a distant infinity.

'Tell me what you see?' asked Swilkin from the door.

I pulled the card out with a start. The painting returned to its original seascape.

He shut the door and came into the room. 'Tell me,' he repeated. 'What did you see?'

'You know as well as I do,' I said, as Andi moved behind Jim and Tebor, a look of fear spreading across her face.

'I don't. I thought I did, but I don't. So why did you kidnap the President?'

'I didn't.'

'Then who did? We sure as hell didn't.'

'You saying you're not part of this?'

'I'm not part of anything. I'm NSA. We were only called in when the President got taken. We were less helpful than you in saving him. I don't like that.'

'But you like the InfoCalypse?'

'Nothing to do with me or my people. What I don't understand is why you? The whole thing, too contrived. And him.' Swilkin pointed at Jim, 'Who the hell is he really?' And you better tell me quick what's going on. Before the Secret Service get here.'

'You called them?'

'No. But last thing I heard was that the President's party was heading in this direction.'

'Who told you?'

'My assistant, back at Langley. I contacted them to get myself past that goon on the Grand Staircase.'

'That means they know.'

'Who knows?'

I paused and looked at Jim. The smile had disappeared again.

'ThemeCorp,' I said to Swilkin.

'ThemeCorp?'

'Who else? Didn't you notice there were no SnoopCams or WebCops anywhere on this section of the Brick?'

'It's a new complex. They'll be in place soon.'

'Web zoning insists that all security facilities are in place before site construction begins.'

'No riddles, please. Either tell me what's going on or I try and keep you here until help arrives.

'When the Brick was being set up, under the auspices of the UN, three very talented US government security agents were seconded to the project.'

'Murphy, Nelson and Keebles?'

'That's right. They were there from day one, right

through inception and planning. Each had specific talents, each headed important divisions. Before Keebles came along, avatars could cross through any wall, pass through anything. Like it was in Alpha World and Second Life. It was Keebles who pushed the protocol so that avatars were automatically blocked from entering any area unless it was through a specified entrance. These guys came up with ideas that the UN then turned into laws. They brought order and control to the Brick. They had seen the potential. They realized they could build a Second World which would make them very rich men. In time they left government service and turned ThemeCorp into one of the biggest organizations in the world, but do you know how they raised the money in the first place?'

'Banks?'

'Yes, up to a point. But no bank would lend the amounts they needed without serious collateral. I think they raided the CIA and FBI data on these banker guys, got to know all their quirks, then blackmailed them. Probably said it was in the name of the government, or national security.' I saw Jim nodding in silent agreement. 'Maybe not Nelson and Keebles, but definitely Murphy and his new security chief, Malcolm Bonham.

'They got into the habit of downloading confidential data. They hacked the Brits, the French, everybody and anybody. Even their Secret Services. It became easier once the Brick opened. Banks, insurance companies, major hotel groups, everybody invested heavily and got involved in Second World. And guess who knew all the security protocols? *They* did. They could tell you about hotel bookings, who was sleeping with whom, how much you paid for a cup of coffee in Albania, if you cheated on your wife, your bank details . . . That last was the easiest. because everyone used credits on the Web, and they were charged back to your bank in RealWorld. That simple. They could access any account they wanted to just by hitting a few keystrokes.'

'The UN changed all those codes – just so that couldn't happen.'

'Too late. They'd embedded nano-cells, microbiological computer cells into the entire matrix by then. They were the CREEPs, quietly going along, maintaining the Web. Totally harmless, everyone thought, except they had other programs built in before the legislations were passed and tighter controls put in. When the UN finally clamped down, it was just closing the stable door. The horse was out and in full gallop by then.'

'That's the InfoCalypse? All that information.'

'And growing all the time.'

'Who uses it?' asked Swilkin, afraid of the answer.

I laughed. 'Whoever they decide they want to use it. Probably even your own government. Ever wonder where those secret tip-offs came from? Those bits of information you readily used, but never questioned the source? And if any government agency – US, British, anyone – got it for nothing . . . well, who would ask questions?'

'Did they sell that information – to another power?'

'Not yet.'

'Meaning?'

'They didn't set out to be traitors. Just greedy.' I saw Jim nod again. Smiling too, even managing to look relieved. Christ, can a robot feel stress? 'They did it primarily for themselves, so they could mailshot clients, check up on their credits, line up the gamblers for their casinos, get people into the theme parks. And worst of all, they could monitor all their competition and thus stay one jump ahead. They formed new corporations in expanding sectors by stealing other people's ideas, or they destroyed the financial base of small innovative companies, then moved in as investment saviours. You read about it every day in the business pages, but ThemeCorp had more information than the US government itself. It probably could react to new legislation on tax and zoning and public grants before the measures became law. They did all that for personal gain, to build their own corporate power. Dammit, even the Good-As-You-Get company that patented the Marilyn Monroe avatars was owned by ThemeCorp. They let someone else get the patents, waited till the company was on the verge of bankruptcy, then stepped in as guardian angels.'

'So why steal the President?'

'That wasn't ThemeCorp.' I was getting restless now. The President's party would arrive any second. 'We need to get out of here.'

'I need the full story.'

'It wasn't an organization, or some powerful RealWorld individual. The whole thing was dreamt up by Nelson and Keebles. They must've had a fallout with Murphy. I think they were straight guys who either didn't know how the information was being misused . . . or didn't want to know. Maybe they just shut their eyes to it, took their cheques and ran.'

'Until it went wrong?'

'They couldn't close their eyes to it any longer. Maybe they imagined the information gathering had stopped. But the news about *Titanic* moving made them realize they'd been hoodwinked – that the information was still being collated . . . on an even grander scale. They lived clean now, having dropped out from ThemeCorp, didn't even have computers at home. But they were rattled, so they set out to protect themselves. With Jim here.'

The big beaming smile told me I was on the right track. I finally smiled back.

'Jim is a robot. He is made up of trillions of nano-cells, individual biological microcomputers that come together under certain conditions. Nelson and Keebles built a lot of their own personalities into Jim: the good-guy bits of their own characters. But Jim couldn't ever talk about the Info-Calypse because he's not programed to do that. If he does, he'd just self-destruct. So Nelson and Keebles came up with a game-plan that would exercise everyone's minds and focus them on the InfoCalypse.'

'Like the kidnap plot?'

'Yes. They must've dreamt it up very quickly. As soon as the First Lady arranged for Marilyn Monroe, they saw their opportunity. They still had a computer somewhere and they used it to confirm the birthday present, and then trigger Jim. I think they arranged Que's death by poison. That must've been difficult for them, because killing wasn't in their nature.'

'Did they really commit suicide?'

'Who knows? Maybe they couldn't take it anymore. Or, just possibly, someone found out and had them killed.'

'Why not tell the authorities?'

'Who'd believe them? And could they risk the NSA not using that information?'

Swilkin ignored that point. 'So the President was always going to come back safe?'

'Yeah, you were always stuck with Teddy Boy.'

Swilkin pulled a face. 'I never put a cross against his name,' he said. 'How'd *you* get involved?'

'I was asked in. I think that was only by chance.'

'You think?'

'Not totally sure yet. But Nelson and Keebles needed a privateer, somebody who'd follow it through.'

Swilkin indicated Jim. 'Did *he* tell you about Theme-Corp?'

'He can't.'

'Then how do you know for sure?'

I then quickly told Swilkin about Alex Mikoyan and how I felt responsible for his death.

'You think it's this Biloxie character?' asked Swilkin

'I picked up on the result of the voiceprint while I was coming up here,' I replied bitterly. 'It matched Biloxie, so he's the guy who killed Alex.'

'I'm sorry,' said Jim.

I leant over and put my arm on Jim's shoulder. 'For a robot you've got a lot of soul.'

'I told you I'm *alive*.'

I grinned. I then looked over Jim's shoulder at Andi and she was still smiling. But her eyes were blank. The final part of the jigsaw suddenly fell into place. I stepped back sharply. *Fuck it . . . not that!*

'Biloxie could be working for someone else, not necessarily ThemeCorp,' I heard Swilkin saying in the background.

'No,' I heard myself reply, my eyes still fixed on Andi. It was inevitable, I suppose. I tore my gaze away from her.

'I also ran the voiceprint of the avatar who killed Monroe,' I said to Swilkin. 'Biloxie again. Only the Good-As-You-Get company could have traced her. They would've known where she was at all times. Biloxie merely accessed their files. It's a no-brainer.'

'I'm sorry,' said Jim again.

'So you keep saying.' I felt the sorrow welling up in me. I pointed at Andi. 'Why her?' I asked Jim.

'The choice was made a long time ago. She was impregnated specially for this moment.'

'Why not you?'

'I have to protect the future. Maybe it will happen again. After you are all gone. When I may be needed again.'

'What's going on?' asked Swilkin, puzzled.

'You'll find out soon enough,' I said, swinging round to face him. 'Are you in . . . or out?'

'In, for now. But I need to know where it is.'

'The InfoCalypse?'

'What else?'

'You're standing on it.'

'Say again?'

'*Titanic.* That's why ThemeCorp bought it all that time ago. And all the land round it in Alpha World. They were managing and organizing complexity. To simplify data storage, they converted all the original structural data that made up *Titanic* into storage data. Then it all got too big, so they ran out of memory. They needed to increase the memory, but it would be too big to go unnoticed. You move something that big around the Web and someone's going to get nosey. So they decided to disguise it. They relaunched *Titanic*. Tidied her up and sent her on her second voyage.'

Swilkin whistled. 'They move all that information into one of their biggest sites? You mean transfer, then store the data under their own protection where no one else has access.' He nodded knowingly. 'That's why they were buying up Alpha World ... where *Titanic* was already based. Only they couldn't get full control of it. Too many small house-holders, like you, who wouldn't leave.'

'Go to the top of the class.'

'Christ, that's cool.'

'We're here to destroy the InfoCalypse,' I warned him.

'Meaning?'

'Not to reroute it into the Telephone Exchange.'

'That's very powerful information.'

'Too powerful for you people to have. We're here to make sure that ...'

A loud cheer came from the deck area outside.

'That's the President getting close,' said Swilkin as the roar grew.

I grabbed Swilkin and pushed him against the wall, pinned him there. 'Tell me about the Dundee Society.'

'Let's get out of – '

'Murphy and Keebles and Nelson were members – like you.'

'Am I?'

'Yeah. Alex told me that you guys are very secretive. And protective.'

'I think we should get out of here ... before I'm faced with a choice.' The sudden urgency focused my mind. If he was the enemy, I now wanted him where I could see him.

I released him. 'Follow me.'

I gripped the SmartCard in my hand and pushed it into the painting. I stretched my other hand towards Swilkin and told him to hang on to it. 'Don't let go whatever you do,' I warned him. 'Come on, you lot, let's go,' I shouted to the others. Jim stood up and waved the two youngsters forward.

I told them to grab hold of Swilkin. Tebor put his arms round Swilkin's waist but Andi rushed over and wrapped herself around me instead.

Our eyes met and held as the Smoke Room door opened and Clancy entered. I heard Clancy yell to the others as the Secret Service man reached for his weapon. As I stepped into the picture and the fireplace under it, I had a last glimpse of Jim disappearing back into the matrix. I knew I would never see him again.

The four of us had disappeared into the walls of the *Titanic* before the weapons that opened fire could do any damage.

Clancy grabbed for the President and punched the man's JetPax. He'd worry about the verbal abuse Dixon might give him once they got back to the White House. He saw one of his team doing the same to Annie Dixon. There was no way somebody was going to steal his President twice in two days.

As he hit his own JetPax he saw two images that alarmed him. One was Murphy screaming abuse at the painting Smith and friends had disappeared in to. The second was Gallagher rushing past, followed by a big gap-toothed man with a grizzled face who was yelling as loudly as Murphy.

'I'll fucking kill him when I get him,' Gallagher's words were the last Clancy heard before arriving back at the White House.

We clung together as we were sucked along the stream of data that was downloading from the *Titanic* to its vast neighbouring ThemePark.

The tunnel twisted and turned but unlike in popular movies, the rush of data was not a visible moving jumble of alphabetical letters or spinning, ever-changing colourful and brilliant lights. It was a rush of energy, a torrent of water that I couldn't see or feel, silent yet more powerful than anything I'd ever known, buffeting us against the soft tissue walls of the tunnel, slapping us against its sides, sometimes cartwheeling us as we tumbled downwards. The bright white light was constant, vivid in its intensity. Miraculously we stayed together.

After a long steep fall, the narrow twisting tunnel suddenly levelled out, and widened, and we four travellers slowed until we fell out into a vast winter mountainscape. We separated and stood in snow, in awe of the breathtaking views of snow-capped mountains that stretched into the horizon. I knew this place; I'd been there before.

'Foo, where are we?' asked Tebor. 'Some place.'

'Valley of the Dragons,' I said. 'The BirthPlace.'

'Of what?'

'Dragons.' I pointed towards what looked like large yellow rocks, each about twelve feet high, protruding from the snow. 'Eggs, ready to hatch.'

'Is this where they're pumping the data?' asked Swilkin.

'Looks like it.'

'Why here?'

'Because this is the centre of a vast space. The Valley of the Dragons is a data area as big as England – the biggest ThemePark there is. The data being transferred here from *Titanic* will be swallowed up into a minuscule part of it. The InfoCalypse could go on collecting for a thousand years and they'd still never fill this place.'

'Risky in such a public place?'

I suddenly remembered. 'It's closed today, for maintenance. They've got the place all to themselves.'

Tebor had wandered down towards the nearest egg to inspect it.

'You were a good choice, then,' Andi said, now standing next to me.

'Because I know this place?'

She nodded. 'You must take me to the lair of the Golden Dragon.'

'I have only achieved that once.'

'At least you know what to expect. Did you reach the Enchanted Palace?'

'Yes.'

'So must we. You have to take me there – right to the heart of the Castle.'

That's what I'd already guessed. It was where this thing would end.

'Jim's gone, hasn't he?' I replied.

'It's all up to you now, Conor.'

'Wowie!' shouted Tebor. 'Look at this.'

Cracks had appeared in the egg nearest to him, and he moved even closer to it.

'Keep away,' I yelled. 'Step back and keep your distance.'

I moved towards Tebor, who backed away from the egg in alarm. It was splintering open now, its top cracking apart from inside. Long teeth suddenly appeared, sharp fangs ten inches long that hacked away at the huge eggshell and ripped an opening nearly three feet across.

Even though I'd seen it a hundred times before, it still impressed me. It was part of the tour I took students on, it was part of their game.

'If they take me . . .' said Andi quietly behind him, '. . . no one will ever stop them.'

'I understand that now,' I said. 'Come back here, Tebor,' I repeated. 'This is a dangerous place.' I turned to Swilkin. 'Are you armed?'

'Yes,' replied Swilkin. 'Heavily.'

'Got a sword?'

'I always carry one when I'm down here.' He shrugged apologetically. 'Which is not very often. I can only do my best.'

'You'll need it. These babies eat bullets for breakfast. From now on in it's hand-to-hand combat. You any good at that?'

'I linked to the ThemeCorp site before I came down. I downloaded their top martial arts programs. Cost me two hundred bucks for the day.'

'Which program?'

'Yours.'

He saw me smile.

'The advert said you were the best,' Swilkin continued. 'Do our JetPax work down here?'

'Yes, but avoid that if you can. Otherwise we'll never get back to this level. We'd have to work our way up from the base level and we'd never get to the Enchanted Castle in time.'

'Where's that?'

'In Portofino.'

'That's Italy.'

'No, that's where St George lives.'

A head now appeared through the top of the egg. A red,

scaly head, with yellow eyes and a reptile's armoured skin. A long brown tongue, forked at the end, flicked out as the monster tasted its first breath of cold mountain air. It lifted its head out further, flared its spiked collar mantle and roared. The sound reverberated down the slope and across the mountains.

Tebor stood with his mouth hanging open; he'd never seen anything like this before. The boy was still too close to it and I grabbed Tebor, yanking him away from the emerging new-born dragon. This sharp movement startled the reptile who swung round and stared at the retreating pair of us. It struggled to break free of the confinement that held it, smashing against the sides of the egg, desperately trying to free its wings. The egg rocked in the snow, then suddenly cracked apart as the beast burst free. Its wings came out first, stretched for the first time to their full width, then flapped as they searched for first flight. The primary movements were weak and inconsistent, like a frantic butterfly with broken wings. Then, as the dragon got accustomed to their power, it worked them together, felt the down force it created, sensed the first moments of lift and freedom.

It beat its wings harder, with more purpose, now realizing their function. It reached upwards with its fore-limbs, ripped the rest of the shell away with sharp claws. Then it teetered upwards as it tested its rear legs for the first time. This baby stood nearly fifteen feet high. It roared at us while it worked the muscles that would break it free.

I pulled Tebor all the way back to where the other two stood, nearly fifty metres from the emerging creature.

'This is too far away,' shouted Tebor. 'I want to see it closer.'

'I've lost too many students up here,' I snapped back. 'Stay here.'

The dragon burst free of its imprisonment and lifted itself into the air above the egg. It tested its wings, flapped them as it experienced first flight, coming to understand the control they afforded. It ignored the four of us who stood and watched.

We were OK. I knew because it was programed to only identify and attack avatars located within thirty metres. We watched as the young Red Earth Dragon flew down the valley to take its place in the Valley of the Dragons. The shattered egg it left behind meanwhile formed itself back into a new one.

'There's another one!' shouted Tebor, pointing towards an egg further down the slope that was starting to crack.

'That's how they're moving the data,' I said as I watched the new birth. I turned to Swilkin. 'With all the new dragons.'

'What gives you that idea?'

'When I get people up to this level, there's only one active egg. If my pupils get too close, the dragon is born and attacks them. Red dragons are pretty ferocious.' I surveyed the mountainside. 'There's far too many eggs here, and dragons only hatch when we reach this level in a game. I've never seen this many before.'

'How do we get off this mountain?' asked Andi.

'The way we normally do.'

'How's that?'

'By air. First class.'

THE SMOKE ROOM
MIDDLE DECK
TITANIC
THEMEPARK
6M432K9212, THE BRICK
REAL TIME: ZERO PLUS 16 HRS AND 40 MINS

Clancy and his team had JetPaxed the President and his First Lady back to the safety of the White House. Once he knew they were safe, he immediately re-entered the Web, heading back to the Smoke Room.

Gallagher was still there with Murphy and the large man. He noticed Gallagher's arm wasn't hanging limp any longer; whatever damage had been caused had now healed itself.

'What the hell's going on?' Clancy demanded.

'You let Smith escape,' was Gallagher's blunt response.

'I was protecting the President. That's first priority – yours as well as mine.'

'You didn't need me there. Now we get Smith.'

'That's not our remit.'

'If we don't, then he stays a threat.'

'Am I missing something? Last I heard from you was that he was innocent. You told me you were after Swilkin.'

'Maybe I was wrong. Maybe you were right all along.'

'There's nothing we can do down here.'

Gallagher nodded. 'You better get back to the White House.'

'And you?'

'I'll hang around for a while. See if they turn up.'

'I'll stay with you'.

'I'd rather you didn't,' said Dom Murphy, from behind Clancy. 'My people can handle it from here.'

'OK, Mr Murphy,' replied Clancy. 'Come on, Paul, time to go.'

'Gallagher can stay.'

'Then I should stay too.'

Murphy shook his head. 'Look, I don't want too many heavies hanging around. It's bad for business. It looks bad on the ship.'

'Why Gallagher?'

'Because he works the Web more than you do. I said, I don't need heavies. I need techies. He'll do fine.'

'I'd really prefer to stay.' Clancy was unsure of his ground.

'This is private property, Agent Clancy, so just go.' Cold, to the point, no niceties.

'Go back, Don,' urged Gallagher. 'I'll debrief you as soon as I'm back.'

Clancy had to agree as Murphy was too close to the President for him to rock the boat. He grunted angrily, then hit his JetPax.

'Where the fuck did Smith come from?' snarled an angry Murphy. 'And how did he get in with the data?'

'Jim Nelson. Who else?'

'Track him. Find him. Destroy him before he gets the chance to inflict any real damage.'

'Nelson's out of it now. Disintegrated into a trillion cells, all with no memory of what they've done.'

'If Smith's hunting the InfoCalypse he'll need support.' Murphy started pacing up and down, slamming his fist into his palm as he thought. 'Finding it isn't enough, though Nelson and Keebles knew that. Smith knows we'll take him out once we get to him. He's not that naive.' He paced for a moment longer, then stopped sharply as the obvious hit home. 'He's pushing on . . . to destroy it.'

'If he finds it.'

'Jim will have worked that out.'

'There's no way he can crack the codes.'

'He's done OK so far,' Murphy said dismissively.

'Only with Jim's guidance. But he's gone. Smith's on his own now. He won't know where to start.'

'Is that a hope or are you sure?'

'I'm sure of it.' Gallagher was genuinely convinced they were safe on that score. 'The one program that runs through every CREEP is that they cannot disclose anything about the InfoCalypse or any information on ThemeCorp. That's how it was all set up. Nor did they have the access or security codes to enter the Dragon's Lair. We have our own CREEPs working our properties, and they have totally different operational requirements. There's no way that can be changed.'

'No. He's not going in there blind, with just his sword in his hand. My former partners will have found a way of getting through – if not Jim, then something else.' Murphy went cold, remembering just how good Nelson and Keebles had been. *Why couldn't they just have been interested in the money?* 'It was your idea to bring in Smith,' he angrily reminded Gallagher.

'Mr Bonham's actually, but I agreed with him. The whole idea, once the President was taken, was to chase Jim with the best operative there was. Smith was the obvious choice, but we didn't expect him to get to Nelson quite so fast. Neither did we expect Nelson to return the President. Smith was in a squeeze. On one side he had Jim loading him with information through those kids ... on the other he had us trying to get him to close down Jim. Dixon coming back to the White House wasn't in the script, but once he was back, we had no choice but to discredit Smith, to protect our own interests. We never expected him to get this far.'

'Conor Smith is the only GameMaster who ever got to the Enchanted Castle,' warned Biloxie. 'That means he can do it again.'

Murphy let out a deep sigh and stopped his pacing.

'Get in there,' he ordered Gallagher and Biloxie. 'Get in there and crush him ... before he crushes us.'

BOOK SIX

ENDGAME

It was a beautiful sight. Every time I saw it. The small Italian bay with its picturesque harbour, its tall terraced buildings coming right down to the water's edge, the hill rising sharply behind with colourful villas perched on its side, the broken greenery between the buildings, the boats in the azure water, the even deeper blue sky speckled with wispy drifting clouds framing the whole vision; the Italian Riviera at its best.

Across the bay, perched on the hill, was the old castle, long since abandoned as a home, now no more than an empty well-preserved monument with a few sticks of furniture for those who would try to reach it. It was a small castle, with ramparts looking over cliffs that fell more than two hundred feet to the forest below on one side and to the sea on the other. It was reached by a steep, narrow, overgrown earth path that meandered down the hill, past the church on the lower level, through the old graveyard and down to the waterside town situated no more than half a mile away across the bay.

This simple castle was the Nirvana of Second World games. It was, in all its simplicity, the Enchanted Castle. In between the castle and the town, half-way up the hill, was the little church, yellow-fronted brickwork with a white surround and roof, and two large narrow green metal carved doors.

That journey, from the town to the castle, had been successfully climbed only once since it came into existence a few years earlier. The route upwards had been perilous and the reward was no more than the right to sit in a small seat at the top of the castle itself. I'd accomplished that climb, and the serenity and achievement I felt when I sat up there was one of the greatest achievements of all.

Portofino was the thirty-third and final level of the Valley of the Dragons. Most GameMasters had only reached level thirty. The sharpest and best of their pupils rarely passed the twentieth.

I now looked up at the castle from Portofino harbour. As usual, there were no people about; after all this was the home of dragons. I was tucked safely into an alleyway, my back to the wall, while I waited for the next red dragon to arrive. In front of me, by the quayside, two red dragons waited their turn to fly up to the Enchanted Castle.

Getting a ride had been easy. I knew how the young red dragons were programed, how gameplayers found their way out of the BirthPlace level. I also guessed that if the dragons were indeed moving the InfoCalypse data, then they would fly direct to their new home and miss out some of the final skill-testing levels.

Six red dragons had hatched and each departed in that same northerly direction before I hitched a ride. I'd watched them turn left just before SunRunner Mountain, the birthplace of the giant red SunRunner dragon. That confirmed that they were all heading for the same destination; the identical timing of each birth proved they were in a program loop. It confirmed the transfer of identical batches of new data. What I hadn't expected was their destination to be Portofino; that they were moving the data to the most sacred place in the Valley of the Dragons.

Tebor had shrieked with excitement when I'd told them what I wanted them to do. Swilkin merely looked shocked, whereas Andi smiled and readily accepted my expertise in dealing with the dragons.

'We're going to ride them out of here,' I'd said. 'These

dragons are young, programed to only attack something that comes too close to their egg during and after they're born. They'll tear you to pieces if they get you, rip you with their claws or their teeth. They don't breathe flames, not these ones. So you have to fool them, kid them into thinking you're part of the egg, part of the shell. Then they'll accept you. You've got to stand on top of the egg, then, as they're hatching, you've got to grab round their necks and hang on. It won't be easy, they're scaled all over and still have egg plasma stuck to them, making them as slippery as hell.'

'You're kidding,' groaned Swilkin.

Not quite what I expected of a top NSA man. 'Once you accept we're in a game, here in Second World, then you realize everything is possible. And everything is programed, but still extremely dangerous. If they get either Tebor or Andi, they'll be wiped out on the Web. You and me, we'll live, only we'll go back to RealWorld with pains and head-aches. These things maul you badly, so you're in bed for a couple of days.'

'You said they're not aware of us beyond thirty metres. That means we must run if we get within that range?'

'If you're lucky. But, remember, while you're running, they're flying. They'll have you within the first few metres.'

'I can't wait,' burbled Tebor. 'This is the best.'

'Just do as I say,' I warned him. 'I need you wherever we end up. Don't be reckless or it'll get us all in trouble.'

'He won't,' said Andi. 'Will you?' she eyed him firmly.

'No,' came the giggling answer. 'I want to see where we're going next. That sounds like a so-so-so adventure.'

'Now, watch what I do,' I said. 'We leave one at a time. If I'm to show you, that means I'll have to go first. The three of you must follow, but I won't be there any longer. Just make sure you do exactly as I do. And when they fly, don't try and guide them. They'll go where they're pro-gramed to go.'

'Which is?' asked Swilkin.

'Directly to the storage area. Normally they go on to the next gaming level ... this is only level twenty-seven. But I think we're going all the way to the top.'

'People pay for this?' Swilkin remarked incredulously.

I ignored that. 'One final thing. I can't tell you what to do at the other end because I'm not sure where they're going. Don't try and jump off unless you're near enough to the ground. Remember, the dragon could turn on you if you do that. Wait until it lands, then slide off, softly as you can. The dragon will be focused on wherever it's going, so just run in the opposite direction, away towards its rear. By the time it's worked out you're there, you should be out of the thirty-metre range. I'll be watching out for you.' I grinned once more. 'Beware it's tail when you slide off. Very sharp with an arrowhead. Could damage your manhood.'

The seventh red dragon had hatched and was lifting off to its destination as I ran down and climbed up onto the rough-surfaced egg that was already showing some preliminary cracks. As before, the head forced its way out first, the dragon snarling and trying to break free. The egg convulsed and I was ready. From a kneeling position on top of the shell, I put my arm round the dragon's neck, from behind, just below the spreading spiny mantle. As the dragon struggled free, I effortlessly slid onto its back.

I saw Tebor whooping loudly, urging me on. I hoped his recklessness was not going to turn on him.

Then the dragon lifted free, its wings beating strongly as it turned towards the white-capped peaks of SunRunner Mountain. I held on, both arms now interlocked round the young dragon's neck as it headed for its destination. The flight, upwards and to the north, took no more than two minutes. It was a bumpy ride, not like in my normal game excursions. I guessed the unusual amount of extra information data being carried by the dragon was affecting its normal programmes. *Near bloody overload.* I clung on tight and hoped the others would do the same.

We flight-landed in the big square and I slid off and ran to hide between the neighbouring houses. The dragon had not noticed me, was instead fixed on its next target. I lumbered towards the rim of the harbour.

Swilkin came next, his body twisted in discomfort as he toppled off the dragon and ran for cover. The dragon spun round but Swilkin just made it out of range in time. I signalled him over.

'Bumpy ride,' complained Swilkin as he hunched down next to me. 'I've been here before. Italy.'

'No, that's in the Italian sector. This place here was specially built, under licence, just for the game. Everything here is designed just for the game.'

'But I've really been there, I mean, to Italy, to Portofino. The real McCoy.'

Silly me. How easily I forget there's a real and proper world out there. 'Then you'll notice it's exactly the same. Including the church up on the hill.'

'San Giorgio. Yes.'

'This will be nothing like you visited before. Bad ride up?'

'Hate coach. I hope that punk kid makes it, he's crazy.' Swilkin saw his dragon join the others, then the one nearest the water stretched his wings and flew out across the bay, up towards the castle.

'Watch,' I pointed across the bay. The dragon reached the top and flapped its wings, bringing its rear limbs forward to perch on the ramparts. It stayed there for a moment, then hopped down, so we saw the top half of it waddling along beyond the rampart wall. Then it halted. Even at this distance, Swilkin saw it become motionless, then it lifted its wings skyward, suddenly turned its head to the sun and let out an enormous roar. One long blast of flame from its mouth, then it disappeared below the ramparts.

The next dragon by the harbour started its journey up to the castle.

'I thought you said young red dragons couldn't blow fire,' said Swilkin.

'I lied,' I shrugged. 'I needed you all up here.'

'I was right not to trust you. So' – he pointed to the castle – 'what was all that about?'

'The dragon's connected, has probably gone into the castle to download.'

Out in the square the next dragon landed and Tebor slid off it. When he saw me waving to him, he ran across the square, shouting with excitement. The dragon he had ridden on heard him and turned round. It bellowed, disgorged a ball of red flame and tried taking flight to pursue. It was too heavy and confused by the extra data inside, and it stumbled, then continued to give chase on foot. Those few extra seconds saved Tebor's life as he escaped from within the thirty-metre range. The dragon, even more confused now, stopped to look round, then headed towards the others already gathered in the harbour.

An excited Tebor skidded to a stop. 'Wow!' was all he could manage. Then he noticed my dark accusing look, swivelled round and went to slouch with his back against the alley wall.

'Is Andi OK?' I asked him.

'Fine,' came his surly response.

She suddenly appeared around the corner. None of us had seen the dragon carrying her arrive. I decided not to question her on how she had got there.

Up above another dragon roared, and spat flames onto the ramparts. More dragons kept arriving, taking up position in turn, waiting to fly to their final destination in a final act of destruction.

'Where next?' asked Swilkin.

'Into the inferno,' I said. 'Straight into the dragons' lair.'

GULFSTREAM N865DDX
3,000 FEET DESCENDING
ATLANTIC CITY
EASTERN SEABOARD
REALWORLD
REAL TIME: ZERO PLUS 17 HRS AND 13 MINS

The GulfStream descended through three thousand feet and turned onto a heading of one-eight-five to intercept the ILS and long approach to Atlantic City International Airport. ThemeCorp's east-coast headquarters were in Atlantic City itself, the top three storeys above their Midas Touch Casino which filled a whole block on the BoardWalk. The company's casino operations were almost as big in RealWorld as they were in Second World.

Bonham was currently only concerned about his conversation with Gallagher over the VideoLink.

'We're in the harbour,' reported Gallagher, the Portofino bay behind him. 'The red dragons are all on schedule. We've downloaded considerable data, but we need another nine hours to get everything transferred.'

'I'm more concerned about Smith,' insisted Bonham. 'He's up there somewhere.'

Gallagher shook his head. 'We know he arrived at BirthPlace. That was the only route in. There's no sign of him there. But I agree . . . he's probably near us, somewhere nearby.'

Bonham ignored the cop-out. 'Biloxie?'

'Looking round the harbour.'

'I suggest you do the same. Find him.'

'Yes, sir.'

Bonham glanced out of the porthole as the plane

descended. 'We're descending in to Atlantic City. Smith'll be jumping levels as we speak. Forget the harbour. Get up to the church. Block him when he gets there. Things have changed since he was last there, four years ago. We've introduced new barriers, new dangers . . . da-dangers. If the dragons hurt him, cut him deep with their talons or their te-teeth, he'll have no choice but to JetPax back to Real-World. If he stays he'll be in a weakened state, and that could lead to him being wiped out in the Web. Just make sure he doesn't get through.'

'Are Biloxie and I in danger from the dragons?'

'No.'

Gallagher didn't believe Bonham. He looked across the harbour towards Biloxie. The bodyguard was crazy anyway, so pain was probably something he revelled in. It didn't need a hacker to work out he was there solely to protect Bonham. Gallagher realized that he himself was the dispensable member on this team. 'You coming down here?' he asked.

'No.' Bonham wanted to get to his offices where he could start to distance himself from any possible discovery of the InfoCalypse. 'You handle it. You and Biloxie. Do what's necessary.'

Gallagher lost contact with Bonham, and knew the security chief had terminated their link. He saw Biloxie crossing the square towards him, shaking his head as he went in. *No good, no contact.* Gallagher pointed up the hill towards the church, and Biloxie stopped, waited for Gallagher, who quick-marched over. Biloxie grinned a gap-toothed grin. At least someone was looking forward to the terrors ahead.

The three-plus hours since they'd commandeered Rose Cottage had passed slowly.

Giles Renreth had twice made excuses to leave the cottage, but John Mathews was adamant he stay put. The small circle of intelligence agents hovering outside justified Mathews's insistence, so Renreth remained, after checking with Norwich.

Mathews had just made another pot of tea for the house-sitters when one of the computers suddenly showed data being accessed and transferred. The farmer watched it, not understanding what was occurring, but aware that this was the first hint of such activity since he'd moved into the house. He hoped it was Conor and not just some outside agency tapping in. He wondered what the GameMaster was up to, but that was a world Mathews knew nothing about, nor wanted to. His world wasn't in this room, but in the country-side where he and Conor shared other, simpler pleasures.

Be safe, Conor.

Come back soon.

Who's going to shop for me?

He grinned and left the room with the tray, to join the others.

The computer continued to transfer data for a few moments more before it finally stopped.

The peace and quiet of the Norfolk countryside returned to Rose Cottage once more.

I felt more comfortable with the weapons I'd just down-loaded from Rose Cottage. I had another forged Hanwei samurai sword with Katana long tangs pinned with bamboo Mekings for security, a black scorch-proof cloak which would provide some protection from a flame-thrower and two high-powered 9mm automatics with explosive heads. I also carried four curved Gurkha kukri knives. My weapons were designed for close fighting and made of cold Chinese steel, as there would be very little warning when the dragons came for us.

I had similarly equipped Swilkin and the others, with the exception that the CIA man had a Chinese Dadio two-handed long-bladed carbon spring steel sword for any Chinese dragon and the two MIWs carried English cold steel broadswords for any European attackers.

'You ever handled one of these?' I asked Swilkin, who was ascending next in line.

'I told you, I already downloaded your program,' came the nervous answer. 'Do I need more software for this one?'

'You're covered.'

'Worth the money, then?'

I grinned. 'Means you'll have to use your own imagin-ation when something comes at you. The sword is strong, it cuts deep, and it'll protect you by leading your arm against those who attack you. But it can't think, only react. If you're under heavy attack, don't rely only on the sword to be able to protect you at all times. Think instinctively, and it'll respond immediately. It's only a program. Sophisticated, but with limitations.'

'Let me download something more sophisticated.'

'Too late. We need to go.'

I took the lead, ordering the others to stay as close to me as possible, with Tebor bringing up the rear, under strict instructions to ensure we were not taken by surprise.

It was a narrow pathway; cracked-terrazzo steps with high stone walls on one side and a sloping tree-lined slope on the other. For all its narrowness, I knew it got worse after we passed the church. Right now we were climbing the steps three abreast, but later we'd be forced into proceeding single file, with high stone walls on both sides. There was no other way to the top, since the rules of play were that any detour off the paths automatically JetPaxed us out of the game, and leave the two MIWs frozen in the Web.

'You've been here before?' said Swilkin.

'This place will have been re-programed many times over since I was last here.'

'What about the other two?' asked Swilkin.

'Street-wise and street-ready. They'll be OK.' Conor understood Swilkin's uneasiness. 'If you want out, now's the time. I won't be able to look after you once we're in the thick of things.'

'No,' came Swilkin's measured response. 'I mean, if I go back now, they realize I know too much. I may not even get a chance to explain what's going on. By the time I get someone to take me seriously the InfoCalypse will be downloaded and impossible to find. Then the *Titanic* will just be another big casino on the Brick. Sorry, but you're stuck with me now, Smith.'

We were nearing the top of the path, more than a hundred feet above the bay, when the first dragon appeared. It was a small earth dragon, fifteen metres long with a fifteen-metre wing-span, its scales lemon-yellow, its teeth bared and snarling.

'Keep in line,' I warned as we moved up the last few steps. 'Watch behind you, Tebor.'

The dragon swayed menacingly towards us. A small flame snaked out of its mouth, towards me. It was a weak flame because earth dragons never have the power of the fire dragons. I crouched down and let my scorch-proof cloak absorb the heat.

But there was no heat. I quickly looked up and caught a glimpse of the small bar-code on the scales under its chest. It was a clone: just a mirror-image of another dragon that was hidden elsewhere. I gave thanks to the ThemeCorp administrators who always insisted on leaving bar-codes in obvious places so that their inventory checks and mainten-ance staff could easily identify the stock. I never told my pupils, but often used the information to my advantage. Tricks of the trade.

'Keep walking,' I said. 'This one can't hurt you. But look out as we go through. There's another one waiting some-where.'

The dragon grew more menacing as we closed on it, beating its wings as we approached. Then it was upon us, tearing at me with its huge fangs. That was to no avail, was only a mirage, so we passed through quickly.

My sword was now in my hand; I slowed as we crested the top of the steps and stood in the small empty square in front of the church. Swilkin bumped into me, swore softly and stopped short. The earth dragon vanished, letting out a final roar of defiance.

'Spread out,' I said, spreading my hands to indicate a line on each side. 'Keep within three arms' length of each other. That way you won't hurt each other while you're swinging your swords. Try and hit the dragon's underbelly, that's usually its weak point. Otherwise just slash at any part of it, keep it protecting itself. Every hit counts, but don't use your guns unless you have to. The noise attracts other dragons and you'll be using up valuable ammunition.'

We spread out, Swilkin on my left, Andi and Tebor on my right.

Tebor saw it first, the same earth dragon, this time much larger, nearly twenty metres long with an equal wing-span. It came at him through the trees and down the slope. He dropped to his knees, presenting as small a target as possible, the scorch-proof cloak wrapped round him to protect him from the flames.

Our formation wheeled round, leaving Tebor on the flank. The youngster's sword tip was just visible through his cloak. He rolled himself up as small as possible and waited.

I realized what Tebor was doing and warned the others to keep their distance, to form in a line behind the teenager. The earth dragon caught a gust of breeze and lifted into the air as it cleared the tree line. It arched its body, lifted its head and released a fireball towards Andi. She shielded herself with her cloak as I jumped up and down, waving my sword, desperately trying to attract the dragon's attention. As it swooped down further, no more than six feet off the ground, it suddenly turned towards me.

'Shit,' cursed Swilkin as the yellow-scaled monster swung towards us.

'Keep the line,' I shouted as I held my sword forward towards the oncoming beast.

Tebor hurled himself upwards, the broadsword lunging into the dragon's chest as it passed overhead.

'Hang on to your sword, hang on, whatever you do,' I screamed as I saw the dragon shudder in the air, the thrust of Tebor's sword cutting deep, forcing it to crash to the ground as it arched its long neck, trying desperately to see what had struck it and caused such pain.

Tebor, hanging on as instructed, was thrown violently into the air, and rolled with the fallen dragon as he refused to let go the sword handle. I rushed towards them and thrust my Hanwei into the dragon's neck, holding it there while blood spurted from the creature's wounds. Swilkin, unsure of himself, tried to join in with his sword upraised, but was knocked away by the dragon's flailing wing. The dragon thrashed, weakened and died, trapped by the two swords that pinned it to the ground. As always, when it died, it vanished into the matrix.

'Well done,' I congratulated Tebor. 'As good as any GameMaster,' I added, genuinely impressed with the youngster's quick instincts.

Tebor smiled, pleased with himself. 'Foo,' he said. 'Foo Foo.'

'Keep away from their wings,' I advised Swilkin. 'Go for areas where they don't have much defence. Are you hurt?'

Swilkin held up his arm. There was a small blood flow from the cut under his elbow. It wasn't deep, but must have stung ferociously. 'I'm OK,' was his response.

I turned to the yellow-faced San Giorgio church, then walked towards its green doors. The others followed me. There was no need to warn them to stay vigilant, since the dragon attack had focused their minds. Their swords drawn, they moved as one across the small square.

'There'll be a key, or a password, somewhere. We need to find that to gain access to the Enchanted Castle.'

'What're we looking for?' asked Swilkin.

'Don't know – but that dragon was only the first line of defence. Just stay cool.'

'Jim's laid the clue,' said Andi.

I looked at her and she smiled back, warm but not totally connected.

'Hey, look at this,' observed Swilkin as he climbed the three small steps, with Tebor following.

'That's the clue,' said an excited Tebor. 'I found the clue. I got the clue.'

I followed him up the steps and peered at the two green doors. The left one had carvings of a crucified Christ and, under it, St George on his horse killing a dragon with his lance. The right-hand door had carvings of Adam and Eve in the Garden of Eden; Adam handed Eve an apple while the serpent wrapped itself round the tree trunk and slid down into the earth. The carving below it was of a shepherd watching his flock while a man approached from behind, clearly intent on bludgeoning him with the club he carried.

'Cain and Abel,' said Swilkin. 'Does that mean one of us is a traitor here?'

I ignored him and told Tebor to calm down. "The clues don't come that easy,' I said. 'Just keep your eyes peeled for trouble.

'We going in?' asked Swilkin.

'Of course.' I decided to leave Tebor on watch. 'Stay here, by the door, and watch the square. If anything comes up, yell.'

'But I want to go in with you,' he grumbled, suddenly.

'I want you here because I trust you, OK?'

Tebor nodded, slightly mollified by the responsibility that I'd bestowed on him.

I was the first to enter the church. It was as stark and simple inside as it was outside; just as I remembered it. Whitewashed walls with simple adornments; the lofty arched ceiling was equally white. The red and white tiled floor led to a white marbled altar at the far end, above which loomed a huge gloomy dark cross. Five rows of pews stretched back towards the doors through which we entered. I took it easy as I warily crossed towards the altar. The other two were still beside me, each facing the adjacent wall as they advanced, crablike, towards the far end of the church.

We climbed the three marble steps to the altar itself, pushing open the small double metal-grille gates that protected it. The cross, embellished with gold crowns on each arm, held the crucified figure of Christ with a crown of thorns. Six large candles stood below his image, three on each side, and between them was a marble figure of St

George mounted on his horse and slaying the dragon. Two marble cherubs, on each side of the altar, completed the tableau, each holding a bowl of fruit in their hands. Nothing had changed from what I remembered apart from those cherubs.

'Look familiar?' I asked Swilkin, remembering that he had visited the actual chapel in Italy.

'Exactly like in RealWorld. Now what?'

'That's for us to find out.' I checked the entrance, saw Tebor crouching behind the door keeping a watchful eye on the empty square beyond. 'Stay by the altar,' I said and went back into the main body of the church.

A painted wooden carving on the left wall attracted me first. I scoured it for clues, then dismissed it. Its centrepiece depicted a man in bishop's vestments; the four side panels were simple images of local dignitaries in biblical dress. Babies emerged from under the bishop's cloak but the other paintings had only adults in each one. Above this carving was an arched painting with a representation of Christ in heaven summoning the little children to him. Religion protected all the babies in the world below whilst those who died in infancy automatically went to heaven. Standard fare of Italian churches: heavy on death and the loss of innocence.

The painting on the opposite wall was much darker, the colours faded in its intensity. There a knight sat on a rock with the head of a monster at his feet, probably another depiction of St George. The knight wore full armour, a white horse waiting behind him, while the setting sun cast a saint-like halo around his head. I remembered this picture from before, and I remembered ignoring it then.

The last time I got here, the dragon had waited for me to enter, poised motionless next to a statue in a wall niche. There it had lain in wait behind a multi-coloured tapestry, then rushed me as I passed.

But there were no drapery to hide behind this time, just

the white walls. And the statue. I approached it cautiously, my hand on the sword under my cloak. Standing on a white marble plinth, the figure was no more than two feet high. Made of metal and painted gold, it showed St George, this time wearing a turban, about to hack at the dragon with his sword. In his other hand, he held a lance, which had pierced the dragon that now lay sprawled under him, one foot planted on the monster to hold it down.

More death. Everything in the church represented death; the crucifix, the paintings, the panels on the doors, even the statues.

In front of the plinth stood a row of twelve electric candles. They were unlit but underneath them was a sign reading OFFERTA, and a creditcard reader. A sign nearby said it accepted American Express, EuroExpress, MasterCard and Visa, but no personal cheques and no cash.

I took out my black Amex card. 'Keep your eyes open, everyone,' I warned. I swiped the card. Fourteen US dollars were charged to my account. Nothing happened until the transaction cleared. The rear right bulb came on.

'You may pray now,' said a microphoned voice from behind the statue. 'No more than thirty seconds is allowed unless you use your card again.'

Death.

Everything was about death.

Except the cherubs.

They were offering food.

They were offering life.

I swung round to face the altar as the lights in the candle holders now lit up, one after another.

'Get away from the altar,' I yelled a warning.

They reacted too slowly, startled by my sudden urgency.

Behind them, another twenty-four candles sparked to life as the cherubs began changing form. The right-one turned into a hydra, that first ever dragon from the days of Greek gods, a monstrous, gigantic, multi-headed beast. Its head split into six heads, as it had done in legend since its origins in the swamps of Lerna, and reared up to attack its closest adversary, who happened to be Swilkin. He jumped backwards, staggering to avoid falling over as he tried to fend it off with his sword.

The other cherub transformed itself into a thick, scaly serpent with a dragon's head. It slid slowly down the altar and snaked across the floor towards Andi. Swilkin regained his footing and slashed wildly at the Hydra, hitting its nearest head, slicing through it from eye to jaw. As he paused, his sword held in front of him, ready to slash again, the head split apart and, where there had been one, there now appeared two gnashing serpents. Swilkin shut his eyes and swung his weapon once more, wild and hard, slashing with all the force he could muster. He felt the Chinese sword's double-headed blade shudder as it met, and cut through scaly flesh. He felt sure he'd hurt the monster, knew he'd cut deep. Swilkin opened his eyes, the sword already drawn back for another thrust. But this time the force of his blow had continued on through two heads, severing the first and gashing deep into the second.

'Yeeaahhh.' He screamed with success, and moved forward, his heart pumping with new found bravery.

The two heads he had destroyed quickly re-formed into four. The Hydra reared up and spread out its now nine heads like wings, ready to attack its aggressor and tear him to shreds. Swilkin spun sideways as the monster swooped, falling against the side wall where the saint's effigy stood.

'All its heads are immortal, except one,' I yelled, as I sprang alongside Swilkin, my sword raised. He pulled himself up again as the Hydra spun round. 'We should spread out, attack it from each side.'

Swilkin lurched away from me, then again stood his ground. The Hydra recoiled, reared up as it prepared to attack its enemies. Four of the heads turned towards Swilkin, and five towards me. It braced itself on its four feet, ready to resume the attack.

'Which head's mortal?' asked Swilkin.

'No idea,' I shouted. As we positioned ourselves for the new onslaught, I heard Andi scream as the dragon-headed serpent flicked its tail and knocked her sprawling. She tried to hack at it with her broadsword but the beast's tail wrapped itself round her, starting to squeeze the life out of her.

The Hydra continued its attack at the same time. In that moment of attack, in that split second, I noticed one head hold back a bit, not lunging with the ferocity of the others. I wasn't sure but I had to take this chance, otherwise all could be soon lost. I ducked under the first two heads, felt their scaly necks grating against me, then lunged my sword straight into the right eye of the third head, which then twisted aside in pain to leave a small gap through which I could see the head that still held back.

The Hydra by now had worked out my ploy, and all the other heads jerked backwards to protect the vulnerable one. They forgot about Swilkin as they swirled round to concentrate only on me, teeth bared and ready to tear me apart. But I'd already thrown myself forward, my Japanese sword thrust forward like a spear, and thus I pierced the Hydra head that shielded itself behind all the others. My sword struck true; the sharp end pierced above its nostrils, slid along the gristle, went under the left eye and entered the brain.

Realizing what I was up to, Swilkin threw himself at the Hydra's diverted heads and hacked away at them furiously. The screaming monster, now under attack from all sides, tried to fight back in panic, then realized all was in vain and finally tried to break free of us. That was useless, as Swilkin, now joined by Tebor, moved in to kill the wounded Hydra.

I squeezed out of the way and rushed towards Andi. By

now the serpent had engulfed her, its large, flat-topped head held high, its bared fangs ready to strike. I couldn't use my sword in case I struck her in error, and didn't have time to reach for either my automatic or my kukris. Desperately I threw myself at the serpent, which was all I could think of doing, a frantic response to the situation. As its head struck down, about to bury its fangs in her unprotected face, I forced my left arm under its scaly neck and tried to throw it off balance with my sheer weight. Adrenalin pumping, I clung on, trying to pull the giant snake's head away from Andi. All the while she struggled to free herself, but the serpent held her tight as it tried to break away from my grip.

Meanwhile it tightened its hold and started to squeeze the life out of her. I slid a kukri out from under my cloak with my free hand, then I arched myself backwards and rammed the knife straight into the snake's mouth. I twisted it sharply, felt a fang gouge my arm, then pulled the knife out and thrust it under the great reptile's jaw, pushing it up until it entered the roof of the beast's mouth. The snake lashed about wildly but I held the knife firmly, saw blood trickling down its scales and onto the floor. Then it stopped writhing. All was over. The serpent slid away, loosening its grip on Andi. She coughed violently, fought to catch her breath, struggled to free herself from its deadly embrace.

By now the Hydra was also in its death throes. I could only lie there, gasping, my energy levels well out of the green, as I watched Swilkin and Tebor finish the creature off. Then there were just four of us in the room again.

The little church had no trace of blood, nothing that might be evidence of the horrors that had just passed. I pulled myself upright. There were now no cherubs on the altar.

'You all OK?' I asked breathlessly.

When I had their assurances, I checked round and noticed a small door behind the altar had swung open onto a bright exterior. It was time to move on.

'It's not over yet,' I warned them. 'Stay close and keep careful watch. It can only get worse from now on.'

I led them out of the church and into the sunlight. A red dragon passed overhead, on its way to the castle above with its valuable data cargo.

THE MIDAS TOUCH CASINO
THE BOARDWALK
ATLANTIC CITY
EASTERN SEABOARD
REALWORLD
REAL TIME: ZERO PLUS 17 HRS AND 53 MINS

Dom Murphy was waiting on the Vue-Link to speak to Bonham as soon as he entered the ThemeCorp Administration offices on the 83rd floor, high above the vast casino and the hotel rooms that served it.

'News?' he asked the Security Chief.

'I have a report that Smith recently used his credit card in the Portofino Church. The next report from the matrix confirmed that they'd crossed into the graveyard behind.'

'Why would they go there?'

'No idea because, logically, I would've expected them to climb straight up to the castle. Smith knows that's where the centre is.'

'Your people?'

'Waiting for him.'

'Why would they go into the graveyard?'

'Either Smith's getting too clever or Jim has set something in motion that we know nothing about.'

'Any ideas?'

'None whatsoever . . . wh-whatsoever. We could stop the download, destroy the evidence, and no one would be any the wiser.'

Murphy thought this through. 'No,' he said finally. 'We haven't come this far to throw it all away. How much longer will the download take?'

'Few more hours.'

'We soldier on. Just make sure your men get Smith in time.'

'And if they don't?'

'Then abort. But only if you're absolutely convinced that we can't protect the InfoCalypse.'

The cemetery, like the church it served, was simple. It looked down on the blue waters of the bay, its white alabaster and marble graves laid out in neat rows, most of them decorated with small, colourful bunches of flowers.

Forming a square around the periphery were simple wall vaults, standing five high, all faced with nameplates for those buried inside. Each of these walls held nearly two hundred coffins, and many had flowers hanging from the nameplates in simple glass containers. I walked round cautiously, searching for any clue, while the others simply meandered about the graveyard.

It was Swilkin who eventually called me over. He was standing next to the only really large mausoleum within the cemetery. It stood six feet high, white marble worn with age, and was crowned with a simple dome on which rested a large bouquet of red and pink roses.

The legend on the side simply read

IRENA MATEO
6–6–1872
10–5–1951

At the front of the tomb stood a marble stone block, across which, in age-stained green marble, was draped a long-haired young girl with her eyes closed. The sad pose, and the girl's tragic demeanour had been well captured by the sculptor.

Under it ran a simple inscribed message:

ANDREA
14–3–2009
14–3–2044

From the similarity of the statue, there was little doubt that the girl on this faded tomb was Andi herself.

'You note the date?' said Swilkin quietly, now crouching at my side.

I nodded.

He stood up. 'You going to mention this?'

'I don't think so. If she already knows, there's nothing we can do. Otherwise, why frighten her.'

'I guess this is the clue we're looking for.'

'Yes, it must be.'

'You don't sound surprised.'

'It's what I feared.'

'So now we just wait.'

I walked back towards the church. It was all coming together. I knew why that tomb bore today's date, but decided not to enlighten the others. I had to keep my emotions in check, as we could only succeed if I stayed dispassionate. Tebor grinned at me, as if expecting something exciting to happen.

I caught up with Andi near the rear to the church.

'What's next on this fun tour you've arranged?' she asked, head cocked sideways, gently mocking.

'Can't tell you. It's a magical mystery tour. Just for you.'

I caught a movement out of the corner of my eye. Tebor was moving towards us, walking fast and with purpose. I saw the automatic in his hand, and he was lifting it towards me. I shoved Andi aside and pulled out my own automatic, swung it up and aimed straight at the teenager. Tebor pulled the trigger and I felt the bullet pass over my shoulder. I heard it explode, and then I had no choice. I shot Tebor in the chest, then in the head, but not before he released one more shot at me. I felt a sharp twinge as it nicked my shoulder, even closer this time. I heard it explode behind me.

Andi screamed as Tebor flipped over backwards, falling across one of the graves. 'You wiped him,' she yelled at me.

'He tried to kill me,' I said. I watched Tebor helplessly. The Hungarian boy didn't even flicker, now frozen in the matrix.

I knew he was gone forever.

'Are you fucked, or something?' cursed Swilkin, running over.

I put my arm round Andi, who was gulping for deep breath as sudden shock took over. She pushed me away, turning aside, her body racked with sobs.

'He came at me with a gun,' I defended myself to Swilkin. 'I had no choice.'

Swilkin pointed towards the church. 'That's why he pulled the gun.'

I swivelled round and saw the serpent. Obviously we hadn't killed it, and it had followed us out into the cemetery. It had been right behind me, probably poised to strike, when Tebor had seen it and took it out.

I slumped to the ground, my head falling to my chest. I felt like absolute shit.

'You wiped him out,' moaned Andi. 'You wiped him out.'

'I didn't see that thing. I thought he was aiming at me.'

'Why would he do that? Why would Tebor ever hurt you?'

'I thought he was trying to kill me.'

She stopped her sobbing, knelt in front of me and lifted my face so she could look straight into my eyes.

'We must finish what we started,' she then said calmly.

'I thought he was – '

She put her finger against my lip to silence me.

'He'll be OK. One day, we'll all be OK.'

'I'm so sorry,' I burbled.

'We can't finish it without you. You've always known what we must do. You must take us there.'

Swilkin stood next to us. 'Where?' he asked.

'Up there,' she answered, pointing to the castle. 'To finish what we started.'

Clancy came through the door to find the President at his desk, with Meisner seated opposite him.

'So what happened?' asked Dixon.

'No idea yet, sir.'

'Where did all these people go?'

'Into the matrix.'

'You don't just go into the matrix,' protested a frustrated Meisner. 'Not unless you've got the necessary protocols.'

'ThemeCorp do have the necessary protocols,' replied Clancy.

'You suggesting that Dom Murphy's people are involved in this somehow?' asked a disbelieving President Dixon.

Clancy spoke carefully. 'We have no other leads right now. Remember, *Titanic* is ThemeCorp property. Conor Smith is a ThemeCorp employee. The matrix they broke was on board the *Titanic*, which is under ThemeCorp maintenance.'

'What about Gallagher and the big nasty he was with?'

'Biloxie, Mr President,' informed Clancy. 'We matched his ID from a picture we took just before he disappeared into the matrix, and he's the third link. He works for Malcolm Bonham, who's head of security and a director of ThemeCorp. He's also a GameMaster. Paul Gallagher didn't work for ThemeCorp, but he spent a long time on the GameMaster induction programs. Under the tutelage of Conor Smith, whom he brought in to this right at the beginning. I guess the final connection is that they also own the copyright to Marilyn Monroe.'

568

'What's in it for ThemeCorp?' asked the President quietly.

'I have no idea.'

Teddy Dixon suddenly slammed his fist on the table. 'I'm the President of the United States and yet I seem to have absolutely no control over what's going on!'

The other two looked awkwardly at each other.

For the first time since it all began, the President had finally spoken the truth.

It wasn't a long climb up to the castle. The path was steep, not stepped this time, but broken-tiled with a red mosaic drain running down the middle. Tall stone walls went up on both sides and the passageway was narrow so that two could rarely move up it side-by-side.

I took one last look down towards the harbour and the town. Even at this moment of drama, when all could be soon lost, when the unnecessary death of Tebor still affected me, I felt the beauty of the view calm and absorb me. Azure water, deep green trees and multi-coloured houses splattered the hillside. DreamVille. PleasantVille. I felt a glow inside me when I realized this was just as it appeared in RealWorld.

Goodbye Portofino. I'll come and visit you for real . . . if I get back. I liked to have a purpose when I entered the unknown, a target to aim for.

I took one last look at the blue sky, with its soft foamy white clouds, then collected myself and turned up the hill leading to the castle. Clouds began to threaten rain at the top of the hill, their dark shadow rapidly cloaking the castle. As we climbed more red dragons passed overhead on their route to the top.

The castle perched on top of the hill at the highest point in the bay. It had a small round keep on the right, adjoining a square residential area with high windows looking out over the town. The sides of the castle dropped to a sheer cliff face nearly two hundred feet high. An inner bailey stretched off to the left, once again with deep battlements following the cliff edge.

Two flat-topped Mediterranean pines grew in the middle of the bailey, both about thirty feet high. It was to this open courtyard that the red dragons were flying. The trees, through which we now followed the narrow path, grew thickly up the sides of the steep hill to protect it from attack.

I went first, Andi second, and Swilkin brought up the rear. We moved vigilantly with swords at the ready, my biggest fear being that an enemy would drop from the hillside and lunge at us when we had little room to manoeuvre. But the narrow path was also our strength, for it would restrict any easy movement by a larger predator.

The one person I didn't expect to see was Gallagher. But I now knew it was him who had targeted me. I'd been part of the plan as soon as President Dixon was kidnapped. The Secret Service man came down the path towards us, holding his arms up, so we could see he wasn't armed. He bled from his mouth and had a gash across his right cheek and ear. He even limped as he approached us.

'Stay where you are, Paul,' I cautioned, tilting my sword up as a warning. 'Keep your eyes skinned,' I told the others. 'Don't be put off guard.'

'I thought you'd never get here,' said Gallagher, his face flooding with apparent relief.

'Cut the games,' I replied. 'What're you playing at?'

'Nothing at all. I came here with Biloxie. He says you know him. They think I'm helping them, but Biloxie attacked me. Have you any idea what's going on?'

'You tell me.'

'They're downloading the InfoCalypse. It's ThemeCorp who are behind it. *Your* people, Conor.'

'Not *my* people. Why did you try and get me turned in, back there on the Brick?'

'I had no choice. I was following my own leads. If I'd

571

stayed down there helping you I couldn't have followed what they were doing. That was my priority.' Gallagher turned to Swilkin. 'Tell him, Dwight. Tell him how we'd decided to follow it through.'

'Keep me out of this,' replied Swilkin. 'I don't know where anybody fits in this business any more.'

'I know all about you and the Dundee Society. And about Nelson, Murphy, even Keebles. Do you know about all that, Conor?'

'I know.' I signalled him to back up. 'Just keep moving backwards, Paul. Right now I am not going to break our formation – not till we're in the clear. I'm not interested in who's doing what.'

'You're crazy.'

'I am. Crazy enough to hurt unless you start going back up that hill. Tell me what's up there.'

'A castle.' He finally retreated, walking backwards, watching his step.

'I know that. But who's waiting for us?'

'Biloxie. I don't know what else. Probably more dragons, more cyber-monsters to send you back to RealWorld.'

'Why did Biloxie attack you?'

Gallagher shrugged. 'Because he didn't believe me, suddenly decided I was on your side. He just went for me with his knife. I was lucky to get away. I need some weapons, Conor. I can't face whatever's up there with my bare hands.'

'You should've thought of that when you came up here with Biloxie.'

'Didn't have time – not to prepare myself. I just wanted to find out what was going on. I see the boy's gone.' I ignored him and he continued, 'Why the girl, Conor? Why's she up here?'

'She's a great fighter, that's why.'

'Like hell. MIWs don't ever go into these games. One mistake and they're wiped out. That what happened to the boy?'

I ignored him as we came to an opening at the foot of the castle entrance, just below the battlements.

'Where'd you leave Biloxie?' I asked Gallagher.

Gallagher pointed to the ten steep stairs that led to a stone-walled corridor sloping up to an open wooden door. 'Last saw him there.'

'So what happened between you?' I repeated, my eyes searching behind him. I saw the ceiling of what looked like a small vestibule, with a window straight beyond. It was, so far, exactly as I remembered it.

'I told you, he got suspicious.'

'Why?'

'He told me he'd killed Nelson and Keebles. Made it look like suicide.'

'He told you that?'

'Yeah. He was very proud that he'd got away with it. Same with your Datakeeper friend.'

'How'd you get mixed up in this?'

'I'm protecting –'

'Don't treat me like a fool, Paul.'

'I know. I . . .'

'Just tell me . . . or get out. I don't have time to mess around.' I moved threateningly towards him, my sword aimed straight at his chest.

Gallagher shrugged. 'I'm in intelligence, Conor. I gave information, about the White House or anything else that might help ThemeCorp. I wasn't spying. I did it because ThemeCorp is a US company interested in protecting its profits.'

'And making some for you, too,' commented a disgusted Swilkin behind me.

Gallagher brushed it aside. 'That's the world we live in. When the President got taken, I never dreamed it was ThemeCorp responsible. But the continuous reference to the InfoCalypse worried me. Then Bonham called, said I had to protect them, that the President hadn't been in any real danger. I asked if it was to do with the InfoCalypse and he wouldn't answer. Just told me to make sure you' – he indicated me – 'or anyone related to you didn't get into *Titanic*. That's when I realized that it was all about the ship.'

I knew he was lying; all built round half truths. But that was for later. 'What's waiting for us up in the castle?'

'You tell us. You've been here before.'

'Things change. Program's are continually re-written.'

'Biloxie's crazy. He suddenly turned on me, claimed I was a plant.'

'Why?'

'I said you guys shouldn't be hurt. But he said you knew too much, then he attacked me. I was near that door' – he pointed to the double doors – 'and I managed to get out. Christ, Conor, I'm trying to help. I hurt like hell. That bastard really hurt me.'

'Prove it, ordered Swilkin. 'Go in first.'

'Why?'

'To keep Biloxie confused. Give us time to surprise him.'

'If you want,' answered Gallagher weakly.

'We do,' I joined in. 'You lead. We'll follow.'

Gallagher took one final look at the three of us, and saw that we meant it. 'Madness,' he muttered, then turned and climbed the stairs.

We kept our same formation as we followed him, towards the open doorway under the round keep. Gallagher entered the castle vestibule, while we kept a safe distance behind.

The hallway was empty. There was one staircase on the right, just beyond the rise of three steps that cut right across the middle of the room. The walls, as in the church below, were simple and white. A chunky blue-and-white porcelain wood-burner stood on legs in front of these three steps. The window I'd seen from below was actually one of a pair, side by side, with arched tops and stained-glass windows. They were at the far end of the hall and I noticed the images on them were of dragons, one an earth dragon, the other a water dragon. These were the only references in the vestibule to dragons – very much like the last time I'd been here. The first attack on me then had come from those windows, when both paintings had erupted into real dragons. That was unlikely to happen now, since they wouldn't repeat the same program for me.

So the wood-burner was the only difference in this room from my last visit. I went past Gallagher to the three steps and looked up the staircase. Nothing. It was there I felt the heat of the woodburner, and was surprised that it was being used on such a warm day.

I then motioned for Gallagher to climb the stairs. I wanted him ahead of me, not behind. The Secret Service man looked nervously around him, then shook his head.

'You're the GameMaster,' he said. 'You go first.'

'Stay close to me.' Having no choice, I started up the stairs. 'You watch our rear, Dwight, and make sure you stay five steps behind Gallagher. If he does anything unusual, just take him out.'

I didn't wait for an answer and started up the stairs. Up above, where the stairs turned left, I noticed a bright, orange glow. I suddenly sensed what was waiting for me, and the hairs stood up on the back of my neck.

I heard the roar, that unique roar, and recognized it. The Golden Dragon was waiting for us in the small round room with the simple round antique table and the four velvet chairs, at the top of the tower.

This was the Room of Peace, the final goal for those reaching the topmost level in the Valley of the Dragons. It was the room that only I myself had ever reached during a game, and where the sole reward was to sit at that table and look out of the small square window on to Portofino below – and know one had achieved the unachievable.

That was the ultimate satisfaction, the ultimate peace.

And for a brief moment, all those years ago, I'd seen the

Golden Dragon, its reflection in the mirror that hung next to the fireplace. It was as beautiful as anyone could describe, beyond perfection, an object of total serenity and peace. And satisfaction. But I'd seen only its reflection in that golden moment when I'd achieved my place in the Room of Peace.

I shook off the memory, took a deep breath and climbed the remaining stairs. Andi moved round Gallagher and closed up behind me. I turned at the landing and opened the door leading into the Room of Peace. Nothing had changed.

I entered cautiously, my sword at the ready. I don't know what they'd planned, but *please don't make me fight the Golden Dragon.* It was one of the purest programs ever written, its purity and very being surpassing the glitz and waste of dreams underlying the ideology that built the Brick.

The room was again filled with a golden glow, but it was empty.

'Can you feel it?' Andi said behind me.

'Yes.'

The presence was still there.

We both sensed its strength, its purity.

'I'm nearly home,' she said, smiling up at me.

We heard the roar together, then Swilkin rushed in behind us. 'Gallagher got away from me,' he yelled.

An ugly, primeval roar surged up the stairs and into the room, telling of anger, fury, hatred. Then Gallagher burst in, too, his face white and full of fear. 'Biloxie,' he screeched. 'The woodburner.'

That was it. Biloxie, with his access to the matrix, had transformed himself into the woodburner that stood in the hall downstairs. That's why it had been so warm; it had absorbed whatever deadly apparition Biloxie had metamorphosed his avatar into.

When it now appeared, it was the worst, most ferocious sight I could imagine. The SatanDragon, shiny black with a thirty-feet wingspan, muscular legs and fore-limbs, fangs over two feet long with hollow cores through which it oozed venom, bright yellow eyes with black centres, a ribbed yellow chest and long talons that could hold and rip through any mortal being. The hood around its thick neck was vast, and its demeanour spoke of only death and destruction. This dragon had no intention of taking any prisoners.

As its head entered the room, it belched a fireball straight towards us. We threw ourselves flat on the floor, covering ourselves with our ScorchCloaks, but even through that resilient material I could feel an intense heat and smell burning. We wouldn't survive another such fireball.

I heard another, but more familiar roar. For a brief moment, there was silence. Then two, very different roars shook the floor we crouched on. I lifted my cloak to see what had occurred. The small room had become like a tight cage as the two dragons began to hurl themselves at each other.

One was the SatanDragon, the epitome of evil. The other was the Golden Dragon, the bravest and purest and most beautiful of all of its kind. It was even more beautiful than I'd ever imagined. And it was defending us against the SatanDragon. That's because the Golden Dragon's program could not be altered; it could only fight for what it believed in, for what it represented and what it had to protect. There was no fear in it, no compromise.

Wrapped round each other in that tight space, the pair of them crunched their fangs ferociously into each other, ripped at each other with their talons, gouged and tore at exposed flesh, and were only united in their hatred of each other. With no room to fly, their wings were crushed against each other and the walls behind. Claws and teeth became their sole weapons. The din was overwhelming, as the blood started flowing and they thrashed around brutally, each with the sole intent of destroying the other.

But the Golden Dragon was at an obvious disadvantage; its superior bulk and size too constrained in the small space.

Then the SatanDragon gained the final advantage as it twisted its head and bit deeply into the opponent's neck, injecting its deadly venom. The SatanDragon clung on, however, gripping its struggling opponent tightly, even whilst the poison took effect. Finally the Golden Dragon gave a final, room-shaking shudder, and died. The Satan-Dragon just lay there, its fangs still buried in the rival's golden scales, desperately waiting for its own strength to return.

Eventually it turned to face us, exuding a vile hatred as it prepared to destroy us. We were clearly now lost; my puny armaments no more effective than a plastic toy against a Panzer tank. I rose and moved towards the SatanDragon, my sword held out in front of me. Maybe, just maybe, while it was still weak, I could pierce its eyes, blind it, just create enough time to give us a breathing space.

'Get out', I yelled to the others. 'Get away from here.'

'Kill it first,' warned Swilkin.

'You can't. Dragons don't die, they just get weaker for a while.'

Then Andi said quietly and simply, 'The Golden Dragon will save us.'

I turned round to stare at her.

'Use the card,' she said.

The card. What card?

'*My* card,' she said.

Jim's card? Jim was still with us. He and Andi had become one.

I reached in my pocket, fumbled around and found it. The card that had cut through the painting in *Titanic* and had been our entrance pass in to the Valley of the Dragons.

'Where? Where do I use it?'

'The Golden Dragon needs space. To beat its enemies, it needs freedom to fly.'

Of course. The small room had put the Golden Dragon at a serious disadvantage. Its very size was its weakness here.

The card glowed in my hand. Andi turned and squeezed my arm from behind, and I saw where we were through her eyes. I knelt down and deliberately sliced the floor with the edge of the card; it was like a hard-steel sword cutting through butter. The Golden Dragon was stirring, even though the SatanDragon still had its fangs buried in its neck. The SatanDragon couldn't hold on to its prey; even in its weakened state it had to somehow stop me. It dragged itself up, releasing its grip. The Golden Dragon thrashed around, still weak, but struggling to recover its balance.

'Get close to the wall,' I shouted at Swilkin. 'Hold on to something.'

Then I ran towards the two dragons, sliding the edge of the glowing card along the floor. It was just like filleting a fish.

The floor burst open under us and I looked down into an abyss. Into blackness. A vast eternal darkness that fell away forever. But this wasn't a Dark Area.

I moved backwards, stepping away from the floor that was opening up under me. Andi still clung to me and I heard a shout from Swilkin somewhere behind us.

As my eyes focused, I could see what filled the blackness below. The sides were supported by Gothic arches that fell away into nothing. There were huge arches with stone stepways that bridged across them. I remembered them: the original Dungeons and Dragons game, now forgotten and locked away under the Portofino castle. Red dragons, with their precious cargoes of data, were lined up on some of the walkways.

Thousands of disks stacked like old vinyl records, each more than ten metres wide, were spinning as they recorded the quantum digital information that was currently being unloaded. I'd seen such disks before at ThemeCorp Utility Center, where they ran the multi-programs for the various games sites. But those disks were smaller, no more than two metres wide, and they could download over five pentabytes a second – that's five hundred thousand terabytes. These babies would be up to five Exabytes, more than half a million pentabytes.

This was unreal.

'Entanglement Arrays,' shouted Swilkin.

He was right. Simple everyday storage was solid state, but for this amount of instant data movement a quantum computer needed photon entanglement. It was a simple system. Each disk was made of diamonds, now mass produced by the Americans from highly refined graphite. These diamonds had a tetrahedral structure of carbon atoms. At regular intervals, some of the atoms were replaced by fluorine atoms – the same stuff that we still used in toothpaste. Then the disks were interrogated by DyeLasers which entangled the fluorine structure in to a readable format.

The disks were now clearly visible, a bright diamond haze covering them. They'd looked black when I first saw them because of the vast darkness they were sealed in. They needed the dark, since any stray light photons would interact with the fluorine and destroy the energy flow. And I had just sliced open this protective darkness with Jim's card.

Two things happened at the same time. Gallagher grabbed my hand and tried to wrench the card out of it. The SatanDragon hurled itself across the void that separated us, its fangs bared, its wings extended, its massive claws reaching towards me. A sword flashed to my right, and Gallagher screamed. His arm fell away though his hand was still wrapped around my wrist.

Swilkin had swung his Dadio carbon steel sword and severed Gallagher's hand from the rest of him. Gallagher swung round, with his back to me, clutching his handless arm with the other. He didn't speak to me, but over my shoulder to Andi.

'It'll kill you,' he shouted at her. 'You'll never get out of here. You'll be wiped out in the matrix. Did Jim Nelson send you? What is it you have to do?'

The SatanDragon hurtled itself through the air towards me. It didn't seem to matter to it that Gallagher stood between us. I held out the Hanwei samurai sword, point first towards the approaching monster.

'She's the destroyer,' Gallagher cried out.

The SatanDragon reached down, grabbed him and spun him onto his back, tossing him to the floor on my right. The cavity was still opening up, reaching out towards all four walls. The dragon crouched over Gallagher and let out another wild roar.

'Help me, help me,' he screamed. 'For Christ sake tell me why you're here.'

The SatanDragon lifted its claw and drove a long talon into Gallagher's stomach.

'Tell him before he kills me,' shrieked Gallagher.

Stupidly, but that's how I am, I threw myself forward, my sword flashing as I ran at the SatanDragon. I slashed at its claws, then rolled over as the monster lunged at me. I grabbed Gallagher's other hand and banged the JetPax that sent him back to RealWorld.

'No, no,' he screamed vainly, but it was too late, and he disappeared from under his tormentor.

He'd led me in to this. He himself wasn't in real danger. He wanted the SatanDragon to get me, and he'd have a lot to answer for when I got back. But the SatanDragon had other ideas. It lunged towards me and I slashed again, making the beast rear back. It was still covered in blood and deep cuts, but they'd heal quickly. The hole in the floor was still expanding; there was now no way I could stop it. The SatanDragon saw the danger, stretched its wings and plunged into the abyss. Its strength had returned; it could now fly.

The creature snarled again, falling away, swooped downwards to build up speed, then turned to attack me from below. I waited till it was close, then rolled over to my left and slid away, pulled my automatic from under my cloak, and squeezed the trigger for rapid fire. The six explosive bullets chewed into the dragon, slowed it down but didn't stop it. However, it was enough delay for me to escape the danger as it turned again, and glided down into the gloom. I stood up and watched it level out and hold its position.

We both knew what would happen next. The floor finally disappeared and the three of us fell into the darkness, tumbling and rolling towards the spinning diamond disks, with their sharp edges. I thought I heard laughter coming up towards me, then I recognized its brutal harshness. The laughter was real. Biloxi was the SatanDragon.

Andi still clung to me, and Swilkin, well out of his normal remit, tumbled alongside me, his sword held ready.

'Use your JetPax,' I yelled.

He shook his head; he was a brave man.

I couldn't do it either. Not until I knew death was imminent. Whatever the pain, I would persevere.

The DyeLaser beams jounced off the disks like crazy lights bouncing off a frenzied ballroom discoGlobe. A red dragon flew past and landed on the first walkway. The damp slate walls and vast buttresses were vaguely outlined in the gloom as the light from above hit the vast space around us. Most of the original dungeons were still in place, entrance holes that opened into passages running back from the walls. The huge area that now housed the spinning disks had been the centre of the immense castle that had once been the core of the game. ThemeCorp must have built the Valley of the Dragons around the castle and re-used much of the existing software to replicate sections of smaller castles in the new game. Then, I guess, they had used the hollowed-out centre to build their new storage facility.

The SatanDragon flew close, but he already knew we were doomed. I swore I could see Biloxi's face staring at me as I tumbled on down. We were now past the first few disks, but drifting closer to one of the stacks. I could hear the whirr of the razor-sharp edges as they flashed closer and closer, They would slice us to pieces as soon as we hit them.

I was more worried about Andi than myself. I could easily JetPax out, but she'd be totally lost to me. At least the damage now being done to the disks by the stray light photons would set their whole operation back by months, if not years. They would never finish downloading during this particular maintenance day. The sharp rims of the disks got closer, and I was facing the stack head-on. I felt Andi grip me tighter, her slim arms wrapped round my waist. I would not JetPax away from her.

I held out my sword, now no more than two metres away from the whirring edge. I could clearly see the pin diamonds that broke up the surface of the disk. Even if I escaped the sharp outer rim, the diamonds would then slit me to pieces. Striking the edge of the disk with my sword I pushed hard. I tumbled away, colliding with Swilkin, which, in turn pushed us further away from immediate danger.

Within a couple of seconds we were drifting towards the next disk, but now we were facing the wrong way. This time there'd be no sword trick; the sharp edges would soon cut slivers of flesh out of our backs. I realized Andi would be the first to wipe out.

It came out of nowhere. I told you, dragons never die. The Golden Dragon swooped down towards us, its strength having returned. Its magnificence could now triumph in the vast new space it found itself in. Like a great golden eagle taking his prey, it scooped me up with its left claw, and Swilkin with its right. Its great face peered at me, studied me as if looking in to my soul. There was a recognition of some sort, then it turned away from the spinning disks and flew us down to the stoned-flagged castle floor. The dragon freed us instantly as our feet touched the floor, yet so gently we didn't even feel it let us go. Then it wheeled away, darting upwards towards the roof.

Andi finally let go of me and she moved alongside.

'Wow!' I heard Swilkin exclaim behind me. 'Wow!' he said again.

Above us the light was invading the dark, some disks had already wound to a stop; the red dragons, with nowhere to go, were backing up onto the stepways and walkways.

A vast shadow blocked out the light. Then it descended towards us. The SatanDragon came swooping in to finish what it had started. There was no new sign of the Golden Dragon. The black monster sent a fireball towards us, but only a rather weak one. I think it was trying just to intimidate us; it wanted to enjoy destroying us slowly. I hardly felt its heat as the fireball passed over me.

I backed up to the other two, my sword once more at the ready.

The black beast touched down, then advanced angrily but steadily, its roar resounding off the ramparts and the disk stacks above us.

'No escape this time,' said Swilkin.

'I'm nearly home now,' said Andi.

Suddenly, over one of the stepways above, appeared the head of the Golden Dragon again. It gave a mighty roar that rumbled and shook the walls around us, even scattered the waiting red dragons with its intensity. It looked down on us and spread its wings. Here it was stronger, stronger and bigger than the SatanDragon, and finally it had room to manoeuvre its natural advantages in bulk and speed. The glorious beast drew itself to its full height, expanded its great golden-scaled chest, and flared its enormous hood. It fixed its gaze on its tormentor and then released a ball of flame towards us. We were safe, however, because the fireball was only for the SatanDragon. The flame tumbled and exploded towards its black opponent, sending it reeling helplessly backwards against the ramparts.

The SatanDragon lifted itself up and rushed me in a last desperate attempt to destroy me and Andi before having to turn and fight its real foe. I dropped to my knee, my sword outstretched. I sensed Swilkin move next to me, realized he'd adopted the same position.

'You really are crazy,' I yelled at him.

'Something to tell my grandkids about ... only I won't tell them I'm currently wetting myself.'

'Go, Andi ... go!' I shouted, urging her to shield herself behind us.

The SatanDragon reared its head, preparing to strike, knowing it didn't have long.

The Golden Dragon, its great wings now fully spread, fell away from the stone stepway and plummeted towards us.

Covering the ground at immense speed, the SatanDragon came snaking towards us. Swilkin and I waited, and when it got close we leapt apart, each waving our swords defiantly and yelling to deflect its attention, hoping to attack it from both sides. But it ignored us and rushed on towards Andi.

I slashed at the dragon's neck as it passed, hoping Swilkin would do the same.

'Slow it down,' I screamed. 'We must slow it down.'

Our swords inflicted deep bloody wounds on it, but the SatanDragon kept heading forward. I heard Andi scream. I heard a wild laugh that I knew was Biloxie.

I lunged one final time at the SatanDragon, only to be knocked sideways by a great force that bowled me over. It was the Golden Dragon, brushing me aside as it landed on its opponent. As I collapsed I saw it sink its long pointed fangs into the back of the other dragon's neck. Tearing at it ferociously, flesh and blood exploded towards me.

Andi rushed over and threw her arms round me, hugged me. 'Don't let me die,' she pleaded. 'One day, one day I'll be allowed back.'

She broke from me and ran towards the two beasts now locked together in savage combat. I stepped forward, wanting to help her, fearful as I saw her slender form approach the two mighty monsters. As she approached, the Golden

Dragon suddenly released its grip and, with a mighty flick of its long neck, rolled the SatanDragon into the base of a nearby disk stack.

The black dragon tried to right itself, but it was already too late. Holding her English steel broadsword high, Andi thrust it firmly into the monster's neck – into that unprotected area just below the head, where no scales grew. The sword, seeming so small in comparison to its target, sliced through black flesh and was swallowed up by the eruption of dark-mauve blood that flowed thickly from the neck wound. It was like lava spewing from an exploding volcano. She stepped back as the blood gushed towards her. Meanwhile the Golden Dragon, sensing its job was done, reared away, its claws scrabbling on the blood-slicked floor.

The black dragon writhed in this slime as it gradually lost power. I watched helplessly as Andi calmly walked round it towards its thrashing head. She stood in front of it, looked deep into the malevolent yellow slits of its eyes, then raised her hands forward, in a welcoming manner, as though offering herself.

'No,' I screamed. 'No.'

I tried to run towards her again, but slithered in the gore and fell onto the stone slabs, my sword clattering uselessly next to me.

The SatanDragon stopped flailing and lifted its head to fix Andi with its cold and deadly eyes. She took a step towards it. The death of innocence. She never even flinched. I cried out her name, but I don't think she heard me.

The SatanDragon lunged at her, with one last defiant roar. Twisting its head to one side, it gripped her by her narrow waist. Biting hard across her back, it crushed her between its enormous blood-filled jaws, grinding its fangs through her flesh till it finally cracked her spine.

Her head was thrown back, but I heard no sound of

pain. Then, just like smoke, she disintegrated and was absorbed by the SatanDragon.

A light exploded from the black dragon's mouth, a shaft of exploding whiteness that hit the stacks and sheared upwards into the vast gothic emptiness of the old castle. Then there was a final explosion and, as the SatanDragon itself shattered, the whole structure of the stacks collapsed towards us.

I saw two things in that instant. One was Biloxie's gap-toothed grin; even that great pain he endured wasn't enough to dilute the big man's hatred and contempt for all others. The other was the collapse of the diamond disks which sliced through the air towards us.

I turned, gave Swilkin a push towards the nearest wall opening and rushed towards it myself, slithering through the gore that still saturated the stone floor. The first tumbling diamond disk sliced into the floor just a few feet away as we both entered the safety of the tunnel.

'Keep going,' I yelled, but Swilkin needed no encouragement.

The mayhem behind us gave us the impetus to run faster as the stacks collapsed behind us. Then we were climbing old sweaty, slippery steps and past mossy walls, as we made our way through the dungeons and narrow corridors of the castle. I now remembered the original game and I took the lead in showing Swilkin the way out of the castle. We climbed into increasing darkness as we moved away from the exploding chaos we left behind us.

We just kept climbing, and the noise of destruction subsided. Then there was light ahead and we pushed through an opening in the cliff face. We stood in sunshine as a warm soft breeze blew across the castle courtyard, rustling the leaves. We were where we had started, in the gardens of the little castle on the hill.

'There are no more red dragons,' remarked Swilkin

eventually, as he stood near the rampart wall and stared down into Portofino harbour.

I sat down there on the grass, and watched the Golden Dragon fly out of the tower surmounting the castle. It looked down at the two of us, tossed its head in defiant yet gentle arrogance, bellowed a roar we would never forget, then turned to fly lazily and majestically into the sky and somewhere beyond.

The Valley of The Dragons was returned to its master.

'Who was she?' asked Swilkin, kneeling next to me.

'She was the virus. The destroyer.'

I didn't feel the need to explain that I had unwittingly passed her the virus when we had made love in the Dark Areas.

'It was designed by Nelson and Keebles to take out the InfoCalypse, to corrupt all that data they've been busy transferring.' I tightened my lower lip for a moment. *Yeah, I signed her death warrant.* 'I was the carrier that brought in the virus.'

'How?'

'Bonham gave me a SmartCard to get into the Dark Areas. Jim realized that, and he needed something from RealWorld that had access to the matrix, something that went beyond his own limited-access passwords. Remember, he was programd so that he could never directly attack the InfoCalypse, not with his protocols, so he had to find an outside source. My avatar was connected to the SmartCard which carried Bonham's DNA. Jim just channelled into my avatar and downloaded the virus into something that would go where he couldn't.'

'You passed that on to Andi?'

'Through touch.' *Did she make love to me because she really wanted to . . . or because Jim had taken her over.*

'Why all the way up here?'

'We had to get the virus into the download conduit, the only place it was truly vulnerable. So Andi had . . . little choice but to lead us here. Nelson and Keebles both knew that, and they just waited their chance. And Jim was solely their creation. Now that it's over we'll never hear from Jim again. He doesn't exist.'

'And kidnapping the President?'

'A trick . . . a device to get us all involved.'

'Gallagher?'

'He's *your* problem.'

'So game over?'

'Yeah. You can back to the Telephone Exchange, while I go back to explaining why I wasn't guilty.'

'They committed murder.'

'You try and prove it.'

Swilkin took a deep sigh. 'I have two personal problems.'

'What's that?'

'The Dundee Society. Nobody's ever quit it before.'

'Your choice.'

'I'm cool about it. My first responsibility was always to my job.'

'And the second?'

'The President. That's a bit more complicated.' He peered round the keep. 'Is anyone picking this up? I mean, are we firewalled here?'

'I think we're pretty safe. Nobody's ever going to admit to what was going on up here.'

Swilkin leant closer and whispered, his two hands encircling his mouth so he couldn't be lip-read. 'I found a way of downloading what went on in the Oval Office, between Monroe and our friend. It gives me – in a slight conflict of interest – an illegal tap that could well cost me my job, even put me in the slammer. So I thought I'd send it to you . . . for safe-keeping.'

I laughed. 'Sure. I'd like that. Stash it away, in case we should ever need it.'

'I did tell you. I never voted for him.' Swilkin looked round at the Mediterranean pine and shook his head. 'I'm sorry about the girl.'

'That's life. Not everything ends the way it should.'
'Very profound.'
But very true.
I stood up 'You want to walk or JetPax?'
'I'm ready to go home.'
We both JetPaxed out of the Valley of the Dragons.

Neither of them went back to the little cemetery behind the church in Second World. The statue of the girl wasn't white any more, but vibrant with colour, flesh-toned and clear in all its detail. It was definitely Andi. There was also a small smile playing round her lips.

BOOK SEVEN

··

CLOSING THE BOX

The island had been every bit as beautiful as it appeared on the Web.

I'd sat on the beach, in shorts, and enjoyed the heat of the real sun, the sound and spectacle of real waves.

I had used up an eight-month supply of carbon credits and taken a plane to Antigua, then caught the boat to Jumby Bay. That was just three days after our battle on the hill in Portofino.

I'd been busy during that time, my main effort in attempting to trace Tebor's cadaver. With Swilkin's help, we finally tracked him down to a Turkish public Catacomb. Tebor Isharak was his full name, no living relatives. I visited the Catacomb through the Web, and found it was a shabby place run as cheaply as possible to bring in the UN's dollars. A little bribery, new export papers from another bribed official, the arrangement of a private flight to carry the cadaver, and I soon had Tebor bound for Jumby Bay.

I spent three days of R & R on the Antiguan beach before Tebor arrived.

The only break from the hot sun and the smoothie fruit drinks involved my visit to Bonham in Atlantic City. But this time we met in Second World.

'Did Biloxie kill Nelson and Keebles?' I asked Bonham.

'Of course not ... not. It was suicide. You obviously haven't been catching up with the news.'

'I've been out of touch, so tell me about it.'

'There really was an Infocalypse. Yes, that quite surprised me. Always believed . . . be-leevved it was an old wives' tale. Apparently it was created by Nelson and Keebles. Hard to believe, isn't it? They were such ordinary people.'

'Very.' But I wasn't surprised; somehow I'd expected Murphy and Bonham would manage to crawl out from under this mess.

'They were also responsible for kidnapping the President. I can't really believe they had it in them. They did it to deflect attention away from the fact they were moving the InfoCalypse on the *Titanic*. Bloody clever . . . cle-verr when you think about it.'

'But why commit suicide?'

'Just what the Chairman asked me. I think they wanted to live forever down there in Second World. I mean become one person, inhabit Jim with their final personalities. Smart little trick. Use the InfoCalypse as their security, something to blackmail with. For them, eternity guaranteed.'

'Sounds a little far-fetched.'

'I know. But it's the story everyone wants to believe.'

'What went wrong?'

'We were lucky. In spite of your interference, my man Biloxie managed to block the transfer.'

'How is he?' I said with a wry smile.

'In a lot . . . lottt of pain. Suffering quite badly, mentally and physically, almost as if he'd had an overdose of narco-juice.'

'Give him my regards.'

'I will . . . and I'm sure he'll want to keep in touch.' That remark went over my head. There was no way they wanted to revisit what had happened. 'Have you decided what you're doing yet?'

'No.'

'Tell me when you've . . . you-uvve decided. I'd hate to lose you.'

In fact I'd already made up my mind, but wanted to keep

them sweating. They would not want to lose me to one of the competitors, and so I'd stay for as long as I had a reason for staying. So far I couldn't think of a reason for going. They were all crooks out there, even the damn President, but they were *my* crooks and at least I could keep an eye on them.

I arranged with Jumby Bay officials to prepare a private villa for Andi and Tebor. Jumby Bay was this small island off Antigua that had gone from being a world-famous luxury resort to the most exclusive Catacomb in the world.

Everything, both life and death, just follows the money.

I arranged them the best medical care and flew in the most expensive CadaverControl units I could buy. The medical care would continue round the clock, while the monitoring units were connected to Rose Cottage so I could keep a constant eye on their progress.

I put them side by side, in two beds which were temperature controlled and linked to the systems that sustained them in their eternal sleep. It was only as they would've wanted.

They weren't MIW anymore, but at least they were both alive. Maybe someone would find a solution to the problem involving all MIWs. Maybe, one day, there'd be a way to bring them back.

I decided not to visit her parents – they'd probably been through too much grief already – but I did pump some of the Reverend Jeremiah Post's unholy collections through to their credit account.

I was glad I'd told her I'd loved her, back when we were alone in the Dark Areas. That had been real; that was before any virus had affected her. Maybe, somewhere in that dark unknown place she now inhabited, those simple words would be recalled and give her the strength to keep going in the constant greyness of wherever she was.

After I left Antigua I flew to Genova Airport, and then on to an overnight stay in Portofino.

I spent the night at the Hotel Splendide, on the hillside above the town and harbour, its windows looking out at the church and the small castle on the other side. I watched a multi-coloured sunset and the battlemented silhouette of the castle disappearing into the dark of night.

The next morning, early with the birds, I climbed the long narrow footpath up to the church and the castle. The church was just like it had been in Second World. I took my time walking through its simple elegance, enjoying the cool interior among the small figures and paintings of St George that now held no hidden dangers. I didn't bother going up to the castle. There seemed little point after I'd walked through the small graveyard.

The real surprise was finding her statue there. But it wasn't Andi now, but a woman called Raggio Paola who had died in 1960. I touched it, feeling the coldness of the marble, but it was still Andi's face, and for a passing instant I sensed her warmth in the cold white stone eyes.

It was only my imagination, my stupid and useless imagination.

It was so peaceful now; there were already plenty of visitors around, real people and not a hint of a dragon. I could smell the Mediterranean below, smell the sea I looked out on. Just like in Second World, but there was now an extra tang here, something indescribable: something . . . real.

I decided then to spend more time in RealWorld. Maybe a lifetime in Second World, and sitting behind computers, had dulled my mind. I'd partially escaped, into Norfolk, but there was so much else to do, so much to really see.

What was it the doctor had said? *Get fit Mr Smith*. I chuckled; *Yeah the old fart was right*, I needed to get back into old-fashioned ways. Maybe I'd get myself a dog, take it walking. Maybe two of them. Yeah, yeah, yeah.

I sat on the grass just above the church and thought of my loneliness and the anger it created within.

It dawned on me that was the reason for my periodic

furies; it wasn't the solitude itself but frustration at my incapacity to do anything about it.

Maybe that's why I'd needed Andi. Because she wasn't real, and because I was incapable of having a relationship with a real woman.

God, I was complicated. *Just go out and enjoy yourself, Smith.* Yeah, easier said than done.

I went back down the hill to the harbour, was driven back to Genova Airport and airmailed myself back to Norwich. By the time I got home, the various outings had cost me two years of carbon trade. So, who cares? I won't now be going anywhere for a while.

The melancholy I feel stays wrapped around me, like a dusty old blanket. So I sit now, alone, on my balcony looking out at the last sunset tatters of another dying day. I am so frustrated that the beauty of end of days merely highlights my solitude. Everyone says I'm cool, but I've accepted I'll never get used to the isolation I've created for myself. And it took Andi to show me that.

I go into the bedroom as night closes. With all that depression, and a strong dash of self-pity, I open the drawer where the Nagan sits. I take out the old revolver, empty the chambers, spin it and reload one bullet. Then, in a final act of desperation I spin the chamber again and slide another shell in, two chambers away from the already loaded one. My pulse quickens, my skin tightens as I decide to halve the odds.

Real Games, Smith. No more hiding in the Web.

I give it a final spin and snap it shut. I stare at the gun, my finger pressed lightly against the trigger. I cock the hammer.

Who gives a damn?

All it takes is a second to turn the revolver, to just gently increase the pressure. Maybe it wouldn't be so bad. I mean, when Mikoyan died, it was all over as soon as the trigger was pulled. Oblivion in a nanosecond.

So easy to rid myself of all the problems.

I feel the rush.

Not so difficult. Not for a GameMaster.

There's a banging on the outside door.

'Where's my bloody shopping, then? I've got your stuff here.' I recognize John Mathews's Norfolk vowels from outside.

I stare down the black barrel with the hole to eternity carved in its end. Such a simple piece of machinery in such a complicated world.

Simple and effective and final. And I remember Nelson and Keebles. Now *they* died for something really important. Not just because they were bored and depressed, but because life mattered to them.

'Come on, you old fart. I'm getting cold down here.'

I grin and uncock the Nagan. I've got to stop playing these games. Why do I always get so carried away? Anyway, my fiftieth birthday is still three months away and I can afford to wait till then.

And who'd look after Andi and Tebor if the techies ever found a way of bringing them back? Who'd protect her from the cops when they went after her for the murder she'd committed years ago?

I feel the furies surge again; she deserved better from the cops, and it hadn't been her fault. How come the victims always become the persecuted?

So that's the result of a world full of the tyranny 'political correctness'.

Except on the Brick. Nobody gives a damn down there.

I hum the words.

> *Oh Rapid Roy that stock car boy*
> *He too much too believe*
> *You know he always got an extra pack of cigarettes*
> *Rolled up in his T-shirt sleeve*
> *He got a tattoo on his arm that say 'Baby'*

> *He got another one that just say 'Hey'*
> *But every Sunday afternoon he is a dirt track demon*
> *In a '57 Chevrolet*

I get the giggles.

Life is good when you've got something to look forward to. So, I guess, was death . . . for Jim.

'Conor, are you coming down?'

I put the gun back in the drawer and go down to collect the bacon.

Visit **www.panmacmillan.com** to read more about all our books and to buy them. You will also find features, author interviews and news of any author events, and you can sign up for e-newsletters so that you're always first to hear about our new releases.